T0248549

PENGUIN BOOKS
DEPLORABLE CONVERSATIONS WITH CATS AND OTHER DISTRACTIONS

Yeoh Jo-Ann grew up in Malaysia and lives in Singapore. As a teenager, she dreamt of being a cat or a rock star, but instead spent most of her adult life working in publishing, somehow ending up as the features editor of a women's magazine before giving it up for a career in digital marketing. Her first novel, *Impractical Uses of Cake*, won the Epigram Books Fiction Prize in Singapore in 2018 and has been translated into German. Her short stories have been included in Singaporean anthologies such as *Best Singaporean Short Stories: Volume Three*, and in 2020, her short story *Dog Tiger Horse* won the *Boston Review*'s annual Aura Estrada Short Story Contest. She is currently working on her third novel and hopes to finish it before she turns into some sort of cabbage.

Deplorable Conversations with Cats and Other Distractions

Yeoh Jo-Ann

PENGUIN BOOKS
An imprint of Penguin Random House

PENGUIN BOOKS

USA | Canada | UK | Ireland | Australia
New Zealand | India | South Africa | China | Southeast Asia

Penguin Books is part of the Penguin Random House group of companies
whose addresses can be found at global.penguinrandomhouse.com

Published by Penguin Random House SEA Pte Ltd
9, Changi South Street 3, Level 08-01,
Singapore 486361

Penguin
Random House
SEA

First published in Penguin Books by Penguin Random House SEA 2024
Copyright © Yeoh Jo-Ann 2024

ISBN 9789815144772

Typeset in Garamond by MAP Systems, Bengaluru, India

www.penguin.sg

For Koh Tsin Zhen.
Love you.

The smallest feline is a masterpiece.
—Leonardo da Vinci

The silly kids next door

have put up paper lanterns for Christmas. Lanterns! And white ones at that. Do they know nothing? *Go to school and learn English, then forget how to be Chinese.* Mr Thiang glares up at the three offensive rice-paper constructions floating moon-like over the narrow walkway in front of the shophouse next door. White lanterns! As if they were putting on a funeral. Pah. This would never have happened while Mr Lee was still alive, while the kopitiam was a proper kopitiam and not some nonsense *cafe.* Why isn't 'coffee shop' good enough any more? Mr Thiang raises the metal shutters of his shop, then unlocks the accordion-style iron grille. He pushes both sides apart and reaches for the fan switch behind the heavy wooden cabinet he's been unable to sell since 1982.

What a morning. And what a day it's going to be. Not even eight yet and already so hot.

It's dark inside the furniture store. It would be even darker if it weren't for the air well in the middle that goes all the way up and through the roof. Years and years ago, when he was a child, he and his elder brother would sleep on the cement floor in the air well on hot days—hot days exactly like this one—and that was heaven, so nice and cool, though sometimes, of course, it would rain and, well, they put in the glass skylight in the late 1970s and no one's been woken up by rain in their faces since. Not that anyone sleeps in the shophouse anymore. These days, the old bedrooms are filled with furniture that won't fit in the store and some pieces that he can't sell but can't part with, like that mahogany sideboard that everyone thinks is so bulky and old-fashioned. But of course what that really means is they can't appreciate these fine things, having been raised on Ikea. And the covered 'air well' is now filled with his wife's potted plants.

Mr Thiang plods slowly towards the back of the store, to the tiny kitchen where he will make himself a nice big cup of coffee. Where did the boy say it was from? He can't recall, but it's good. Mr Lee raised his boy well—maybe he should talk to him about the lanterns? So inauspicious. Not that he's the superstitious type, no, not at all, but no point tempting the gods, right? Mr Thiang isn't sure even Jesus would approve of white lanterns for Christmas. Surely all the red and green everywhere meant that those were his favourite colours. And good for him—red and green are good colours.

A flurry of bright red passes by the store. 'Morning, Mr Thiang!'

The old man turns but it's too late. She's gone. He hears her key turn in the heavy old lock next door. Maybe he should talk to her about the lanterns instead? Maybe. But kopi first.

* * *

'The quaint Singaporean quarters of Joo Chiat and Katong, those kissing cousins—who knows, really, where one ends and the other begins? Who cares? Perhaps the government and the local town council. There are, after all, reams and reams of rules to enforce in any heritage zone. Mammon help anyone who dares damage a pre-war facade. But maybe all you want to do is gut a building and eat its soul for breakfast with your kopi-C?

'Then, welcome—take a walk on these old mosaic pavements, admire the old architecture, say clever things about the local businesses and slow living, and congratulate yourself. How cultured you are! How sweet your faint praise; how unlike the babble of others.'

Meixi shakes her head indignantly, frowning. Wow. Some people can be such cynics. Maybe she'll stop reading this architecture blog, even if it's really helping her get on with her boss. She switches off her phone screen and looks around her, sighing, smiling. Joo Chiat is *so* pretty in the morning, in that still-sleepy hour right after the sky has lightened, when things are just beginning to move, and hum and click and roll and purr. Most of the shophouses still have their shutters down, and as she walks down Joo Chiat Road, towards the corner at Duku Lane, she can see Mr Thiang in his store, straight-backed and regal even in Bermuda shorts and an old white shirt.

The air conditioner is already humming when Meixi unlocks the door and walks into the cafe. In a way, this is nice—it's so warm outside, and she's sweaty from the walk from the bus stop, so stepping into a nice cool room is . . . nice. But also not, because this means the boss is already here. She locks the door behind her. They only open at 8.30, and Shawn is fussy about people walking in and finding that they're not ready to serve coffee. 'Creates a bad impression,' he says. 'And coffee addicts are nuts in the morning.' Nuts enough to leave a one-star review on Google is what he means, of course—Shawn checks every week to make sure their five-star rating is intact.

'Shawn! Morning!'

He's not behind the counter, but there are sounds coming from the storeroom at the back of the cafe. Meixi switches on the espresso machine and the coffee grinder beside it.

'Shawn! I'm making us coffee!'

The bag of organic West Javanese coffee beans on the shelf is nearly empty, so Meixi grinds up some Vietnamese Arabica instead; it's now Shawn's second favourite—is he fetching more Javanese beans from the storeroom? Must be more than that—he's not even answering her. What can he be doing, though? They just finished inventory three days ago, and it's been a quiet week. Plus, it's Christmas Eve, so it'll be even quieter today—most of the locals have gone on holiday, and all the tourists are downtown on Orchard Road frittering away money on things they don't need. Like that new Chanel bag she's been desperately pretending not to want but stalks on the brand's Instagram when the crowd is thin and the boss isn't around.

The door to the storeroom slams shut as Meixi pours frothy milk into the second cup of coffee.

'Meixi, where's that instant camera . . . what's it called . . . the . . . starts with a P—'

'Lucky!'

Lucky looks a little sleepier than usual—well, she's never seen him at the cafe before noon, let alone before eight—but he's still the only man Meixi knows who can pull off track pants and flip-flops. And Lucky's lucky—on shoulders like his, that rumpled Care Bears T-shirt, faded to the point at which its original colour isn't quite discernible (could be blue, could be grey, could be purple) looks like something a Japanese designer crafted to look 'distressed'. Maybe it's that scar on his face? In any case, a less lucky man would have just looked like he was wearing his sister's old clothes. (Lucky is in fact wearing his sister's old clothes.)

'Oh, good. You made coffee.' He smiles, sighs, runs a hand through his hair. 'I couldn't sleep. I had this idea for this thing I'm making, and I printed out some pictures but then I thought, wait, we have that camera, and that would be so much better, right?'

Meixi has no idea what he's talking about. She almost never has any idea what Lucky is talking about. But she hands him a cup of coffee, smiling and nodding, because, really, Lucky is her boss too, even if he never orders her around and isn't, well, bossy.

'Thanks,' He takes a seat at the counter, frowning, tapping his fingers against the ridge of his eyebrows and then against his right cheekbone, along the scar.

She puts a plate of home-made biscotti in front of him, then goes to check the fridge to see if there's enough milk. There is: full fat, low fat, evaporated, condensed, soy, almond. Meixi does a quick survey of the self-serve counter—teaspoons, napkins, sugar sachets, water jug. All good. Tables and chairs—wiped down the night before, but always good to check again—all good. On the long, cast-concrete table in the middle of the cafe, Meixi rearranges the magazines into what she hopes is an artful jumble, with the latest issue of *Apartamento* close to the top but not too close. Well, Shawn will redo this later anyway.

Lucky puts his cup down and slaps the counter. 'Polaroid!'

'What?'

He stands up. 'Polaroid! Where's the Polaroid camera we got for that party in September? It's not in the storeroom. I searched . . .'

Meixi hopes he hasn't messed around too much with the stock. She and Shawn have a system, refined through months and months of trial and error, and if Lucky does anything to upset it, she will scream. Even if he's her boss, even if he's not bossy, even if he's the hottest thing she's ever seen in a Care Bears T-shirt. And hopefully he hasn't looked behind the carton of cleaning supplies.

'. . . even under the shelves, and in that box with the pink plates, the ones we got for that thing in July—'

'Dinah took it, I think . . .'

Lucky raises his eyebrows. 'Dinah? Really? What's she doing with it?'

The lock on the front door turns with a sharp click, and Meixi hurries to make another cup of coffee. Arranging his face into an expression of mild disapproval, Lucky turns towards the door. 'Ah, finally. I thought you were never coming in.'

Shawn stares. Lucky grins. It's so much fun messing with Shawn. It's been one of his favourite things to do for the last fifteen years.

'Okay, what's going on?' Shawn looks at the clock. 'It's 8.15. Are you okay? And you know we open at 8.30, right?' He narrows his eyes at Lucky as he goes behind the counter and starts to check that everything is exactly how he likes it, left to right and top to bottom.

Lucky decides to ignore the cattiness of that last question. Shawn can pretend all he likes to be bitter about being stuck with the opening shift, but there's no way to hide the fact that he is, in fact, one of those strange creatures rarely sighted but generally assumed to exist—a Morning Person. Lucky, on the other hand . . .

'Couldn't sleep. I came in looking for that Polaroid camera. I have to make this thing, you see, it's going to be made of all these little photos and I've got some wire and it's going to be so cool—'

Shawn puts on a black apron and throws one at Lucky. 'If you're going to hang around, at least look like you work here!'

'Heyyy! I do work here!'

'So put on the apron.'

'I will. You're forgetting I designed it.'

Holding up one hand for silence, Shawn reaches out the other and takes the cup of coffee Meixi's holding out to him. He sniffs it, then takes a sip. He pauses, then nods. Lucky grins. A more fearful beast than the Morning Person—the Morning-Person-Coffee-Snob. Meixi resumes regular breathing then goes to check the water filter one last time before they open. They're trying out a new one made with coconut-husk carbon because Shawn didn't like the last one—the crazy expensive one he ordered specially from Oslo. 'It makes the water taste kind of too clean,' he kept saying. In the end, Dinah snapped and told him to 'buy whatever. I don't care. I just don't want to hear another word from you about water or water filters.' Dinah is hardly around, often grumpy, and Meixi's least favourite boss.

Shawn unlocks the front door, then darts behind the counter and checks the water filter. Lucky puts on the apron, then sits back down and finishes his coffee, wondering if it's too early to call Dinah and ask about that camera.

She could already be in a meeting—she's always complaining about early-morning meetings with contractors—and if she were and he called, she'd be so pissed. But if she weren't? What if she could pass it to him today? Maybe it's in her car. Dinah keeps everything in her car. It's like a wardrobe-junkyard-hardware-store on wheels. And if he had the camera, he could get started on the thing—what should he call it? A photo sculpture? But would that make him seem pretentious? Pretentiousness is so unattractive in a man. At least two of his most recent Tinder dates have said this. Maybe there's no need to call it anything. What's in a name?

> What's in a name? That which we call a rose
> By any other name would smell as sweet;
> So Romeo wou'd, were he not Romeo call'd,
> Retain that dear perfection which he owes
> Without that title. Romeo, doff thy name,
> And for that name which is no part of thee
> Take all myself.

Damn, did he actually remember all of that nonsense? Why? Miss Parimala would be so smug, knowing her attempts to drill Shakespeare into the unsubtle minds of the boys in his Secondary Two class actually worked. What did they use to call her again? The Walrus? No, no—it was something else. The Seal? Nope. Too cute.

'You okay, Lucky?'

'What?'

'You're mumbling to yourself.' Shawn hands him a glass of water with a slice of cucumber in it. 'Can you go sit in the corner? I don't want you scaring customers.'

'Oh, Shawn, Shawn.' Lucky puts the glass, then his head, on the counter. 'I need that camera.'

Before he can stop himself, Shawn rolls his eyes and sighs. He does, however, manage to refrain from saying, 'What is it now?' No point—with Lucky, it's always something. Something he has to do or has to make or has to have, or someone he has to meet—or do. And with Lucky, it's always urgent, always a matter of life or death or madness, hour of the day be damned. It's because of Lucky that Shawn began sleeping with his phone turned off.

Shaking his head, he slides onto the stool next to Lucky's and puts a hand on his shoulder. What the hell. It's Christmas Eve. It's going to be a slow day anyway.

'So, what's going on?'

Lucky keeps his head on the counter. 'I have a date with Rosalind when I'm back from Bali.'

Shawn tries to remember if he should know who Rosalind is. 'And you're going to give her the camera?'

'No. I need to take photos of Joo Chiat.'

Lucky doesn't explain what photos of their neighbourhood have to do with this Rosalind. Unsurprising but annoying, but not as annoying as it used to be. It's been like this since their days in architecture school. Shawn feels he really should be better at this by now, but it's still so damn hard to knit Lucky's stress-scattered thoughts together. It's freaky how the guy unravels every time he's excited or agitated, and suddenly his perfectly articulate friend is replaced by a babbling five-year-old. Shawn takes a deep breath. What would Pearl do?

'Lucky. Begin at the beginning.' Yes, yes, definitely sounds like something Pearl would say. Gentle, but firm.

'She's amazing, Shawn. Amazing. You have to meet her.'

'Rosalind?' Ah, must be a new one. Okay. This is starting to make sense. He doesn't ask what happened to Jamie, last month's amazing woman.

'Yes!'

Meixi watches from behind the espresso machine as Lucky lifts his head and nods, his hair falling over his eyes. She sighs. Another woman?

'. . . and she cooks! She can make nasi lemak. Sambal from scratch and everything.' Lucky fishes his phone out of his pocket. 'Here, look. Wow, right?'

Shawn takes the phone from him and swipes through a few photos. Wow, indeed. The nasi lemak does look good.

'Where did you guys meet? And why did she make you nasi lemak?'

'Someone's birthday thing. Potluck. Rosalind brought nasi lemak.'

'And when was this?'

'Last week.'

'Ah.'

Lucky laughs and slaps his friend on the back. 'Say it. You think I'm mad,' he sighs. 'But I think this might be it.'

'You said that about Jamie.' There, he said it. Shouldn't have, but he couldn't resist. Shawn waits for it to bite him in the face.

Lucky waves it off. 'Oh, that woman.'

Her with the K-pop perm and the big boobs. Oh yes, Meixi remembers *that woman*. She remembers how she came in with Lucky and kept her hand on his arm the entire time. She remembers how she ordered a decaf soy latte. She remembers Shawn trying not to snap when he told her they didn't do decaf, how he grumbled after they left: 'We've called this place Caffiend—*how* much more obvious do we need to be? And why was I the one who had to tell her no when he was right there?'

'What happened?' Shawn isn't doing a great job hiding his delight, but lucky for him, Lucky doesn't care.

'Did I tell you she's a teacher?' Lucky shakes his head. 'Never date a teacher.'

'I'm married, but go on, what happened?'

Lucky makes a face. 'The trouble with teachers is that they really like to point out what's wrong with things. I mean, it's their job so I get that it's useful and all, but I don't think I want that kind of rubbish energy around me all the time, you know?'

'Ah, what did she say was wrong with you?' Shawn grins. This is too funny.

Another dismissive wave. 'I've forgotten most of it. Who cares, anyway? But can you believe she said it was unmanly that I can't drive? Unmanly!'

Shawn thinks it's unmanly that Lucky can't drive. *Doesn't* drive— sure. *Can't* drive—lame.

'But Rosalind—she'd never say that. She really *gets* me.' Bright-eyed, Lucky launches into details. He and Rosalind talked about food the entire night at the party, particularly about how difficult it was to get a decent sambal sotong anywhere, and then shared a taxi home. 'And we've been texting. She's hilarious, Shawn. And she said yes to dinner! Should I cook or take her out or order in?' If Lucky had a tail, he'd be wagging it.

The front door opens. A woman walks in. Shawn catches her eye and smiles; Lucky continues gushing about Lady Amazing.

'Okay, Lucky—'

'. . . and you know what she said, she called it the flying buttress of kuih . . .'

'I should get to work. Pay our bills, you know.'

'. . . and I said, how do you know what a flying buttress is . . .'

Watching Meixi take their first customer's order—the woman isn't one of their regulars, which is odd for this time of the day— Shawn absently pats Lucky's shoulder. 'She sounds amazing. And it's going to be fine whatever you do—you'll have all that time in Bali to figure it out.' *And maybe meet some other amazing woman to be an idiot about.*

'You know what? This is special. *She's* special. I'm going to cook.'

The light from the windows suddenly changes—a passing cloud? The interior of the cafe takes on more of the blue and green tones of the antique glass panes in the top half of the French windows. Lucky and Shawn watch as, duped by the temporary softening of the tropical glare, their lone customer walks across the room and takes a seat at a table next to a window. Lucky wishes the light could always be like this—it's like being in an aquarium. Or the sea—he would be a pufferfish. Or an octopus. He once saw a video of an octopus moving with the current, its body billowing like a sail, and it looked like it was enjoying itself. Are there octopuses (octopi?) in Bali? Doesn't matter, but it would be quite a treat to see one while snorkelling.

The cool, dappled light keeps Lucky thinking of the sea. And by logical extension, the beach hotel in Bali he's booked for a week. 'God, I can't wait for Bali.' The sea, hopefully the octopuses or octopi, the coffee, the food. And the chocolate! 'Shawn, I'll bring you some chocolate. Balinese chocolate is superb. You'll love it. There's one they make with coconut milk . . .'

Shawn's managed to drift off, though, and by the time Lucky realizes he's missing, Shawn is crossing the room, bringing the customer at the window her coffee along with a tiny plate of lemon cookies. Very important, these thoughtful touches, Shawn is overfond of saying. Lucky wishes he could take a picture of this and, assuming the availability of a working time machine or his ability to build one, show it to Shawn and Lucky and Dinah of two Christmases past.

'See?' he imagines saying. 'That's our cafe, still in business in a couple of years.' And to Dinah: 'Check out that gorgeous light. Are you happy now that I insisted on keeping the old windows?'

* * *

Meixi fiddles with the box she hid in the storeroom a week ago behind the carton of cleaning supplies. Should she or shouldn't she? Maybe she shouldn't have wrapped it up. Now it looks too . . . planned. And obviously he didn't get her anything. Does Lucky even know it's Christmas Eve? He's still at the counter as she slinks behind it and hides the box behind a row of coffee cups. Smiling to himself, he checks his phone. Probably a text from *her*. The new her.

Meixi stares down at her new dress, its red pleats half hidden by the stiff black apron. What's the point? But still, she ventures forth. 'You're going to Bali?'

'Yes, in a couple of days.' On the counter, Lucky's phone screen lights up with another text message, but he doesn't look at it. 'You? Heading anywhere for the new year?'

She shakes her head. 'Not this year. I'm working late shifts until you're back. Well, me and Dinah.'

Lucky grins. 'Really? You're the best, Meixi.' He winks. 'I'll remind Shawn about your Christmas bonus.'

He looks at his phone. Don't forget to pack your travel adaptor.

He rolls his eyes. The next text reads: Feed the fish. And the cat.

He stares at the phone until the light from the screen goes off. Another text arrives, but he doesn't read it. It's nearly 11.00. How long could cats go without food? He definitely fed it on Monday—that was two days ago. And the fish—he's almost sure he fed them last night. Jesus. Pearl would be so pissed off if something happened to the cat.

Lucky hops off the stool and waves to Shawn, who's back behind the counter next to a rather morose-looking Meixi. Poor girl needs a break. Maybe he should get her a spa voucher or something? 'Hey, I'm off. See you guys later? I'll come back around two?'

Shawn shoos him off. 'Ah, forget it. I'll close up. You know we're closing early today, right?'

'Yes!' He'd completely forgotten, but what a nice surprise. And good for Meixi. Lucky beams at her, but she's too busy staring at a row of coffee cups. 'Thanks for closing up, Shawn. See you tomorrow!'

'Come over at 2.00. And come hungry. We'll have food for an army.'

* * *

As Lucky bounds out of the cafe and walks down the street, he finds himself thinking, *Shawn—what a guy.* He's going to have to get him a really good gift this year—but what? And what did he get Shawn last year? Some sort of book? A video game? Vouchers? Clearly he didn't make much effort. Better ask Pearl. After he gets home and feeds the cat, that is. Wait—do shops close early on Christmas Eve?

As Shawn makes the next customer of the morning a flat white, he finds himself thinking, *Lucky—what a kid.* And what exactly did he want with the Polaroid camera? Shawn sighs. Well, as long as it's got nothing to do with mushrooms . . .

The cat and the fish

are fine. But just to be safe, and because he feels a little guilty, Lucky feeds them both a double helping before he leaves for Shawn's on Christmas day.

'Happy Christmas!'

The cat gives him the briefest of glances. The fish don't deign to notice him.

His phone vibrates. Pearl again. `Just had the most awesome bakso. What are you up to?`

He texts back: `Going to Shawn's. No bakso.:(`

As he slips the phone into his pocket, it vibrates again, but he ignores it. First, his sister ditches him over Christmas and goes off to Surabaya, and now she wants to rub his face in all her bakso-scoffing? Seriously. She better bring home something nice or at least illegal. Maybe some sort of home-brewed rice wine, like the one they had had in Sabah a few years ago? Or a shrunken head. Yesterday, he came across a video on how shrunken heads are made—really quite time-consuming stuff. Do they do shrunken heads in Surabaya? If Pearl wasn't careful—and she never was, she could and would say random nasty shit if she didn't sleep enough or if the food wasn't good or if she just felt like saying random nasty shit—she'd end up with her head chopped off, boiled, and dried out until it was half its size, and maybe turned into a keychain or a doorstop. Then there would be no bakso for her either.

It's only five minutes past one. Plenty of time for a coffee. Lucky is relieved. Having a coffee first means he won't have to ask Shawn for one, which means he won't have to get into a discussion about whatever extraction technique or beans or roast or water or milk or grinder Shawn's currently hating or loving. Seriously, why take coffee so seriously? Lucky just wants to make it and smell it and drink it and do it over and over again. Shawn calls this half-assed; Lucky is happy to agree. Half a donkey is amusing in a way a whole donkey could never be.

The espresso machine in the kitchen is nearly forty years old, once the little prince of his father's office in Chinatown. Lucky wasn't even allowed to touch it when it first arrived home to begin its retirement years, lovingly carried into the kitchen by two of his father's delivery men as the boss himself looked on. His mother had been told to clear a place in the cooler part of the kitchen for it, and after much bargaining, had been persuaded to allow the espresso machine to usurp the microwave oven's prime spot. After the delivery men left, his parents, his sister, and Lucky stood in the kitchen, forming a semi-circle around the new addition to the family.

'Works like a horse,' boasted the proud Papa. 'Built like a tank.' It was like the son his father wished he was.

The old Italian lever machine is in fact a tricky thing to operate, but Lucky has learnt to relish his daily arm-wrestling with the horse-tank. Pulling an espresso shot should be about, well, *pulling* an espresso shot. The semi-automatic machine at Caffiend took a little getting used to, and Shawn used to yell at him to 'just press the damn button, dumbass'. And then, 'Turn it *off*—you have to turn it *off*.'

But now, as Lucky pulls on the piston lever, working hard for his one espresso shot, he almost wishes for a button. He neighs, wishing his father could hear him. *Who's the damn horse now?*

* * *

Traffic all over Singapore on Christmas day is as quiet and uneventful as it gets, unless your taxi driver decides to take the scenic route down

Victoria Street and Penang Road, through Orchard Boulevard, to get to Farrer Road. Lucky watches the fare meter jump, grateful that Pearl isn't with him, staring down the red digits and wondering out loud why the driver felt it would be better for them to crawl through the legion of taxis ferrying tourists between shopping centres in the middle of the city, instead of taking the PIE. He can almost hear her stage-whisper, 'Why? Will the car be lonely on the highway? Does the car feel better going slow and surrounded by many, many friends?'

'Wah, so many people . . .' The taxi driver gestures at the hordes of shoppers waiting to cross the street. 'Traffic damn *jialat*, yah?'

Pearl would have lost it. Lucky tries to smile. It's Christmas, and the cat didn't die, and he's about to be treated to a very nice lunch that will probably include curry kapitan and plum pudding and a glass or five of Valpolicella. He can certainly afford to be indulgent—if the driver really feels the need to state the obvious, Lucky will listen. Lucky will commiserate.

Lucky sighs dramatically. 'Yah, why so bad ah? Siao lah, all these people. Nowhere else to go ah?'

'You want I take shortcut?'

'Can ah?'

'Caaaaan. I show you.' The driver makes a sharp left turn into an unfamiliar residential estate. The houses are oldish and quietly proportioned, aside from a few ugly modern things, and the road is flanked by tall saga trees—very popular with urban landscape architects in the 1980s.

Lucky finds himself instinctively checking the ground under the trees for bright little red seeds as the taxi rolls past, bringing his face as close to the window as he can without pressing his nose against it. There was a big saga tree right outside Pearl's primary school and some days she would bring home handfuls of saga seeds, gleaming red and perfect, and the afternoon's play would begin.

'Look. I've got us some gold.'

'Gold isn't red.' Lucky was seven but he knew this.

'This is a special gold, idiot. Red with the blood of dwarves who perished in the ancient mines.' Pearl seemed completely sure, and the words 'red with the blood of dwarves' thrilled him and scared him at the same time.

'Are we protecting the gold? From pirates?'

Pearl looked at the little seeds in her hand. She closed her fist. 'No. We're pirates, and we're travelling far away to sell it to a king who likes red gold.'

Lucky produced a tablecloth he'd taken from the laundry line. 'This can be our pirate flag! On our boat.'

'Our ship,' Pearl corrected. She took the tablecloth from him. 'And this is my secret cloak. I'm also a princess, and when I put this on, I'm invisible. You can be my bodyguard.'

Another sharp turn jolts Lucky out of his recollection. Looking around, he marvels at how quickly the chaos of the shopping district has been left behind. The houses are further apart now, and set far back from the road, surrounded by large, leafy gardens. Gates are mostly stately and prominent, and Lucky looks enviously at some of the more elegant ones. One in particular makes him stare—a curvilinear, postmodern thing with vertical slate-grey metal slats arranged at different angles within a heavy black steel frame so that no one walking or driving past the house would have an unobstructed view of it and the garden beyond.

Bewitched, he jerks upright in the backseat and claps the taxi driver on the shoulder. 'Can we stop here? I need to take a picture.'

After repeated assurances that he won't take long and that yes, of course, the driver must keep the meter running, after the driver comes to the conclusion that his smartly dressed customer is a bit weird but isn't trying to run away without paying, Lucky hops out of the taxi. Hoping he won't look too suspicious and knowing he will anyway, he paces in front of the gate, staring at the slats, taking first a few pictures and then a video to try and capture how effectively— and how beautifully—the changing alignment of the slats hides the house and the garden from all angles. Neither the photos nor video are very good, but Lucky doesn't notice, and by the time the taxi drops him off at Shawn's apartment building five minutes later, all he cares about is lunch.

Will there be assam pedas? Is that too un-Christmassy? Would Anita even give a shit?

Lucky goes up to Shawn's apartment, presents his wife with wine and chocolate and finds out: Yes. No. No.

Slightly sweaty but obviously in a good mood, Anita is all dressed up, but the effect is somewhat dampened by the large dish cloth she's tucked into the collar of her blouse. Lucky notices she's put on more weight, but of course he will never tell her. Let Shawn—it's his husbandly right to dig this hole and bury himself in it. He, Lucky, will deny, repeatedly, on pain of death, that she looks any different from the skinny thing who married his friend five years ago—it isn't gratuitous honesty that has secured Lucky his top spot in the ranks of Anita's Husband's Friends.

'I'm making assam pedas fish pie—is that bizarre?'

Yes. 'No!'

'Really? Shawn says it's super weird.'

Across the room, Shawn is chatting intently with a vaguely familiar couple. He spots Lucky and raises a hand. Lucky waves back. He turns to Anita and rolls his eyes. 'God, sometimes Shawn has so little imagination—thank goodness he has you.' He takes a step towards the kitchen. 'Come, show me this pie.'

Shawn watches them head into the kitchen, hoping Lucky will say something about the ridiculous pie. He thanks god that the turkey is a regular, normal roasted thing and not some try-hard fusion horror. He thanks god for supermarkets in general, and for Cold Storage in particular.

A photo from Pearl—a large bowl of noodles in a dark, spicy-looking soup full of thick chunks of stewed beef, topped with spring onions and half a salted egg. Lucky gnashes his teeth at his phone screen.

A text message pops up in the chat window under the photo: `How was lunch? Look what I had. Rawon! So good. Beef is super tender.`

His thumbs fly across the screen keyboard. `Damn that looks good! Rawon! I want rawon! Lunch isn't ready.:( Waiting for the assam pedas fish pie. 10 mins more.`

WTF. It's almost 3.00.
Yes! Hungry as hell.
I've had two lunches. WTF is assam pedas fish pie.
Anita's being creative.
Well don't let her poison you.

Lucky sees Shawn coming towards him and slips his phone into his pocket. His stomach rumbles loudly, roused by thoughts of rawon. This is all Pearl's fault. If she hadn't run off to Surabaya, she'd be here. And they'd be Christmassing together, at home, with beer . . . and . . . and beef noodles. *Damn it, Pearl.* Beef noodles are all he can think of now.

* * *

The living room is perfect. Lucky's heart fills with the same mixture of awe and envy every time he's here. Perfect proportions—what a length-width-ceiling-height ratio! Perfect natural lighting—could the windows be better placed? No. And, of course because it's Shawn, self-described *Apartamento* addict, the furnishings are painfully tasteful—soft grey walls, shelves in polished wood, antique mirrors, vintage prints. Large potted fig in the corner.

'It's like he needs people to say, "Oh my god you have such great taste, are you a designer?"' Pearl said to Lucky years ago. 'And then he can tell them, "Oh yes, I'm an architect," and everyone just *gushes*. You know, maybe it's a good thing you didn't end up practising.'

Which was nonsense, because for years, all she did was lecture him about wasting all that time getting a degree he wasn't going to use. Which was silly, because clearly all the stuff he learnt at school was useful because architecture is *everywhere*.

'Lucky? Don't *stare*—go, go.'

Shawn has armed Lucky with two glasses of wine and now aims him in the direction of the new arrival, Nisha. She is smallish and pretty, even if her dress is a little too tight and her eyeliner is already smudged. She's Anita's colleague, Shawn tells him, and she's single.

Lucky lopes over and hands her a glass of wine, introducing himself. 'So, Nisha, you're also in the HR department?'

'Oh no, we call it Talent now. We're in the Talent team.' She smiles up at him and blinks. He finds the smudged eyeliner distracting. It makes him think of . . . motor oil.

'Talent?'

'Talent management. Because, well, everyone in the company is considered a talent, right, not a resource, right, and we manage the talent.'

'Right.'

Lucky smiles and takes a sip of wine. It's all a bit daft, these new names dressing up tedious things. And talent management sounds to him like a euphemism for running a brothel, or maybe a seedy karaoke joint.

Nisha smiles back. What a nice smile he has. She tells him how glad she is to be here. 'Isn't Christmas so sad when your family doesn't celebrate?'

Lucky nods, looking into her smoky eyes, thinking of Uncle Thiang's old motorcycle—does he still have it? Would he be willing to sell? Lucky sniffs the air. Ah, that damn pie is just about done.

* * *

'Pearl Lee is your sister?'

He should have known that it would come to this. It always does. But, as usual, Lucky is caught completely off guard, and today he is caught off guard and in between mouthfuls of assam pedas fish pie. He chews, keeping his face down and his eyes in the middle distance. Can he pretend not to have heard her? More thoughtful chewing. Lucky loads more pie onto his fork—it's much, much better than he expected. Assam pedas fish pie—who would have thought? Well, actually, Anita—he wonders if she will share the recipe.

A clatter from the other end of the table—the woman who is half of the just-barely-familiar couple he met earlier now dramatically puts down her spoon. 'Is Pearl Lee your sister?' She has raised her voice a little, and now everyone at the table is looking at Lucky.

In front of him, Shawn shrugs. Next to the woman, Anita shoots Lucky an apologetic look. Lucky turns his head slowly to face the woman, quickly noting the widened eyes, the expectant expression, the way she's leaning in his direction. Her name—is it June? Jill? And where has he seen her before? Lucky smiles his lazy smile. Well, grab the bull by the horns, eh? The cow. Do cows have horns?

'Yes.'

She gasps. 'Wow, that's amazing.'

Lucky laughs. 'Well, I don't know what Anita's told you—but Pearl's just like any other elder sister. You know—bossy, mean, never ever minds her own business . . . but she feeds me well.' *And occasionally abandons me at Christmas.*

Lucky turns away, but she presses on. 'I'm such a big fan—I love her show! And I just bought her book on dumplings for Anita here.' She beams.

'Book *of* Dumplings.' Lucky smiles. Pearl would have growled.

'Oh yes, of course—*A Book of Dumplings*. A book on dumplings called *A Book of Dumplings*.' She giggles. 'She kept saying that on the show.'

Nisha smacks the table in front of her. Rather unnecessarily, Lucky thinks. 'Wait, is your sister the one on *Oodles of Noodles*?'

'Yes.' He hates the name. His own idea for the name of that series on Southeast Asian noodles was *Bowled Over*, but Discovery didn't think it was quite noodley enough.

'That's so cool.' Nisha's turn to widen her eyes. 'I just finished the first season—is there going to be another one?'

'Could be.' He gives her a conspiratorial wink. 'She's always working on something.' In fact, it is the second season of *Oodles of Noodles* that has stolen his sister from him and compelled him to spend Christmas at Shawn's. But Lucky doesn't bother to say this— it's time they talked about something other than the wonderful, clever Pearl Lee, who's managed to monetize her compulsive eating, cooking, talking.

'I hope everyone has space for dessert!' Anita (when did she leave the room?) sets a large dish on the table. Plum pudding! Lucky brightens up. He dreams of Anita's plum pudding from time to time—tart with preserved plums and sultanas, drenched in plum brandy. 'Hang on, so your name is Lucky Lee?' The woman's husband now, grinning like he's told a huge joke. 'And Pearl Lee—oh my god.'

Lucky Lee. Pearl Lee. Luckily. Pearly. *Is it really that funny?* Lucky smiles and waves his fork. 'I dare you to find two cuter names in all of Singapore.' He wishes Pearl were here—she'd pick this up and run with it.

Anita wishes she hadn't said anything to Jenna about Pearl. It was so silly, but she just felt like she had to say that her curry kapitan had a pretty famous fan . . . and Pearl did like it and, well, Lucky was right there—exactly the kind of proof a story like that required. She cuts him an extra-large slice of plum pudding to make amends.

'So, Lucky, in that episode in Myanmar—'

'Oooh yes, yes, that's my favourite!'

Lucky crams his mouth full of pudding and pours himself another glass of wine.

* * *

The apartment is finally quiet again, the sink is full of dishes, and the leftovers have all been stowed away in the fridge. Obviously, they'll be eating kapitan curry and turkey and fish pie all the way until the new year. But the plum pudding—well, there's not that much left after she set aside that slice for Lucky to take home, and Anita can't see the point of saving it for tomorrow. Or tonight.

As she wears down the remaining chunk of pudding on the serving dish, Lucky turns on the tap and starts rinsing bits of food off the plates.

'Oh, leave it—I'll do it later.' This is an auto response. Anita knows quite well that Lucky will insist on washing up. For this, she loves Pearl. 'So what do you think?'

'About what?'

'Nisha. My colleague.' Anita swallows a mouthful of pudding. 'The one in the black dress.'

Lucky shrugs. 'She seems nice. Are you guys close?'

'We're okay. I think she's pretty cool.'

Anita looks at her phone. Half an hour ago, just five minutes after she left, Nisha texted her: I like him! At first I was like, hmmm sounds like he's all over the place, but I like him! Reading the message again, Anita smiles to herself. She didn't doubt it for a second. Like so many women before her, Nisha has fallen into The Lucky Trap. It's a bit like the Bermuda Triangle—they wander in, they lose all sense of direction, they wander around for some time, and then maybe, maybe, they break free. Every woman meets Lucky and feels a connection—Shawn thinks it's a mystery; Anita thinks it's the disarming grin and the long lashes.

The first time she met Lucky—Was it eight years ago? Seven?—was at the launch of some very fancy restaurant on some remote beach on Sentosa, perched at the edge of the sea. Shawn was so thrilled. He was still new at the firm, and it was his first time seeing something he'd helped design actually exist for other people. Anita almost didn't go. She really liked Shawn, but swanky events made her nervous and she didn't know what to wear—and then when she arrived, there they were on the terrace, Lucky and Pearl, laughing, arms waving and sinuous, demonstrating some very odd bird-like dance moves as Shawn and a few others looked on, laughing and clutching each other while everyone else sipped champagne and tried not to gawk. It was hard work, not gawking—he and she looked so alike in their dark suits and skinny ties, tall and reed-thin with the same long limbs and the same wide mouth and that same thick mop of hair falling over their eyebrows, and from a distance, it was like looking at a crazy, two-headed spider. At the entrance to the restaurant, Anita stopped and stared at the spider and thought, *wahhh*. She might have even said it out loud when they were introduced. Thankfully, Shawn was skipping about like a child and didn't notice. Neither did Pearl. In those days, she was still—what was it? Food editor? Food critic?—at that snooty magazine, and never paid attention to anything or anyone she didn't have to write about. And Lucky just leaned over and told Anita that seriously, he was starving from the effort of eating so many tiny little canapes.

Still soaping up the dishes, Lucky turns to face her. He raises his eyebrows. 'Are you trying to set me up?'

'I'm trying to set *her* up.' Anita rises from the kitchen table and goes up to him. She leans back against the kitchen counter. 'She's really fun—lots of cool stories. Very adventurous. She's travelled quite a bit ... I think she was in Bhutan last month.' What else? What does Lucky want in a woman? 'And she likes to cook.'

He flashes her the disarming grin. 'She sounds wonderful. Good luck.'

'We can all hang out over New Year's? I think she's free—'

'I won't be back from Bali until after New Year's. But Pearl will be around. She's back on the twenty-eighth.'

'And you're heading out on the same day?'

'No—I fly the day after tomorrow.' He sighs happily, thinking again of the sea and all the things he will eat and the octopuses or octopi he might see. 'Can't wait.'

Anita texts her friend: He's in Bali for New Year's but let's figure out something for the week after. BBQ?

* * *

All packed?

Nope. Tomorrow.

Don't forget your trunks and meds and adaptor. Did you feed the cat?

Yes!

Pearl's next message is a grinning cat emoji. Very good!

Lucky rolls his eyes. Meowrr! The best.

Night. Off to get kopi. Ratna says hi. XX

Hi back. Night.

He runs downstairs and, in the darkness, fills up the cat's fish-shaped enamel dish. The cat watches him from under the papaya tree, eyes narrowed.

The airport

is one of Lucky's favourite places in the world. In the space of four wondrous terminals, cocooned in cladded concrete and plush carpet and soundproof glass and bespoke scent, interspersed with hanging orchids and bubbling fountains and even butterflies, Changi Airport brings together Lucky's favourite restaurants, his favourite fro-yo chain, his favourite Japanese lifestyle brand, his favourite electronics store, his favourite fast food, luggage, skincare, shoes, bak kwa, durian cake, salted egg crisps . . . To Lucky, the airport is a wonder of the world, and if he were a poet, he'd write it a sonnet.

But today there's no time for Lucky's post-customs, pre-flight routine of coffee and a round of the duty-free stores, no time to check out the new Bose headphones, try on shoes and sunglasses, poke at the designer bags and wonder if he should bother, pick out a couple of magazines—let alone write a sonnet. Instead, he's dashing like a madman through Terminal 2, dragging his trolley case behind him, his backpack bouncing uncomfortably against his tailbone. Why, why did he think it was a good idea to stop for dim sum before the flight?

Dinah had thought him a fool and said so. 'Stupid—there's no time. I'll just drop you off.'

'But we have nearly two hours—plenty of time, and the har gao at that place, what's it called, is so good. And you love the carrot cake. Come on, Dinah . . .'

The food was sublime—the dumplings, plump with juicy prawns, and the fried carrot cake almost made up for having to wake up at 7.30, shower half-asleep, and be picked up by a grumpy, grumbling Dinah who was bitterly and vociferously regretful about promising to drive him to the airport. But he was wrong about there being plenty of time. By the time the dumplings arrived, piping hot, there was only an hour left before his flight, and in the end he had to leave Dinah with the bill ('Go, you dumbass, just go!') and run to catch the inter-terminal train from Terminal 3 to Terminal 2, check in his large suitcase, clear customs, and rush to the gate before it closed.

The carpet makes it hard to move quickly—the soft, luxuriant pile provides just enough friction against the wheels of his trolley case to keep him from tearing down the corridor to gate C11. Struggling through the crowd, trying desperately not to slow down, Lucky resorts to picking it up to run around a dawdling family of five and their parade of matching designer suitcases and then decides he may as well just continue to run, suitcase held above his head like a trophy, all the way to the gate.

The security guards at C11 eye him curiously as he heaves the suitcase onto the conveyor belt of the X-ray machine, but Lucky doesn't care. He flashes the guards a triumphant grin and walks through the metal detector. No beeps—yes! He grabs his suitcase and backpack, then jogs towards the entrance to the plane. And now for Bali!

'Two suitcases? For a week in Bali? What the hell did you pack?' That morning, while they rearranged the junk in her backseat to accommodate the smaller suitcase, Dinah told him yet again how she managed Europe for three months on just one forty-litre backpack. This is one of Dinah's favourite quick-and-easy anecdotes—she uses it to prove that she's efficient, resourceful, minimalist, unmaterialistic, low-maintenance, and organized, that she's a veritable, verifiable Uberwoman. 'You know what your problem is, Lucky? You're so spoilt.'

Safely on board now, leaning back in his seat, Lucky contemplates the small suitcase tucked in the overhead compartment, the large one nestled in the depths of the plane's underbelly, the backpack resting under the seat. Spoilt? Seriously, how unfair! It isn't like he's packed gourmet hot chocolate or one-thousand-thread count Egyptian cotton pillowcases or his own plates or anything ridiculous like that. Can't a man be fond of a few basic creature comforts?

Speaking of creatures . . .

Lucky takes out his phone and texts Dinah, quickly, before the flight attendants make their final rounds prior to take-off. `Remember to feed the cat. Thanks!` He slips the phone back into his pocket. He stops. He sighs. He takes it out again. `And the fish.`

He pauses, then types out another message in a different window. `Off to Bali. See you next week!` Should he ask if there's anywhere she wants to go, or just tell her he's cooking? Perhaps better that he should commandeer the situation and that kind of thing. Some women like that—would Rosalind?

'Sir, please switch off your phone or put it on flight mode. We're preparing for take-off.' The steward's steely smile assures Lucky that he means business.

'Sure, sorry.' He turns off his phone and tosses it into the pocket behind the seat in front of him, where it lands between the in-flight magazine and the sick bag.

Outside, the sun is beating down on the tarmac, and in his window seat, Lucky drifts off to sleep. Minutes pass. His shoulders sag, his head dips forward, his jaw slackens. He misses the safety demonstration; he sleeps through the chief flight attendant's reminder for passengers to keep their seats upright and seat belts tightly fastened for take-off; he doesn't hear her final caution against smoking in the toilets at any time during the flight.

But heat-induced sleep is no match for the roar of the plane's engines as it hurtles along the last hundred metres of the runway, the sudden force of the lift-off throwing everyone back against their seats—Lucky leaps awake, eyes flying open, heart slamming against his ribcage. For a moment, he is lost.

The engines quieten as the plane eases into a more horizontal position. A few more minutes and they are cruising. Just beyond the window next to Lucky, the aeroplane's left wing gleams in the bright sunshine. Far below, the clouds are white and pillowy and inviting. Like a giant soufflé, or a mattress made of meringue. Or a field of cotton candy. Or a great big bubble bath. The seat belt sign goes off with a prissy little ding, jolting Lucky wider awake and back into the plane.

The man on his right lets out a big, attention-seeking sort of sigh. He lets go of the arm rests on either side of him, leaving behind, Lucky notices, a thin layer of sweat. The woman in the aisle seat on the other side of the man curls her lip and looks away, pointedly edging away from the arm rest between them. Wiping his palms down on the knees of his jeans, the man turns to Lucky.

'I hate flying.' He manages to sound quite calm, but there's a sheen of sweat on his forehead. 'I wish there was another way to get to Bali.'

'Well, you could always take a boat.' Lucky loves boats. He and Pearl spent a lot of time canoeing when they were kids. Wow, if there were a ship or something that could get him straight from Singapore to Bali, he'd take it. Was there such a thing? 'There's a ferry to Sumatra from Malaysia, I think, and from there you can probably take another one to Java, and then to Bali? There's definitely a ferry from Java to Bali.' Lucky wishes he had thought of going to Bali by boat.

'I don't know. Sounds like it would take a long time.' The man shakes his head. 'And who has so much time?'

Actually, Lucky does. He never has to think about things like annual leave or running out of vacation days, not since his days as an intern, fresh out of university. Ten years ago, that was—no, twelve. The thought makes him feel a little guilty, so he continues to talk to the man for a little longer than empathy and good manners demand, listening with well-placed nods about his plans for his holiday.

'. . . lots of good walks—some very nice hills and rice fields near my friend's house.'

'Sounds amazing.' This is a lie. The idea of walking for pleasure is incomprehensible to Lucky, whose idea of a holiday is days on end at a beach or on a terrace of some sort, with great food close by and a view he doesn't have to work for and some magazines and movies on his iPad.

Encouraged, the man tells him about the birdwatching that awaits him in Bali—has Lucky ever tried birdwatching in Bali? The best time is near dawn, on the marshes. Would Lucky like to go? He could recommend some epic birdwatching tours or perhaps Lucky would be happy to go with him on an excursion to the nature reserves on the western coast?

Lucky wonders where the refreshment cart is—he'd like a coffee now. Or perhaps something a little stronger. Is it too early for gin?

* * *

For the second time in the space of an hour, Lucky is jolted awake by the same beast of a plane. He blinks, foggy-headed, frowning. What the—? The plane, it's bouncing up and down in a very unsettling way, jerking everyone around in their seats. The seat belt sign is on. Lucky scrambles to fasten his as the pilot's voice comes on overhead, imploring everyone to please, stay calm and keep their seat belts on— it's a bit of turbulence, nothing to worry about. Lucky sits up straight, feeling suddenly dizzy, wondering if he should be worried. But plane crashes are super unlikely, aren't they? Sometime, somewhere, he's read that there's a much higher chance of dying in a car accident on the way to or from the airport than in a plane crash. As if in response, the plane suddenly lurches forward. In the overhead compartment, suitcases collide. The lights flicker. Someone shrieks.

It's the man next to him. He's bent forward, breathing in shallow gasps, his hands gripping the arm rests. The plane jumps. The man shrieks. Another jump. Another shriek.

'Oh my god oh my god oh my god.'

The plane begins to jerk around more violently. Lucky puts both hands on the seat in front of him and pushes against it to keep from being thrown about like some helpless toy.

'All passengers, brace! Brace!'

Brace? The command from the pilot sends everyone into a momentary frenzy, but quickly, thankful for something to focus on, they get into whatever versions of the brace position they can manage. The man next to Lucky begins to cry—a pathetic, stricken sort of half-whine-half-cry, like the sounds of a small trapped animal. Lucky watches him, frozen, struggling between horror and pity. The man turns to Lucky, bawling open-mouthed, babbling in between sobs.

If this is the end, am I okay with it? Lucky wishes his last text to Pearl hadn't been about the babi guling he thought he'd be having for dinner tonight. If this is the end, he'd like to have said something worth remembering. *So long, and thanks for all the papaya salad. And it was me who broke Papa's clock.* Pearl would laugh at that—and she'd have to forgive him for not admitting to the whole clock business and getting them into so much shit when they were kids. He thinks about Dinah—she would remember the cat and the fish, whether he lives or dies. Shawn will be fine, though hopefully upset. The electronics voucher he bought for Shawn's Christmas present that he forgot to bring to Christmas lunch— he left that in his desk drawer in his bedroom; hopefully someone will find it. The plum pudding and the leftover curry that Anita made him take home that day—at least that's all in the freezer.

The man beside Lucky continues to weep. The plane lurches again, tossing Lucky off his seat for a second. *Okay. Just do it just do it.* Lucky sighs and holds out his hand to the man, who just stares at him and continues to cry loudly.

Lucky grabs his hand. It's cold and wet and gross. He gives it a squeeze. 'Come on. Let's do this.'

* * *

The babi guling is delicious. Juicy, perfectly spiced, just a hint of smoke. Incredibly crispy skin. And that green chilli sambal—still the best he's ever had. The last time they were here, three years ago, he and Pearl brought ten bottles of it back to Singapore with them.

Lucky orders another bottle of beer—last one. There's no way he's going to be hungover tomorrow, on the first proper day of his vacation.

Besides, he's agreed to go birdwatching.

* * *

It better not rain. She's left her umbrella in the car.

Frowning, wishing she hadn't agreed to help Lucky, Dinah looks out the kitchen window into the back garden. It's two in the afternoon, and the garden is full of shadows. No sign of the cat—but it could be anywhere. Jesus. How many gardeners must these people have?

'Coconut!' She squints at the large thicket of pandan, hoping to see some sort of movement possibly indicative of a cat. 'Coconut! Coconut!' Should she just leave the food out? But then it might attract ants, right? And Pearl could be so weird about ants.

'Coconut!' Dinah is beginning to feel ridiculous. Coconut—what a stupid name for a cat. If she had a cat—but she wouldn't, because cats are awful and mean and totally useless—she would never give it a stupid name like Coconut. It would at least be something cool and Egyptian. Like Hapshetsut. Or maybe an Asian queen. Like Lakshmi Bai.

Fine. She'll put out the food first and see how it goes. Tearing open a foil packet of premium cat food, she makes a face. The greyish brown lumpy paste smells weird and looks nothing like the real fish and seafood the packet promises. Well, whatever. She studies the pack. 'Princess. Because they're your little royals.' Oh, god. And it probably cost more than the thosai she had for breakfast.

She looks around the massive kitchen, at the rows of stove tops and cooker hoods, the wall of floor-to-ceiling cupboards, the industrial-size oven, the two fridges larger than her wardrobe at home, the herbs growing in pots on a shelf next to the window, the vintage coffee machine, the antique kitchen table bigger than her bed, the massive granite island smack in the middle, presiding over everything. Incredible, that people actually live like this. Incredible, that her mother's spartan kitchen—the kitchen she still thought of as her mother's, with its tiny Formica table and narrow shelves and cupboards so cramped they had to keep their largest pot on the stove and move it around whenever they needed to use the second hob— and this kitchen, Pearl's kitchen, could both go by the name 'kitchen', and incredible, that there should be nothing odd about this.

'Coconut!'

Well, she has better things to do than stand around waiting for the cat to show up. Dinah walks out through the kitchen door and puts the cat's fish-shaped dish next to a large potted cactus on the back patio.

'Coconut!' *Stupid cat. Where the hell is it?*

A rustle from the mango tree makes her look up. Nope—squirrels. What's that brownish thing up among the leaves? Dinah squints. Is that Coconut, watching her, taunting her? Cats are such devilish things.

A sharp, shrill clanging from inside the house. For a moment, Dinah stands still, puzzled. The clanging continues. *Oh, fuck.* It's her phone—she changed the ringtone to a more annoying one yesterday. Well, annoying—yes; actually recognizable—not yet.

The phone is on the kitchen island, vibrating and flashing like a crazed jellyfish. She looks at the screen. It's Shawn. Dinah frowns. He never ever calls her.

'Hello?'

'Have you seen the news?'

She hasn't, but Shawn doesn't wait for her reply. He charges at her, loudly, speaking far too quickly, everything tumbling out in a confused jumble of sentences. Dinah goes to the window. In the garden, everything looks exactly the same.

'When? When? Shawn, slow down.'

He's crying now. She's crying now, even if she isn't sure she understands him. The sobs coming out of her don't sound like any sound she's ever made—she's surprised at how coarse and guttural she sounds, how like a . . . pig, or a duck.

Outside, the cat is enjoying its lunch. Sensing her at the window, it looks up briefly. Its eyes narrow, sizing her up. Satisfied that she isn't dangerous, perhaps even recognizing her, Coconut blinks and returns to its little blob of paradise.

On the phone, Shawn has stopped speaking. He's still crying, but Dinah refuses to say anything as stupid as 'Don't cry,' or worse, 'It's going to be okay.' Pearl would slap her.

Dinah takes a long, deep breath. 'Have you called him?' She's sure he hasn't, but it's something to say.

'No.'

Outside, the rain has started. Now she can hear the raindrops on the roof. Faster, and faster.

Damn. She's left her umbrella in the car.

Lucky

looks very small. Dinah watches him through the great glass walls of the arrivals section as he waits for his bag at one of the luggage belts. She spots his suitcase before he does—it's neon green and she chose it at that warehouse sale that they went to last year, deep in the belly of Sembawang. It was ridiculously crowded, even in the middle of the afternoon on a weekday, and she had laughed at the thought of so many rich idiots driving out into the middle of an industrial estate just to buy luxury luggage.

Lucky's managed to spot his suitcase. She waves. He doesn't see her, but she's waiting for him when he passes through the automatic doors. She takes his suitcase and he lets her. She takes his hand and he lets her. They walk to the car park two levels down and throw all his stuff into her car, and then she drives him home.

Dinah wants to ask if he's eaten anything, but she's afraid she will sound like Pearl.

They arrive at the house unscathed, against the odds that that damn plane couldn't defy—how true can it be that they're likelier to die on the way home from the airport than on a plane? Shawn's waiting outside the gate. They go in together. They get very, very drunk, and then they tumble into Lucky's bed, dizzy and dumb. They wake up the next morning, dry-mouthed and groggy, forgetful for the tiniest while, and then they remember. They sit in the living room and watch the news for the rest of the day and the day after, eating random things from the fridge at odd intervals. The news channels show the same footage over and over—the map with the dotted line moving across it, starting from the black dot marked 'Surabaya' and stopping somewhere in the blue bit meant to be the Java Sea; the representatives from the airline saying they still don't know what went wrong or how the crash happened; the list of passengers, with little flags next to the names to show where they're from. The newspapers online are pretty much the same, repeating the same vague, incomplete tale with gusto and from as many points of view as they can manage.

Lucky feeds the cat and the fish. Shawn and Dinah go back to work.

Two days later, her body is still missing. But Pearl is such a strong swimmer, and Lucky imagines her cutting through the water like a razor. He imagines her climbing onto a rescue boat, gritting her teeth and demanding a towel, asking what took them so long.

He takes the sealed containers of dried squid and the bags of rice crisps and the tins of salt-and-pepper cashews and the many, many packets of dried mango out of his suitcases. He'll leave some of everything for her, of course—she'll want to stuff her face when they finally bring her home.

The towel

is what gives him away.

He takes a few steps away from the window, but it's too late. He knows he's been seen.

The towel is bright yellow with a faint pattern of ducks. Of course the ducks aren't visible all the way from the gate, but the blob of yellow behind the gauze curtain must be. And now the man at the gate is staring right at him and waving.

Lucky raises his hand to touch the towel, then realizes that now he looks like he's waving back. Damn. The man is a stranger—it's hard to see his face, but the figure is unfamiliar. The towel is fluffy as hell, and so . . . soft. He takes the bit dangling over his face and nuzzles it.

The man keeps waving. He presses the bell switch on the gate post, then presses it again. Something in the way he's holding his head still, eyes presumably fixed on the blob of yellow in the window, strikes Lucky as predatory. A small predator, not a big one—like Coconut going after an insect. Lucky watches him for a few more minutes, incurious. The doorbell rings again and again and again and again.

Quite suddenly, as the predator at the gate continues to stare, the yellow blob at the window disappears. Moments later, the door opens and the blob reappears, now with a head attached to it, along with a neck and a torso and arms and legs.

The thing calls out, 'It's not locked. Pull down.'

For a moment, the man at the gate doesn't move. Lucky can imagine him thinking: Really? Not locked? *This* gate? Pull what down?

Then the man spots the lever near the middle of the gate, on the inside. He reaches through the bars and pulls it downwards. The latch lifts and one arm of the gate slowly swings open.

Later, Lucky will wonder why he opened the door for the stranger, but he won't dwell on it. For now, he watches the man approach, walking down the long, wide driveway of pale yellow stone tiles. He looks taller now than he did at the gate and younger—a kid, really. The clothes are neat and unimaginative—dark jeans, collared T-shirt in a bluish hue, sneakers. A large, worn-out satchel hangs from one shoulder.

'Hello madam, thanks for letting me in.' Lucky raises an eyebrow; the boy stops and stares. 'Sorry, sir.'

'It's fine.' And it is—what can he expect, really, from a stranger? The towel, wrapped around his head, its ends knotted, bow-like, at the top, has no meaning for the boy.

Even under the porch, it's far too bright and far too warm. One hand on the door, Lucky inches back into the house. He wishes he hadn't opened the door. Or stood at the window. Or gone to the window to check when the doorbell rang the first time. Or come downstairs. Or wrapped her towel around his head. Or showered. Or got out of bed. Behind him, the monstrous cuckoo clock his parents dragged home from Germany forty years ago begins to cry out. Today, the cuckoo sounds louder, pushier, than usual. Embarrassed, a little distressed, unused to feeling embarrassed or distressed, Lucky smiles widely, even encouragingly, at the intruder on his doorstep.

Who started to introduce himself while Lucky's mind wandered, who is now explaining why he's here. '. . . architecture school. I'm doing some research for my professor and he mentioned this house . . .'

'*This* house?' Lucky's smile widens. 'Your *architecture* professor mentioned *this* house? What exactly did he say?' He wonders which professor.

'He said it was interesting—lots of contrasting elements, unusual materials . . .'

How very PC. For once, Lucky would like to have someone say it like it is—that the house is not so much interesting as it is horrifying. Crude. Crazy.

'Cuckoo!'

Well, yes.

He can't remember actually inviting the boy in, but he steps back and the boy steps forward and suddenly they're both inside and the boy is looking around, eyes darting everywhere, and then the door swings shut and Lucky is offering to get him a glass of water.

'Thanks. Wow, it's much bigger than it looks from outside.'

'Well, it's a long sort of house. And I suppose you'd like a tour?'

Two yeses, two eager nods. Lucky doesn't know why he brought up the subject of a tour—he's getting tired again and he wants to go back to bed, but it feels like good manners. And this guy had come all the way from wherever it was he came from just to see his father's house. If Pearl were here, she would laugh—and she would give this guy a tour.

He leads the way towards the kitchen—better settle that glass of water first—and the boy follows, staring. Lucky smiles to himself. *Cool it, or those eyes may never go back into their sockets.* Lucky wonders what the guy is thinking. People never, ever say what they're thinking about the house. Maybe they can't—he imagines it's like walking through a large chamber full of people throwing things at you. Not pointy, dangerous things, but a random assortment of big, bright, bouncing objects.

'Wah . . .'

The boy is staring past Lucky's shoulder, his mouth slightly open. Lucky sighs. Oh, right—the stairs.

The boy walks across the living room and into the long, narrow courtyard-like space that punctures through the middle of the house, from about halfway down the living room right up to the kitchen at the back and all the way up to the skylight in the roof. The stairs, which connect all three floors, have been constructed to cantilever out from the stone wall on one side of the courtyard so they would appear to be floating. Gave his father quite the kick.

'First in Singapore, Lucky—*first*. Your Uncle Desmond told your mother it was a stupid idea but look at it. Who's stupid now? Lucky, in life, you cannot simply listen to people because they say you're stupid, okay?'

Lucky heard this so often he grew to expect it every time one of these subjects came up at home: 1) Uncle Desmond, 2) architectural marvels, 3) good ideas, and 4) people who couldn't see good ideas until they were forced to stare at the physical manifestation of these good ideas.

The architecture student—whose name Lucky didn't catch but they were past that now—has stopped moving, mesmerized by the physical manifestation of his father's good idea. But not quite for the reason that his father intended. All sense of propriety abandoned, the boy rushes up to the stairs and walks up a few steps, stroking the little spines on the dragon's back with an expression of child-like awe.

This was not just a floating stair—it was a floating stair with a floating dragon for a handrail. At the bottom of the stairs, it greeted you, its massive, menacing demon-like head raised, its bulging eyes, flared nostrils, twisting horns, open mouth and sharp teeth just at eye level if you were, say, five years old. And as you climbed up the stairs, it went with you, its sinuous, scaly body leading you up and up and up. Only his father, the man who never cared if anyone agreed with him, could have wanted and ordered something like this for his home. Carved out of the finest Malaysian teak, he told everyone. Lucky isn't sure how many people remember this—no one remembers the teak when they're trying to forget the dragon, right?

Lucky never liked the dragon. When he was five, Pearl told him to swear not to tell anyone she'd told him, but that the other brother had been fed to the dragon for being naughty. She sighed, one hand stroking his head, 'I could hear the dragon crunching his bones up all the way from my room. He was so small—just about your size.'

'But it's not a real dragon.'

'Silly Lucky—dragons only come to life at night. When we're all asleep.'

'But you said you heard it eat the other brother.'

'I woke up! It was so loud.' Her eyes widened. She covered her mouth. 'So horrible.'

'Were you scared?'

'Super scared!' She took his hand. 'But if you listen to everything I say, I'll make sure the dragon doesn't get you.'

And so he had her protection. But for years, he climbed the stairs crab-like, his back flat against the wall so he could keep an eye on the dragon, just in case it decided to strike. And some nights from his bedroom, he would hear a noise from downstairs, a sound that wasn't the usual furniture creaks, a sound that could have been something stirring, something shifting, something hunting for something to eat, and he would lie very, very still in bed, frozen, certain that if he made any sudden moves, the dragon would hear him and finish him off before even Pearl could stop it.

'Is it okay to take pictures?'

Lucky wants to say no. He feels suddenly, curiously, protective of this ridiculous dragon, and he doesn't want it—or any of the other possibly more ridiculous things here—captured for posterity in someone's research paper.

'No.'

Lucky's 'no' is, as usual, perfection—calm, mild, no offer of an explanation, and then a pause and a brief smile. The boy looks disappointed, but he doesn't protest. He gives the dragon's head a kindly pat and follows Lucky across the rest of the courtyard and into the kitchen.

Lucky fills a glass with water from a bottle in the fridge and hands it to the boy. 'You can bring this with you. I'll show you the other floors.'

The other floors aren't quite so interesting. Mr Lee didn't really expect to give most guests a tour of anything but the ground floor, so the living room, the kitchen, and the garden received most of his attention. But he did have a study–library built on the third floor, with an adjoining tea room opening out into a garden of bougainvillaea and bamboo. Lucky decides he will show this to the student, though perhaps he won't tell him that his father wasn't much of a reader at all and didn't care for tea, being, after all, in the coffee business.

'Wow.'

The jar on his father's oversized mahogany desk hasn't been touched for years, but he lets the student pick it up. Who cares, really, if the boy drops the pickled snake? Who cares if the jar breaks and all of that snake stuff gets all over the old parquet? He'd just Google a solution—Google nearly always has a solution.

'What is it?' The boy holds it up to his face, then up against the light.

Lucky isn't sure. Pearl was always changing her mind about what it was—once, she said it was a hibernating alien worm, but another time she said it was a shrinking potion, like the one that Alice drank.

'But that's in a bottle!'

She gave him a knowing look. 'Yes, and someone made it, right? Everyone knows you need a snake in a jar to make a shrinking potion.'

The snake coiled at the bottom of the jar is small and whitish, surprisingly intact after so many years of swimming in whatever the hell that clear yellow liquid is.

Lucky watches the student put the jar back on the desk, wondering where his father had got it from. Vietnam? Indonesia? Had to be one of the coffee countries. 'Hmm. Some sort of snake wine, I think.' And who knows why his father thought a jar of snake wine would be an amusing thing to have in the library? Thankfully, he'd left his wife to pick out the books or they might have ended up with—whatever. It doesn't matter.

The student doesn't appear so keen on the garden, but he comments on the odd pairing of bougainvillaea and bamboo. 'Very different textures. What an interesting contrast.'

'Yes.' Also, they're the only two plants that manage to survive up here, in direct sunlight. His mother used to try so hard to get that soft, wispy look going, to keep the bamboo company—she tried dog fennel, ferns, some sort of dwarf pine, but nothing stayed alive. And then she gave up and brought in pots and pots of bougainvillaea she had bought for cheap somewhere and that was that.

Well, the plants are definitely alive, in spite of the recent neglect. In fact, the bougainvillaea's in full bloom and the garden is a riot of pink and purple. The bamboo doesn't seem to mind. Lucky watches the bamboo plants sway in the wind, oblivious to the poky, psycho exuberance of the bougainvillaea and decides he must come up here more often. There's a lesson somewhere here that he's been missing out on.

'Where's your room?' the student asks as they go down the floating stairs, just as they're about to pass the second floor—it's the level Lucky's excluded from the tour, so it's quite obvious to the boy that it's where the family actually lives.

Lucky points at a closed door, hoping the boy won't ask to see it.

He doesn't. He points at another closed door, further away from the stair landing. 'And whose room is that?'

Lucky shakes his head. It was a terrible idea, showing the boy around their house. 'We can't go in there.'

'Okay.' The boy starts walking down the stairs.

Lucky follows him. 'I'm really sorry—it's my sister's room, and I don't really know what to do with it now, you know. I mean, after my father died, we cleared out most of his stuff and my mum's, and my sister used their room to keep her clothes and things. But now—'

The boy stares. He fiddles with the empty glass he's holding. He looks away from his host, who's now mumbling to himself. Up until now, besides the fact that he's wearing a towel around his head, the man has been really normal and nice and polite, but suddenly he sounds like he's freaking out a bit. Should he offer to get him a glass of water? Would that be weird? Confused, the boy stays exactly where he is and says nothing. He studies the long rectangular pond below the stairs—what kind of fish are those? Probably carp. And what were those little statues at the bottom? Dogs?

Lucky sits down with a loud sigh on the bottom-most stair. 'You know, I'm really tired.' He rubs his face against a bit of towel.

'Are you okay?'

Lucky thinks of all the things he needs to do for the wake in a couple of days—the flowers, the canopy, the food, the tables and chairs and all of that, and does he need to get someone to clean up the house or is cleaning up for a wake considered unlucky and should he ask someone about that or just do whatever he likes, and is he really supposed to call up everyone personally to invite them? And honestly, why are they bothering with a wake? Also, photos, fucking photos.

'Of course we must have a wake,' Aunty Maggie kept saying last week, when he made the mistake of calling her with the news that the search had been called off. Aunty Maggie never said exactly why they must have one, but then Aunty Dolly called and said Aunty Maggie called and of course they must have one, and he said yes because Uncle Desmond always agreed with them both, so why fight it?

Well, screw them. He's going back to bed. Good thing he's still in his pyjamas.

He stands up and crosses the room, then fishes around in a large bronze bowl in the middle of the coffee table. 'Here, in case you need anything else for your project or anything.' He hands the boy a card: 'Caffiend: Coffees from Southeast Asia'. 'Can you let yourself out? Drop by the cafe whenever, okay? If I'm not there, just leave a message.'

Lucky turns and starts climbing the stairs. He should probably drop by the cafe himself, soon.

* * *

Mr Thiang has always liked the lions. Standing opposite his old friend's house, he stares at them and thinks—that Mr Lee really knew how to get people's attention. Such a clever man. When people were drinking kopi at home, he started his kopitiam. One shop, then two, then three. And then when there were so many coffee shops everywhere, he started selling coffee powder in small packs so people could make their kopi at home. Always, always, Mr Lee had to do something different—*like these lions lah.*

Mr Lee, if he were alive, would have laughed loudly and clapped his friend on the back—he was the kind of man who laughed loudly and clapped people on their backs. He had the lions made in 1977, five years after he bought the house and business was, as he liked to say, boom-boom-booming. He didn't mind that no one else said boom-boom-booming; he didn't mind that his brother-in-law the doctor openly grimaced every time he said it; and he definitely didn't mind that the neighbours on their evening strolls stopped to stare at the massive stone lions flanking his gate.

It was partly a feng shui thing—lions of this kind (the male with one paw on a sack of money, the female with one paw on a cub) were meant to bring luck. Luck was always a good thing. No businessman would ever discount the role of luck—if you did, it abandoned you, and then where would you be? Living off your brother's family, like his friend Jit back in Ipoh. But aside from making sure the stars aligned, Lee Joo Meng also really, really wanted a way to announce to the smug, old-money, English-educated pigs who were his neighbours on Swan Street that he had not only arrived—he was here to stay.

Lions on gate posts were not new to Swan Street. A few houses had them—haughty things the size of cats, usually in marble, eyeing passers-by from their perch with coolly detached interest. *Nice lions*, Mr Lee thought, careful to meet the lions' gazes whenever he passed by, noting how they added an air of superiority to the houses they guarded.

But lions *as* gate posts—that would make people pay attention.

There is plenty of opportunity for this tonight, and for the next couple of days—the house on Swan Street hasn't seen so many visitors since Mr Lee's own wake and funeral eighteen years ago. As Mr Thiang walks through the gate, he can't help but notice how similar it all looks—an identical white canopy hangs over the front porch; under it, about fifteen tables have been set up, covered by white tablecloths; even the buffet table is in exactly the same spot. And they've probably hired the same brass band for the funeral.

Aiya, when we die, we're all the same lah.

It's been years since Mr Thiang has seen most of the people here, who are now sitting around the tables eating peanuts and sipping various hot beverages from little paper cups—and he's surprised a few of them are still alive. Old Madam Khoo must be a hundred by now. And was that Cikgu Firdaus? Must be long retired—he was Mrs Thiang's youngest brother's history teacher, and that must have been, what, forty years ago? Mr Thiang feels very, very, very old tonight.

'Hi, Uncle Thiang. Thanks for coming.'

Mr Thiang squints up at Lucky, then grabs his hands. 'Must lah. Of course must come.'

Mr Lee's boy is just as tall as his father was. But he looks like his mother. Betty Chong—how they all used to stare. How they used to dream—that voice, that hair, that figure! Everyone thought she was going to end up with Old Khoo's son, the fellow who had come home from England with a law degree and very shiny shoes. Old Khoo definitely thought so when he started building that second house on the family stretch off Frankel Avenue. And then Betty married this poor coffee seller from Ipoh—he wasn't even the owner of the coffee store back then; he was just the owner's poor nephew, some kampung boy helping out at the store on Smith Street, lugging sacks of coffee powder and driving the lorry around to deliver them to the big grocery stores and the hotels and the ang moh restaurants.

It was Mr Thiang's mother who broke the news to their family. She had learnt it at her weekly mahjong outing with the other Peranakan bibiks. They were having dinner, and his father was so shocked he stopped eating. The strip of pork hanging from his chopsticks halted in the middle of its journey from serving plate to mouth; a drop of sauce was allowed to drip onto the table.

'*Apa? Anak Chong kahwin itu budak jual kopi? Aiyo, chio see lang.*'[1]

Well, the dead could laugh all they wanted. Mr Lee certainly never cared. And Betty Chong married her coffee-seller boy.

Accepting a cup of coffee from Lucky, Mr Thiang goes with him to take a look at the display of Pearl's photographs on the stage-like area set a little apart from all the tables and the peanut-chomping guests.

There's a photograph of Pearl as a child, standing outside the house. A sunny day, and she's squinting into the camera. Another photograph is of her on the beach, her teenage face inscrutable, her hair down to her waist. Lucky was surprised to find that photo tucked away among his sister's things; she always said she hated her long hair. A photo of her and Lucky and their parents at their very last vacation together

---

[1] In Malay and Hokkien, 'What? Chong's daughter married the coffee-seller boy? Even the dead will laugh.'

in Hokkaido. The last photograph is the most recent—a Polaroid snap of Pearl on a motorcycle in Vietnam, grinning like a mad thing, probably taken some time while shooting that noodle series. This was taped to the inside of her wardrobe. Lucky wonders who took it.

Mr Thiang sips his coffee. Only forty, wasn't she, if he recalled the obituary correctly? At least her father had made it to fifty-five. And Betty, too, was gone. And now her girl. Forty is far too young. Not even married yet. And to die like this . . . not even a body for the family to cry over. Mr Thiang stares at the photographs of Pearl, wishing he could turn around and go home. It's too much for an old man, and he really shouldn't have come.

He turns to face the boy. 'So much like your mother, you two.'

'Really?' Lucky never thinks of himself as being very much like his mother, or his father—or anyone.

'The same nose, the same eyes. The same mouth.' Mr Thiang moves his face a little closer to Lucky's then steps back. 'Yah.'

Ah, he meant the physical resemblance. Okay then. There are worse things than looking like his mother. And it was good for Pearl— television is television.

'I look so nice on camera,' Pearl often said, especially if any of Lucky's friends were around. 'Just like Mum.' She would pause, strike a pose, bat her lashes. 'You too lah, Lucky. So lucky!' And then she'd pat him on the cheek and giggle. Everyone but Lucky found this funny.

'More kopi, Uncle Thiang?'

He drinks more coffee himself. He's already tired, and the aunties aren't even here yet.

The brass band

arrives in a little van—six old men in stiff black trousers, white shirts tucked into waistbands pulled high, their jackets over their arms. They shake hands with Lucky and his Uncle Desmond, muttering condolences, and sit down on the chairs Lucky has arranged for them next to the photo display. The aunties Dolly and Maggie come out of the house with trays of coffee and biscuits.

'Oh, thank you.'

'So kind, thank you.'

Amid the niceties, Lucky wanders off to feed the cat and the fish. Coconut is waiting for him, tail swishing—probably hungry, even though he fed it twice yesterday. Greedy thing. He opens a packet of Princess and shakes it out into Coconut's dish, sighing. It must be so nice to be a cat. Cats don't do funerals. Cats don't have shitty relatives staring at them and asking weird roundabout questions about why there isn't a body. Cats don't have to explain that, sometimes, after a crash, not all bodies are found. Cats don't have to explain why the airline and the Indonesian authorities decided to call off the search after three months. Cats don't have to serve coffee and be nice and respectful of their elders while explaining all of this. Cats don't care.

The cat, having gobbled up its breakfast, looks up at him.

'I'm tired,' he tells it. 'And people are shitty.'

Cats have no problems sleeping.

He reaches out and pats the cat tentatively, softly, on the forehead. It squints and moves its head backwards, away from his hand. He tries again, and this time, Coconut walks away then turns around and sits down, staring at him.

He lies down on his side on the floor. The terrazzo is cool and surprisingly comforting against his cheek. If he closes his eyes, will he fall asleep and miss the funeral? He stretches out an arm. 'Come back, Coconut.'

Cats never have to go anywhere they don't want to.

The cat licks its paw and starts to clean its face. From the other side of the house comes a long, loud wail, followed by another. Trumpets. And then a cry, startling in its sharpness—the saxophone. One by one, the old men, their cups of coffee emptied and their jackets buttoned up, pick up their instruments and begin. Lucky recognizes the first song. 'Bila Larut Malam'. One of his father's favourites.

> *Bila larut malam*
> *Suasana sepi*
> *Tiadapun insan*
> *Yang ku lihat lagi*[2]

'Now this is music, Lucky, not this nonsense you keep listening to. Terrible, these Durian Durian fellows. But Saloma, wahhhhh! Have I told you I heard her sing at a nightclub once? In KL. My cousin was working in that club . . .'

And the record would play on, and his father would go on and on. Pearl would sometimes chime in, 'Oh yah, Papa, she's so good. Play it again—I love that.'

And they would all know she was just priming him for some big favour or some big purchase, maybe a trip to Malacca for chendol, or a pasta machine or, that one time, a skiing holiday to rub her classmates' faces in. But their father would play the song again anyway and smile, even though he knew he was setting himself up, and Lucky would join in the singing, even though he only knew half the words and almost none of the meanings.

---

[2] In Malay: In the middle of the night/ It's lonely/ There's no one here/ That I can see anymore

Mengapa hatiku
Merasa terharu?[3]

Something about feeling confused. Pearl would know. When they played this at his funeral, she cried. But maybe it wasn't the song.

Probably not. Eighteen years on, the old Malay classic—ridiculously upbeat, with that cha-cha-cha rhythm so popular in the 1960s, a song that made anyone who grew up on P Ramlee movies want to giggle or dance or sing—is just as inappropriate for a funeral. But the band plays on, stoic in starched collars and shiny buttons. People are starting to arrive, but Lucky can't hear them from the back porch. Observed only by Coconut, he flips onto his back on the floor and stretches out. He closes his eyes.

* * *

'Oh my god, Mummy, what's happened to him?'

'Yah, so sad, right? Such a handsome boy, and now . . .'

'He looks like a . . . zombie. And Daddy says he won't let Lucky carry the umbrella himself, can you believe it?'

'Can't blame him. Look at him—looks like he can hardly stand. You know, I heard he hasn't left the house in three months.'

'Three months? That's crazy.'

'Yah! He wouldn't even open the door last week, you know, when your father went over.'

'Poor thing. Maybe he's going nuts . . .'

'Choyyyyyy! Bad luck lah, don't talk like that!'

* * *

Shawn and Dinah leave last—someone has to shut the gate—and take their place at the tail end of the parade of mourners moving slowly down the road. Lucky has ended up at the head of the procession, holding a framed photograph of Pearl. Next to him is Uncle Desmond,

---

[3] In Malay: Why does my heart/ Feel so confused?

who's wielding a large black umbrella, and right behind them is the lorry carrying the band, seated in reinforced chairs on the open truck bed, now belting out a particularly up-tempo version of 'Stand by Me', and then the aunties in trishaws, then the cousins, and then everyone else. All Shawn can really see is the black umbrella bobbing up and down in the distance, and he can't recall if the umbrella is part of the ritual or if it's just there for shade. In any case, the funeral rites have been quite the cut-and-paste job (well, more like cut-and-cut), seeing as there's no coffin, no cremation or burial, and no strong religious inclinations anywhere in the family. The band and the march are really all there is, in true Lee family style. He allows himself a small smile, knowing Pearl Lee would have approved of the commotion, the congestion they're causing on these narrow, single-lane roads—and, of course, the passers-by gawking at it all.

The funeral march from the house to the columbarium is a long one by Singaporean standards—it takes them down the length of Swan Street and then Joo Chiat Road, then through Koon Seng Road and into a fleet of hired minibuses that takes them to a small road about two hundred metres from the columbarium, where they troop off the bus, rejoin the lorry carrying the band, and pick the march up again.

At the columbarium, in a white room that smells of incense and detergent, everyone watches Lucky put Pearl's picture into a hole in a wall and light a candle in front of it as the band strikes up a slow, sleepy 'Somewhere Over the Rainbow'. They watch him hesitate just before he puts down the framed photo; they can see his lips move but no one can hear him over the music. Dinah bursts into tears.

The next day, two newspapers publish stories about the funeral.

'Grand Send-off for Surabaya Crash Victim in Katong'. This is accompanied by a photo of the procession as they pass the old shophouses on Koon Seng Road—very nice contrast of the mourners in white against the bright pastels of the shophouses—and a good photo of the band, which the newspaper files into its photo archives to throw out at the next old-folks-local-culture story opportunity.

'TV Chef Pearl Lee's Funeral Causes Traffic Jam.' This one has a photograph of Pearl, a still from *Oodles of Noodles*, and a photograph of cars being forced to stop along Joo Chiat Road to allow the procession to pass. That day, more people stream *Oodles of Noodles* than in the last six months and many more click on the outdated ad for the first-season trailer—this leads the network executives to decide to release the half-complete second season a month after the funeral, padded with out-takes and behind-the-scenes footage.

After the funeral, Lucky sleeps for two days, waking up intermittently, unwillingly.

The bar down the road

is dark and cool and not yet swarming with the after-office drinkers, and Lucky feels happy—suddenly, deliriously, deliciously happy— that Shawn decided they should close up early and get a drink. It's Wednesday, after all, and they're never really busy on Wednesday evenings. And it probably helps that the day-shift bartender, Veen, is rather attractive. She looks up as they enter the bar and tilts her chin at them.

'My favourite coffeemakers!'

'Hey, Veen.' Shawn lifts a hand. Lucky nods, grinning.

She wipes her hands on her apron and picks up a couple of glasses. 'Long day?' She wags her eyebrows. 'Must be five o'clock by now.'

Shawn rolls his eyes, leaning against the bar. 'Wednesday lah. No one needs coffee after five.'

Lucky shakes his head. 'Says you—you're asleep by, what, ten?'

Veen puts down two pints on the bar counter in front of them and goes off to attend to another customer. Shawn and Lucky clink glasses.

'Hey, another year survived!' Shawn takes a large swig of beer.

Lucky laughs. 'Already?'

Shawn's right, he realizes. It will be three years in a couple of weeks. Funny how surprised he always is at the quick passage of time, no matter how many times before time has passed quickly. It really does feel like not so long ago that they were busy doing up their cafe-to-be, painting the walls and polishing the floor tiles and building their own shelves and doing all sorts of everything they could do themselves to save money. They had driven around in a borrowed van for weeks, picking through piles of discarded furniture on the sides of the road and under HDB blocks, salvaging anything they thought they could reuse. They went to the Salvation Army stores to buy pots and jars and plates and cups. Shawn had quit his job at the firm. Dinah had taken three months off. Lucky had convinced Pearl to let them have their father's old defunct coffee shop in the gentrifying bit of Joo Chiat rent-free for a year in return for a share in the business. His sister had given him a long lecture about getting his life together ('A cafe? Are you trying to be a cliche, Lucky?'), but in the end, she threw up her hands and said fine and made him papaya salad—exactly as he knew she would.

Lucky grins. 'Heh. Do you remember what Dinah said, the day we opened?

Shawn shakes his head. 'God, yes. "What are we doing? This neighbourhood doesn't need another cafe. We're going to lose everything. We're idiots. Let's just go home."' He mimics her clipped, rapid way of speaking perfectly. 'Seriously. I wanted to strangle her.' He laughs. 'Well, if we hadn't made it, I might have!'

The beer is nice and cold. Lucky takes a long gulp, suddenly yearning for papaya salad. He pushes the thought away. Probably won't go with beer.

He takes out his phone and sends a text. I wonder if beer goes with papaya salad?

'Lucky?'

Lucky swivels around on the bar stool. For a moment, he stares at the woman next to him, searching his head. *Oh, god.* 'Hey, Rosalind.'

Shawn frowns. Where has he heard that name before? He looks at the unhappy-looking woman talking to Lucky now, arms crossed, mouth in a tight smile.

'Well,' she's saying, 'I kept wondering what happened—if something happened—to you.'

Lucky looks sheepish. He taps his fingers on his cheekbone. *Clearly nervous*, Shawn thinks. *Good job he doesn't play poker.* 'I'm so sorry, Rosalind. Really sorry. I should've got in touch.'

Shawn's eyes widen. *Rosalind! It's the woman Lucky was going on and on about some time ago—was it last Christmas? Before he went off to Bali, before—*

'. . . I'm really sorry. I just got caught up in a bunch of things.'

Rosalind shrugs. 'Okay. That's fine. Sorry I jumped at you; I was just so surprised to see you.'

'Oh no, this is nice.' Lucky wishes he could think of any other word besides 'nice'. 'Nice' makes him sound so . . . limp. 'Do you come here often?'

Rosalind takes a drink of her beer. It's nearly gone. 'No, my friends chose this place.'

'Anyway, how are you?'

'I'm okay.' She shrugs. 'Busy.'

He wants to ask her what she does, and what she's been busy with, but Lucky has a feeling he should know, so he says something trite, brightly. 'Well, busy is . . . good?' At least he didn't say 'nice'.

'Yes.' Rosalind smiles.

She has good teeth, he notices. And she's pretty—still pretty. Not that he expects her to have changed. He doesn't know enough about her to expect anything. She adjusts her hair, arranging it across her neck and over one shoulder, and he's struck by how familiar this is. But why? He can only recall, vaguely, meeting her at a party and maybe once or twice after. But he's quickly remembering how much he liked her. She's funny, he recalls. And a bit of a know-it-all—a tiny snippet of a conversation returns to him, something about the correct use of the word 'wherewithal'.

She puts her empty glass on the counter. 'Well, I'll see you around. Anyway, I'm here with friends, so I better go join them.' She gestures at a table at the back of the bar.

Lucky buys another round for himself and Shawn, feeling a little lost. A little later, he turns around and openly watches Rosalind talking to her friends, laughing, enjoying another beer. It's a bit like seeing a ghost, which is funny, because obviously she's very much alive.

'Hey, you okay?'

Lucky smiles. 'So, what else do we do to celebrate? Three years—crazy. We should call Dinah!'

* * *

At the edge of the fish pond under the stairs, Lucky sits down and checks his text message history, pulling up the chat window with Rosalind's texts. He reads his last text to her.

Off to Bali. See you next week!

Right, he does remember sending that. Well, he meant it at the time. He scrolls through her replies, one after another.

See you! Have tons of fun.

This he remembers reading. He didn't reply because he thought he'd wait until the next morning and send her photos of something cool.

The rest of her messages—did he ever read them? He can't remember.

Happy new year! How's Bali? We're having a BBQ. In this heat! My parents have the worst ideas.

Two days later: Hey, back yet?:) Guess who made pineapple cake yesterday?

Three days later: Everything OK? I tried calling but you're not picking up. Let me know if you need anything?

A week later: Can you call me back when you have the time? Just want to know if you're OK.

Two days after that: Hey if you're OK, can you let me know?

And her final message, the day after: It's fine, Lucky. Sorry to bother you. Have a nice life.

That last bit was rather passive aggressive. Has anyone ever said 'have a nice life' and actually meant it? But he can't blame her. He checks the date—21 January. What was he doing at the time? Nothing much. Just waiting. Hanging around the house. Feeding the cat and the fish. Maybe overfeeding the cat and the fish. Watching the news. Waiting.

It was a lot of waiting.

God, he's tired. Lucky checks the time. Past two—unsurprising, considering how long they stayed at the bar earlier. And then of course everyone got hungry and they had to go get something to eat. Which of course meant Dinah wanted her mee goreng at Simpang Bedok, which of course meant they had to drive all the way there and drive round and round the car park before they found a spot. Which made them all hungrier and they ordered too much food and now he feels gross and bloated. Gah. Because no one at his age needs a second plate of mee goreng at any time, let alone after midnight. Lucky pats his tummy. We should take it easy tomorrow, he tells it.

As he climbs into bed, still feeling gross and bloated, Lucky finds himself wishing he explained things to Rosalind at the bar. A proper explanation, not that rubbish about being caught up in a bunch of things. Which in her head is probably a jackass excuse for ghosting her. And he does feel like a jackass, so she wouldn't be wrong. Anyway, it's done, *so* done. But maybe not—she could have just ignored him at the bar. Well, now she thinks he's a jackass, so what does it matter?

He takes out his phone and types out a text, then sends it. `Really blew it with Rosalind. Maybe I should call?`

If he hadn't ended it with a question mark, he probably would have just called, even at two in the morning. Lucky Lee in love, or in some semblance of love, has done odder things—usually with good results. Instead, Lucky goes to sleep.

* * *

It's a cold morning. At seven-thirty, far, far earlier than he's used to, Lucky wakes up and is unable to go back to sleep. Stupid dreams. He's spent the whole night chasing a tree down narrow corridors, trying to get it to eat from a plate of cookies. There was something else about a swimming pool, but he can't remember it now.

But he does remember Rosalind, and now he wonders if he should text. Or call. Or keep going back to the bar, on the off chance—

He throws off the blanket and climbs out of bed. He may as well get an early start.

It must have rained all night. Through the kitchen window, the back garden looks sopping wet. And rather unkempt—he really should call Mr Chee soon and ask him to send his boys over. Lucky turns on the water boiler on the espresso machine, then shuts it off again. Maybe he should just go down to the cafe, give Shawn and Meixi a hand. But he's sleepy now and he really, really wants his coffee. Lucky turns on the boiler again. Later—he'll wait for them to open the cafe first. No point getting in their way, after all.

He takes his coffee out to the back porch and sits down on a bench he's put out there. It's become one of his favourite spots in the house. The cat is lying down near the bench, looking grumpy. Must be all the rain—cats hate water, don't they? Or is it hungry?

'Where is she?'

What? Lucky looks about, but there's no one around. It's just him and Coconut. He stares at the cat, who stares back. He takes a deep breath and a sip of coffee. It's the lack of sleep—he's clearly hearing things. Lucky grins and takes another sip of coffee. Geez. For a moment there, he actually thought—

'Where's Pearl?'

The voice is soft and scratchy, a little high-pitched. Like Bonnie Tyler, but squeakier. How bizarre—it's exactly how Lucky imagines a cat would sound, if a cat could talk. This makes him suspicious. Lucky squints at the garden—is there anyone out there? Wow, that thicket of pandan is definitely overgrown—anyone could hide in there.

Coconut jumps onto the bench. Lucky jumps off it.

His eyes flit from cat to pandan to cat to pandan. He calls out wildly, 'Who's there? Shawn? Is that you?' Shawn isn't the kind of guy who plays practical jokes, but Lucky really, really wants him to be right now.

Coconut sits down, looking straight at Lucky. 'Did I frighten you? I just want to know where she is. She's been away for so long.'

Lucky stands very still for a few minutes, staring at the cat, his mind a big white blank. Then he turns and walks into the kitchen, finishes his coffee, and washes up. He opens a cupboard, takes out a packet of Princess Tuna Supreme, and empties it out into Coconut's fish-shaped dish.

Coconut hops off the bench and starts on its breakfast. Lucky takes a long shower, gets dressed, and goes to the cafe.

* * *

'What? Why can't *you* feed the cat? What are you doing?'

'I'm super busy this week, Dinah. Super crazy busy. Please.'

Dinah glares at her phone, wishing he could see her. Lucky cannot be busier than she is. She's got a tender submission to check and run by her boss on Monday, and the building contractor for one of her projects has just asked for a meeting later—she's sure he's going to ask for some sort of change to the schedule, again. Plus, she's a little hungover from last night, in spite of drinking all that water when she got home.

But it's Lucky, so . . . Besides, he does sound a little scattered. She hopes it's a new business idea. Lucky hasn't had a stupid business idea in a really long time—as long as it has nothing to do with mushrooms.

'Fine. Just this week.'

* * *

Meixi watches as a morose, limpid Shawn alternately sips coffee, water, and orange juice to 'rejuvenate rehydrate raise glucose levels'. He mutters this to himself over and over again as he checks the bar counter supplies. If only—if only he could un-drink some of the beer he drank last night, he moans.

There's no sympathy to be wrung from Meixi this morning. She's still annoyed that they didn't press her to join them the night before. 'How much did you have?'

'I don't know . . . five pints?'

'At your age?'

Shawn can't muster enough energy to tell her off, so he hunches over the counter and drinks more orange juice, hoping he'll look weak and frail enough to make her feel bad. Bloody Gen Z. He would never have dared to speak to his boss this way when he was in his twenties.

And on Saturday (Saturday!) she left early to get her hair done (her hair!) and wasn't the slightest bit apologetic. The nerve. The colossal nerve. Shawn drinks more orange juice, and then a bit of coffee. Please, please let him be better soon so he can make jokes about her hair.

The door swings open and Lucky walks in wearing sweatpants. It's barely nine, so it's not his shift for another five hours. Also, sweatpants on Lucky—to Meixi, always a sign of distress. But then he grins and starts talking about a new coffee plantation in the Philippines he's heard about recently, and it looks like he's fine.

Lucky feels much better now that he's here. And much safer. He'll make coffee, talk to Shawn, get stuff done, maybe do some research on that plantation. It's good to be around people. And it's going to be a good day. He's not going mad. He's not going mad. Not going mad. Not. Going mad.

'Lucky, shall I make you some coffee?' Meixi asks, reaching for a mug, delighted to have him in so early. She missed him quite a bit all that time he was away and has been fussing over him since he started working regular shifts again about two months ago. Unfortunately for Meixi, Lucky hasn't noticed this.

Also, unfortunately for her, it appears to be one of those days when Lucky is determined to Get Shit Done Himself. 'It's okay,' he tells her. 'I'll make it myself.'

Must keep busy. Must keep busy. Must keep busy.

He does. For the rest of the day, Lucky is the most productive he's been in a very, very long time. To Shawn's alarm, he offers to do the week's inventory checks, and then, to Shawn's surprise, he's done by lunch *and* he's placed all the orders for the supplies they're running low on. He takes their Vietnamese coffee supplier out for lunch and manages to negotiate a lower price for an increased volume order over the next year. After lunch, he schedules a servicing for their espresso machine—something even Shawn hasn't thought of doing. Then he cleans the coffee grinders, taking them both apart and putting them back together again. At four, he tells Shawn to go home and takes over cashier duties until six, when Meixi leaves and Lucky does both cashier and barista duties until it's time to close. And though it's been years since Lucky pulled a double shift, he doesn't feel the least bit tired.

He sends a text, five minutes before closing time. `Pooped. Really long day at the cafe.`

As he locks up the cafe, he decides he might as well head to the bar before going home. Just one beer. After all, he's in no hurry.

* * *

`Fed the cat. You owe me.`
`Thanks, Dinah!:)`

* * *

Lucky would have liked to stay out much later, but the bar shuts down at midnight and nothing else is open except the karaoke pubs on the seedier end of Joo Chiat Road, so he slinks home. It's a cool night— it rained again in the afternoon—and he walks towards Swan Street as slowly as he can. But fifteen minutes is all it takes, even with all his dawdling.

As he unlocks the front door and pushes it open, he feels queasy and afraid. A quick look around the living room and the courtyard reveals no intruders. Nothing odd at all—good. He moves quickly and quietly to the back of the house. He scans the kitchen—nothing. Still looking around the kitchen, he pours himself a glass of water and gulps it down quickly. Absolutely no sign of the cat—good, very good.

Lucky feeds the fish and dashes upstairs, forgetting to glare at the dragon, nearly stubbing his foot on the top stair. He locks himself in his room and doesn't emerge until the next morning.

* * *

Meixi twists a tendril of hair around a finger, watching Lucky take a customer's order. She was going to do it, but he beat her to the counter. Practically ran across the room. The man is like a maniac these days.

'Yes,' Lucky is telling the customer, 'I'm sure soy milk is lactose-free.'

The customer isn't convinced. Narrowing her eyes, she presses him, 'You're *sure*? How?'

The interrogation continues as Meixi and Shawn do their best to pretend not to listen. The customer, a young woman in her twenties dressed in pastel-toned athleisure, demands to know exactly how Lucky can be certain of the lactose-free-ness of the soy milk he's about to put in her coffee. There's no telling, she tells him, what kind of havoc any amount of lactose will wreak on her system.

Lucky blinks. He looks up at the ceiling. He sighs. He takes the napkin from his shoulder and folds it twice. Shawn takes a step towards the counter, ready to step in.

Lucky leans conspiratorially towards the girl. 'Okay, here's the thing. Sometimes—rarely, but sometimes—and people don't usually tell you this—there's just a little lactose in soy milk.'

She nods, looking smug. 'I knew it.'

'Yah. Like I said, people don't usually tell you.' He pauses. 'But we've got a special sort of machine at the back that gets rid of all of that stuff—just to be safe, you know. German design, very cutting edge.'

'Really?'

'Yah, we ordered it last year and we were on the waiting list for *six months.*'

'Six months! Wow. Cool.' She nods. 'I'll have that soy latte then. Um, Javanese. To go.'

They wait for her to leave, and then they laugh and laugh, Lucky and Shawn and Meixi, until their eyes water and their bellies hurt. Shawn is surprised, afterwards, at how relieved he is. It's been such a long time since he's seen Lucky like this—cheeky, slightly malicious, funny. And far too long since they've laughed like this. He watches Lucky hum to himself as he makes the next customer a Vietnamese flat white. 'Eye of the Tiger'? Geez! Shawn grins. It's so good to have him back. Properly back.

* * *

Meixi knows from the dating website she's been checking out that you shouldn't tell boys they're funny, but she tells Lucky anyway. And she forgives him for not noticing her new hair, though she doesn't tell him *this.*

'That was so funny.' She wishes she had something funny, or clever, to say.

Lucky raises his mug at her and takes a sip of coffee, trying not to stare. But hair grows out, so—well, he'll be kind and say nothing about what appears to be a really frightful mistake. She can't have possibly meant to get it dyed *that* colour.

* * *

It's difficult not to think about it.

Every time Lucky finds his mind wandering back to that morning and to Coconut, he stomps on it by forcing it to think of the next thing on his to-do list. Or by humming 'Eye of the Tiger'. It's the most distracting song he knows.

* * *

'How's Lucky?'

'He's great.' A pause. 'So am I.'

Dinah laughs. 'Ah, right—well I was just a bit worried. He asked me to help feed the cat for a week. He said he was going to be busy.'

'Well, he *has* been pretty busy. He pulled double shifts on Friday and over the weekend, and I think he had plans yesterday.'

'So, nothing's wrong?'

'Nope. In fact, I think he's much, much better now. I mean . . . it's been nearly a year. You can't go on worrying about him forever, you know.'

She knows. 'Fine.'

* * *

After dinner, Dinah drives Lucky home. She was actually going to skip dinner tonight—so much to do, always so much to do—but it was such a lovely surprise when Lucky called after his shift and suggested dinner at the late-night ramen place next to her office. So she caved. And she's happy she did—Shawn's right; Lucky does seem much better.

Energetic and cheerful and chatty and so excited about this new plantation he's just ordered a small shipment of beans from.

When they stop outside his house, he leans over and gives her an unexpected hug.

'Thanks for helping to feed the cat. It's been insane.'

'Ah, no big deal. You're okay to do it tomorrow, right? I stopped by this afternoon on my way to that meeting—so today's done.'

Lucky nods, getting out of the car, waving goodbye. It's been a week. He's been keeping busy, sleeping well, eating regularly, spending time with his friends. Thinking positive thoughts. Getting a bit of exercise. He's even gotten back on Tinder and gone on one date—a bit of a dud, but whatever. So he should be good. Obviously, it was sleep deprivation and maybe the alcohol or loneliness or whatever that was getting to his head. And maybe it's the house, he thinks as he goes inside—so large and so obviously empty. And all these *things*—so much fodder for the imagination. Maybe it's time he moved.

He heads into the kitchen and looks out the kitchen window. Coconut's nowhere to be seen. Lucky feels a little silly—and the tiniest bit guilty—for avoiding the cat for a whole week. Maybe he'll get it sardines or something as a treat.

* * *

Lucky wakes up just a little after eight, a few minutes before his alarm is set to go off. He feels bright, alive, refreshed. *Okay. Everything's going to be okay.*

He heads to the kitchen and makes himself a quick breakfast of scrambled eggs and toast. He plays a little music on his phone, putting it on speaker, humming along. One song ends and another begins, its bright opening chords rushing quickly to fill the room.

'I'll Follow the Sun', one of Pearl's favourites, and the last time he heard it, she was singing along. The memory hits him so suddenly that he feels his chest expand into a deep breath before he realizes he's taken one.

I'm fine, Lucky assures himself as the old Beatles song continues to play. *Perfectly fine.* He goes out onto the back porch and picks up the cat's dish, then takes it inside and empties a packet of Princess Shrimp Dream into it. When he goes back out with the dish, Coconut is waiting.

'Good morning, Lucky. Are you feeling better?'

Lucky puts down the dish as quickly as he can and runs up to his room. He locks himself in and wonders what he will do now that he's gone mad.

The house on Swan Street

hasn't changed very much since Pearl went away. Slyly tucked among stately homes of the old rich, it stares out onto the street, its view partially obscured by the large casuarinas in the front garden and, of course, by the lions and the tall, lace-like wrought-iron gate. On the facade, the house appears prim and mild-mannered, set a demure distance away from the street, with pale grey walls and simple louvre windows that went out of style sometime in the late eighties. But, on the inside, it's a troubled soul, the love-child of the ménage à trois between Mr Lee's money, his imagination, and his very limited grasp of the Art Deco movement.

The vine motifs across the high, corniced ceilings, the antique chandelier, the parakeet-pattern wallpaper in four different colours, the large potted palms in the courtyard, the crystal doorknobs, the Peranakan tiles, the herringbone parquet, the velvet curtains, the zebra rug, the swan-shaped sofa, the ornate mirrors in all sizes, the diamond-shaped windows in every bathroom—all of these are exactly as they were nearly a year ago, on the day Pearl turned her key in the front door for the last time, wheeled her suitcase down the driveway and closed the heavy gate behind her. The only addition to the house is the thin layer of dust over everything—not that its sole human inhabitant has noticed. When the cleaning lady, Aunty Lakshmi, retired a few months ago, Lucky wrote her a generous cheque and forgot to hire a new one. He also keeps forgetting to call the gardener, Mr Chee, and the back and front gardens have begun their rapid transformation into tropical jungles.

As he sits in his room, protected from the world, contemplating the newly speech-gifted Coconut, Lucky decides that one of these things must be true:

1.   He's gone mad
2.   He's dreaming
3.   The cat is really talking

The first option is the likeliest; the second the most attractive. The third is just . . . *desperate*. A talking cat—surely the stuff of dreams. Well, someone else's dreams. Lucky isn't really that fond of cats. Sure, he's become used to Coconut, but they're not *friends*. It'll always be Pearl's cat. He slaps himself lightly on the cheek a few times and flicks a finger at the corner of one eye. Well, he *feels* awake. He goes to the window and looks out. The view of the back garden is the same as ever. Nothing seems dream-like, or even slightly more interesting than usual.

Feeling lost, Lucky takes a second shower to clear his head.

* * *

Post-second-shower, his head wrapped in the yellow towel with the ducks, Lucky stares down into the back garden from his bedroom window, watching intently as Coconut chases a butterfly. The cat, he decides, looks perfectly normal. Completely unchanged. Still the same tortoiseshell thing that's been living in their garden and kitchen for years, amusing Pearl with its unamusing antics. As he continues to stare, his phone rings.

'Lucky, everything okay?'

'Hey Shawn, yea yea of course. All good.'

'You coming in today?'

Lucky checks the time. Damn. It's already eleven, an hour past the start of his shift, and Shawn sounds worried. Well, he's not the only one. 'Sorry, Shawn, I'm . . . I'm not feeling so good today.' He manages something between a cough and a growl. 'Is it okay if I stay home? Sorry, I should have called.'

'What? Okay. Okay. Fine. I'll see if Meixi can come in earlier.'

Of course, now Shawn's annoyed, but Lucky will make it up to him. There's no way he's going in today. He's not going anywhere until he decides what he's going to do with this horrible, ludicrous thing with Coconut. *Damn that cat.*

'I'm really sorry. Something . . . odd . . . happened this morning.'

'What happened? Are you okay?' A clatter from the other end of the line. 'Shall I come over?'

For a moment, Lucky is tempted to say yes. Maybe Shawn will know what to do—but what would he tell him? *Hi Shawn, the cat has started talking. And it's asking about Pearl. I think I'm going mad.*

Nope. Far too early to go down that road. Also, why would Shawn know what to do with a talking cat, or impending madness? 'Don't worry, I'm good. I just need to lie down a bit, maybe.'

It's absurd. This is all so absurd. Yes, absurd—Lucky decides he'll go back to bed.

He does, pulling the blanket over his head, shutting out the world. It would be so nice, he thinks, if he could just lie here forever. Or if he could go to sleep and wake up, having forgotten that Coconut ever spoke to him. That would solve everything, except that if he did forget and Coconut spoke to him again, then he'd be back exactly where he is now, walking the line between madness and sanity, not knowing if he's already crossed over. Assuming, of course, that he hasn't been mad for some time—the talking cat may really just be a sign that he's getting worse. Which may mean that he could expect a whole host of other things to start speaking to him.

Lucky forces himself to take long, deep breaths. This is often helpful, but right now it doesn't make him feel any better.

He drifts off into a fitful sleep, and when he wakes up, still completely under the covers, he's shocked to discover that he's been asleep. Gasping, he throws the blanket off.

He doesn't dare to check the time. The sun is streaming in through the window at an angle now, so it must be mid-afternoon. Already!

How much longer can he stay up here? He can't leave—he still hasn't figured out what to do about the cat and his very possible descent into madness. But he's also starting to get hungry, and there's nothing to eat up here in his room.

He rewraps the towel around his head—it came undone while he slept. The towel always makes him feel better, and thus recharged, Lucky has an idea.

It's quite clear now that none of this is a dream, which means Option 2 is dead, which leaves him Option 1, madness, or Option 3, the existence of Coconut as a cat with the power of speech. This is where Lucky's idea comes in—he will call Shawn and ask him to come over, and then perhaps Coconut will speak to him as well.

* * *

'Okay, sure, I'll head over now; Meixi can close up later. Anything I can get for you?'

'Ooh. Yes, yes. That chicken rice from Five Star—that's the one with the red-and-white signboard, not blue and white. Thigh or drumstick.' Lucky wonders if he should get the fried tofu. Nah. 'Hmmm get extra chilli. No cucumber.'

'Okay. Red and white. Got it.' Shawn doesn't sound surprised or irritated at being asked to get food—he must really be quite anxious.

Lucky feels a little guilty, but . . . 'Hmm get two portions. And extra rice. Thanks, Shawn!'

Might as well get enough for two meals while he's at it.

* * *

The phone buzzes with a text from Shawn. Hey, I'm at the door.

Lucky grabs his phone and dashes downstairs. In the half an hour or so that it's taken for Shawn to arrive, Lucky has managed to turn a few scenarios around in his head. While part of him is still very, very much afraid that he's gone mad and is now hearing voices, he's also beginning to be entertained by the situation. Or rather, Lucky is now determined to derive some entertainment from his situation.

It's like the time he and Pearl had chicken pox when they were children. They woke up achy and feverish one morning, itchy little red spots popping up all over their legs and arms and backs and even faces. Their mother responded with a bizarre list of rules she vaguely recalled from the time she herself had chicken pox, thirty-something years ago (Mrs Lee was unable to even recall when she'd had it). After some intense bargaining between their mother and Pearl, three hard rules remained: the children weren't allowed out of the house, they weren't allowed to eat anything with soy sauce or shrimp in it, and they were not to scratch at those stupid maddening spots.

'Go put on some snake powder.'

Even Lucky knew by then that snake powder wasn't really made from snakes. It came in a tall metal tin and the label wasn't very exciting—white, with some Chinese letters and, in English, 'Snake Brand Prickly Heat Cooling Powder'. There was a snake on the tin, of course, but even that failed to impress the children—it was bright green and slithering through a patch of grass with an arrow through its head, but somehow it still managed not to seem like a very fearsome or even interesting sort of snake. Mrs Lee wasn't entirely sure what 'prickly heat' was or whether the powder would help with the chicken pox spots, but she had had to dust herself all over with snake powder when she had had chicken pox, so it must be the done thing.

The children, weakened by disease, didn't put up much of a resistance. Under their mother's watchful eye, the pair stood in the middle of her bathroom and rubbed handfuls of snake powder all over their legs arms tummies faces and each other's backs. They were seven and eleven—it was the year that every 7-Eleven convenience store seemed significant—and mortified to be stuck at home, away from their friends and the development of classroom politics for a whole week. Pearl declared that 'Sarah is going to steal my seat next to Liling', while Lucky fretted about the shiny flattened thumbtack he'd found in the teachers' car park and hidden at the back of his desk drawer under his exercise books. Would someone find it and take it?

But they paused, after their mother had gone off, and they looked at each other and then at themselves in the bathroom mirrors, their bodies streaked and splotchy with snake powder, their spots still managing to show through the white coating, and it made them laugh like a pair of young . . .

'Dalmatians! We're dalmatians!' Like the cartoon, he didn't have to add.

'No. We're lepers.' Pearl had just read the abridged-for-kids version of *Ben-Hur* and was very much taken with the illustrations of the leper duo that turns out to be Ben Hur's mother and sister.

Lucky and Pearl pored over the illustrations of the robed lepers walking through the desert wilderness, noting how they wore cloths draped over their faces and heads and necks, how their hands were swaddled in rags, how one of them needed a stick to walk with.

'You be Tirzah. I'll be your mother. We've been turned out of prison for having leprosy and now we have to find the Nazarene so we can be healed.' She pronounced it Na-zah-ray-nee and would continue to pronounce it this way for years.

Pearl flipped through the pages of the book and showed Lucky the drawing of Jesus touching the shoulders of both lepers, and the next one, showing their amazement at being healed, and then the drawing of their reunion with Ben Hur, who's been standing around and suddenly recognizes the ex-lepers as his mother and sister. Leprosy, she told him solemnly, was a lot like chicken pox. But with leprosy, the sores were bigger and sometimes you lost a hand or a foot or an eye—this is why lepers sometimes needed a walking stick.

They found towels in the bathroom to tie around themselves and clean dishcloths in the kitchen to wrap around their hands and feet. They found tea towels in the linen closet to go around their heads. And finally they found a walking stick in the same place they found their Nazarene—the guest bedroom on the third floor, in the front section of the house. A bridge suspended two floors above the courtyard connected this seldom-used room to the passageway leading to the library-study, and this bridge alone made it obvious that their route to the Nazarene would have to include the guest bedroom. This was serendipitous—it was also the room where abandoned projects lived on, alongside other things that their parents weren't ready to donate or throw out in the garbage, so Pearl and Lucky found their father's golf bag with its full set of clubs and took one of them for the walking stick, then put a sheet over the bag and made it their Nazarene.

Tirzah and her mother made the pilgrimage a few times a day, tramping across the living room and then around the courtyard twice and up the stairs, stopping to drink from the faucet in Pearl's bathroom ('Oh, Tirzah, how good the water from this oasis tastes!'), climbing up to the third floor and crawling across the bridge to make sure the Roman soldiers didn't see them, and ending up at the guest room to play out a dramatic scene that involved them flinging off the various parts of their leper costumes, yelling 'We're healed!' over and over and over and then falling to their knees close to the sheet-clad golf bag, shouting, 'Thank you, Na-zah-ray-nee, for taking away the leprosyyyyyy!'

It was all very time-consuming stuff—and the ten days of chicken-pox quarantine passed in a thrilling blur of white cloth, snake powder, and near-hysteria.

Of course, Lucky isn't going to swathe himself in towels today, but he will find a way to entice Coconut into speaking with Shawn. Hopefully, this won't be too difficult—and Lucky is very hopeful. After all, if he were a talking cat, he'd want to be appreciated by an audience of more than one.

Yes, Option 3 is the most entertaining.

As Lucky stops halfway down the stairs to send a text (Feeling better now. And yay Shawn's here with food), Shawn, weighed down by bright blue plastic bags full of chicken rice wrapped in brown paper, wonders why it's taking Lucky so long to let him in. Like Dinah, he has keys to the house, but unlike Dinah, he doesn't carry them everywhere just in case Lucky has a meltdown or panic attack or whatever else Dinah thinks might strike him down. That's the trouble with Dinah—she's fixated with the notion that Lucky would have a breakdown after Pearl died and now she's just waiting for that axe to fall. Of course, today he seemed a bit weird over the phone, but that happens to everyone. So what if he's a little anxious or upset about something? He did say something happened that morning, right? Feed him chicken rice, talk to him, maybe put on a funny movie, and he'll be fine . . .

. . . or not. Lucky opens the door with his head still wrapped up in the yellow duck towel, and Shawn takes an involuntary step backwards. *Shit. This again.* He takes a quick step forward to try to hide that first backwards step and ends up nearly nose-to-nose with Lucky, who hasn't moved at all.

'Hey, Shawn.'

'Hey.' Shawn steps inside, trying to sound upbeat. 'I got four packets. In case you're really hungry.'

'Thanks, really sorry to trouble you.'

'Ah, no big deal.' Shawn waits for Lucky to lead the way to the kitchen, but he doesn't move, so Shawn starts walking towards the back of the house. Lucky follows, one hand playing absently with a trailing bit of towel.

He lets Shawn enter the kitchen first while he lingers near the doorway, checking for the cat. Nothing. The back door is halfway open, but Lucky doesn't have the nerve to approach it. The smell of chicken rice fills the room as Shawn unwraps a brown paper packet and slips its contents—two chicken drumsticks and a large mound of steaming rice—onto a plate. He goes to a cupboard and takes out a small bowl, then empties a sachet of chilli sauce into it.

'Lucky, is this enough chilli? There's more.'

He turns and finds Lucky still standing at the kitchen door, staring at the corner of the kitchen where the back door is. *Okay.*

'Lucky? You okay?'

Still no answer. Shawn watches Lucky watching the back door for a while, wondering if he should wait for him to snap out of this daydream by himself or try to shock him out of it. Lucky's clearly a bit off today—even ignoring that towel, he's dressed strangely. Okay, the T-shirt is just one of his silly Care Bear things, but where the hell did he dig out the denim cutoffs?

'Lucky!' He raises his voice and finally manages to get Lucky's attention. 'Nice shorts.'

Lucky looks down at the cutoffs. 'Oh, these. Funny story.'

He tells Shawn about the time he and Pearl went to Bali after his graduation and she fell into a paddy field while trying to get a closer look at the tiny fish swimming among the rice plants. So she got soaked and muddy and then refused to get into the rented car soaking and muddy—which, Lucky agreed, was wise. They looked around and found a villager running a homestay who was willing to sell them clothes left behind by guests, but nothing fit except the cut-offs and a ratty T-shirt that had 'I Love Langkawi' printed in a virulent shade of green on the back. Of course, Pearl didn't want to wear them, even though she was the one who had fallen into the rice field in the first place, even though all they were about to do was drive two hours back to their hotel and there was zero chance of bumping into anyone they knew along the way. So it fell to Lucky to wear them and give her his own much less retro-ratty jeans and T-shirt. He had been really annoyed—the cut-offs were awful and the T-shirt smelled weird—but rather than argue with Pearl in front of the friendly, kind, opportunistic villager, he had given in.

He doesn't know what's happened to the T-shirt, but he still has the shorts. Obviously.

'Oh yes. Funny story.' Shawn grimaces. God, that Pearl was always such a bully. Not to speak ill of the dead or anything, but what a nasty specimen of womankind. 'Okay, I queued for ten minutes to get you your chicken rice, so can you get over here and eat this?'

Lucky approaches the kitchen table. *God, he's slow today*, Shawn thinks, taking cutlery out of a drawer. Maybe once he's eaten he'll be less sluggish.

This would have been a good bet. The moment he begins to eat, Lucky realizes how hungry he's been. He forgets to watch the back door; he can only focus on tearing into the chicken and shovelling rice into his mouth, grateful that Shawn brought all of this gorgeousness to him. *What a guy!* Lucky looks up to flash a grateful grin at his friend, who's now making them coffee, before going back to his very late lunch.

Shawn brings two mugs of coffee to the table. Lucky is finishing off the last of the chicken (*Wow, how do they get it so tender?*) and doesn't look up.

'Oh, hey, Chocolate.' Shawn looks down and smiles politely. He passes Lucky a mug. 'Is it Chocolate? I can't ever remember the name.'

Lucky almost chokes on his last mouthful. He swallows in a hurry, looking around as calmly as he can. Is the cat in the kitchen?

Yes.

The cat is lying under the table, sphinx-like, blinking slowly. Barely managing to keep from shouting out, Lucky jerks backwards in his chair, nearly falling over in his hurry to put more distance between himself and Coconut. He stands up, then sits down again.

Shawn stares. 'Hey. What's up?'

Lucky tries to sound calm. 'Sorry, didn't expect to see the cat.' He makes a face. 'So quiet, these cats.'

Shawn looks under the table at Coconut. 'I'm not much of a cat person. Cats are a bit creepy, yah?'

Lucky's eyes widen. *Hmm. Very good.* Maybe Coconut will have something to say about that. 'Oh, yes. What's creepy about cats?'

'Oh, everything.' Shawn gestures with his mug. 'All that sneaking around, all the climbing, you never know where they are. And they've got these judgy little faces, like they're waiting for you to do something stupid.'

'You've never had a cat?'

'Oh, no—Anita wants one, but no, no, never. Cats would just kill the furniture, won't they? And they're not even fun, like dogs.'

Lucky checks under the table. Coconut has gone to sleep.

'Oh, Shawn, sorry, can you help me feed Coconut?' He goes to the sink and begins washing up.

Shawn looks up from his coffee and frowns. He's never fed Coconut. Or any other cat, for that matter. 'Why can't you do it?'

'I've forgotten to.'

'What? But you've just remembered!' Shawn blinks, baffled.

'Right. But I . . . I stepped on its tail this morning.' Lucky pauses midway through soaping up the sauce bowl. What else should he add?

'And I think I frightened it. So I'm worried it hates me.' Even as the words come out of his mouth, he has to fight the urge to snicker. He sounds like such a nut. Hmm. Maybe he should go further. Be more compelling. Really cry for help. 'I feel like Coconut needs some . . . space, you know. From me.'

Shawn nods, now afraid to say anything that might encourage Lucky to explain himself any further. Is this the odd thing that happened this morning? Jesus. Maybe he'll call Dinah and tell her to come by after work. Just in case. But sure, he can feed the cat.

He forces himself to smile. 'Sure, I can feed the cat.'

* * *

Lucky lies in bed, under the blanket. It's late, and his friends have gone home. He made them sit in the kitchen and then on the back porch for ages, making sure there was ample opportunity for Coconut to make contact. And because Lucky has read somewhere that cats are very much motivated by food, he made Shawn feed it, and then he poached a fish and de-boned it and made Dinah feed neat little fillets to the cat for supper.

He even brought up Pearl a few times to try and rouse the cat's interest in their conversation. He even told them about the letter he'd found among her things, which he had never told anyone about before.

At some point, Lucky addressed the cat directly. 'Coconut, you like Dinah, don't you? She took you to the vet that time you messed up your paw, remember?'

Coconut ate the Princess Seafood Delight and the fish but refused to say a word. It hung around for a while while he was talking about the letter but didn't even stick around for the end of the story. It didn't say whether or not it liked Dinah, or whether it remembered her taking it to see the vet.

So basically he could still be very much mad, and Coconut could still be a talking cat.

Lucky pulls the blanket over his head. It would be so nice, he thinks, if he could just lie here forever.

The cat of the house on Swan Street

licks its bowl clean. Breakfast, as usual, was unexciting but delicious but unexciting but delicious but unexciting but at least delivered early today. It is difficult to predict the arrival of food. Most of the time, the man of the house puts food in the dish sometime in the morning, while the air in the garden is still cool and before the sun strikes the back of the house, but sometimes it's already warm and sunny in the back garden by the time he delivers the food. Other times, the man leaves food in the dish when the sky is already dark and the moon is out and the cat is out too, surveying the neighbourhood. Even the frequency of food is impossible to predict. Most days, food appears in the dish once a day, but sometimes the man puts out another helping at night, and yesterday there were two servings in the daytime, and at night there was even a fish.

Lucky watches from the kitchen window as the cat licks its bowl clean, then proceeds to clean itself. It still hasn't said anything to him. He was expecting it to when he went out to feed it about ten minutes ago, but it didn't. He had been so fearful, and so aware of how brave he was being as he dished out this morning's Princess Tuna Supreme, that now, now that the cat hasn't troubled itself to speak to him, Lucky finds himself displeased.

He makes himself some coffee, wondering if this, then, is all there is to this weird little drama—a few words maybe spoken by the cat, maybe not, a few days of quiet horror, and then, then life goes back to normal. He sips the coffee. Not bad, this coffee from the Philippines—

not too acidic, very robust flavour. Lucky heats up a bit of milk in a saucepan, careful not to bring it to boil. He splashes a little into his mug, tastes the coffee, then adds a little more, tasting it again. Hmm, good with milk as well. He wonders what Shawn will think. He finishes the rest of the coffee.

Just as he's about to wash up, he realizes there's a bit of milk left in the saucepan. Well, no point wasting it. Lucky carries the saucepan out to the back patio and pours the milk into the cat's water dish. As he turns and walks back into the kitchen, he hears behind him a now-familiar voice.

'Thank you.'

Lucky freezes. He drops the saucepan, frightening both himself and Coconut with the resulting clatter—enamelled steel on terrazzo can make a hell of a din. Cat and man dash off and away from the small saucepan, one into the kitchen and one up the mango tree.

Lucky peeks from behind the kitchen door. The saucepan sits upended on the floor, looking like a rather stupid hat. He calls out, 'Coconut, are you okay?'

Nothing.

He comes out from behind the door and takes one step onto the back patio. The back garden is completely still. The pandan, thicker and lusher than ever, doesn't appear to be harbouring anything. The ginger flower has grown quite a bit, it must be at least waist-high. *Yikes.* He never knew those plants could be so tall. Nothing among them either, except for a few ferns that have taken up residence. Ferns! Mr Chee is going to be pretty upset.

Fuck the ferns—where's the cat? He doesn't see it in the mango tree, looking down at him, so Lucky squints at the rest of the garden riot, hoping to spot Coconut somewhere among the hibiscus, the aloe vera, the pink frangipani, the blanket of morning glory over the grass.

'Coconut?' He's starting to feel a little silly.

'I'm here, Lucky.'

So it is—licking a paw, cleaning its face, on the floor right next to him.

Lucky nearly jumps. But he doesn't. This morning, another option presented itself when he woke up: 4. The cat only talks to him.

The more he thinks about it, the more attractive—and logical—it is. He finds his tongue. 'You're so quiet, Coconut.'

Coconut continues cleaning its face. 'It's the paws. If you had my paws, you could be quiet too.' It looks at Lucky's feet. 'Those don't look very useful.'

Lucky looks at his feet. How big and clumsy they look next to the cat's dainty little white paws. 'Well, I'm used to them. And if I have to run or climb or anything, I just wear shoes.'

'Yes, you would need them.' Coconut looks up at him. 'And you have many, many shoes.'

Lucky frowns. Not true. He knows lots of people who own many, many more pairs of shoes. Shawn, that one is a shoe freak. Lucky owns maybe ten pairs. He counts them in his head to make sure. One for running, which he doesn't do often. Two pairs of loafers, for everything else. A pair of sneakers. Maybe two. Three pairs of flip-flops. Two pairs of dress shoes, and maybe a pair of moccasins . . . or two?

'Are you counting your shoes in your head, Lucky?'

Lucky stares. What the fuck? Does Coconut read minds as well as speak? Shit. 'How do you know?'

Coconut cocks it head sideways. 'I don't. I'm asking you. And isn't it easier if you just count them?'

'What? Like, on the rack?'

'Yes. The one near the big door.'

Well, his shift doesn't start for another two hours. 'Okay, let's have a look.'

Lucky and Coconut walk into the kitchen and through it to the courtyard and through that to the living room. Lucky loves how cool it is in the middle of the house. He wonders if Coconut likes it too. And does Coconut like the William Morris wallpaper, rife with parakeets and roses and tulips and twisting vines, so beloved by his parents that they plastered the entire length of the living room and all the upstairs corridors with it?

'What do you think of the wallpaper?'

'The birds don't look like any bird I've ever seen. Are there really birds like these?'

Lucky and Coconut study the parakeets on the wallpaper, all gorgeous creatures in red and blue and yellow. Some have spotted chests; others have grand, crown-like tufts at the top of their heads. Some perch at the ends of vine tendrils; others are in eternal mid-flight. Lucky hasn't really ever paid attention to birds, and the only parakeets he's ever seen were green, but he doesn't know if out there somewhere there aren't birds like these.

'I don't know. Maybe. Maybe just not here, but elsewhere.'

This seems good enough for Coconut, and the subject is considered closed.

Next to the front door is a system of cabinets for keys, letters, shoes, umbrellas, shopping totes, paper bags, and other odds and ends, but there is no actual system for how any of these are stored. Lucky opens a few cabinets to show Coconut his shoes.

'See? There aren't that many.'

They count them together and find that Lucky owns fifteen pairs of shoes. He's almost forgotten about the new snakeskin loafers he bought on a whim and has never worn, and the boots he bought on sale while he was in Tokyo in winter a few years ago. And a few other pairs he wishes he never bought but is too ashamed to give away.

Coconut hops into a cabinet to get a closer look at a pair. 'These look strange.'

'Oh, those are special shoes. For hiking and climbing.' Lucky doesn't know why he bought them, really—must have been a really good sale. He turns one of the shoes over so he can point out the ridged soles to Coconut. 'See? This helps me climb over rocks and things.'

'I've never seen you climb anything.'

Lucky feels a little indignant. 'Well, not recently . . .'

'I've never seen you climb anything, Lucky.' Coconut jumps into another open cabinet. 'And what are these?' It nudges its head against a pair of high heels.

The high heels are very high and very sparkly, and they are, of course, Pearl's. They look brand new—she probably bought them for an event and changed her mind. Or maybe she never got to go. Lucky takes the shoes and puts them on. They fit—he and Pearl have always worn the same size shoes. He snickers, remembering that she sometimes had to buy her shoes from a New York web store for drag queens.

'These are Pearl's shoes, Coconut. What do you think?'

'They look like weapons. And she'll be very, very tall.'

'She's not coming back soon, you know, Coconut.' Lucky walks to the nearest sofa, still wearing the shoes. He almost falls over, but he manages to fling himself onto the sofa just in time. The cat jumps up next to him.

'Where's she gone, Lucky?'

'Far away, Coconut. Really, really far away.'

'Where?'

Lucky stretches out, flips onto his stomach and buries his face in the white leather softness of the sofa. He doesn't know how long he stays this way, but by the time he turns over, the cat is gone.

* * *

In between preparing a Vietnamese drip coffee for his first customer and signing off on the day's delivery of pandan cake, Lucky realizes that he's had his first proper chat with Coconut and that he's not freaking out. Should he be freaking out? But it isn't really so weird after all, a talking cat. Aside from the fact that he's never heard a cat speak, there's nothing supernatural about it. The cat seems really nice, actually.

He will get sardines. He doesn't know if the cat will like sardines, but if it doesn't, he can eat them all himself—he has a nice recipe for grilled sardines that he hasn't made for far too long. Perfect with green chilli sambal—he'll get some green chilli on the way home from work. And Thai basil—Pearl always made that sambal with Thai basil.

* * *

Lucky stands at the massive kitchen counter, pounding lightly roasted green chilli in the large stone mortar that his mother used to use. Coconut walks into the kitchen, possibly lured by the smell of grilling sardines.

'What are you doing?'

'I'm making something to eat with the fish.'

Coconut jumps up onto the counter and stares into the mortar. 'What is it?'

'Chilli, basil, lime. Do you know what those are?'

'Yes. I don't like them.' But it pokes its head into the mortar anyway. 'Smells bad. This smells so bad.' Coconut takes another sniff and sneezes.

Lucky laughs. How do cats make sneezing look so cute?

He sniffs the air. The sardines should be done pretty soon. He's done them in two sets—salted for himself and plain for Coconut. It's a bit sad, the thought of unsalted sardines, but he's found a cat nutrition website and it's very, very adamant that cats shouldn't eat salted things. Poor Coconut. Plain sardines! He picks the sardines off the grill pan with a pair of chopsticks and puts Coconut's four little fish into its dish.

'You be careful, very hot.'

'Yes. I saw you take them off the fire.'

They eat their dinner together in the kitchen—it's raining outside and Lucky's moved Coconut's food and water dishes indoors. He watches the cat eat, nimbly picking the flesh off the bones, crunching up the heads. He's never noticed that cats eat while sitting down on their hind legs, and now that he has, it does seem the logical thing to do. Gravity, and all that.

`Coconut liked the sardines`, Lucky types. `I'll get more next week.`

The phone rings just as he clicks send. Lucky makes a face. Uncle Desmond—what does he want? Lucky makes more faces as he finds out.

* * *

'Cats are such logical things, you know,' Lucky tells Shawn.

Shawn doesn't know and doesn't care.

* * *

'Cats are such logical things, you know,' Lucky tells Dinah. 'They eat on their haunches. It helps get the food down into the gut properly. I wonder if lions eat on their haunches too?'

Dinah frowns. There's definitely something odd about him these days.

* * *

'Cats are such logical things, you know,' Lucky tells Meixi.

Meixi wonders if she should tell him she likes cats too or if that will seem desperate.

* * *

For the next two weeks, Lucky and Coconut dine on sardines cooked in every way Lucky can think of—grilled, roasted, baked, fried, poached, and even raw in a ceviche, which Coconut refuses to eat, so Lucky has to give it a packet of Princess instead.

'Shrimp Dream, Tuna Supreme, or Seafood Delight?' Lucky fans out the packets, waving them in front of Coconut.

Coconut yawns. 'Doesn't matter. They all taste the same.'

'But are they good?'

Another yawn. 'Good enough. And Pearl likes to say, a girl's got to eat.'

'Boys as well.'

Coconut sniffs. 'Pearl didn't say anything about boys.'

Lucky watches Coconut finish the Princess Tuna Supreme, deep in thought. *Right, so Coconut's a girl.* It's weird, but he never knew this.

It's a comforting thought. *This house needs a girl.*

The mess with the mushrooms

really began with Pearl, Lucky tells Coconut. It was Pearl, after all, who first said they should find a way to do something profitable with all the used coffee grounds.

'You guys should find a way to do something . . . profitable with all the used coffee grounds,' she said, apropos of nothing.

Pearl and Lucky were in the kitchen, chopping up spring onions and chilli, and pounding lengkuas and cekur and turmeric and lemongrass and coriander root. As always, Lucky was de facto sous chef, prep chef, and general kitchen dogsbody in Pearl's convoluted kitchen experiments, and the most trying times were the weeks she spent cooking all day and all night, compiling and testing recipes for her books. The first one, *The Tao of Bao*, and the second, the much more lazily titled *Book of Dumplings*, had done unexpectedly, disturbingly well and had been translated into Malay, Bahasa Indonesia, Portuguese, and Spanish. So of course she was going to do another one, and its working title was *Pearl's Noodle Journal*, which Lucky thought was rather rubbish. And rather too obvious a plug for the television show.

But he loved the idea of a book about travelling and eating and making noodles. He wished he had thought of it first and wished even more that he too could do something like this, though of course the whole point of the book was that it was Pearl Lee's views on the subject, not that of some random guy who just loved eating noodles and seeking them out. Lucky had, as publishers would put it, zero weight and even less pull, and even he knew this.

Pearl, on the other hand, was convinced that fans would 'absolutely lap up, of course they would' a book about her favourite, most fondly remembered noodle dishes from Southeast Asia, with notes and maps and recipes and photos that she had herself written and drawn and cooked and compiled. She had some rather good photos of her own, taken on her trips, but the plan was to travel back to some of her favourite sites to take more and better ones.

'What does this have to do with mushrooms?' Coconut walks off for a bit to investigate a massive chest of tiny drawers.

'Nothing. That's my grandmother's Chinese herb chest.'

The cat turns back and gives him what Shawn would call a judgy look. 'No, Lucky—what does the noodle book have to do with mushrooms?'

Nothing there either, Lucky is forced to admit. But it's the way he remembers the whole thing starting, with he and Pearl making some sort of dipping sauce for some sort of Vietnamese noodle dish for the nth time, and she had been in the middle of telling him off for not slicing the chilli finely enough when, quite suddenly, she began going on about coffee grounds.

'How much coffee grounds do you throw away every day at the cafe?' she pressed on when he hadn't immediately latched on to her idea of making money from used coffee grounds.

'I don't know.' He didn't. 'A lot.' It was.

'Just think, Lucky. What would Papa do?'

Lucky didn't know and couldn't guess. He knew that his father used to sell his used coffee grounds for cheap to be mixed in with fertilizer on farms in Johor, but that was a very long time ago, before he'd leased out the coffee shops and focused on the import and wholesale aspect of the business.

Pearl gestured with the pestle, scattering tiny bits of pounded coriander root and lengkuas. 'I think you need to find a way to reuse them for a new product. Something totally different so that you're not too obviously selling a by-product of the cafe.' She paused. 'Is the cafe even making money yet?'

Lucky shrugged. What a nag she could be sometimes, and her quarter stake in the cafe gave her licence to nag him as much as she wanted about it. Was it making money, and who did this and who did that, and had they thought of this and that and the other? Utterly aggravating, though of course it helped to have Pearl around—it meant he didn't have to worry too much about anything. Of course, sometimes he got in trouble for worrying too little.

'You worry too little, Lucky,' she told him, after making sure he was slicing the chilli to correct levels of skinniness. 'This cafe, you have to really try to make things work this time, okay?'

Pearl worried a lot when it came to Lucky—it felt like she never trusted him to get anything right.

'Did Pearl worry a lot?'

Lucky stared. It's as if the cat is reading his mind sometimes. Coconut jumps onto the kitchen counter and stares into the baking dish Lucky is shredding cheese into. 'And what are you making?'

'Mac-and-cheese pie. Dinah's coming over to dinner.' Lucky continues to grate cheese onto the first layer of macaroni. 'Pearl didn't really have to worry most of the time. She just got things done, you know? Pretty amazing.' He pauses. 'Sometimes a little too amazing. Made me feel a bit, I don't know, not so amazing . . .'

So in order to shut his sister up and to quell rising feelings of not-so-amazingness, Lucky collected two days' worth of grounds from Caffiend and put them in little plastic containers on the kitchen table and stared at them and poked at them and wondered whether it was worthwhile to try growing something in them. This was, in hindsight, a side-effect of his most recent misadventure, in which he'd tried to make something out of being an urban farmer after visiting a rooftop farm somewhere in the hipster part of Tiong Bahru.

Pearl could and should have told Lucky that he didn't have the makings of a successful farmer, urban or not—he kept strange hours, he didn't like messing about in the dirt, he wasn't even that fond of gardening—but she didn't. Instead, she threw some of the family money his way and was the first to sign up for a weekly mystery herb subscription. Meanwhile, Lucky threw himself at their back garden and trusted that things would somehow work out. Eight months and the price of a small car later, Lucky was bored out of his mind, and Pearl had started looking for ways to shut the whole thing down. But in the end, it was Lucky's terror of snails that brought Blue Box Herbs to an end.

'You're afraid of snails?'

Lucky realizes that admitting this will make Coconut think less of him—the cat appears fearless. Only this morning he saw her leap from the top of the garden wall onto the roof of the house next door, and for no good reason. So he lies: 'Only the big ones.'

'The snails in the garden are all big—so it's a good thing you gave up gardening.'

'Farming.'

After Lucky's urban farm went back to being the back garden, the blue boxes remained. Piles and piles of them, ordered at significant cost from a crafter in Malacca who made boxes out of old egg cartons and then hand-painted them in non-toxic vegetable-based dyes she cooked up herself. So of course he decided he had to incorporate them in whatever he decided to do with the coffee grounds. Anyway, Pearl wouldn't let him throw them away.

'So, it really was her fault, the whole mushroom thing.'

Coconut yawns. 'I've heard nothing about the mushrooms. And it's nearly time for a nap.'

'You're always napping.'

'I like naps.'

Coconut yawns again and Lucky speeds up his storytelling, aware he's losing his audience.

In the end, the Internet showed Lucky a way to grow mushrooms out of coffee grounds. He bought some oyster mushroom spawn, cut up some of the cardboard boxes that their coffee shipments came in, tinkered with various proportions of cardboard bits to mushroom spawn to coffee grounds, and made a mushroom-growing mixture that he stuffed into fine string mesh and then into a blue box.

Lucky was rather proud of himself. He showed the mushroom kit to Pearl, then to Shawn and Dinah. 'See? All you have to do is make slits in the mesh and spray water and wait for the mushrooms.'

He had really enjoyed making the kit—cutting up cardboard, trying out different kinds of mesh, fiddling with the design until it worked. It reminded him of his days in architecture school, and all the models he'd had to make. Indeed, Lucky had enjoyed making models much, much more than he enjoyed designing the schools or homes or hospitals or hotels for any of the imaginary briefs his professors dreamt up. Also, for whatever reason, he always forgot about the toilets.

Anyway, the whole thing with the mushrooms and the coffee grounds really should have been an easy side business, but it wasn't. Lucky ended up spending all his time making mushroom-growing kits instead of making coffee, and Shawn had to put in longer hours at the cafe. But at least the kits sold out every week, which surprised everyone.

'Except me,' Lucky adds. 'What's not to love about mushrooms? And being able to grow your own mushrooms—how cool is that!'

They were thrilled when the organic supermarket on their street agreed to stock the kits, but that was when things slowly but surely began to spiral out of control. First, they had to supplement their own supply of coffee grounds with grounds from some of the other cafes in the neighbourhood, and very soon Lucky and Pearl found their kitchen full of garbage bags full of damp coffee grounds. Then they had to start buying fresh cardboard because there wasn't enough from the boxes they got from deliveries. Other little things began to go awry—some of the kits they sold didn't sprout any mushrooms ('Complete mystery, Coconut!'), and once an entire sack of coffee beans was contaminated when a kit fell into it and managed to split open.

'There were *spores* in the coffee—Shawn was practically barking!' Lucky grimaces. He sighs. 'And then we had the leak. Final straw. Shawn made me pack all of it up the same day.'

It started one stormy night, that leak in the ceiling in the storeroom, and by the time they got in the next morning, about two hundred mushroom kits were soaked through and there was nothing they could do but wait for the mushrooms.

'We ate mushrooms for weeks and weeks after all those kits started to sprout,' Lucky tells Coconut. 'Mushrooms in everything. Can you imagine?'

'No. Why would I?' Coconut looks offended.

'You don't like mushrooms?'

'No.'

'Why not?'

'Pearl says I mustn't eat them, and she's always right. She wouldn't let me eat a prawn once. She said it was off and she threw it out but I dug it out of the bin and ate it anyway. And then I was sick. So, I'm not eating mushrooms.' The cat gives him a haughty look. 'You don't seem to know very much. Definitely not as much as Pearl.'

Only later, while consulting his trusty cat-info website, does Lucky learn that many mushrooms are toxic to cats. But for now, as Coconut goes off to take her nap, Lucky sits at the kitchen table, waiting for the mac-and-cheese pie to be done, thinking about what he didn't tell the cat.

That it hadn't been all that funny. That he resented—still resents—how everyone talked—still talks—about the mushroom incident like it's proof that he's some sort of ridiculous buffoon, and how Pearl always seemed happy to join in. That at some point during the weeks of enforced mushroom-bingeing, he had thrown a sprouting kit at her, telling her to go fry her stupid smug face.

Pearl, being Pearl, had started it by losing her temper. 'God, how much more of this crap are we supposed to get through? I feel like I've eaten nothing but mushrooms for two weeks.'

They had just sat down to dinner, and she had stir-fried some mushrooms to go with the mushroom fried rice left over from the night before.

Lucky had shrugged. 'I don't mind. I like mushrooms.'

'Of course you don't mind.' Pearl slammed her chopsticks down on the table. 'You know what your problem is? You never appreciate the rubbish I have to put up with for you.'

'For me? This whole thing was your idea.'

'Are you joking? I only told you to do something useful with the coffee grounds, and you came up with this!' She waves her hand at the kitchen counter, at the mushroom kits piled up all over it.

'Mushrooms are useful. And delicious.' He ate one to prove his point.

'You know what? *You* eat them! You eat them all!' She flung a mushroom into his bowl of rice. 'I'm so sick of fucking mushrooms.'

'No one's asking you to fuck them!'

She threw another mushroom into his bowl. 'Oh, Lucky, that's so funny. You're a funny one, right? So fucking funny! You know what's really funny? You! Living off money you don't have the slightest idea how to make, never feeling the need to do . . . *anything*. *You* fuck a mushroom!' She threw another mushroom and it hit him in the face.

Lucky stood up. He snatched up one of the many kits on the kitchen counter. It was bursting with white blossom-like oyster mushrooms, and Lucky remembers taking a moment to think about how pretty they looked. And then he hurled it at her.

'Go fry your stupid smug face, Pearl.' He started to walk away before he felt inclined to throw anything else. 'Go drown yourself.'

And then she kind of did, didn't she? Going to Surabaya, plunging into blue-black depths in that stupid plane. Of course, that was months after he told her to drown herself, and of course, the morning after the blow-up, things between them were back to normal, but it's still hard to think about, most days.

Lucky pops open a can of beer. Twenty more minutes until the pie is ready.

* * *

Shawn looks up from counting cash. 'You're late.'

'Sorry, traffic was so bad.'

'Coffee?'

It's six. Normally, Dinah doesn't drink coffee after five if she isn't working late, but she feels like Shawn would be happier if she had some, so she says yes and then wishes she hadn't when he promises her 'a nice strong one, yah, the way you like it'. He's obviously trying to be nice, and it makes Dinah feel like more of an ass. She hasn't had the time to work any shifts at Caffiend lately because the new apartment complex she's working on has been delayed yet again and there are a million things to fix and figure out. *Look at him—actually whistling while he works. What the actual fuck.* Some days, Dinah wishes that she too had quit her job, like Shawn did, to work full time at the cafe. And Shawn still manages to take on quite a few freelance projects—like the series of sculptures for East Coast Park last year, and that restaurant in Siglap. And Shawn has a wife, and a *life*.

Meanwhile she hasn't dated anyone since, well—what's the point? It's been a long time. And she can't recall the last time she hung out with friends who weren't Shawn and Lucky. Seriously, at this rate, she's definitely dying alone with a freezer full of pies and ice cream and a fridge full of beer. All she's eaten this week—five consecutive dinners—is tinned chicken curry. Two weeks ago, she went shopping and bought chicken, meaning to actually make chicken curry, but every night when she got home at ten or so, the last thing she wanted to do was cook—she ate frozen pies while the chicken turned green in the fridge.

But tonight will be different. Tonight, Lucky's making mac-and-cheese pie. He thinks it's her favourite, and in a way it is, but only because they ate so much of it together back in architecture school, when she only had money for one meal a day and he was her hero without quite knowing that he was, bringing her home to eat in that great big kitchen, to watch him and Pearl muck about and make heady, hearty, delicious things.

'What do you think?'

Dinah takes a second sip of her coffee. The first one didn't register. 'That's a really dark roast. Too dark?'

Shawn picks up her mug and takes a sip. 'Hmm. That's a bit burnt, my bad. Maybe it's better as a drip.'

'Maybe.' Dinah shuffles in her seat. 'Anyway, what did you want to talk about?'

Shawn's lovely, but she knows there's no way he just wants to chat. If he did, he'd have suggested drinks. Which is why when she received that silly text asking her to `drop by later if you're free, would be` nice to catch up, she cancelled her last meeting of the day and told him she'd see him at five-thirty.

'Wow, Dinah, so . . . business-y.' He rolls his eyes.

'Aiyah, don't be an idiot. I can't stay long—Lucky's expecting me for dinner.'

'Ah. That's what I wanted to talk about.'

'Are you coming for dinner too?'

'No, no! I mean I want to talk about Lucky.' He sighs. 'I think you're right.'

Dinah waits for him to tell her what about.

'He's getting weirder. Maybe he's having a breakdown. But he was getting better just weeks ago, so I really don't get it.' Shawn runs his hands over his face. 'I don't know, Dins. Maybe it's not even about Pearl? Maybe it's something else—who knows? Maybe it's a woman. We did bump into that Rosalind woman a few weeks ago. He's just really off these days.'

He tells Dinah that Lucky's been even more distracted than usual—mixing things up, forgetting things, drawing unidentifiable objects on scraps of paper.

'I don't know what they are—roundish, like eggs, I guess.' Shawn throws up his hands.

Dinah flinches. She's accustomed by now to his dramatic gestures, but sometimes she wishes they weren't quite so . . . explosive. Shawn should come with a helmet for anyone who has to be within arm's length.

'And I caught him eating biscuits off a plate . . . Dinah, let me finish . . . with his hands behind his back.'

'What?' Dinah hates people who say 'what' to register surprise, but she can't help herself this time.

'And he keeps talking about cats. What the hell is up with that?'

* * *

The house is completely dark as Dinah walks in. Not a single light has been turned on in the living room or on the front porch. She switches on one of the living room lights. No Lucky—good. It would be really weird to find him sitting here in the darkness. Dinah makes her way through the house, thinking for the nth time as she avoids treading on the zebra skin rug, what the hell were they thinking when they furnished this house?

The kitchen light is on—she can see it from the courtyard. 'Lucky?' she calls out.

He doesn't answer, but as she approaches the entrance to the kitchen, she can hear his voice. At first it's hard to make out what he's saying, but when she's right at the doorway, she hears him say, loud and clear:

'Well, Coconut, it's easy for you to say. Cats see much better in the dark than people, you know. I can't see a bat coming at me from, what, twenty metres away. And they're so fast! Ick. Okay, let's please stop talking about bats.'

A clatter of dishes and things. Some footsteps. Then Lucky, sounding annoyed: 'You could have said so earlier. How am I supposed to know you prefer salmon half-cooked?'

He's having conversations with the cat now. God. Dinah shakes her head. This from a guy who never even looked at the cat before Pearl died, who could never be trusted to even feed the damn cat while she was away on her trips. Clearly, so clearly, he's not himself. Dinah stands quite still, unwilling to enter the kitchen, wondering if she should call out his name again. *Of course I should! I'm in his house!*

But just as she's about to shout for Lucky, he pipes up: 'Don't look at me like that. You know you can't have mac-and-cheese pie. I told you, it's the cheese. Too much salt.'

Feeling like she's sneaking up on him, Dinah enters the kitchen, trying to stomp a little on the polished ceramic tiles to give him fair warning.

Ever since she met Lucky, Dinah has been unable to think or say 'lucky' and mean 'fortunate'. Being (L)ucky has come to mean much more than just being fortunate, even if statistic-defying good fortune—winning both the economic and genetic lottery—was perhaps the start of Lucky being Lucky and lucky. But careless, silly, strange, charming, creative, clueless Lucky and his no-fucks-given, madcap, manipulative sister and their crazy house and their fucking huge kitchen—it was the movie she wanted to see over and over again in their uni days, a movie she was thrilled to be an extra in (*Hungry Friend 2, House sitter 1*) whenever it suited them.

But as Dinah walks into the cool, bright kitchen and looks at Lucky now, standing at the oven with Pearl's ridiculous towel wrapped around his head, her acid-yellow oven mitt on one hand, her floral apron over his shorts and Hawaiian shirt, her cat at his feet and shadows under his eyes, the only thought that pops into her head is: *Fuck, he looks like the ghost of a 1960s housewife*. Actually, he looks like Pearl doing a parody of a 1960s housewife. Dinah blinks back sudden tears, just in time to put on her widest smile as he sees her and announces:

'You're here! I've made your favourite—wait, have I already told you?'

She says hello, wishing she knew what her role in this new film is.

An interventionist god

is what Lucky wants, some days. Someone to yell 'Stop that!' or 'What a dumb thing to do, Lucky.' Or, right now, 'The blue jacket with the grey shirt makes you look like an unimaginative paper-pusher.'

'It does, doesn't it?'

'What?'

'This shirt. Does it make me look like an unimaginative paper-pusher?'

'What kind of paper? Like that ball?'

Lucky sighs, shrugging off the jacket. 'It's fine, Coconut. I won't wear the jacket.'

The tropical dress code is a hard-to-please, unforgiving bitch and today Lucky feels like her prize whipping boy. How is it possible, he wonders, that in a region that's basically always hot and damp, there isn't a properly thought-through, modern dress code for occasions such as this part-Christmas do, part-poncey engagement party hoo-ha tonight at Uncle Desmond's? Something that isn't some sort of traditional costume or the damn batik shirt, which always makes him feel like he's about to impersonate his father at some Chinese businessmen's guild event. He wishes he could do something quick, much like putting on a jacket without actually putting on a jacket, that would signify he's being what his parents would call 'properly respectful' and Pearl would call 'not being a dick'. At least women have earrings—Pearl used to wear her enormous vintage chandelier ones to all the Big Family Functions.

Lucky wishes he could put on one of his mother's pearl brooches and a silk shawl and just be done with it. He snickers. If only.

Lucky hates the Big Family Functions. The food is never much good and the conversation is rubbish, and now that Pearl isn't around, there's also no one to stand in a corner and commiserate with or say inappropriate things to. Having to wear a jacket makes it so much worse, so no, no he will not wear a jacket today. Uncle Desmond will just have to deal with Jacketless Lucky.

'Stuffy old fish,' Jacketless Lucky mutters, wondering if he should change his trousers.

Now, an interventionist god might have told Lucky to change his trousers—they don't fit well any more, not even with his tightest belt—or to at least hold off on calling his uncle a stuffy old fish, but the cat has other priorities. She jumps off his bed and rubs her face against his knee.

'What's for dinner?'

'Princess? Any flavour you like. I was going to steam a fish, but I have to press these damn pleats again. Just look at them! Gah. I look like I slept in my clothes.' Lucky wishes he could just put on jeans, but he can't let the side down now that he's the only one left, can he?

'Okay. Now?'

Lucky looks down at Coconut, who's busy studying a dark spot on the parquet floor. 'Right now? Are you hungry already?'

She looks up at him and narrows her eyes. 'Pearl never has to ask if I'm hungry.'

Lucky rolls his eyes. What's the point of a talking cat who can't give him a nice, straight answer?

Not that anything about Coconut being able to speak is nice and straight, of course. The more Lucky thinks about it, the more confusing it is. Should he be more alarmed? More cautious? Somehow he feels like he's not responding to this situation in quite the right way, even though he's not sure what the right way is. Obviously, while there isn't an authority on what to do with a talking cat, common sense suggests not talking back or at least not encouraging it with grilled seafood. Unfortunately, common sense also suggests he check himself into a mental institution or at least talk to a doctor. More unfortunately, the family doctor is the stuffy old fish, who is both family and doctor.

Just for fun, he Googled 'talking cat' last week. *Four hundred million* results, but mostly cat videos edited and dubbed over by people with far too much time on their hands, and blogs by people who want to be cats. But after refining the search to 'article talking cat', he found an article in a psychology journal on people–cat interactions.

> The emerging science of cat cognition offers plenty of evidence that cats have highly developed socio-cognitive skills. Unlike dogs and dog–human interactions, however, which have been extensively studied, cats and cat–human interactions are much less understood. Much less is known about who cats are, what skills they have developed to understand and communicate with humans, and how to ensure the success of human–cat relationships within the home. Using some of what we've already learnt about dogs, researchers have begun to explore human–cat communication and the human-directed cognitive capacities of cats.

Lucky read the article twice, bookmarked it, read it again yesterday and still can't decide if it's saying it's possible for cats to develop the ability to speak. It doesn't say it's impossible, but then again, perhaps that's not something that needs to be said.

Also, he's discovered that Coconut can *read*. Or at least he thinks she can—she scoffed at the packet of Princess Chicken Feast that he bought in a bid to provide some variety.

'If I wanted a bird, I'd catch it myself.' She sounded so offended that he felt compelled to grill a few large prawns for her dinner.

God, what the fuck is going on?

The interventionist god of Lucky's dreams, he believes, would have answered him by now.

* * *

A silver Mercedes jerks along Swan Street as its driver scrutinizes the houses, noting the more recent additions with contempt. All these new-money idiots, tearing down the old bungalows and putting up their massive blocks with no soul. Dolly Chong can't believe that Old Chew's house is gone and along with it the verandah she spent so much time on as a young woman, buttering up Suzy Chew while trying to catch Bobby Chew's dark brown eyes. What's Bobby doing these days, she wonders, and does he still have all his wonderful hair?

The car comes to a sudden stop outside the house with the enormous lions. Dolly wrinkles her nose. So crass. Her late brother-in-law had absolutely no taste. Bought the house for a proper bargain when the previous owner (wasn't it Siew Fong's cousin?) went bankrupt, then filled it with all these horrible things from goodness knows where. Like that zebra rug. Dolly shudders. She can't say exactly why, but a rug like that feels decidedly un-Christian. What to do? All these low-class kampung types—when they get rich, they just don't know what to do with their money. It's been so many years—forty-five?—but Dolly still can't believe her sister Betty went off with that riffraff.

Thank goodness the children take after her. As her nephew walks towards the car, Dolly notes with satisfaction the Chong nose, chin, and cheekbones. But the boy has definitely gone to seed, poor dear. It's a good thing his mother isn't here to see this.

'Hi, Aunty Dolly.' He gets in the car and puts on his seat belt. 'Thanks for picking me up.'

Lucky would have much preferred to take a taxi than suffer his Aunty Dolly one-on-one for the twelve minutes it takes to get to Uncle Desmond's house. But she insisted and insisted, and then she sounded like she was about to cry or choke and he decided putting up a fight wasn't worthwhile. He'd see her at Uncle Desmond's anyway, and then he'd have to endure an entire evening of melodramatic comments about how she wished Betty was here to set things right. His poor mum, always conveniently conjured up by Aunty Dolly every time he or Pearl or their father behaved 'like unsociable barbarians'. Unsocialized, he's always wanted to yell, barbarians are meant to be unsocialized, you daft owl.

'You look like you haven't been sleeping properly,' says the daft owl as the car jerks forward.

'Careful—' He inhales sharply as she makes a sudden left, narrowly missing the curb.

She clicks her tongue. 'Wah, these streets are much narrower than I remember.' She drives on, scowling. 'Why aren't you getting enough sleep? Watching too much TV, I'm sure.'

Lucky blinks hard. Does she think he's five? 'I'm getting plenty of sleep.'

'You look so tired.'

'I'm fine, Aunty Dolly.'

The trouble with everyone nowadays, Dolly decides as she manages to beat the red lights at the end of Koon Seng Road, is that they all have to be heroes. It's all this modern nonsense about being strong and independent and forging your own path and being your own person (who else's person would you be?) instead of just admitting you need help, please, and thank you very much. Even her nephew Lucky, who's never had any ambition or drive, who's never done anything even vaguely memorable, who's so hopeless that the family jumped on this cafe idea because at least it would give him something to do, who is so obviously not fine—even *he* needs to be a hero.

'No man is an island, Lucky,' she reminds him.

'So true.' He wishes he were an island. Something off the coast of Terengganu, maybe, something small and hard to get to. Something with a tiger on it.

'Are you eating enough? You look like you're not.'

'I'm eating a lot.'

'Maybe you have worms.'

'Maybe I have worms,' Lucky agrees pleasantly.

Dolly can't tell if he's making fun of her or trying to be agreeable. She sighs. Betty's children were always difficult. That Pearl, such a little dictator. And Lucky—a fool. Probably Betty's fault, though. Spoilt them rotten.

When they get to her brother Desmond's house on Frankel Avenue, all the porch and garden lights are switched on even though it's barely six-thirty and the sun hasn't set. *So wasteful.* The red Lexus parked outside tells her that her sister Maggie is already here, probably with her husband and her daughter Gillian. Lucky should really try to be more like Gillian or any of his other cousins. Like Andrew, who's a surgeon now, or Anne, who's just made senior partner at the law firm, or Anton, who's doing so well at that computer company and is getting engaged to Loo Wen Shi's daughter. It's probably too late though. He's thirty-seven and potters around in a cafe—which heiress would even look at him?

* * *

The duck is dry. All around the table, the aunts and uncles and cousins chew politely, everyone taking turns to help themselves to more of the sweet soy sauce, lime, and chilli dip. Sensing his deteriorating value as host, Uncle Desmond opens a bottle of wine to distract his guests and begins to pour it into glasses.

'I hope this is good.' He hands Aunty Maggie the first glass. His sister accepts with a brief nod. As the eldest, she's used to having the first of everything. 'Had it shipped from Portugal. Someone on the hospital board of directors recommended it.'

His wife nods indulgently. Caroline Chong can't tell and doesn't care if the wine is any good, but it's always reassuring to know her husband is rubbing shoulders with the hospital big-shots. Next to her, Lucky gives the tip of his spoon a quick, discreet lick. At least the kicap manis is of good quality. He drowns his chunk of duck in dipping sauce, wondering how long he'll have to stay at this dud of a party to 'give face' to Uncle Desmond. On the other side of the table, his cousin Andrew is struggling to open a second bottle of wine. He tries not to stare. Funny how a man who can take off the top of people's heads without killing them can't find his way around a stupid bottle of wine. Lucky would offer to help if it didn't mean drawing attention to himself.

Just drive that corkscrew in! It won't bite.

'Aiyoh.' Aunty Dolly shakes her head at Andrew. *Another hero, it seems.* 'Careful, Andrew.'

'Lucky, go help him.' Aunty Maggie doesn't look up from wrestling with her slab of duck. *Betty's boy drinks like a fish, doesn't he? Might as well be useful then.*

Everyone is watching Andrew now. He's standing up at his seat, his face stricken as he renews his efforts at coaxing the corkscrew into the bottle. Next to him, his sister Anne rolls her eyes. Next to her, their brother Anton smirks.

'Lucky, help me.' Andrew tries not to sound desperate, but his voice is an octave higher than usual.

Fuck. Lucky smiles to keep from swearing out loud. Walking over to Andrew, he takes the bottle and the corkscrew from his cousin and deftly eases the latter into the former. Pulling out the cork, Lucky holds it out solemnly for everyone to see, then does a comical little bow before going back to his seat. Anne giggles. Andrew manages a laugh. The aunties shake their heads and smile.

Lucky waves his chopsticks at his audience. 'That one's free, but I'll have to charge for repeat performances.' He can imagine Pearl rolling her eyes, saying how kind it is of him to always play the fool for their benefit. *Isn't it nice for them, knowing they can count on you if they need a laugh?* He helps himself to the steamed cod in an attempt to distract himself from her voice in his head.

Not quite Pearl's fault, though—she was just echoing Papa. His father hated his mother's family. 'Too much money and no substance,' Mr Lee frequently pronounced, refusing to see his wife's side of the family unless it was a matter of marriage or death or the Chinese New Year. 'Never *really* worked at all, that Desmond—have you seen his hands? Smoother than his wife's.' And not just his wife's—his brother-in-law the doctor's hands could have put any woman's to shame.

Uncle Desmond raises one of these smooth, shame-inducing specimens, and everyone stops talking. Lucky wonders if it is true, as his father liked to say, that his uncle sleeps with special gloves on. What kind of gloves, though? And did he slather his hands in Vaseline, like that guy in that book, what was it? *Of Mice and Men* or was it *Of Men and Mice*? He looks down at his own hands. They're long and thin and ordinary. No calluses or spots or scars. Would his father have been fine with these? He never said anything but probably not.

'Takes after your side,' he heard his father tell his mother once when he was fourteen and got into trouble at school for skipping the cross-country meet. 'Only good in air con.'

Lucky had never been so ashamed. He made the mistake of telling Pearl, who found it hilarious and taunted him for weeks afterwards.

By the time Lucky's mind returns to the dining table, he realizes he's missed half—hopefully more—of his uncle's welcome-to-the-family speech. The stuffy old fish sounds even stuffier than usual, having dusted off his old British accent (acquired while he was at Oxford) for Anton's fiancé's benefit.

'I hope you won't find us too tiresome, Xiying.' His uncle beams. 'But we're all looking forward to getting to know you even better, now that you're going to be one of us.'

The girl winces slightly—Lucky's guess is that his uncle has probably mispronounced her name—but quickly hides it with a bright smile. 'I'm sure I'll enjoy getting to know everyone. You've all been so wonderful to me.' Her voice is on the squeaky side and her accent is American-ish.

Lucky blinks hard as she continues to talk. *So grating.* Pearl would have said something snide and he would have laughed. Left to his own devices, though, Lucky decides that it's entirely Anton's problem. Poor bugger.

As the conversation begins to fragment and scatter, Lucky finds himself the target of his Aunty Maggie's intrusive brand of concern. He pretends to be distracted by the cart of desserts being wheeled in by the waiter hired for the evening (fancy hiring a waiter for a family dinner!) but all this does is force her to raise her voice. Talking across Anne and Andrew and their mother and Aunty Dolly, she booms, 'Are you still working at that cafe?'

'Yes,' he chirps. 'Making coffee seems to be one of my superpowers.'

'Your what?'

'Superpowers!' Seeing her baffled expression, he tries again. 'I seem to make very good coffee.'

Maggie eyes her nephew. Why does he look like he's wearing someone else's clothes? She sniffs. 'Still seems like a waste of the architecture degree.'

Please, not this again. It's been nearly fourteen years since he graduated and this topic still hasn't lost its lustre for her. *I know what your superpower is, Aunty Maggie.*

His eldest aunt raises her eyebrows. 'At least your sister found a way to put her degree to good use.' *And she must have dressed the boy. He never used to look so . . . shabby.*

Aunty Dolly surfaces from her conversation with Anne and Andrew about one of the other senior partners at Anne's firm, whose mother was a classmate of hers. 'I'm still not sure I like the thought of her being an actress, but she did it well.'

Lucky helps himself to another glass of wine. 'Aunty Dolly, she wasn't an actress. Pearl was a TV chef. And a food writer.'

Dolly shrugs. 'There's not much difference.'

'I'm sure there is.' Lucky has to work very hard to keep the edge out of his voice, but he succeeds. This, he's always felt, is his real superpower.

The waiter sets a dome of meringue aflame with a long match. Every head turns to watch it burn, including the aunties'. Lucky exhales and takes a long sip of wine, watching the bluish flames leap and dance on the snowy meringue peaks. Flaming desserts, what marvellous things! There's still some fruit cake from somewhere in the freezer at home, maybe he'll set that on fire. Lucky grins to himself. Everyone starts taking photos of the fiery dome perched on its fancy glass plate, and he joins in, managing to get a poorly framed shot with his phone just before the flames die out. He sends it off in a text message: `Flaming thing with cherries!`

As Lucky digs into his slice of meringue, he hears his name being called in a squeaky, American-ish accent. He pretends to be occupied with portioning out his share of the cherry syrup, but the woman is persistent. Her rounded, nasal tones claw at his ears.

'Lucky!'

He looks up, putting on a confused air. 'Sorry, yes?'

'Hi!' She leans towards him from her side of the table, smiling. Lucky notices she has a good smile. Very straight teeth. Shoulder-length hair, recently trimmed. Skin with a pampered glow. Clothes in muted colours. No jewellery except for the monster ring on her left hand. Lawyer? Banker? Lucky wonders what her hands are like up close.

He smiles back. 'Hi, Xiying.'

'Your sister is Pearl Lee?'

'Yes.'

'I'm sorry. I didn't mean to eavesdrop . . .'

He waves off her apology, exactly as the socialised script demands. 'It's fine.'

'It's just that I'm such a big fan . . . I've always wanted to meet her.' She stops and puts down her spoon. 'I just remembered. Oh, I'm so sorry. I hope you're okay. It must have been so hard.' She looks flustered, waiting for him to reassure her that he's okay.

So he does.

Then, as she turns to talk to Anton, Lucky takes his glass of wine and, sipping from it, makes his way into the kitchen. Alone in the kitchen, surrounded by dirty dishes and remnants of dinner, he sighs, long and loud and a little drunkenly. He raises his glass theatrically and takes a long drink, then a deep bow.

The hangover

is intense. Lucky wakes up to find the bedroom spinning. He tries to sit up, but a wave of dizziness sends him crashing back onto the bed. So he stares at the ceiling instead, thankful he managed to crawl into bed the night before. He can't remember much. He remembers saying goodbye to everyone and getting into Aunty Dolly's car, but after that—nothing.

Lucky lifts the blanket and looks down at himself. He's in his underwear and the clothes from the night before are in a tangle around his feet. Whatever. He spreads out his arms and legs. He's definitely alone in bed—very good. Not like that time with whatshername after that karaoke session to celebrate the end of the third year at architecture school. That was so bad. Especially when he had to ask her what happened. And then he found her panties in his *pocket*. Cringing at the memory, he buries his face in his pillow, gathering his blanket around him, trying to ignore the pounding in his head and the churning in his gut. Please. Stop. Please. Stop.

'Stop what?'

Fuck. Lucky jerks upright, sending the room spinning faster. 'Shit.'

'Drink.'

Lucky takes the cup from Dinah and obeys. He wants to ask her why she's here, but he hasn't got the energy. At least she's fully dressed, and there's no chance of that anyway, though weirder things have happened to him and he's still living to . . . nope, he's not telling anyone *those* tales. He finishes the water and hands the cup back to Dinah.

'Thanks. Can I go back to bed now?'

'It's already two. And your aunt's downstairs.'

What? This may be worse than the panties-in-the-pocket situation. He taps his fingers against a cheekbone, trying to calm himself. He fails.

'What? Why? You called her?' Lucky lies back down. He can't process this. He is all head and gut and nothing else.

Dinah gives him a nasty look. '*She* called *me*, dumbass.'

He can't, *can't* process this. He doesn't want to.

* * *

The dragon stares back at the woman, untroubled by her obvious contempt.

'Madness,' she said just seconds ago, looking it straight in the eye, her eyes flitting across its horns, its mouth, its great big teeth.

The workmanship is quite exquisite, Dolly notes unwillingly, but what a waste. All that hard work and for this? At the foot of the stairs, she steps back to take another look at the floating dragon handrail. 'Madness,' she pronounces again. Her late brother-in-law really was the most ridiculous man. Poor, dear Betty should have married Khoo Wai Keong when she had the chance. Old Khoo's only son would have made a proper husband, and she wouldn't have had to raise her children in this *jungle* of a house.

Dolly starts to walk up the stairs, then decides against it. Let Dinah deal with him first—hopefully, he's in better condition this morning. She sighs. Thank goodness Betty isn't here to see this.

Or this—she runs a finger over the doors of the shoe cabinet and it comes up thickly coated with fine brownish-grey dust. The place was at least clean when Pearl was around, but her nephew just doesn't seem to understand the first thing about keeping a house: keeping a housekeeper. It's obvious no one's dragged a duster or mop or a vacuum cleaner through this madhouse in months. And this thing— she nudges a toe against the stripy, bushy tail of the zebra-skin rug— looks like it needs to be shaken out and aired.

The kitchen, at least, is as clean as it ever was, and, apart from the modern appliances, isn't much different to how it used to look when Betty was its mistress. Ah, you—Dolly pats the old medicine cabinet fondly, remembering how it used to stand in her grandmother's parlour. Red Chinese teak, and probably more than a hundred years old—and living on. And unappreciated—she frowns as she considers her nephew, still in bed upstairs in the middle of the day. Disgraceful. And yet—to be all alone after a lifetime of mollycoddling! The nitwit must be so frightened.

She will make the nitwit some porridge.

Staring into one of the double-doored fridges, she curls her lip. Goodness, is there no end to his depravity? Aside from a bundle of Thai basil, a large plastic container of fresh prawns, several packets of what smells like fish wrapped in newspaper and half an onion smothered in cling film, all available space in the fridge is occupied by bottles of wine, and bottles and cans of various types of beer and tonic water. Clearly, last night was no one-off—not that this possibility had even crossed her mind, given what she knows of the children's drinking habits. Her brother-in-law's fault, of course, raising them uncivilized, encouraging them in their disorderly, arrogant ways.

'My Pearl can do whatever she likes,' he said when Pearl got it in her head to take up theatre studies, of all things, at university. 'She's a born businesswoman.'

'Lee Joo Meng, for once in your life, be reasonable.' She'd come to beard the lion in his study. Betty would have wanted her to.

'Aiyah, Dolly, going to university—only for show, right?' He'd laughed. 'She wants to do this for a few years, so what? My girl will find a way to make money.' He tapped the side of his head. 'She's very sharp, my Pearl. Unlike her name.' He laughed again.

He was right. But he could have been wrong, and what a mess that would have been. Two wastrels to feed and tend to, two to fret over, two to be continually disappointed by—even pig-headed, thick-skinned Joo Meng couldn't have withstood that. He couldn't even do it for one—he left it all to Pearl, his sharp, smart girl. And now, now who will do his donkey work?

Burning with righteous indignation, Dolly unwraps a random packet of fish and stares at the three small silver fish inside. Ikan kuning. Why is her nephew eating ikan kuning? She wrinkles her nose. Poor man's fish, her mother used to call it. 'Only fit to feed the cats,' she would say. Dolly wraps the ikan kuning back up and pushes the packet to the back of the fridge. Unwrapping another parcel of fish, she discovers a chunk of batang and decides to use it for the porridge.

As the rice simmers, she chops up spring onions and ginger, wondering how the boy is doing. *Nitwit.* She's still shocked at how poorly behaved he was last night, in front of Anton's fiancé too. Poor Desmond must be so mortified. Thankfully, he didn't say anything awful, but it was quite, quite enough to have him sitting there, drinking glass after glass of wine—even when Maggie told him that it was time he stopped—muttering and giggling to himself. Has he always been this bad, or is this part of coping without Pearl? Dolly stirs the porridge, adding ginger, then soy sauce and sesame oil. Thank goodness she had the sense to take that girl Dinah's number at the funeral. Such a sensible girl. Didn't even panic last night or anything, just said she'd arrive in half an hour and then did exactly that. No fuss, no complaints, no drama of any kind. Like a man.

Dolly sighs. If only she and Lucky . . . but that girl's too smart for him anyway. Too smart to spend her life looking after someone like Lucky Lee.

A loud mew at Dolly's feet interrupts her mental tirade. She looks down at the cat, surprised. So it's still around, this clever little thing that wandered into the garden one day years ago and decided not to leave. Pearl's little Coconut. She remembers her niece calling her out of the blue, frantic and aggressive, asking what kittens ate and whether it was okay to give them baths. A very small cat had decided to live in their garden, Pearl said, and it seemed to be her responsibility now.

'Hello, dear. Remember me?' Dolly stoops and pats it lightly on the head, making mewing noises. The cat narrows its eyes at her.

She goes to the fridge and it follows her. 'You want some ikan kuning, darling?'

* * *

'Oh, no.'

'Oh, yes.'

Lucky shakes his head. Oh, no. He cannot believe that he had to be dragged out of the car and across the porch and up the stairs and into bed by his Aunty Dolly and Dinah. He also cannot believe that he can't remember any of it. Why, why? And *how*?

'How did you guys do it?'

'I used the trolley thing in my car for a bit.' She grinned. 'Aunty made sure you didn't flop off. Heh. You did fall off at one point, but we just folded you back up on the trolley.'

'God.'

Dinah laughs. 'Well, you're quite pliable when you're drunk, so it wasn't that hard. We said, "Curl up and stay still." And you did.'

'And you got me *up the stairs*?' It's too horrible to imagine.

'Yah. That was basically just me sans trolley sans aunty. She's seventy, for fuck's sake.'

'God, Dinah, I'm so, so sorry.'

Lucky wants to shrivel up and turn into a prawn or a rock or—Coconut pokes her head through the door and gives him a look that manages to be both steely and serene—a cat. He watches her jump onto the seat of the big bay window and settle among the cushions. She yawns and blinks slowly a few times, then stretches out as Lucky looks on, envious. Probably time for another nap—cats spend so much time napping. He read somewhere that the average cat spends sixteen to twenty hours a day sleeping. Sixteen to twenty! What a life. Lucky shakes his head and then wishes he hadn't—it feels like a block of concrete is knocking about on the inside of his skull. A nap would be really nice right now. But Aunty Dolly's downstairs and probably waiting to give him a brutal dressing-down for last night—though she might leave if he stays up here long enough.

'Lucky!'

'What? Sorry, sorry.'

'I said, happy Christmas.' Dinah rolls her eyes.

Lucky would love to roll his eyes too, but he's afraid it will make him dizzy. Instead, he shuts them and wishes he were a cat.

Dinah wishes she could smack him for getting so wasted he couldn't even crawl out of a car. She wishes there were a way for her to tell him off without getting angry and shouting, but there probably isn't—not for her, anyway. She smirks. She will leave him to his aunt.

* * *

'You're nearly forty.'

'I know.'

Dolly makes an impatient noise. 'Yes. But do you know that that's far too old to be behaving like a silly teenager? You're old enough to be someone's father, Lucky.'

But I'm not. I'm not anyone's fucking father.

He's only come close to getting married once and that was some time ago. He's been in love, he's done his share of running after girls and being thrilled by the newness of a new person a new face a new set of hobbies books thoughts dreams favourite things legs. But he's never really felt the need to do anything more, and getting married seemed so grown-up and frightening when he was younger. Not that it's any less frightening now, just a lot less likely, now that even the thought of dating anyone makes him feel queasy.

'You're drinking too much. You have to have better self-control.'

'I don't drink that much, Aunty Dolly.' He stirs his bowl of porridge listlessly. 'I don't know what happened last night. I'm really, really sorry.'

He can hear Pearl in his head: *Keep at it! They just want to hear you apologize.*

'I'm really sorry, Aunty Dolly. And thank you for checking on me and making me porridge.' Lucky lowers his head in what he hopes to be an abject manner and eats a mouthful of porridge. It's quite good, and he's starting to feel a little better.

His Aunty Dolly, having lost hours of sleep the night before over a drunken, shameless nephew, is in no mood to be placated. She raps on the table impatiently, making him wince. 'Lucky.' She says his name in the way his PE teacher in secondary school used to say it, with that calculated mixture of disdain and bewildered pity only a true master of elocution can manage. 'Lucky, look at me.'

He does, feeling like he's a child of five again, cowering from the dragon at the bottom of the stairs.

'Lucky, you can't spend your life being an ostrich.'

'Okay.'

'What are you going to *do*, though?'

'Not be an ostrich.' He giggles.

'Lucky! Be serious,' Dolly snaps. If he were a child, she would have slapped him. 'Stop behaving like you're some sort of little prince.' Her face is red with effort as she struggles to keep from raising her voice. 'You know, this is exactly why we've all been worried sick about you. You have no sense of responsibility, Lucky. Or reality!'

Lucky hangs his head. It's spinning again.

His aunt keeps going, her voice sharp, every sentence ringing like a slap. 'Wake up, Lucky! Your sister is gone. When will you start taking care of yourself?'

Coconut leaps onto the kitchen table, purring loudly. His aunt's face softens. Lucky, pale, unsteady, sensing an opportunity for an impasse, picks up the cat and puts her on his lap. Usually, Coconut hates being picked up and put on laps, but today she sits still, allowing him to stroke her head and hum at her to calm himself. Lucky, impressed by this show of solidarity, makes a mental note to get more sardines from the market tomorrow.

'Have you even been to see Selvam?' Dolly's voice is gentler now, but still firm.

'No.'

'And when will you do it?'

'Next week?'

'Good.' Aunty Dolly nods. 'I'll take you.' She reaches out and pushes his bowl closer to him. 'Now finish your porridge and go back to bed. You look terrible.'

* * *

Coconut and Lucky lie in bed, under the blanket. Her tail taps against his shoulder.

'Is Pearl really gone, Lucky?'

'Yes.' He sighs, stroking the back of her neck.

'I miss her, Lucky.'

'Me too.'

The morning

is like any other. The alarm goes off at 8.15 and Lucky wakes up alone in bed with the sun creeping in, the room cold from the air conditioner's all-nighter. He picks up his phone. No messages. Good.

Lucky stretches. Back to the grind, quite literally. Today he will put in an order for the coffee from the Philippines, and there's a sample to try from that new Malaysian plantation. And that delivery of soy milk is coming today, isn't it? He picks up his phone to check his calendar and quickly puts it back on the nightstand. *Fuck.*

27 December. A year to the day.

Lucky flips over onto his belly and buries his face in his pillow. He stays like this until he falls back asleep.

Later, he dresses and goes to the cafe, and makes many, many cups of coffee. At night, he comes home to his sister's cat and they have sardines for dinner, before Coconut goes off into the night for a prowl. Lucky stares after her, feeling like maybe he too should go for a walk. But he doesn't.

Instead, he goes to the freezer and rummages around among the assortment of containers inside until he finds a tall rectangular box that should have been returned to Anita ages ago. *Well, I'm sure this stuff doesn't go bad.* He upturns its contents into a glass plate and defrosts the brown, brick-like object in the microwave, then puts it in the oven for a short while, until the smell of plum pudding fills the kitchen.

Then he douses it with brandy, turns off the lights, and lights it with a match. Watching short blue flames lick the cake, he feels his chest expand, as if a clamp has been loosened. Lucky wonders if this is what death does to the fuckers left behind—turn them into weepy idiots who set fire to cakes and eat them.

The door

is open. Which is startling, because no one has been in Pearl's bedroom for months and months, not since the funeral. Lucky moves a little closer. Yes, it's open—ever so slightly, just enough for a cat to enter and for a sliver of sunshine to stray out into the corridor.

'Coconut? Coconut, are you in there?'

No answer, so he gently pushes the door wide open and steps inside. 'Coconut?'

No answer and no cat. But the room is exactly the way he remembers leaving it—the bed made up with her favourite sheets, the curtains drawn, the dressing table and her make-up and the desk and the bookshelves and her books left exactly the way she'd left them, helter-skelter, higgledy-piggledy. The chaos of her surprises him in the same way it always has, ever since they were children, because Pearl was neat everywhere else but here. Lucky picks up a tube of mascara and puts it down again on the dresser, next to a stack of *Vogue* and a small pile of seashells. The blue plush seal sitting on the stack of magazines beams at him.

Lucky opens one of the dresser drawers. Earrings. So many of them. He picks up a pair, one of the vintage chandelier ones she used to wear so often. He puts it back and picks up another one of her favourites, a pair made of bright blue feathers glued together in the shape of a fan. A bigger drawer reveals a jumble of headphones, travel adaptors, spare buttons, and a surprising number of calculators. He wanders away from the dresser, towards the tall bookshelves lining the

121

wall on the other side of the bedroom. She was always reading when they were children, he recalls, and she never ever lent out her books or gave them away. He scans the shelves, looking for her copy of *Ben-Hur*, but when he eventually finds it, at the bottom of one of the shelves, he decides against touching it. It's okay, he tells himself, he only wanted to make sure it's still here.

There are a few gaps in the bookshelves, some large, some small, but Lucky can't recall if they were there when he last looked. He also can't recall when he'd last looked. Well, clearly these gaps haven't always been there, but did she pack up a few books? Lucky eyes the gaps for a while, trying to remember what books used to be there, but he can't recall. Clearly, his memory has been fucked over by age.

There are gaps among the clothes in her closet as well, but these could have been just her. He hasn't looked in here at all before now. Lucky shakes his head, amazed as ever by the volume of her clothes. Insane. She could have gone for a couple of years without repeating an outfit, and why the hell did she own so many sweaters? Sweaters! In this heat! And she hardly travelled anywhere cold. And her coats—oh, but he does like that bright red one, and the grey trench looked so good on her in the store that he convinced her to buy it.

Hey. With a frown, Lucky reaches out and takes a pair of wide-legged drawstring linen trousers off the closet rail. *These are mine!* He grits his teeth as he takes them off the hanger and slings them over his shoulder. That devious woman. Devious, deceitful, *thieving*.

He'd bought those trousers at a sale and gleefully showed them off to her the moment he arrived home. She loved them, and then of course she decided she had to have a pair too. So off they went to the store, even before he'd had time to stretch out a bit and rest his legs and have a coffee, just so that she wouldn't have to wait any longer. But the store no longer had their size, which meant he had to deal with Pearl sulking all the way home and all through dinner. He offered to lend them to her, but she was in a bit of a state so he dropped the subject. And three weeks later—it could have been more—he couldn't find those trousers, and he searched everywhere, even the kitchen, but they never turned up. Pearl denied she'd seen them anywhere—

And yet here they are. In her closet. With the price tag and labels still attached! *Seriously, Pearl.*

Feeling indignant, he goes through the entire rail of clothes, but finds nothing else belonging to him. Before he shuts the closet, he takes one of her T-shirts off its hanger. It's from the Depeche Mode concert she snuck out to when she was a teenager. He's always liked that T-shirt. Plus, he'd stayed up to let her in, so it's only fair that they share it. He slings the T-shirt over his other shoulder, feeling smug. Later, he will return to his room, put on the stolen T-shirt and the retrieved trousers and take a selfie, then send it in a text message: `My morning has been unexpectedly bountiful #achievementunlocked`

Her desk is a rat's nest of papers, folders, books, paper clips, cables, Post-its, pens, pencils, string (what the hell was she doing with so much string?) and other random items of stationery. A wine glass stained with lipstick stands at the edge of the desk, looking like it's about to tip itself over the edge. A lonely little sock peers out of a large book, the unfortunate stand-in for a more appropriate bookmark. Feeling suddenly, inexplicably miserable, Lucky looks away and walks across the room.

The windows in Pearl's bedroom overlook the front garden. Lucky draws aside the curtain and looks out, blinking at the glare. The street looks the same as it does every morning—quiet, still, sleepy, except for the odd passer-by cutting through it on their way to the next street. If he squints slightly, he can see the house at the corner with its enormous cempaka tree. What a prim little gate! So poised. He smiles, shifting his eyes to the lions at his own gate. Lucky for Lucky, he likes the lions.

What's that? He squints at the prim little gate again, at the small figure emerging from between two of its slim horizontal slats. A woman follows the figure to the gate, waving. Is that . . .?

Coconut!

The cat walks slowly across the street and into the shadows of the trees and out of sight. Lucky continues to stare. Moments later, she reappears, leaping onto the border wall at the side of his garden, trotting along the top of the wall towards the back of the house. Lucky watches until she disappears from his line of sight.

* * *

The phone rings and it's his Aunty Dolly.

'Feeling better?' Does she never say hello to anyone or is it just him?

'Yes. Don't worry, Aunty Dolly.'

'Good. Don't forget our appointment with Selvam on Monday.'

Lucky puts down the phone and bares his teeth at it. Ugh. If only *she'd* forgotten their appointment with the family lawyer. But, clearly, there's no hope in hell of that. Lucky sighs as he wipes down the countertop with grapefruit-scented disinfectant. The pompous, meddling daft owl. What exactly gives her the right to stick her nose in his face? He imagines calling her back now and telling her off. *Ostriches are fine birds, Aunty Dolly. If I really were an ostrich, I wouldn't have to go see Mr Selvam. And ostriches don't drink coffee or work in cafes.* He quickens his speed of wiping in tandem with the angst rising in his chest.

Shawn sidles up next to him, sniffing the air. 'I think that's quite enough, Lucky. It's beginning to stop smelling like coffee in here.'

'Only now? I thought your cologne's taken care of that.'

'Shitface.' Shawn snatches the spray bottle away from Lucky. 'And stop that. You're the third person to clean this counter this morning—you're making it look like we've got a hygiene issue.'

'Or trying to get rid of traces of that guy you murdered yesterday for wanting a soy caramel latte, venti.' Lucky laughs at the memory, owls and ostriches forgotten.

Shawn grimaces. 'Oh, that ass. Trying to be funny for his girlfriend.' He shoots Lucky a stern look. 'And you. Please tell me you've recovered from your drunken antics over Christmas.'

Lucky groans. Dinah! Why did she have to go and tell Shawn? Shawn probably wouldn't have cared if he heard it from Lucky himself—he might have laughed, he might have cracked a few jokes, but he wouldn't have cared enough to bring it up a week later—but Dinah tends to infuse things with her own brand of fretful urgency.

Pearl used to say that architecture was a waste of Dinah's gifts—she should have been a fire-and-brimstone preacher. Lucky blows out his cheeks, refusing to answer Shawn. He knows he should be used to this by now, but he finds himself annoyed and resentful.

'Anita misses you.' How like Shawn to change the subject. Thank god!

'Does she? Maybe you guys should come over for dinner sometime.'

Shawn thinks about the last time he was at Lucky's, and the weirdness with the cat. 'Nah. You come to ours. When was the last time you ventured out of the east of Singapore?'

Lucky can't remember and doesn't care to. Especially when he knows he's being dragged into the CBD on Monday by his aunt. He takes a deep breath, suddenly feeling like a trapped animal. Why are people so bloody difficult? He doesn't want to go to see the lawyer. He doesn't want to have dinner at Shawn's. He doesn't want to flatter Anita and maybe endure another ill-disguised set-up with another single colleague or friend or whatever. He just wants to stay home and talk to Coconut and watch TV and sleep, and not meet anyone on any sort of social errand. The Christmas party at Uncle Desmond's—fucking hell. No more of that fucking rubbish. Except—*god*, the wedding. Anton's fucking wedding. Well, except for the wedding then—no more fucking rubbish with fucking people and their fucking rubbish. Fucking people. Fucking rubbish.

'Lucky, are you okay?' Shawn takes a step closer.

Lucky smiles. 'Of course.' He turns away from Shawn, walks behind the counter, and picks up two large mugs. 'Let's try that Malaysian coffee again? It's from Ipoh, you know, kind of my father's kopi hometown.' His smile widens. 'We should have it with condensed milk. Old school.'

He, Lucky Lee, can be just as poised as that prim little gate across the road.

* * *

Coconut leaps off the window seat and begins to walk towards the back door of the kitchen.

'Coconut, where do you go? When you're not here.'

She turns around and sits down. 'I just go where I like.'

'Anywhere in particular?'

'No. I just go to all my places. Waving my wild tail. Walking by my wild lone.'

'Your places?' Lucky wants to ask if she can show him and he wants to know if the house across the road is one of them, but he's afraid to seem needy. Being needy, Pearl always said, was a surefire way to lose a woman. And what's all this about a wild tail?

Coconut starts making her way towards the door again. Lucky watches, wondering if she's annoyed at him for being inquisitive. But cats are supposed to be curious, right? Surely she should understand. Maybe she does—before her tail disappears through the doorway, he hears her say, 'I'm always close by, Lucky. If you call for me, I'll be home very quickly.'

'Okay.'

* * *

Lucky feels dizzy, but he hasn't had a drop to drink. In about an hour or so, this will be rectified. At the moment, though, he's walking home in the uncomfortable dress shoes he thought would make him feel better about being dragged to Mr Selvam's office, dying to open the bottle of primitivo he's been saving for a special occasion. Special occasion be damned—his mind feels like it's tied to the rest of him by the thinnest of threads, and it's time to dip that skinny filament into some full-bodied Italian red.

It's a long way from Mr Selvam's office at a swanky law firm at Raffles Place to the house on Swan Street, but Lucky knew this when he walked out of the office and out of the building and onto the street and decided to walk home. A walk, he thought to himself, will clear my head.

As he makes his way towards the Esplanade Bridge, his shoes making ridiculous clip-clop noises on the concrete pavement, Lucky isn't sure if his head is any clearer, but he's definitely . . . sweating. Back in Mr Selvam's office, it was almost unbearably cold—how else could the man have worn a suit? And if he hadn't been wearing a suit, how could he have managed to be quite as elegantly unpleasant? But out here in the open, the tropical sun is unrelenting, beating down on everyone, making Lucky and all his fellow pedestrians wonder why they hadn't dared damnation and worn shorts today.

The Merlion, standing three storeys high at the edge of the water, looks miserable. Poor thing, Lucky thinks as he passes the statue of the national monster, which, for some reason, spits cascades of water into the river. It looks like it needs a hat. Or maybe even an umbrella.

Lucky clip-clops over the bridge and past the Esplanade. His phone is ringing again, but he's not going to answer it. He's not even going to look at it. He doesn't have to. It's going to be his aunt, demanding to know where he is and why he left so suddenly and telling him how terrible his manners are and how like an ostrich he's being. Hah! He would like to be an ostrich now—he would be home much, much sooner. Or a cat—he'd find a shady spot and take a nap, and saunter home later.

The phone continues to ring. Lucky turns it off.

Perhaps he shouldn't have left like that, Lucky concedes, glad for a passing cluster of clouds that gives him a breather from the sun. He could have just sat there and nodded and then he could have shaken the lawyer's hand and left, gracefully, quietly, his Spanish leather soles barely whispering on the soft carpets. But he really couldn't sit there any longer and hear any more.

It was probably Mr Selvam's tone of voice that got to him first. Dry, monotonous, all-knowing in its dryness and monotony. 'Your sister left everything to you, of course.'

Lucky hadn't known that Pearl even had a will. He made the mistake of saying so.

'Of course she did.' Was there a hint of disdain in Mr Selvam's reptile eyes? Lucky believed there was.

His aunt shot him a look that very pointedly demanded he shut up, and so he did. He listened as the family lawyer listed his sister's personal assets. The house on Swan Street, the beach chalet in Changi, the warehouses in Macpherson, the shophouses on Smith Street, Joo Chiat Road, and River Valley Road—

'Wait, sorry,' Lucky interjected. 'Those are my father's properties.'

Mr Selvam paused and cleared his throat. 'They *were*.'

The reptile and the daft owl exchanged a look. Lucky began to feel like a weird sort of joke was being played on him. He crossed and uncrossed his legs. He tugged at the cuffs of his shirt. He swallowed the lump growing in his throat.

The lawyer cleared his throat again. 'The properties belonged to your father, and upon his death, they became the property of your sister.'

Lucky shook his head. 'That's . . . wrong. I've always understood that my father left his estate to be divided equally between Pearl and me.'

'No.' The lawyer waited a few seconds for this to sink in. 'Your father left everything to Pearl, on the condition that she would be required to provide for you, up to a stipulated annual maximum. And he made a provision that the family home on Swan Street cannot be sold in your lifetime.' In response to the frown on Lucky's face, he added, 'Your father wanted you to always have somewhere to live, Lucky. And he left you a third of his cash assets, which you of course have already received.'

He had. He and Pearl had been surprised to know his father had left the remaining third to a cousin in Malaysia they had never even heard him mention, but at the same time it was so like their father to pull a final dramatic stunt like that.

Mr Selvam repeated, 'The rest of your father's estate passed to Pearl upon his death nineteen years ago.' He paused. 'Shall we proceed with the list of her assets?'

Lucky took a deep breath. Nineteen years. Incredible. He felt like such a fool. No wonder they all laughed at him; no wonder they called him an ostrich and fuck knows what else.

'I'm sorry.' He hated himself for apologizing, but he did it anyway. 'I'm going.'

And then, ignoring the look of confusion on Mr Selvam's face and the look of horror on his aunt's, he stood up, turned, and walked out the door. He didn't shut the door behind him, and he didn't stop to think or look around until he was out of the building, and then he decided he'd walk home.

What a stupid idea this was, he thinks, but he walks on anyway. Having never seriously exercised but having always imagined it to be vaguely spiritually invigorating, Lucky had assumed that the walking would lead to some sort of epiphany or at least some sort of happy calm. How wrong he'd been—it's only managed to tire him out and convince him that, no, he'll never exercise enough to be fit. He stops for a cold drink at the hawker centre on Old Airport Road and the woman behind the counter gives him an odd look. He must look frightful, he realizes, trying to look casual as he gulps iced lemon tea from a bright pink plastic cup. *Like I've been dragged through a menswear store and then a carwash.* The hobbling can't be helping the look very much either.

But luckily no one sees him hobble down Swan Street in the middle of the afternoon, and the lions seem pleased to see him. Lucky gives them both a pat on the nose. The first thing he does when he gets home, after kicking off his scuffed shoes, is head to the kitchen. He grabs the bottle of Primitivo di Manduria and a glass and a corkscrew and, thus armed, heads up to his father's library–study on the third floor. The room feels like a furnace, but it's nothing the air conditioner can't handle. Lucky puts on an old record, pours himself a glass of deep red wine, then leans back in his father's black leather chair at his father's mahogany desk, and waits for the music to start.

Bila larut malam
Suasana sepi
Tiadapun insan
Yang ku lihat lagi

Mengapa hatiku
Merasa terharu?
Di malam ini
Terasa sunyi[4]

---

[4] In Malay: In the middle of the night/ It's lonely/ There's no one here/ That I can see any more/
Why does my heart/ Feel so confused?/ Tonight/ I'm suddenly lonely.

When the song ends, he plays it again, turning up the volume. And then, unable to hear himself, he shouts out his sister's name and a string of curses. He shouts and shouts and shouts, turning the volume up louder and louder so that Saloma and her band can sing over his rage.

'Fucking control freak!

'Stupid lying madwoman!

'Why did you have to lie to me? Did it feel good, having me live on your charity?

'Is this why you took the trousers? Fuck you!'

But most of all he shouts her name, again and again and again.

The man behind the counter

doesn't notice him enter the cafe. He's too busy typing into his phone. Naresh isn't in a hurry, so he stands a little way off and studies the menu above the counter, trying to decide what to get. How much does he have in his wallet? He had fifteen dollars yesterday, and he had instant noodles for lunch and a cheese sandwich for dinner, and then this morning he bought tea for one-twenty, and lunch today was three-fifty, so that means if he needs to eat his Friday mee goreng and teh tarik tomorrow, he should spend five dollars here, maximum, and have a cheese sandwich for dinner today as well. Naresh sighs quietly. How can coffee be so expensive? His mother would be horrified. Back home, five Singapore dollars will pay for the week's marketing.

The man slips his phone into his pocket and Naresh tries to get his attention by moving a little closer to the counter. This doesn't work. The guy has opened the fridge and begun inspecting its contents, picking up bottles and putting them back, evidently looking for something.

Should he go and come back another day? Maybe he should have called in advance or something. And what if the guy doesn't recognize him? That would be so embarrassing. Maybe he should just go now, before the guy sees him.

A girl suddenly pops up from behind the cash register—has she been there the entire time? 'Hey, sorry! Hope you haven't been waiting long. What can I get you?'

'Oh, um, what would you recommend? Is the Javanese coffee like Malaysian coffee?' Naresh hopes he doesn't sound like some village idiot. Being actually from a village has made him a little over-cautious of seeming provincial, especially in a place like Singapore where, to his horror, he's discovered the term *sua ku*—literally meaning 'mountain tortoise', metaphorically meaning 'village person'—which all the city folk (well, they're all city folk here) use to refer to anyone ignorant of the latest trends or technology. He doesn't understand why. It seems unfair to tortoises, which live long, are hard to kill, and generally don't bother anyone. Naresh would happily be a tortoise, which would mean having his home built into his back and being able to live rent-free in Singapore.

The girl smiles reassuringly. 'Not really. Malaysian roasts are darker and Javanese coffee tends to be a bit more acidic.'

'Is that the same as sour?'

She laughs. 'We don't like to say that, but yes . . . let's say a little sourish. Fruity.'

Naresh grins, relieved. He takes out his wallet. 'Okay, I'll try the Javanese. Thanks.'

'We can do it as espresso, or in a drip. Which one would you like?'

Naresh frowns, his earlier unease quickly returning. 'What would you recommend?'

The girl tugs at her pale orange hair. 'I'd say drip, if you like it strong.'

'Okay, drip is fine.'

'With milk?'

'Yes, please. Thanks.'

She nods. 'No problem. Full fat? Low fat? Condensed? Soy? Almond?'

Naresh blinks a few times. What? Isn't milk just milk? He bites his lip. Will it be very village idiot of him to suddenly say he'll have it without milk, and is it cheaper without milk? Because if it is—

'Hey, it's you!' The man behind the counter steps up next to the girl, taking both her and Naresh by surprise. 'Nice of you to drop by.'

Naresh waves, feeling a bit shy. 'I was in the area. Another school project. So, I thought I'd check this place out. It's cool, sir.'

The man makes an impatient, grunt-like sound. 'Jesus. Please, I'm Lucky.' Seeing the hesitation in Naresh's face and mistaking it for disbelief, he adds, 'Lucky's my name.'

Naresh knows this. After being shown around the Swan Street House, as his professor calls it, he found himself so fascinated by it and by his strange tour guide that he read everything he could find on the Internet about the house and its inhabitants dead and alive. Lee Joo Meng, coffee seller turned coffee tycoon, who grew up in a village just twenty kilometres from where Naresh's parents live. Betty Chong of the 'Lychee' Chongs (her father sold his fruit-processing business in the late eighties for millions). Pearl Lee, host of food shows *Pearl About Town* and *Oodles of Noodles*, plane crash victim. Lucky Lee, co-owner of a cafe. Naresh tried to find out more but nothing turned up. The guy didn't even have a LinkedIn account.

'I'm really sorry, but I'm terrible with names—'

'I'm Naresh.'

'Hello, Naresh.' The man called Lucky Lee lifts a hand in mock salute. 'So, what are you having?'

The girl jumps in before Naresh can answer. 'Javanese drip.' She turns back to Naresh. 'Have you decided what kind of milk you'd like with your coffee?'

'Full fat?'

Lucky nods. 'Sure. Meixi, I'll take this one.' He smiles at Naresh. 'My treat. You take a seat, and I'll bring it over.'

Naresh feels a rush of gratitude. Now he won't have to have a cheese sandwich for dinner. 'Thank you.' He knows he should try to refuse, but why be insincere?

'Oh, don't worry about it.'

Spotting a small table near the back of the cafe, Naresh makes a beeline for it. It's nearly four in the afternoon, but most tables are taken and the clientele is a smorgasbord of idlers. Three women in yoga attire talk quietly at a table near the windows. At the next table, a young couple giggle over something on one of their phones. A few people occupy the long concrete table in the middle of the room, flipping through magazines or watching something on their iPads. Naresh never fails to be surprised by people sitting around cafes in the middle of the day, just whiling away time. It must be a city phenomenon—he doesn't understand it, and he's only ever seen it happen here and in Kuala Lumpur, where his brother lives.

But what a space this is, this beautiful old shophouse. Naresh's face lights up as he examines the high ceiling and exposed wooden beams and the small butterfly-shaped vents near the ceiling, meant to let the warm air out in the old days before air conditioning. From the back of the cafe where he's settled with his worn-out satchel, he's perfectly positioned to appreciate the long floor plan, his favourite feature of the traditional shophouse. It's like sitting at one end of a tunnel, or a cave. The length of this particular shophouse looks at least ten times its width, and he loves how, about halfway through, three short, shallow steps lead down to a small, light-filled central atrium. In the middle of this sits a rattan armchair, flanked by a low wooden table with a couple of books. Naresh sighs. Five dollars for the pleasure of a place like this for an hour or so is probably a fair price—if one has five dollars to spend on pleasure. Naresh doesn't. He hopes the coffee is good, so he'll at least have that excuse to return.

His host suddenly appears and lays a tray down on the table. 'I got us some cake, hope you like pineapple. And try the biscotti. We're quite well known for ours. Meixi's mum makes them.' He takes two plates and two mugs of coffee off the tray and sets them on the table.

'You've got a really nice space here.'

'You think so? Thanks.' Lucky Lee's smile is lazy and strangely encouraging. Naresh feels the urge to say something witty, but he's never been a witty guy, so he ventures forth with more compliments on the space. Lucky accepts them without adding very much, like a man very much accustomed to hearing good things.

How different a man can look without his head in a towel, Naresh thinks. He says, 'I really like how you've left most of it alone. I keep seeing shophouses renovated to death, especially in Chinatown.'

Lucky laughs, turning around to look behind him so he can see the cafe from Naresh's viewpoint. 'Honestly, we were afraid to spend too much money doing up the place, so we just kept everything we could and fixed anything that was broken. If we'd had any idea we would make money, it might have been very different!' He pushes a mug towards Naresh. 'Don't let your coffee get cold.'

'Thanks.' Naresh takes a sip of his coffee. 'Oh, this is good.' He means it.

'Great, next time you have to try a Vietnamese coffee.' Lucky leans back in his chair. 'So, how's your project going?'

'It's okay. I'm still doing the research. It's due at the end of next semester.'

'Ah, the third-year project. What a horror.' Lucky makes a face. 'Mine was a disaster.' He paused. 'I did archi too—I can't remember if I mentioned that when you were at the house.'

He didn't, but Naresh is aware of this. He wasn't when he visited the house, but then he'd gone back to school and told his professor that he was absolutely right, that the Swan Street House really was an incredible specimen of local architecture. That's when Professor Wijono told him that quite a few of the more *incredible* additions to the house were made by its last owner, the father of an old student of his, Lucky Lee, who probably still lived there now. The knowledge that he'd been in the company of a fellow sufferer of the shitstorm that is architecture school made the strange house and the strange man who showed him around it even more attractive to Naresh.

Which is pretty much why Naresh has ended up here today at Caffiend, but he doesn't dare to dive right into things. 'I haven't really done much work on my project, actually.'

Lucky takes a sip of coffee. 'I left mine to the absolute last minute. I did something about gates, but I kept building models, and I kind of forgot about the paper I was supposed to write.' He shakes his head. 'I think I bombed it pretty badly.'

He did. Professor Wijono told Naresh that Lucky Lee would never have made a good architect. 'Very keen sense of space and proportion, but too easily distracted,' he pronounced. 'But a very pleasant young man.'

Naresh leans forward in his chair. 'How have you been? Everything okay?' He hopes he doesn't sound like some horrible busybody. His online research has told him that Pearl Lee died in that plane crash last year and that around the time he'd gone to the house, they had stopped looking for the bodies. One hundred and six bodies were found, out of the one hundred and sixty-two people who boarded the plane that morning. Fifty-six forever missing, including Pearl Lee. He wonders how Lucky is doing. He looks so much thinner than he did the last time they met.

Lucky leans forward too. 'I'm good.' He picks up a fork and eats a bit of cake. 'I buried a bird yesterday.'

Lucky had not meant to say this, but he has. Tricky. The boy in front of him frowns and looks confused. Lucky doesn't blame him. He wouldn't know what to do either if anyone told him they'd buried a bird the day before. Perhaps he should elaborate?

'I didn't kill it,' he adds conversationally.

The bird was already dead, lying just outside the kitchen door when he opened it yesterday to check on Coconut and get her her breakfast. The cat sat next to the bird, cleaning herself. She looked up at him and mewed loudly. He wondered if she was waiting for him to say something about her bounty, but all he could do was stare at the little brown lump, thinking, *it's a bird and it's dead and it's on the back porch.* The little brown lump's little brown eyes stared back at Lucky. One of its little brown wings appeared broken.

'Coconut, did you do this?' He realized he sounded like he was pleading, and he was.

'It's for you, Lucky.' Coconut got up, circled the dead bird, and sat back down next to it. 'The early cat catches the early bird.'

Lucky raised his eyebrows. Was she making jokes now? And then he saw the bird again. He sighed. 'What am I supposed to do with it?'

Coconut mewed again. She sounded terribly pleased with herself. 'Whatever you like. Pearl wraps the birds up in newspaper and takes them away. I think she likes to eat them in private.'

Lucky went into the kitchen and came back out again with a large tea towel. He slowly approached the little brown lump and, as the cat stood by watching, lay the towel over it, feeling like a mortician. 'Coconut, this is terrible.'

Coconut sniffed the towel-covered lump. 'Do you want a different bird? I can get you a bigger one tomorrow. I've noticed that some people like big things better than small things. That man with the long arms, the one who lives in the house with the water bowl out front, has just bought a bigger car.'

That would be Dr Chan at number twenty-five, the house with the fountain. It's funny how Coconut knew some words and not others.

'No! No more birds!' Lucky scooped her up and carried her into the kitchen. He shut the door behind him. Ignoring her mewing protests at being handled, Lucky walked through the kitchen and put the cat gently down on one of the chairs at the table, then sat down next to her.

He felt rather foolish. How does anyone tell a cat that birds are much better left alive? 'Can you promise me not to kill any more birds?'

'Why? *Pearl* likes the birds. She always says, "Thank you, Coconut, how sweet."' Coconut glared at him. '*Pearl* knows what to do with birds. If she were here, I'd give the bird to her.'

God, Pearl. He took a deep breath, exhaled. 'Well, if you're not going to eat something, you shouldn't kill it.'

Her eyes narrowed. '*You* eat it.'

'No!' Logical reasoning had never been one of his strong points. Lucky forced himself to try another tactic. 'Would you even eat a bird?' He hoped she wouldn't. 'Have you eaten a bird, Coconut?' He hoped she had not.

Coconut assured him that she hadn't eaten one in a very long time. In general, birds don't taste very good, but she'd eat his bird if he really wanted her to.

'It's not my bird, Coconut.'

'I got it for you. So, it's yours.' She rested her head on her paws. 'I wanted to get you a fish, because you like fish, but I didn't know where to get one. And the ones in the pond are too quick for me. And too wet.'

The fish were in danger too? Lucky shook his head. 'Please. You don't have to get me anything.' He stroked her head, hoping she wouldn't be offended. 'And now we've got to do something about this bird. We can't just throw it out.'

Coconut didn't understand why anything had to be done about the bird. The bird, she pointed out, wouldn't care. And birds died all the time, she told him. What made this one special? Lucky struggled to explain to Coconut why they couldn't throw the bird away in the rubbish bin, like they did with the fish bones and fish heads. It had something to do with giving the death more meaning, he told her.

The cat didn't look convinced, and Lucky was forced to continue. 'And respect, we have to show it a bit of respect.' Because she killed it, he said, and she shouldn't have.

Respect, and often love, was why people had funerals for the dead, he told the cat, and why people buried bodies or burnt them or whatever else people did when other people died. 'I don't know why we do it exactly. Maybe we're just trying to make death less ugly? Or maybe less scary?'

'The ancient Egyptians,' he told Coconut, 'had very elaborate death rituals. When people died, their organs were removed from their bodies and put in special jars. And then the bodies were sewn back up and wrapped up in strips of cloth and allowed to dry out. These were called mummies.'

He thumbed through the photos folder on his phone to show Coconut the cat mummy he'd seen on display at the British Museum. 'Look, here's a cat that was wrapped up and dried when it died. They really liked cats in ancient Egypt, Coconut.'

Coconut didn't seem to like the photograph of the little mummified cat, with its elaborately woven shroud and the solemn, sad face that had been painted onto it. She sniffed at the screen of his phone and then turned away.

Lucky put the phone away and went on. The mummies of people, he told the cat, were often put into large stone boxes called sarcophagus ('no, not a kind of asparagus, Coconut') and sealed into tombs. 'We're talking about tombs the size of a room. Maybe the size of this kitchen.'

Coconut looked around the kitchen and seemed impressed.

'And if you were a king,' he continued, 'you had a tomb the size of a house—or bigger. The size of ten houses! The ancient Egyptians also liked to be prepared. The dead were buried with jars of oil and grain and jewellery and things they liked very much when they were alive, in case they needed any of it in the afterlife.' Lucky was about to tell Coconut that sometimes people had servants buried with them too, and pets, but he decided against it—too much explaining to do afterwards. But he did explain that the afterlife was where people believed the dead went—where they didn't need their bodies, obviously.

'But they needed oil? And all the other things? What about birds? Did they need birds?'

'I don't know if they needed birds or oil. Maybe.' Lucky thought about it. He didn't really know that much about Egyptian rites beyond what he read on placards at the British Museum when he ran into it for shelter from rain while he was in London a few years ago. 'Maybe people weren't sure what they needed, so they just made sure the dead had supplies in case they needed them.' He sighed. 'That seems wise, right? Once someone's dead, you can't really ask them if they need oil or anything. Or if they meant to lie to you. And you can't shout at them and you can't tell them you're angry.'

The cat cocked her head sideways. 'Are you angry with the bird?'

Lucky cackled in spite of himself. 'Nope. But I'd feel better if we buried it.' He added, 'And can you please leave birds alone?'

Coconut said she would try, and Lucky felt this was probably a big step for a small cat.

But he doesn't say any of this to the architecture student who's dropped in to see him. 'My sister's cat killed the bird. And we buried it.'

'You and . . .'

'The cat.' Lucky sighs. 'Poor little bird. But I gave up my favourite tea towel so it would have a pretty shroud.'

Naresh isn't sure what to say to or think of Lucky Lee. It isn't as though the man makes him uncomfortable, but even without the towel around his head, he's a little strange. Maybe he just likes birds? Or maybe this isn't a good day? But Naresh decides to press on anyway.

'I'd like to write my paper about your house,' he says before he loses the nerve.

Lucky looks surprised. 'My house? But why?'

Naresh has prepped for this, and he launches into a modified version of the raving description of the house he gave to Professor Wijono six months ago. 'It's totally crazy,' he told his Southeast Asian architecture professor, thrilled that he'd actually been inside this bizarre mash-up of tropical vernacular architecture and some sort of eccentric Asian take on the Art Deco and the Arts and Crafts movements.

'It's such an eclectic house. And I heard that your father built a cooling system into the walls? That's super . . . cool.'

'That's right. He did.' He wonders where the boy heard this. Lucky hasn't talked or thought about it in years. 'We've got a network of pipes in the walls that used to carry water from the roof down through the walls and into the pond.' But then Pearl had wanted fish, so, of course, she got fish. Their father turned off the pipes—the water from them was too warm for keeping fish—and then he bought a dozen koi and popped them into the pond and installed an air circulation system for the stupid fish and now, more than twenty years on, Lucky has a pond full of fish and a house that doesn't cool itself down.

'Are you okay with this? And may I see the house again?' Naresh hurries on to his next question before Lucky can answer: 'And please, may I take photos this time?'

Lucky doesn't feel the slightest bit torn. He wants to say no outright and tell the boy to find some other dysfunctional house to write his paper on. But something holds him back. Perhaps it's the pathetic look on the boy's face. Perhaps it's the rumble of distant memories of agonizing over papers in his own days at university. Perhaps it's the not-distant-enough memory of the burial he and Coconut held yesterday under the mango tree.

The earth was soft and wet from rain when he dug the hole and put the tea-towel-shrouded bird into it. Coconut watched and got in the way, peering into the grave as Lucky carefully placed two little parcels on top of the bird—raisins and sunflower seeds wrapped in paper—just in case it was a long journey to bird afterlife.

'We're very sorry, bird.' Lucky refilled the hole before Coconut could get her paws into it. 'Rest in peace.'

'I'm hungry, Lucky.'

Cats could be quite awful. He had begun to feel teary about the bird, but clearly Coconut's tummy couldn't wait for him to have a cry about death and mortality.

And so, feeling a little fragile, a little starved for human sympathy, Lucky agrees to let the earnest student into the house he grew up in. Again. 'But I need your help with a few things while you're at my place.'

'Okay.' Naresh would have cheerfully agreed to anything short of crime that will keep him in Lucky's favour.

'Great. Do you know anything about gardening?'

The market

is crazy every morning, but on weekends it is a special sort of madhouse. As Lucky approaches it from the bus stop, he can already hear the vague clamour of people and things, and as he enters the market, this solidifies into hundreds and hundreds of distinct sounds—stall-keepers and customers shouting over each other, flip-flops and gum boots squeaking against the wet floor, water gushing from taps, ladles clanging against pots, spoons striking bowls, chairs scraping, rubber bands snapping, coins clinking, fans whirring. The mee pok man tossing noodles in his great big sieve. The butcher slapping fresh hunks of meat onto his scale. The cleaver coming down hard on the fishmonger's wooden chopping board.

The fishmonger's wife sees Lucky before her husband does. 'Eh, handsome, today you want ikan siakap? Just came in this morning.'

The barramundi laid out on the ice in front of her does look good. Lucky reaches out and presses two fingers against the belly of the fish nearest to him. Nice and firm. He checks its eyes—yellowish, turgid, no sign of bleeding. Good.

'You make steam fish lah—very good, very easy.'

It's quite a large fish. Lucky wonders if it will fit into the wok at home. 'Got a smaller one? My wok not so big lah, *makcik*.'

A loud thump from the fishmonger's cleaver. A fish head flies off the chopping board and lands on the floor with a wet plop. It stares at Lucky, all glistening glassy eyes and gaping mouth, while the fishmonger deftly pulls the sloppy entrails out of its body. Lucky gives the head an apologetic look as the fishmonger's wife picks it up and drops it into the bin.

She dips her hand in a bucket of water, then examines the dozen or so barramundi she's got on the ice. 'This one?' She lifts one up slightly by the head.

Lucky and the fish lock eyes. The fish's dark grey scales tell him it's likely to have been caught wild at sea, rather than farmed. A Malaysian fish, probably. Lucky pictures it swimming with its friends in the blue-green waters of the Malacca Straits or the South China Sea, smacking its lips, chomping down prawns, and then a fishing net comes along and ruins everything. He gives it a sympathetic look. *Bad luck, chum.*

'How? This one okay?' The fishmonger's wife lifts the fish up a little higher. 'Can lah, boy.'

Lucky nods. At least he will give it a proper ending. Some people out there can't cook fish properly. 'Okay.' He hadn't intended on steaming fish, but he can—and maybe ask Dinah over for dinner? It's been a few weeks since he's seen her.

'Steam it! Very good. You trust me.'

Lucky grins. 'I trust you, makcik. Can I also get three ikan kuning for my *kucing*? She loves it.'

'Your kucing, good life!' The makcik wraps up the barramundi in a few layers of newspaper, then the ikan kuning.

As Lucky gets on the bus home, the parcels of fresh fish safe in Pearl's extra-large marketing basket, he wonders if Coconut will agree with the makcik's pronouncement. Do cats think about things like happiness and personal fulfilment and quality of life? Or is it all about food and naps and being able to chase birds and insects and jump onto walls? And watch television, which Coconut tells him is one of her favourite things to do.

'Pearl lets me watch whatever I want,' she informed him yesterday, as Lucky changed the channel while she was watching some crappy documentary about penguins. And then, to his amazement, she used her paw to knock the remote control out of his hands and changed the channel back to penguins.

Do cats really have favourite people or is it all about the hand that feeds them? Or at least the hand that gives up the remote control? He'd like to think he's Coconut's favourite person now, but she's Pearl's cat, after all, so can all his efforts to win over Coconut be considered some elaborate form of betrayal? Obviously nothing like the way Pearl betrayed him (psycho mean bat spider!), but the emotional theft of a cat must rank somewhere in the scale of larceny.

It's a short walk home from the bus stop, through a lane next to the house with the prim little gate, which is shut. But there's someone in the garden, pruning a hibiscus bush. The woman looks like she might be his Aunty Dolly's age. But, of course, she could be younger. Anyone gardening at ten o'clock in the morning, even in partial shade, is clearly unaware of the detrimental effects of the sun. Lucky is very, very careful about sun protection.

'Hello!' The woman has seen him. 'Are you looking for someone?' she asks in Hokkien.

Lucky's Hokkien is rubbish, but he manages to string a few words together with only the barest regard for structure. 'Hello. No. My house across road.'

'Ah, so we're neighbours. I was thinking you look familiar. How are you?' She nods at the basket. 'Going somewhere?'

'Bus. Go market.' Lucky struggles to recall the word for 'fish', then gives up. 'Go home now. Hot.'

'Oh yes, it's very hot. But I couldn't find my hat today.'

Lucky wishes he could ask her whether she's put on any sunscreen, but he can't. 'Very hot.'

Just as he's about to go, a cat appears from behind the woman, brushing against her legs. His heart leaps. It's Coconut. She looks at Lucky for a moment, then walks towards the gate. He stares after her as she steps daintily through the vertical slats, one leg at a time.

The woman waves. 'Bye bye, Mimi.'

Mimi?!

Lucky forces himself to smile. 'Nice cat. Your cat?'

'When it likes.' The woman laughs. 'It treats our house like a hotel. Comes here every day expecting food.'

'Ah. You give food.'

'Very picky! Only eats one brand of cat food.' The woman laughs again. 'My daughter calls it a little queen.'

The little queen says nothing as Lucky walks into the kitchen two minutes later, sulking, his steps deliberately loud against the floor. Stretched out on the kitchen floor with her eyes half closed, she doesn't even seem to notice him. She yawns, baring her little teeth. *How convenient! It's time for another nap.* Lucky rolls his eyes a little resentfully as he chucks the parcels of fish into the fridge. When she doesn't stir or look in his direction, he sends a text: `Coconut is cheating on me with a neighbour. After all the fish!` But a moment later, as he watches her curl up into a ball under a chair, he's pleased that she's here instead of across the road.

Mimi, indeed.

* * *

Looking out the kitchen window, Lucky is seized with a sudden terror.

'Coconut!'

The cat doesn't hear him or pretends not to. Outside, in the garden, at the edge of the herb cluster, she lowers herself on her front paws and arches her back, wiggling her bottom. About a metre away, a few tiny sparrows hop about among the new chilli plants. Why can't they see her? Honestly, what the fuck is wrong with these birds?

Lucky taps on the window. 'Coconut! Get away!'

She jumps, sailing through the air, a little tortoiseshell missile shooting over the mint seedlings, the butterfly pea shoots, the young lemongrass. At the very last second, the birds fly off in different directions, scattering themselves. Coconut sits down, looking as if she meant to miss. She licks a paw and begins to clean her face.

Lucky watches her. Perhaps it was unfair—and quite, quite silly—of him to ask a cat not to terrorize birds. He'd have to tackle this himself. Upstairs, in Pearl's bedroom, he collects an armful of things and brings them down into the kitchen. In the storeroom, he finds an assortment of sticks and old mops he can use, and some raffia string left over from architecture school days. And then, as Coconut watches, Lucky assembles everything together while sitting on the kitchen floor.

'What are you making?'

'Something for the garden.'

'I don't like how it looks. It's ugly, Lucky.' She paws at his creation and gets her claws tangled in string.

Lucky untangles her, then puts her on a chair. 'Well, Coconut, you don't have to look at it.'

'Tell it not to look at me either.'

Why does she always have to have the last word? Must have got that from Pearl.

* * *

'Are you eating the whole thing yourself?'

Lucky is making long incisions in the side of the barramundi for it to better soak up the sauce he's made. 'No. I told you Dinah's coming for dinner.'

Coconut nudges his elbow with her nose. 'Tell her not to come. You have to eat more, or you'll fly away in a storm, like that woman.'

Lucky puts down the knife. 'What woman?'

'The woman,' Coconut repeats snootily, 'who flew off in a storm. Aren't you listening?

'She could have been a teacher. Always carrying armfuls of books around. Lived close by, near the school with the tall trees that rained little red seeds.'

'The saga trees?'

'Yes. Don't interrupt if you already know what they are, Lucky.'

The woman, according to Coconut, was tall and thin, like Lucky. Far too thin, also like Lucky. Didn't eat enough, her cat always said. Too many vegetables and not enough fish. And she was always running around and around the neighbourhood, as if a large dog was after her, which made her even thinner.

'And one day, there was a big, big storm. Rain and thunder and lightning and wind, wind, wind. And the wind picked her up and took her away.' Coconut gives Lucky a stern look.

Lucky stares. 'That's nonsense.'

'Her cat saw the whole thing.'

'It's not possible, Coconut. The wind isn't strong enough to pick people up. Not in Singapore, anyway.'

Coconut mews loudly, waving her tail from side to side. 'You weren't there, were you? Her cat saw the whole thing. He never saw her again, Lucky.'

Lucky turns his head away so Coconut can't see him roll his eyes. He selects a couple of bird's eye chillis from a bowl on a shelf and starts to slice them up. Coconut sits down in front of his chopping board, watching his knife move in minute increments across each pinkie-sized chilli.

'So you have to eat more. I don't want you flying off.' Coconut jumped from the countertop onto the floor. 'Who knows where you'll end up?'

'Maybe Bali?' He would like that.

'Maybe a rubbish heap somewhere.'

Coconut walks up to the kitchen door and sits down at the doorway, looking out into the garden. 'That's a very ugly thing that you've made, Lucky. What's it for?'

'It's decorative.' He adds the sliced chilli to the mixture of sesame oil, soy sauce, Shaoxing wine, coriander, and lemongrass he's put together in a small bowl, stirs it all together with a pair of chopsticks then licks it off the tips. Much better.

The cat makes a derisive noise that sounds like a half snort, half sneeze. 'Decorative? No wonder you're not an architect.'

God, she's like an emissary for Pearl or Aunty Dolly. Lucky wishes he never told her about architecture school and how he never ended up practising—he did a couple of internships and enjoyed them, but he didn't see himself spending a few years sketching up toilets and car parks and pipes and doing detailed technical drawings of senior team members' designs and taking minutes at meetings. He knew it was how everyone cut their teeth, but it was just so, so dull and he was afraid it would make him dull too. So he quit to join a graphic design firm, but he didn't like that either, so he took a break and that went on for quite a bit . . .

Lucky sighs. He lays the barramundi gently into a shallow dish, pours the sauce over it, and pops it into the wok, in which he's set up a wire steamer rack and water is already simmering.

'I'm fine with not being an architect, you know,' he tells the cat. 'I like what I do now. The coffee and everything.'

'And making garden decorations?'

Lucky decides to ignore the sarcasm. He sets his phone's timer for twelve minutes. 'That's right.'

'What if Pearl comes home one day? She'll be so angry that you've taken her things to make silly decorations with.'

God. That cat is so obsessed with Pearl. It's always Pearl this, Pearl that. It makes him sad and somewhat bitter. Poor little thing, though. It's probably time he dealt properly with this. Lucky goes up to the cat and sits down next to her. She moves her tail so that it lies against his knee. 'You know she's dead, right, Coconut?' He says it as gently as possible, ignoring the tightening in his throat.

She moves her tail away. 'You never said that.'

'You asked if she was gone, and I said yes. Remember?'

'Gone and dead aren't the same thing. The cat who lives near the church was gone for a long time but he came back. He was thinner and he'd lost the tip of one ear, but he came back.'

'You're right.' He paused. 'But sometimes we like to say "gone" instead of "dead",' Lucky takes a deep breath and tries to focus on being very clear with Coconut, 'because "gone" sounds better. But it's the same thing.'

The cat looks up at him. 'Did you bury her with seeds and raisins, too? And oil? And jewellery?' Coconut's voice sounds scratchier than usual.

Lucky presses his palms against his eyes. 'No.'

They're silent for a moment, the cat and the man. He picks her up and carries her out to the back porch, where they sit on the bench and look out at the garden. The sun has just set and the shadows are quickly deepening.

'What about her journey to the afterlife?'

'The sea took her, Coconut. So, she had plenty of fish.'

'You're lying, Lucky.'

Coconut starts to pace the border between the garden and the porch, two paws on the grass and two on the terrazzo floor. Then, she sits down, tail curled around herself, raises her head, and yowls and yowls and yowls. Alarmed, Lucky rushes up to her and tries to pick her up, but she doesn't let him, scratching him on the cheek as she struggles out of his arms. Coconut runs to the middle of the garden and continues to yowl, loud and enraged and accusing, her head thrown back and her tail pointing up like an old television antenna. Unable to take his eyes off the little tortoiseshell figure in the middle of the herb patch, Lucky sits down on the floor, knees against his pounding chest. When he can't stand to watch any more, he covers his face with his hands. But he can still hear her.

* * *

There's no one in the kitchen, but the door to the back porch is open. Dinah goes towards it. As she passes the kitchen window, she stops and stares. She blinks. She squints. Even in the half light, it's obvious that the garden has been tamed—the mango tree pruned, the ginger flowers cut back, the ferns among them removed, the grass trimmed down, the morning glory pulled up. And there, in the middle of the garden—what the hell is that? The frame-like structure looks disturbingly like the gallows, and from it hangs a trio of . . . jellyfish? From each billowing mass of fabric hang tentacle-like tendrils, and everything dances and floats about in the light evening breeze. The effect is rather hypnotic. Dinah stares for a while longer, her mind emptying, before she realizes she's seen that bright red fabric with dark splotches before and where. *Fucking hell.* It's one of Pearl's dresses. The jellyfish are *all* Pearl's dresses, and their tentacles . . . are those scarves?

And is that the cat, sitting on the grass in the middle of all of this floating fabric?

From the back porch, through the door, she hears Lucky's voice but she can't see him.

'. . . should have told you earlier, but it's been very hard, okay? But I should have said something, I should have. I'm sorry. I really, really shouldn't have kept it from you. Of course I should have told you she's dead, of course I should have known you were waiting every day for her to come home. Oh god, I'm awful, I'm so sorry, Coconut.'

Silence. The cat is very still on the grass. The dresses continue their dance.

'I'm sorry. I'm sorry. Of course you're angry with me now, but please, please try not to be, okay? Come here, let's talk about this. Why are you so quiet, Coconut? Say something.'

Quietly, Dinah opens the back door and finds Lucky lying flat on the porch. Belly down, limbs splayed, cheek against the floor, head turned towards the garden, towards the cat, who is staring at him from the middle of the garden and doesn't move.

'Come here,' he says. 'Let's talk about this.'

Dinah stays at the doorway, staring at Lucky. He doesn't notice her. A whole minute passes before she finds her tongue. 'Lucky, are you okay?'

He turns towards her, his face wooden.

'What are you doing?'

'Looking at the moon.'

A series of beeps pierces the distance between them. For a moment Dinah is unsettled, but then she realizes it's the timer on his phone.

Lucky rolls over and stands up in a quick, fluid motion. 'Dinner's ready,' he chirps. He steps quickly past her and goes into the kitchen. There's a long scratch on his left cheek, a thin bloody line from near the corner of the mouth to the outer edge of the eye.

'Lucky, you're bleeding.' But he doesn't hear or won't answer.

* * *

'You have to pick yourself up or go see someone.'

Lucky stares at Dinah over the remains of their dinner. The fish is no more. He's given it the most honourable, spicy end he can manage, and they've picked it clean in a silence that Lucky assumed to be rooted in hunger and perhaps some dumbstruck appreciation on Dinah's end for his mastery in the kitchen. But now he realizes she's just been quietly stewing over this stupid, dramatic ultimatum.

Careful not to make any noise, he rearranges his cutlery on his plate. Chopsticks across the top, spoon in the middle with its handle pointed towards him. How shall he respond? A shrug is irritating but too ambiguous—she'll just assume he acknowledges she's right but wants to be stubborn. He can casually ask what she's talking about— but that will only allow her to go into detail about what it means to pick himself up, or worse, who she thinks he should go see. As he turns the spoon's handle slowly, slowly, away from him, something in his head clicks and he almost smiles.

'I don't know why you're talking like this.' This should irritate her *and* redirect things towards her behaviour. Her melodrama, her presumptuousness, her inability to mind her own business.

Dinah doesn't sound irritated. She sounds calm and measured and prepared. 'We've been watching you for months.' Aha—'we'. So typical of her to have already started rallying people to her cause.

Lucky grins. 'I hope I've been entertaining.' He picks up her plate and stacks it on top of his, then carries them both and the long dish full of fish bones to the sink.

She follows him. 'Lucky, listen to me. You're not well.' She starts to say something else but stops herself. 'You're not well,' she says again, sounding small.

Lucky turns on the tap and begins to rinse the plates. 'I appreciate your concern, Dinah.' He doesn't. 'But I'm fine.' He pitches his voice low—much, much more reassuring.

She stands next to him, close enough for him to hear her breathing. Dinah has always been a heavy breather when anxious. In those awful semester-end presentations they had to do back in uni (what were they called? Meets?) she sometimes sounded like she was on the verge of an asthmatic attack. (Crits! They were called crits. Into which they went one by one, like lambs to the slaughter, to present their projects, along with models and drawings and whatever else they managed to vomit out in those dark days, and then waited for the axes to fall as the professors cleared their throats and then tore it all down. Shawn used to say that maybe Dinah should bring an oxygen tank with her into crit and milk the professors for sympathy points.)

Lucky soaps up the dishes, fighting the urge to fill the silence, determined that he won't be milked for sympathy points. Sounding like a cow running uphill, Dinah swivels the tap over to the adjoining sink and begins to rinse off each dish as soon as he's done soaping it. Lucky sets his teeth. *Meddler. Such a meddler.*

'I know you're still upset about Pearl but try to have some perspective. You know, there are much harder things to deal with than . . . this.' She makes a sweeping gesture with a wet hand, indicating the kitchen. 'You've got so much more going for you than so many people.'

What the actual fuck? Lucky scrubs at the rice pot, splashing soap suds all around the sides of the sink. When he speaks, his voice is pleasant and even. 'Dinah, I don't get it. I'm not asking you to feel sorry for me.'

'I'm just saying . . . you have a lot to be thankful for.'

Lucky turns to her and smiles. 'I do. Two fridges, four cooking hobs, a freezer unit, that monster oven. What more can a man possibly want?'

Soap, rinse. Soap, rinse. If only they could go on like this forever.

'I've got a friend you can talk to. I haven't told her anything, except that I've got a friend who's had a tough year.' She pauses. The breathing stops. 'And he's having trouble picking himself up.' And the cow continues uphill.

There it is again. What is with Dinah and her . . . her fixation with him picking himself up? He is up. He's up. Up. Up. Up. Damn her and her . . . toxic positivity. Why can't she see? See Lucky. See Lucky stand sit talk walk. See Lucky steam fish feed cat plant things make—

'Coffee?' He washes his hands and dries them on his second-favourite tea towel. He remembers the bird and shakes his head to dispel the memory.

'Are you okay?'

Lucky taps on the scar along his cheekbone, forcing himself to think about coffee. Strong, milky coffee. 'Yes. Do you want any coffee?'

Dinah shakes her head but follows him closely as he puts on the kettle, then goes to a cupboard, and takes out a small sack of Vietnamese coffee beans. He measures out three heaping tablespoons into the hand grinder and begins to turn the handle, humming 'Eleanor Rigby' to set his pace, as his father taught him to. Round and round and round he turns the handle, relishing the pressure of the burrs against the beans, the minute little cracks, the final give as the last of the beans falls through the burrs and into the drawer-like compartment at the bottom of the grinder. *All the lonely people, where do they all belong?*

'Are you listening?'

No. No, he's not. He's making coffee. Isn't it odd, how little attention she pays to what's happening around her? He takes out his phin and puts the coffee grinds into its cup-like brewing chamber and presses them down gently with the perforated filter press. Carefully, he places the little vessel over a glass and pours hot water into it. His mind follows the thin stream of water into the filter. She moves her lips, and he can't hear her. She wipes her eyes with the backs of her hands, and he lets her. She touches his shoulder, and he turns away.

The coffee drips into the glass, and he watches it.

The woman surrounded by cats

makes low clicking sounds as she squats on the pavement, unwrapping newspaper packets of rice and fish. There must be at least thirty cats in the crowd, of different colours and shapes and sizes, and every cat waits for its own packet. The woman, hunched over her task and dressed in matching blouse and trousers of a dull green, works quickly, snapping the elastic bands off each packet and over her left wrist in one fluid motion. Next to her are two red plastic bags full of newspaper packets. As Lucky watches, transfixed, more cats arrive, mewing in response to her click-click-click.

'Putih, this is not yours. Be patient!' She picks up a large white cat and sets it firmly down next to her, away from a brownish-grey cat and its dinner pack.

Putih gives her an insolent stare, which the woman returns. 'You be patient.' Her voice is low, gentle, and authoritative. Putih looks away.

Lucky, standing by himself barely an arm span away, goes unnoticed by the woman, Putih, and all the other cats. He's become so accustomed to talking to Coconut and having her talk back that he's a little confused at first that none of these cats are talking. And then, seized by the horror that he's become the kind of nut who expects cats to talk, he almost turns and runs away.

'Gajah, *mari sini*.' The woman waves at a large grey cat, larger than Putih, larger than all the other cats. Gajah steps up, princely and handsome, slowly blinking its amber eyes. The woman shifts a few cats and their dinners to make room for Gajah and the packet she unwraps in front of it. Lucky notices it's at least twice the size of the other cat dinners. *Lucky Gajah.*

A sudden gust of wind sweeps across the wide walkway they're on, blowing Lucky's hair into his eyes, flattening the woman's blouse against her back, rustling the red plastic bags and the many, many newspaper packets of fish and rice. It makes an odd picture, the lanky man in the Depeche Mode T-shirt and wide linen trousers lurking near the woman in green and the feeding army of felines with their heads buried in newsprint and tacky headlines, but no one takes the snapshot. Behind them, a ceaseless stream of people move into and out of the MRT station, impatient to end their homewards commute. A couple of schoolgirls stop to remark to each other how cuuuuute the cats are; neither cats nor woman pay them any attention.

Lucky takes a step closer. They don't pay him any attention either.

He's seen this woman hundreds of times before, maybe more. She's been here for years, the crazy cat lady of Eunos station. Every evening, at around six-fifteen, she appears with her plastic bags filled with neat piles of carefully packed portions of food, and every evening the stray cats of the neighbourhood wait for their benevolent queen and eat their dinner. As Lucky looks on, the woman waits for the cats to finish, and after each cat licks off the last of its dinner and saunters off, she folds up the bit of newspaper it leaves behind into a neat little triangle. When all that's left is a mound of neat little triangles and a scattering of cats giving themselves a bit of post-dinner grooming, the woman stands up, gathers all the newspaper triangles and throws them into a nearby garbage bin. The cats look up from their toilette, their heads following her as she walks away. Lucky watches her as she walks past the now-empty market and disappears around the corner.

For five days, he takes the bus to Eunos station and waits for her, then watches her feed the cats and clear up and walk away. Then he goes home and makes Coconut's dinner. On the sixth day, after she unwraps Gajah's dinner, the crazy cat lady of Eunos station stands up and faces Lucky. She is taller than he assumed, and though she's shorter than he is, she manages to stare down her nose at him, her shoulders deliberately thrown back and her chin lifted.

'What do you want?' Her voice for humans is a lot less gentle and a lot more authoritative.

'Hello.' Lucky feels like he's a kindergartener again, caught for peeing in the sand pit. 'I'm Lucky.'

Her eyes narrow. For the nth time in his thirty-seven years, Lucky regrets his name being what it is. Right now, it just sounds like he's making a really weird statement—a total non sequitur, and a stupid one at that. If he really wanted to drop a non sequitur, he'd have chosen something a little more amusing. Like maybe, 'In Hartford, Hereford, and Hampshire, hurricanes hardly happen.'

The woman repeats her question–challenge–dare. 'What do you want?'

They stare at each other across the sea of cats and Lucky takes a step closer, doing his best to keep his face pleasant. She is also younger than he assumed. He's been fooled by the grey in her hair, but up close, he realizes she can't be much older than he is. Her skin is smooth, her eyes unlined. In fact, she could be a little younger. What does she do, he wonders, when she's not feeding cats? Who is she?

'It's very nice of you to feed the cats.'

She frowns. 'Why are you watching me?' Her accent is that familiar flat-toned sound cultivated at all the good schools. He frowns, unhappy to be surprised. Why, indeed, should he be surprised? What education is guarantee against . . . whatever it is that turns anyone into the crazy cat lady of Eunos?

'I was hoping to talk to you.' *Please, please don't let her think this is a pick-up.*

'Why?'

'I have a question about cats.'

Her face relaxes slightly, but her posture remains defiant.

'And you know so many.' Lucky takes another step towards her.

Instinctively, she looks down at the cats around her. Gajah is at her feet, making loud purring sounds in between mouthfuls of fish. She smiles at it. She looks up at Lucky and her smile disappears. 'Okay.' Not exactly an invitation, but not a rebuff either. Lucky smiles. He'll take it.

Some of the cats are done. Some begin to wander off, tails swaying. Others linger, cleaning themselves daintily. Lucky squats down beside the woman and begins to fold the newspaper cat-plates into neat triangles, as he's seen her do every day for the last five days. She gives him a snooty look, and a few passers-by stop for a moment and stare, startled to see two crazy cat people instead of the usual one. But Lucky is unfazed. He continues to squat and continues to fold, until all the cats are done with their dinners.

The woman and Lucky throw their triangles into the bin, and then she thanks him for helping. This is perfunctory, without warmth. As she begins to walk away, he falls into step with her. Softly, his head lowered, he asks if he can buy her coffee.

'Are you from the SPCA?'

'No.'

'The church? I'm not helping you look for Jesus.'

'No.'

'The town council?'

'No.'

'Did Sofia send you? Tell her I didn't eat the cashews.'

'I don't know who that is. I just have a question . . . about cats.' He waits for her to fold her red plastic bags into neat little triangles and put them into her pocket, then asks her again if he can buy her coffee.

She walks up to one of the stone benches in front of the station and sits down, crossing and uncrossing her arms. 'I want a Coke.' There's a challenge even in this, a pointed edge in every syllable. It makes him think of Pearl. Why does even the crazy cat lady make him think of Pearl? *God, I'm turning into Coconut.*

At the nearest kopitiam, Lucky buys a can of Coke and a cup of kopi-O, and as he pays the bored-looking boy in the Wolverine T-shirt behind the counter, he snickers. He wishes Dinah could see him now, buying Coke for the cat lady instead of working, instead of picking himself up, instead of going to see Dinah's psychologist friend, whose card she left behind after yelling something at him he couldn't quite make out. He stares at the can of Coke and the cup of black coffee. What's the point, really, of any of this?

But he takes the Coke to the woman and asks, 'Do any of the cats ever talk to you?'

The woman doesn't answer right away. She pops open the can and takes a sip. She tugs at the collar of her green dress. She takes another sip. She whistles. She bites her lip. 'Who's talking?'

Lucky tries rephrasing his question. 'Have you heard any of the cats speak?'

'Not me.' The woman shakes her head. 'My hearing isn't good enough.'

Okay. 'Do you know anyone whose hearing is good enough?'

More sips of Coke. She looks into his cup and shakes her head again. 'Cats shouldn't drink coffee.'

Lucky nods. 'You're right. They shouldn't.'

Before he leaves her, her dark skirt floating as she drifts past the market, he looks at every single cat to make sure, again, that none of them are Coconut.

He's searched everywhere, every morning, every afternoon, every night, but she's nowhere to be found. He walks circuits around the neighbourhood, looking into storm drains and under cars, checking the narrow alleyways between rows of shophouses, looking up into trees just in case.

'Coconut!' He shouts her name like it's a call to arms. 'Coconut!' It's the movie *300*, and he is Leonidas. 'Please, Coconut!' *This is Spartaaaaaaaaa!*

People stare. They can't help it. This morning, a mother walking her children to school crossed the street when she saw him. A tall, unshaven man in pyjamas, hair wild and wayward, loping down the street, stopping to shout up random trees—it would have been unwise not to.

'Coconut!'

She's been missing since he told her the truth about Pearl. He finds her dinners untouched every morning, but every evening he grills more sardines and puts them in her fish-shaped dish. He leaves the back door open, just a crack, so she can always slip in. He checks his father's study every night even though he's never seen her up there and he leaves one of the windows open. He called out of it last night, 'Coconut, you can have this room. You won't even have to see me.' To tempt her, he's put an array of boxes in the study after watching a video of cats looking like they were having fun jumping into and out of boxes.

It's been more than a week. In between combing the neighbourhood for Coconut, Lucky forgets to comb his hair and shave, he drifts in and out of the cafe. Every evening, he takes the bus to Eunos MRT to watch the cat lady feed her cats. At first, he had only wanted to check if Coconut had joined the legion of stray cats around the train station. But now, he goes back every day, out of some inexplicable kinship he feels with the woman who seems to have made herself guardian and commander of this feline legion. He wishes he had her purpose.

* * *

Don't you think you've grieved enough?

Dinah. Who, in spite of leaving his house in a huff that night, has not been able to stay quiet. Who has appointed herself his dragger-upper. Who won't give up until she declares him happy and cured and irrefutably Up.

Sighing, Lucky turns off his phone screen. What does a man have to do to get some peace?

More importantly—what does a man have to do to get his cat back?

'Lucky! Two Vietnamese drips and a Javanese latte.' Shawn shoots him a frazzled look. It's their Sunday morning brunch rush, and he wishes Lucky would wait until later to daydream. 'Come on, another hour and we should be able to take a break.' Seriously, sometimes it's like working with a child.

Lucky salutes apologetically and, whistling, reaches for the phin filters on the shelf behind him.

Heigh-ho, heigh-ho.

* * *

Under a purpling evening sky that neither of them notices, Lucky is giving the crazy cat lady of Eunos station as detailed a description of

Coconut as he can. He holds his hands a little less than chest width apart. 'About this big.' He touches his right eye. 'A brown patch over one eye. The rest of her face is white. But dark nose. Tail mostly dark brown and black, white tip. White paws, white belly.' He pauses. 'Her name is Coconut. She's my sister's cat.'

The woman frowns. 'Sorry. Haven't seen her.' Her voice is clipped, her eyes dart around.

Lucky sighs and nods. 'Just thought I'd ask. She's my sister's cat.'

When the cat commander speaks again, she is gentler. 'I'm sorry. Do you want me to help you look?'

Her voice is soft and kind, and it makes him cry. He puts his face in his hands, horrified and horribly ashamed. He stands there for a long time, head bowed, face covered, chest heaving. When he looks up again, the sky is dark and she is gone.

∗ ∗ ∗

One of the cats went missing a year ago, the cat lady of Eunos station tells Lucky.

She hunted and hunted for Mochi. She searched the market, the bus stops, the MRT station, the hawker centre, the playground. Days passed, then a week, and still no Mochi. She asked the hawkers, the hairdressers, the veggie man, the fish man, the fruit man—

Lucky cuts her off. 'That's a lot of people. You were very busy!'

—the sugarcane man, the kopi uncle, the makcik at the nasi lemak stall . . .

Lucky gives up and listens.

When no one could remember having seen Mochi in the last week, the cat lady looked under all of the cars in all of the car parks nearby. She looked into the recycling bins. It made her very, very upset. She was afraid she wouldn't find Mochi, but she was also afraid she would.

'What if someone had run her over and left her for dead? Or . . . worse?'

And that was when her sister stepped in and got in touch with a cat psychic.

'You have a sister?' He almost laughs at how surprised he sounds. *Jesus. Why do you think you have the monopoly on sisters?*

'Two. It was my elder sister who called the nice lady. And paid.'

'The cat psychic?'

The cat lady nods. 'Very powerful. I've heard so many stories about her finding missing cats and even chasing away cat ghosts. Quite famous, actually—sometimes the police have to ask her for help when there's a crime involving a cat.'

Lucky raises his eyebrows. The cat lady is too caught up in her story to notice.

The powerful cat psychic said she was really busy, but she agreed to help after the cat lady's sister offered twice her hourly fee. So off they went to see her in her flat in Yishun, a forty-minute drive away. There was no furniture, and they had to sit on the floor. The cat lady had expected to find the psychic living among cats, but there weren't any cats either. The psychic didn't keep any cats herself—it interfered with her work.

'She said that?'

The cat lady shrugs. 'She said she used to have one, but he didn't like that she was friends with other cats, so he left.'

Lucky leans back on the bench they're sitting on and looks up. The sky is streaked with pink from the setting sun, and everything—the pavement, the cats, the woman, the station, his hands, his coffee cup—has taken on a reddish hue. It's a little past seven and Lucky's usually home by now. But today feels different. It is she who wants to talk, who's done most of the talking. He still doesn't know her name, but he can tell she's getting used to his visits.

'So, did the cat psychic manage to find Mochi?'

'She didn't find Mochi herself, but she helped us get in touch with the cat network.'

The what?

Seeing the incredulous look on Lucky's face, the woman offers an explanation: 'It must be like Facebook for cats. She told a few cats and told them to tell other cats, to spread the message about Mochi.'

Lucky marvels at how sane and yet insane the woman sounds. 'And it worked?'

'Yes. That's Mochi.' She points out a small black cat with pale green eyes. As if on cue, Mochi turns and stares at the both of them, then yawns. 'She came back two days after I spoke to the psychic.' She sighs. 'But of course she never told me what happened.'

On the bus on his way home, Lucky folds and unfolds and folds and unfolds the small slip of paper the woman pressed into his hand. The cat psychic's name and number. Ryn—what kind of name is that? Cat psychic? What the fuck. He puts the slip of paper back into his pocket. Maybe. Maybe in a few days he'll be desperate enough.

He takes the usual shortcut to Swan Street, through the small pedestrian lane cutting through the streets. It's shady here, even at high noon, the result of being hemmed by the side gardens of houses, each of which has grown its own border of trees, shrubs, and high hedges to keep out nosy stares. Lucky comes to the part of the lane that meets his street and he takes a sharp right, walking past the house he can see from Pearl's window, the one with the elegant little gate and the cempaka tree. She's there, the woman he spoke to some time ago, the one with the hibiscus bushes. Lucky lifts his hand in a wave, then stops and walks up to the gate. A thought strikes him. He wonders why he never thought of it before.

'Aunty, how are you?' he ventures, in Hokkien.

She looks up from a plant Lucky can't identify. 'Ah, hello. Haven't seen you in some time.'

'Busy. Many busy.' God, he wishes now he had bothered to learn the language from his parents.

'You young people, always busy! My daughter is the same.'

Yes, yes, the daughter who feeds Coconut. The bitch who's stolen my cat. Lucky smiles to keep from scowling. 'Aunty, cat here? Cat.' He pauses, thankful he can remember the Hokkien word for cat. 'Cat here?'

The woman looks at him strangely. Clearly she wasn't expecting this sudden line of questioning. 'What? What cat?'

Lucky takes a deep breath. Another smile to hide another scowl. 'Mimi. Cat. Mimi here?'

'Oh, Mimi?' She laughs. 'Yes, in the garden. At the back.'

What the actual fuck. Here! All this time!

The woman comes up to the gate and now, looking up into Lucky's face, she seems a little worried. He realizes how odd this must be for her. 'Everything okay?' she asks.

NO. You've taken my cat. MY CAT. Lucky swallows. *MY SISTER'S CAT.* 'Yes, yes, Aunty. Long time I no see cat. Sometimes cat go my house. I give food.' He nods vigorously. 'I give fish. Many fish.'

She beams at him. 'Wah, what a nice boy. Thank you so much. So kind!'

Kind, my ass. Take me to the cat! he bellows in his head. Lucky– Leonidas, helmeted and sword in hand, slick in armour and leather, throws his head back and roars. *Coconut! Coconut!*

Lucky bends his head a little closer to the old woman's. He smiles. 'Aunty, can I see cat? See Mimi?' What a fucked-up name for a cat. *She's a cat, damnit, not a French courtesan.*

She opens the gate for him and they walk through the garden, his neighbour warning him to look out for her plants and pots and random garden decor. A multicoloured pinwheel stuck into a pot stand at eye level nearly stabs him in the eye, but he plods on, trailing behind her like the proverbial sheep. When she gets to the edge of the back portion of the garden, she stops and points.

'There. Mimi.'

Mimi is indeed there. She's circling a large flower-pot, peering into it, her tail waving. Lucky watches her, deciding she must be after some sort of poor small creature. Some sad little gecko or an innocent snail. Lucky walks up to Mimi and goes down on one knee.

'Hey, Mimi,' he says loudly for his neighbour's benefit.

The cat stops midway around the pot, keeping herself behind it. She regards Lucky with cold eyes.

'Coconut,' he whispers. 'I'm so sorry. I've been looking everywhere for you. Come home, please?' He says loudly: 'I bought some nice sardines for you this morning.'

A snarl and bared teeth are all he gets in return. And then, a flurry of brown-black-white as she runs off and up onto the wall between this house and the next. Here she sits and stares down at him, her tail waving threateningly.

'Aiyo. Looks like she's in a bad mood.' The aunty sounds apologetic and Lucky feels like an ass.

He sighs, lifting his hands in surrender. 'Cat difficult, Aunty. Difficult cat.'

* * *

Coconut's run away.:(

'Who are you texting?' Shawn comes up from behind Lucky, his head cocked sideways, a grin on his face. 'New girl?'

'Nope.' Lucky puts his phone face down onto the table and turns his attention back to the grinder he's been cleaning. 'No such luck.'

'Really? Come on.' Shawn pulls up a chair. 'No leads on Tinder?'

'They're called matches, Shawn.' Lucky removes the grinder's outer burr, twisting it gently until it comes off in his hands.

Shawn watches Lucky set the burr aside, and they both peer into the grinder. 'Looks okay.' Even if Lucky doesn't—everything about him looks ragged. And why is he cleaning the grinder? Shawn ran some fast-cook rice through it himself two weeks ago—there's no way the grinder needs cleaning.

Lucky takes a cloth and begins to wipe down the inner burr, rubbing carefully. Cleaning the grinder used to be such a pain, but these days he finds it quite relaxing, taking it all apart and putting it back together again.

The pompous salesman who sold them their top-of-the-line grinder had been so horrified when he heard they wanted to grind up 'awful Southeast Asian roasts, with all that oil and even sugar, for fuck's sake, guys'. He had even tried to find a clause in the manual stating that 'lame, tacky roasts' would nullify the warranty. There was nothing.

'Dinah says you guys had a fight.'

Lucky looks up. 'Yah.'

They lock eyes for a moment. It's obvious Shawn wants to say more, but he doesn't. He sighs and claps Lucky on the back. Lucky nods and continues cleaning.

'It's going to be fine. I'll make you a cup of something, okay?'

'Thanks, Shawn.'

* * *

It's 2.00 a.m. and the human inhabitants of Swan Street are asleep. Except Lucky, who is lurking outside the house with the prim little gate and the cempaka tree and the hibiscus bushes. The house where Coconut has holed up. It is dark and quiet, and a car parked in the driveway obscures Lucky's view of the garden.

'Coconut?' he calls out softly, careful not to raise his voice. The last thing he needs is for the neighbours to call the police. 'Coconut? Come out, Coconut.'

No answer, no cat.

Lucky walks around the side of the house, along the thick bamboo border. 'Coconut? Coconut, are you there?'

Still nothing. Lucky sighs. He waits five minutes and calls out again. 'Coconut, Coconut.' His tone is low and coaxing, an unconscious imitation of Pearl's way of calling her cat home for dinner in the evenings. 'Coconut, Coconut.'

A rustle of leaves, and then: 'What do you want, Lucky?' Two little discs peer at him from among the bamboo stems.

Lucky sits down on the pavement in his pyjamas. 'I want you to come home.'

'Why?'

Why, indeed.

'I'm supposed to take care of you.'

'I can take care of myself.'

Lucky sighs. 'I know. But I like taking care of you.' Another sigh. 'And you take care of me.' He realizes as he says this out loud that it's true. 'You like taking care of me, don't you?'

She doesn't answer.

'Come on, Coconut. We're supposed to take care of each other . . . because—' He doesn't want to say it.

Coconut does. 'Because she's dead?'

'She would have wanted us to take care of each other, Coconut. She would, wouldn't she?'

The eyes look a little larger now as Coconut moves a little closer. She lets out a meow, frail and sad. 'I stayed for you, Lucky. You looked so sad when you said she was gone and wasn't coming back.'

Lucky gets on his hands and knees and begins to crawl towards the gleaming little eyes in the bamboo hedge. His insides feel hollow and crumpled, like a semi-crushed-up beer can. It never occurred to him that Coconut stayed to make sure he was okay. In his head, he's been the big guy here, feeding and fostering his dead sister's cat.

His throat feels a little weird. Dry. Choked up. 'Come back, Coconut. I still need looking after, you know.' He does. What's the point of denying this, when even a cat can see it?

Coconut steps out and walks towards the crawling Lucky. She stops when they're face to face, her pointed dark nose looking up, his pointed pale one looking down.

'Why did you lie to me, Lucky? Why didn't you just tell me she's dead?'

His mind flies back to that morning months ago, to that crazy startling moment when Coconut looked him straight in the eye and demanded to know where his sister was. He remembers the confusion, the horror, the unspeakability of it all. And it wasn't just because Coconut had started talking. Sure, he had run from the little cat, but he realizes now he would have run from anyone who had come up to him and asked where Pearl was.

'I couldn't say it. I didn't want to think about it.'

'Because you miss her?' Coconut comes closer.

'More than that.' Lucky blinks. His face is wet. 'More than that. But yea, I miss her.' He pauses. It's so hard to explain. But her cat is waiting, so he tries. 'It's like this. I wake up every day and everything's okay. I'm good, I'm thinking, yea this is fine, yea I'm going to the cafe, I should get some coriander later. But then, while I'm eating something or just walking somewhere or I'm at the supermarket or cooking or washing the dishes or anything, anything, she just pops up. Well, actually, she *doesn't* pop up, right, she can't, and it's like suddenly finding a hand or a foot or my nose missing.' Lucky sighs. What a rubbish way to put it. Pearl would have done a much better job even at this.

Coconut touches her nose to his for the tiniest while. 'I don't understand. But it's okay. I miss her too.'

'I don't think I'll ever stop.' *What about her*, he wants to ask, but he's suddenly too tired. How long do cats stay sad?

Coconut rubs her face against his. Her fur tickles his nose. 'Lucky, it's okay. She won't mind.'

Lucky rubs his face against hers, then picks her up and takes her home.

The letter from Mr Selvam

arrives on a Tuesday morning. The postman slips it into the red
letterbox tied to the gate as the lions look on benevolently. An hour
later, as he leaves home on his way to the cafe, Lucky sees it poking
out of the letterbox and gives it a sharp tap so that it falls all the
way in. He forgets about it even before he arrives at work.

It is Naresh who brings it into the house, two days later. You have
mail, he tells Lucky, who reluctantly takes the thin, white envelope and
leaves it on the table next to the front door. He hates receiving letters in
the mail. Anything that can't be sent by email, in Lucky's opinion, must
be either 1. a threat 2. a summons 3. a wedding invite 4. some sort of
special horror devised by a government official.

All four are equally unwelcome at the house on Swan Street.

The letter sits idly on the table as Naresh roams the house, taking
photographs. Lucky, casting an annoyed glance in its direction as he
lets Naresh out a couple of hours later, decides it cannot be 2 or 4. The
envelope is too high-quality for these. And yet too low-quality for 3.
And although 1 is a possibility, he's never actually received a threat by
mail. Or at all.

By virtue of the mystery now surrounding the letter, it is moved
to the kitchen island. Here it sits for another two days, leaning
against the wire fruit bowl, watching Lucky hand-pull his espresso
in the morning, enduring Coconut's curious sniffs on her way to
investigate a beetle.

On the third day, just before he makes his first coffee, Lucky decides he will not be turned coward by a piece of stationery. He flips the envelope over and tears it open. He reads the letter, feeling cold all over. *Damn it, Pearl.* As he reads through the list of her assets, carefully itemized by the family lawyer, Lucky is horrified. Are these all his now? Fuck. Fuckity fuck. He allows himself a grim smile. All his to squander. *Rest in peace, Papa.*

One item on the list makes him stare. He frowns. He reads the list again. A minute later, he is running up the stairs, two steps at a time.

* * *

'What are you doing?'

'Nothing.'

Lucky is on his back on the floor in Pearl's room. His head hurts. He shuts his eyes.

Coconut nudges his shoulder. 'Why are you up here anyway? Get up, Lucky.'

'I was looking for something.'

But, of course, he won't find it here—why would she keep it among her things? Knowing Pearl, it's in a safe somewhere or hidden in the storeroom that used to be their parents' bedroom. He shouldn't have come in here. He should have just called the lawyer or one of the aunties or something. But now that he is here, in her room, he just wants to lie down. So he does, spreading out his arms and legs, waving them from time to time. *Floor angel!* Pearl would have laughed.

So Lucky laughs for the both of them. He laughs and laughs, waving his limbs against the old parquet floor. He laughs until he chokes on his tears, then he goes back down into the kitchen and makes himself a cup of coffee. Coconut watches him, eyes narrowed, tail waving.

* * *

Another day. Another can of Coke. Another cup of kopi-O.

'My sister's cat talks to me.'

'What does it say?'

'Quite a lot of things.'

The woman nods but doesn't speak. She takes a sip from her can and looks at him, waiting for him to continue. So Lucky tells her the story Coconut told him a few days ago, about the man who only ate cabbage.

'I hope you know that cabbages can be bad for you,' Coconut said, apropos of nothing, as she watched him prepare a drip coffee.

Lucky stared. After the chat with Dinah, it had struck him again that perhaps something could be wrong with him. He'd tried not to think too much about it while Coconut was missing, but technically, this . . . thing . . . with Coconut was impossible. Intelligence aside (and it was a lot to put aside), cats did not have the physical capacity for human speech, which depended entirely on the shape of the mouth cavity and the tongue and the teeth and . . . even on having lips. And yet, here she was in his kitchen, a cat lecturing him about the nutritional value of cabbages. Surely, *surely*, there was something wrong about this. And if he was indeed hearing things, why, why, why *this* sort of thing? Why not a treatise on sustainable living or some conspiracy theory about the government, or a prophecy foretelling the overthrow of the human race by cats? Or something useful—something to compel him to behave better work harder reduce his carbon footprint save the rainforest rob the rich feed the poor. Instead, his possibly deranged subconscious—if he were to accept that it was his subconscious talking to him and not Coconut—instead, his subconscious preferred to sling cabbages at him, and women swept off by the wind, the odd wisecrack, and a bit of Kipling (he had finally figured out where Coconut got the line about waving her wild tail by her wild lone from). And Pearl. Of course his subconscious needed to talk about Pearl.

'Don't make faces, Lucky,' Coconut warned him with a slight baring of teeth. 'If the wind changes, you'll get stuck that way.'

And now stupid Western superstitions.

But he rearranged his scowl into something more pleasant and sipped his coffee as Coconut told him about the man who only ate cabbage.

He ate it for breakfast, for lunch, and for dinner. He had it in all forms. He had it stewed and stir-fried. He had it in soup. He made it into soup. He pickled it. He made coleslaw. He put it in pies. He bought a spiralizer and turned it into noodles—or coodles, which perhaps sounded worse than they tasted.

'How do you know what a spiralizer is?'

Coconut's tone was crispy. 'Everyone knows what a spiralizer is.'

The man who only ate cabbage turned paler and paler every year. This alarmed his wife, his cat, and his doctor. In vain, his wife slipped pork bones into the cabbage soups and spooned slivers of chicken into the coleslaw. In vain, his cat mewed and yowled and sharpened her claws on every cabbage head she could find. In vain, his doctor spoke of balanced diets.

'Fish. He told him to eat fish.'

'Of course he did.'

One morning, the man woke up to find that he couldn't move. He shouted out for his wife, but by the time she and the cat appeared, all they found was a large head of cabbage underneath the covers.

'And that's what happens when you only eat cabbage.'

'I don't get it. He turned into a cabbage?'

'Or a large cabbage ate him.' It was impossible to tell if Coconut was being sarcastic.

Lucky finishes his kopi-O and begins to compress the paper cup into a more 2D version of itself. The cat lady of Eunos tells Lucky that Coconut was definitely being sarcastic. It's very clear from the story, she says solemnly, that the man turned into a cabbage.

'Your cat,' she continues, 'is funny.'

'My sister's cat.'

'Still funny.'

* * *

The funny cat is not amused with the thing Lucky has made out of Pearl's clothes. The birds don't come into the garden any more, she complains. Not even the large stupid ones.

'Pigeons? Peacocks? Ostriches?'

'Whatever. Take it down, Lucky.'

Lucky watches as his cat–subconscious struts into the garden to glare menacingly at his scarecrow–sister. Who knew that deep down, somewhere in the underbrush of the forests in his head, he could be so obsessed with . . . birds?

* * *

'Did you ever call Ryn?'

'Who?'

'The cat psychic.'

Lucky stifles a sigh. This again? This Ryn clearly made an impression on the cat lady with her feline-Facebook stunt. There's no way he's going to call this nutjob, but he doesn't say so—no point hurting her feelings. It's a relief to talk to her—she accepts, without question, that Coconut talks to him, and she doesn't care who he is or why a cat might want to speak with him. It's so refreshing, Lucky muses, to have open-minded friends.

Anyway, why would he even need the psychic now? Coconut's back and even more queenly than ever.

But before they part that evening, his new friend tells Lucky again that he really should call Ryn. It will be good for him, she assures him earnestly, to talk to someone else with the gift. He almost asks her what gift, then realizes that, of course, this is how she sees it. Of course she must want so badly to speak with her cats. If he thought she would listen, he would tell her that it's not talking to Coconut that is his problem. Lucky's seen a lot of people talk to their cats—and why not? Everyone needs a good listener—and Coconut is a pretty good listener. No, his problem is that Coconut talks to him. So, even if he did call the cat psychic, who's either a lucky fraudster or a shrewd woman somehow able to make herself understood by cats, what would he say?

Hi, I'm Lucky. I hear you talk to cats. Has a cat ever talked back? Asking for a friend.

* * *

Three phone calls and Lucky isn't much wiser.

The aunties Maggie and Dolly claim not to know anything.

Uncle Desmond hesitates, then says, 'I can't remember what he said exactly, but I think your father did mention something about Teluk Intan . . .'

Lucky cuts his uncle off before he can make up some dreadful excuse for not bringing this up before. 'Do you know anyone from my father's family I can get in touch with?'

'No . . . but maybe Selvam has a number somewhere.'

The reptile does. Over the phone, he sounds pleased, like he's been expecting Lucky to call. He's clearly prepared and doesn't have to look up the number of that distant cousin Lucky's father left a third of his cash to. As Lucky writes down the number on the back of the envelope that the reptile's letter came in, he feels like kicking himself. Of course, how could he have forgotten about *her*? Lucky imagines Mr Selvam in his expensive suit, leaning back in his big black chair in his chilly office with its view of the heritage district, reading off the number he wrote down on a Post-it right after he got his secretary to send off the letter. After he puts down the phone, the reptile will congratulate himself. He will think, I made that gormless Lee boy call me after all—I knew that the house in Teluk Intan would get his attention. All families keep things from their black sheep.

Seething at this imagined slight, Lucky mutters a thank you and ends the call. Now what? This could be worse than speaking to the cat psychic.

Hi, any chance you know anything about your cousin's house in Teluk Intan, and why he kept it a secret from his blameless son, who never ever ever knew the house existed until his sister died? Asking for a friend.

* * *

This is all Pearl's fault, really. The secret house—hers. The secret of his non-inheritance—hers. The talking cat—hers.

And now this.

Lucky stands at his sister's dressing table. He can feel it—something is different, somehow. The seal—that ridiculous blue thing that used to be right here on this stack of magazines—is gone. He opens a drawer. It's half empty—but the last time he opened it, it was so full of her earrings and accessories, it was difficult to shut properly. He rummages through the drawer. The vintage chandelier earrings—they're gone. So is the pair with the blue feathers. He can't tell what else is missing, but obviously quite a bit. And the top of the dresser looks suspiciously bare—very, very unlike Pearl.

He goes to her closet and opens it. Everything here looks the same as it did the last time he looked, the day he rescued his linen trousers. Her red coat is here and so is her weird chequered prom dress, and the green cheongsam she wore to that television awards show, and her collection of misspelt knock-off T-shirts. D&D—check. Fenbi—check. Channel—check. Stellar McCartney—check. Her bags are still on the rack he made for her years ago—the ridiculous one that looks like a pineapple, the one shaped like a skull, the vintage doctor's bag she got on eBay, the numerous messenger bags she was always buying but never used because they never went with any of her clothes.

So where did the earrings go? Frowning, wondering if he could have been mistaken, he checks the dresser drawers again. Nope. The chandelier earrings and the stupid feathered ones are definitely missing. Her bookcase looks a little sparser too, but he can't remember enough to say for sure. *Gah*. Grumbling, unsettled, Lucky takes photographs of everything—her bookcase, her dresser, her closet, her desk—just in case. In case of what, though, he's not quite sure.

In one of the desk drawers, he finds a stack of notebooks crammed under a DVD box set of *'Allo 'Allo*. Grinning, he remembers trying for years to discuss the show with people at school and at university and even at random events and always, always, coming up against quizzical frowns or confused faces, or quizzical frowns on confused faces. And then he would try to convince them to watch it, recounting jokes and telling them about his favourite episodes, and very often, they would quickly find a way to leave or end the conversation

'Why you watch this kind of thing, ah?' A make-up artist at a television station asked him once, at some sort of party for the crew of a food show Pearl was in. What was that show? He frowns, unable to remember. He can only remember that she was really very attractive in that edgy, badass way he didn't usually go for, and that he wished he never brought up *'Allo 'Allo*.

Because the short answer to her question, and to many, many others, was 'because my sister does', and every man knows that no woman will touch him even with sterilized tongs after he says something like this. The long answer involved him trying to explain the finer points of *'Allo 'Allo*, which ended with him doing a poor impression of an English actor's poor impersonation of an Italian soldier. The attractive make-up artist left with a man in a leather jacket who spoke derisively of the food show they were meant to be celebrating and referred to his new BMW as 'the boss ride'. Lucky watched them leave, wishing heat stroke upon his rival.

'Anyway, we both know it's a good show,' he says conspiratorially, shrugging at the empty bedroom.

Lucky leafs through the notebooks, trying to make out Pearl's loopy, chicken-scratch handwriting and badly drawn sketches. These are notes for another book, he realizes . . . about *coffee*? *Really?* What did Pearl even know about coffee?

He takes the notebooks down to the kitchen and spends the rest of the evening poring over them. He finds sections dedicated to a few countries—Vietnam, Indonesia, Laos, Cambodia, Malaysia—and there are notes on coffee plantations, growing methods, plant varieties, soil and terrain, roasting techniques, brewing methods. There are maps, addresses, phone numbers, sketches of beans and sieves and filters and terraced hills and cups and mugs and pots of coffee. There are Polaroids of and notes about coffee shops, cafes, roasteries, recipes. Next to a photo of what looks like a glass of frothy milk marbled with coffee, he reads:

'Sounds super strange but is really delicious. Cà phê sữa chua— drip coffee with condensed milk AND yogurt. Creamy as hell. Shits all over every affogato I've ever had.'

There's a recipe. He has to get yogurt, but that doesn't take him long. When he returns from the twenty-four-hour supermarket, bearing the yogurt, a tub of ice cream, a six-pack of beer, and salted egg instant noodles, Lucky makes a cup of Vietnamese coffee with a phin. As the coffee drips into a glass, thick and dark and completely opaque, he combines one and a half cups of yogurt with a tablespoon of condensed milk in a small bowl. He pours this mixture into the coffee once it's done and adds ice chips. Looks good, just like in the photo. He stirs it with a chopstick and takes a sip. His eyes go wide. *Gorgeous.* He takes another sip, reading Pearl's notes again. Shits all over . . . *yes, definitely.*

Lucky raises his glass in triumph and defeat. She knew more about coffee than he did, it appears. But she's sleeping with fish, and he's the one enjoying yogurt coffee in the wee hours of a Wednesday, and he's going to wake up later and have another one.

* * *

'Did you check for fingerprints?'

'Fingerprints?'

'Yes, fingerprints.' The cat looks up at him from her new blanket-lined basket (courtesy of the lovely Naresh, who has also fallen under Coconut's spell) and yawns.

It's a rainy morning, and the kitchen is cold. Lucky's feeling very lazy, but his shift at the cafe starts in an hour. There's time for another cup of coffee, though.

'Detectives always dust for prints when things go missing. I thought you'd know that, Lucky.' Coconut yawns again. 'You should check for fingerprints in Pearl's room.'

Pompous little know-it-all. Lucky grimaces as he puts the kettle to boil. She's been watching more television than ever since he got her that television box thing with a hundred different channels, and now she's insufferable, forever treating him to random bits of useless, unnecessary, often completely irrelevant information. If she's a manifestation of his subconscious, an idea that still clings to the external protrusions of the roof joists of his mind, if his mind were a wooden kampung house from the early 1900s, then . . . then he should be thrown into an asylum. Or, at the very least, made to pay a fine. If everyone who had a misbehaving, errant subconscious could be made to pay a fine, the Singaporean government could probably fund a space programme. Lucky would love to be part of a space programme, particularly now that there are ways to make coffee in space.

'No, I didn't take any fingerprints.' He pours hot water into a French press, into which he's measured out a porcelain-soup-spoonful of ground coffee. Every time he does this, he remembers his father telling him, 'no need for weighing scale, boy—medium grind, five grams, is one soup spoon, flat. Rounded soup spoon—seven grams.'

'Do you think she came back for her things?' Coconut chirps, interrupting his thoughts.

'What?'

'Pearl. Ghost Pearl. Maybe she decided to come back and get her earrings. And the seal.'

'Ghosts don't need earrings and stuffed seals.'

'But they might want them, right? Like you're always wanting more coffee.'

Lucky rolls his eyes. This is the last thing he needs now—a talking cat who believes in ghosts and wants to discuss them. What kind of crap is she watching these days on television? Well, he won't encourage her. 'Do you know that coffee can be made in space now?'

Coconut wriggles under the blanket and pokes her head out from under it. 'Yes. Are you talking about the ISSpresso?'

Lucky has forgotten the name of the space coffee machine he read about a couple of years ago. A quick Google search reveals that yes, the know-it-all cat-fiend is correct. If she doesn't turn out to be part of his messed-up head, he might sell her on eBay—a talking cat will fetch a lot of money, and all this trivia may be entertaining for someone else. Meanwhile, Lucky entertains himself by watching a video demonstration of the ISSpresso extracting espresso from a regular capsule (damn, what amazing PR for Lavazza) and spurting it into a bag. Another video shows him how some engineer decided that he couldn't allow space coffee to be served in bags and developed a zero-gravity cup to funnel coffee into the mouths of astronauts. How cool—it makes Lucky yearn for space travel, and it makes him regret not paying more attention to his physics teacher, Mr Kamal, while the poor man valiantly tried to explain how gravity affects fluid mechanics. Instead, he and his friends rolled up paper balls and tried to toss them into the wastepaper basket in the corner of the classroom every time Mr Kamal turned to write something on the whiteboard. Lucky shakes his head. Well, the next time some busybody asks him if he has any regrets, he will have a ready answer.

He sends a text message: `Space coffee cup looks like the love child of a jug and a bed pan.`

'What do you think ghost Pearl looks like? Is she transparent, translucent, or just invisible?'

'Coconut! I don't want to hear anything more about ghosts.'

'Are you afraid?'

Of Pearl coming back as a ghost? Lucky snorts. As if. His sister was too smart to do something like that. She'd know he'd want to grill her about the whole inheritance sham, and this house in Teluk Intan he's never been told about. And those trousers she stole. And these notebooks—Lucky keeps them on the kitchen table now, reading them every evening, sometimes adding his own notes. If she were here, he'd ask her about this coffee plantation in Lam Dong in her notes. He remembers them talking about Vietnamese Arabica years ago, and he still orders a regular supply of Lam Dong Arabica for the cafe but did she actually go to this mountain region somewhere in Vietnam just to see the coffee grown, to taste it? Pearl wasn't even a fan of Arabica. Like their father, Lucky and Pearl preferred the earthier 'low-class' Robusta, roasted to near-black, the way most Vietnamese roasteries do it. To travel all the way to Lam Dong seems really quite unnecessary, even if she was probably shooting her noodle show in Vietnam at the time. But she was always doing that—the unnecessary. Lucky sighs. What was it like, he wonders, to be so determined to do and know and see everything that crosses your mind? Did it ever get tiring for her?

'You should get going. It's nearly ten-thirty.' Coconut is staring at the kitchen clock. 'Do you know that means it's nearly eleven-thirty in Japan now?'

'In Japan?'

'Yes. Japan. The capital of Japan is Tokyo, and they eat a lot of fish. And noodles. And seaweed. And soybeans. Do you know that Mount Fuji is an active volcano?'

'Really? How nice for Mount Fuji—great way to keep fit, you know.'

Damn that television.

* * *

'You're like that too, you know.'

'No.'

'Yes.' Shawn opens the door of the dishwasher, releasing a warm waft of air. 'You're just as bad as she is . . . was.' He waves a little wildly, whether out of apology for using the wrong tense or to disperse the warm emissions of the dishwasher, Lucky can't quite tell.

Lucky throws up his hands in echo of Shawn's. 'Okay, are we talking about the mushrooms again?'

Shawn gives him a hard look. 'No. But remember when you first tasted a primitivo?'

Lucky does. 'That was different.' He crosses his arms and casts a wary eye at the door. Why is it so quiet this afternoon? Thursday afternoons aren't usually so bad.

'No, it's exactly the same.' Shawn reaches into the dishwasher and takes out two mugs, which he passes to Lucky, who puts them on the counter shelf. Four more mugs into the relay, Shawn pipes up again: 'Remember how you talked about nothing else for two weeks? Remember how you called every wine shop in Singapore asking if they had the goodness knows what specific primitivo from that one vineyard from that specific year? Remember when you thought you should start a wine import business so you'd have a reason to bring in all the different primitivos you liked and whatever else that kept popping up on your hourly—no, don't deny it—Google searches? Remember when you convinced us to order that case for Christmas, and you doubled the order without telling me? Remember when you went off to Manduria?'

Wow. Lucky does remember, but he never realized that Shawn had been so irritated by all of it. He didn't say anything back then, but Lucky can tell from the set of his jaw and the increasingly extravagant hand gestures that his friend is growing more and more agitated with each new 'remember . . .?'

'Yea so you and your sister—same horse, different cart, okay? I never saw two people more . . . relentless in their pursuit of . . . of whatever strikes your fancy. It's like a light goes off in your heads and you can't turn it off.'

'Same horse . . . what? Did you just make that up?'

'Yea. And here's another one—people who live in glass houses shouldn't whine about people staring into their bathrooms.'

'What?!'

'You do what you want, Lucky. I get that life isn't great and you miss her and all of that and I'm here for you, but if you're going to be weird and pretend to have conversations with your cat and make sculptures out of your sister's clothes . . .' Shawn takes a deep breath. 'If you're going to be weird, then you need to accept that people are going to be weirded out. Okay?'

Shawn puts the last of the mugs onto the counter shelf and walks off to rearrange the magazines on the large concrete table.

Wow.

* * *

'Coconut, my friends hate me.'

'Please, Lucky. You think you've got problems?' The cat sounds grumpy.

He reaches out to stroke her head. 'Do *you*?' He rolls his eyes.

Coconut puts her head on his knee. 'I've never seen a mountain, Lucky. I've never seen the sea.'

Damn that television.

The bus

is full. Lucky has managed to get a seat next to the window. He looks out the window as the bus slowly rolls along Tanjong Katong Road, at the old tailor's shop, at the hardware store that's been there since before he was born, at the pet store that used to be a fish and chips shop that used to be a karaoke bar, at the organic grocery that used to be a brothel, at the hipster bicycle shop that used to be the mini mart that used to be called a sundry shop.

As the bus passes a block of apartments in a mock-Georgian style, Lucky rolls his eyes. If Pearl were here, she'd stick out her tongue at it. Chelsea Lodge—what a blot on the page of Katong. What a fart in the face of heritage. A poo on the plate of vernacular architecture. *Mock-Georgian. Seriously.* Lucky rolls his eyes again. He wonders for the nth time which idiot Europhile decided sometime in the late nineties that this jarring, random *mock-Georgian* thing that looked like some caricature of European townhouses would be a fitting addition to the neighbourhood. He remembers the plain, practical 1960s shophouses that used to stand in its place—poor things weren't old enough to come under any sort of heritage ruling. They weren't particularly eye-catching or charming, but they belonged here in their own laid-back, lazy way.

The bus turns left onto East Coast Road and it's more of the same. More and more of the old shops gone, and new and new-fangled things taking their places. Is this what it means to grow old, Lucky thinks, watching a girl with a kingfisher-blue streak in her hair walk into a yoga studio where a kopitiam used to be. Seeing every change less and less as something to be excited about and more and more as something trimmed off your world?

'She looks like a bird,' says the basket on his lap.

Lucky glares at it. An ear, then an eye emerges from the folds of the blanket he put into the basket earlier. He quickly adjusts the blanket. Now it's just a lump again. The man next to him hasn't noticed a thing, thank goodness.

'This isn't fun.' A whisper, but he can still hear her.

Lucky bends closer to the basket. 'Quiet,' he hisses. 'This isn't the fun part.'

'I want to look out the window.'

'No.'

A series of short, small mews follows. Lucky looks up, alarmed. The old man next to him turns to stare. Lucky smiles at his neighbour as another mew escapes from the basket. 'Hello.'

'You have a cat in the basket.'

Lucky very briefly considers if he should lie. But he doesn't. 'Yes.' Slowly, he pulls back the blanket. Coconut's dark, pink-tipped nose pokes out.

The old man reaches out to pat it. She mews softly. The man giggles. 'Aiyoh. So cute.'

Lucky shakes his head, refusing to agree. It will make her vain. He covers her back up, ignoring the next pitiful mew and the man's disappointed face. Well, it's not like he wants to keep her covered up, but pets aren't allowed on public transport in Singapore. Quite ridiculous. What do they think a cat will get up to? And if the news stories he's read are anything to go by, it's people who need to be kept off buses and trains. Someone pooped on a train a couple of months ago, and last week, some jerk was caught taking upskirt photos of women in a crowded bus. Pooping, maybe, but no cat, no dog, no parakeet, no gerbil would ever take upskirt photos of anyone, so doesn't that make them relatively less of a menace on public transport?

In any case, when they get off the bus, he is taken to task by Coconut for keeping her in the basket. 'Not fair! I want to look around too.'

'And you will.' He lifts her out of the basket and puts her on the pavement. 'Don't wander off.'

She sniffs the air. 'This place smells different.'

A bicycle whizzes by. Coconut jumps and looks cross. Humming softly, Lucky picks her up and carries her in the crook of his elbow, her tail curled against his chest, as he walks away from the bus stop and the road, taking a narrow path between two rows of tall casuarinas. The sound of birds overhead makes Coconut look up with much interest, but Lucky tightens his grip before she can manage to leap out of his arms to start a detailed investigation. The concrete pavement they're on soon gives way to grass, and the grass gives way to sand.

He puts her down. 'Here you go, Coconut. The sea.'

'It's big.'

'It is.'

'Bigger than any puddle I've ever seen.'

'Bigger.'

'Bigger than the fish pond at home.'

'Much, much bigger.'

The little cat is quiet for a very long time as she sits on the sand and stares at the wide expanse of green-grey sea and the container ships scattered across the horizon. A large bird flying overhead squawks at her and she hisses back. And then, looking a little scared, she trots towards the edge of the sand and puts a paw in the water. She mews indignantly. Lucky laughs. Then he takes off his sandals and sits on the sand and watches her chase a tiny crab and laughs again as she jumps back in confusion as the crab burrows into the sand and disappears.

'Where does all the water come from?' She's back at his side.

'I don't know, Coconut. It's always been there.'

'Really? So much of it? How?'

Lucky doesn't know. He shrugs. 'It's a mystery.'

'Everything's a mystery when you don't read enough. Pearl read *a lot*, so she was very clever. When was the last time you read a book?'

He ignores her. Having a cat talk to him is one thing, but taking self-improvement advice from her would be a different level of weird. As she trots off again, Lucky stretches out on the sand, shielding his eyes with his hands. He wishes he had taken Coconut to another beach. This one is completely fake—part of a 1980s land reclamation project—and he hates the concrete jogging paths and the public barbecue pits and the small strip of sand imported from either Vietnam or Indonesia. Only in Singapore could a beach be such a crashing bore. But it's close to the house, so . . . anyway, Coconut seems impressed enough.

He sits up and looks around. It's crowded for a Tuesday. No picnicking families, but a surprising number of people jogging along the paths. And rollerblading. Lucky recalls he has rollerblades stashed somewhere at home and cringes at the thought. Those rollerblades, then top-of-the-line and the epitome of cool, now shamefully gathering dust, were incredibly hard won.

No other kid in the neighbourhood—certainly no one in his class— ever had to deal simultaneously with the shame of being absolutely rubbish at rollerblading and having his mother and his sister insist on watching him be absolutely rubbish at rollerblading. It was bad enough that he had to practise in Pearl's rollerblades because his father refused to buy him a pair until he passed Pearl's stupid test—involving twenty non-stop figure-eights and an obstacle course that had her chasing him and yelling as he tried not to hit any of the random objects she threw in his path.

Once, as she charged down the driveway at him during a practice test, she started to yell, 'You think you're faster than a girl, Lucky? You think you're faster than me?'

What was she going on about? This wasn't fair. He knew she was faster. She knew she was faster. She knew he knew she was faster. So, for the first time in rollerblading-practice-test history, he yelled back, 'Is that all you can come up with? You think I care that you're faster? You're stupider and uglier! And you have man-feet!'

In retort, she hurled a large spherical cushion in his path. Pearl had a very, very good arm and that cushion might as well have been a thunderbolt. He quickly changed direction to avoid it, but another cushion came flying at him—of course she had predicted, accurately, his change of direction. He tried to go in yet another direction, but managed to trip himself up, sending himself straight into the arms of his mother's largest bougainvillaea. Pearl came running up to help but, still annoyed, he waved her away. Sadly, the arm motions upset his balance and he fell down again, face first, against the terracotta pot.

'Shit.' This was Pearl.

'Shit.' This was Lucky, realizing he had blood all over his face and it was getting into his mouth.

But it all ended well, in spite of the three hours they had to spend getting him stitched up at the hospital. He did eventually pass Pearl's stupid test and get his own rollerblades, and now he's got this cool scar across his right cheekbone, at the edge of the eye socket.

He shows it to Coconut. 'Cool, right? And all because some boy at school told Pearl she would never run faster than he did and of course she had to take it out on me. Honestly, I think the idiot had a crush on her.'

Coconut inspects the scar. 'Looks like a cat got you. Did you ever get faster than her?'

Than *Pearl?* Lucky laughs, digging his bare toes deeper into the sand. 'Nope. Never.'

* * *

Coconut has licked her ceramic fish dish clean and is about to tell one of her stories. Lucky can tell by the way she's sitting upright, shuffling her bum back a little (for better balance?) and swishing her tail very, very slowly back and forth. He's washing the dinner dishes, but he turns his head so she can see that she's got his attention. Has he heard, she wants to know, of the man who tried sailing to the edge of the world?

'You know the world is round, right?'

'And you know very little about the world, Lucky.'

The man who tried sailing to the edge of the world was a little older than Lucky—maybe fifty years old.

'I'm hardly *fifty*!'

'Okay. Maybe forty.'

The cat continues before he can interrupt again. The man, she repeats, was a little older than Lucky and just a little taller. He didn't like his house or his bicycle or his neighbours. He didn't like his job, or his boss, or the people he worked with. He didn't like his parents or his mother's dog or his brother. So he bought a little sailboat and took it out to sea and then decided he would keep on going until he reached the edge of the world.

'Again, the world is round. There's no *edge*.'

The man sailed on for quite a long time. He sailed until there were no birds in the sky any more, and the waves were bigger and bluer and blacker than any wave he had ever seen. He sailed for three days without seeing a trace of land, and he started to think, *Excellent. I'll soon be at the edge of the world.*

'Dumbass.'

'Be quiet, Lucky.

But on the fourth day, a speck of land appeared in the distance. It grew and grew as the man and his sailboat approached, urged by the wind, and suddenly the man found himself on the sandy shore of an island. There was no one around, but there were coconuts on the sand and everywhere he looked, there were trees heavy with ripe fruit, and the man realized how hungry he was.

'He hadn't eaten, in all that time?'

'Just a sandwich and a tube of Oreos. He wasn't planning on staying out at sea for so long, remember?'

So he ate the fruit and managed to break the coconuts open and drink from them, and then he took a nap. When he woke up, he was surrounded by cats.

'Cats?!'

'Yes. He ended up at the little-known island of Cat.'

'The island's called Cat?'

'I just said that, Lucky. You really must pay attention.'

The island of Cat was populated by thousands of cats, all living happy lives. They had never seen a man before, but cats are by nature gracious hosts, so they shared their fish with him and they let him sleep in their cave at night while they hunted and roamed about the island. But the man grew sick of fish, and he missed his bed and his house and his bicycle more and more, so one day he said goodbye to the cats and got back into his boat. He was never seen or heard from again.

Done with the dishes, Lucky has resumed poring over Pearl's notebooks. 'Wait, really? That's it?'

'He should have stayed with the cats.' Coconut lies down on the kitchen table, her tail tapping against the thin cardboard covers of two of Pearl's notebooks. 'He was lucky to have fish.'

Lucky looks back down at the page he's on and rereads his sister's notes on coffee in the Malaysian state of Perak. Why didn't Pearl take him with her when she went to this roastery in Ipoh to check out the famous Ipoh white coffee? He would have wanted to go—he wants to go. He will go. He should go. One day. Soon. The cafe orders a small shipment from Ipoh every couple of weeks, but Lucky is suddenly filled with the need to *really* see this 'golden' roast that his father grew up on—smoky and strong, more fragrant than the darker, sugared roasts elsewhere in Malaysia. He stops in mid-flight-of-fancy. *This* is it, isn't it? That charging horse thing that irritates Shawn so much. But he does want to go. But to what end? Is there a point to any of it? He's probably better off spending the rest of his days holed up in his kitchen, cooking for his sister's cat.

Lucky sighs. 'I feel like that man, Coconut.'

'You don't like fish any more?'

Lucky sighs. Is she being literal on purpose, or does she just enjoy having him spell things out? 'I feel like I don't really enjoy anything any more. Not like I used to. Something's missing.'

'What's missing? Is it somewhere in the house? I'll help you look.'

He reaches out and rubs her head. Again—literal on purpose or just a bit perverse? 'I don't know what's missing.' He pauses. 'But it's probably not here.'

'You know what you need to do, Lucky?'

'What?'

'You need to go on a journey.'

'What?' Lucky rolls his eyes. 'Like sail to the island of Cat?'

'No. You won't be able to find it.' Coconut's voice is patient. 'But all heroes go on a journey at some point, Lucky,' she explains. 'So, it's time for you to go on a journey. Maybe that's how you become a hero.'

Lucky sits up straighter, nodding. What a clever cat. And if she were his subconscious . . . *what a clever boy am I*. Yes, he can see how the

Greek hero thing could work for him, metaphorically as well as literally. Noble but flawed man seeks out challenges and discovers new lands, maybe saves a few princesses, kills a few monsters. 'Like . . . Odysseus? Hercules?'

Coconut gives him a sideways look. 'Like Doctor Strange.'

* * *

Well, there are definitely fewer books now.

Pearl's copy of *Ben-Hur* is missing. In its place, an inch-wide gap in her bookshelf winks at him from between the copy of *Romeo and Juliet* they both used in secondary school and her old dictionary. He compares the current state of the bookshelf with the photo of it he took with his phone last week, frowning. Two cookbooks—one on Vietnamese cooking and another much dog-eared one on Chinese dumplings, one or two recipes from which she may or may not have ripped off for her own cookbooks—have gone missing too, along with her author's copies of *Tao of Bao* and *Book of Dumplings*. Her old school yearbooks have also disappeared.

What the fuck is going on? Lucky can't think of anyone who would want Pearl's school yearbooks.

Her closet is less populated too. Gone are the silly Channel T-shirt, the pineapple bag, the stack of plain white tank tops she always wore while travelling. Her large black suitcase isn't in its spot on the shelf any more. Lucky makes a face. What, really, is he supposed to do now? He can't even think of a way to talk about it without sounding like he's lost his mind. For a moment, he amuses himself thinking of what the aunties will say.

'Lucky, you really mustn't let your imagination run wild at your age.'

Or even better: 'Lucky, I hope you haven't told anyone outside the family about this?'

And the stuffy old fish Uncle Desmond will say, 'Oh dear, I hope they haven't taken anything valuable? Have you checked on your mother's jewellery?'

How, why, is he related to these people? Hard-boiled, unimaginative, always worried about how much money other people had what cars other people drove what other people's children were doing. No wonder his father detested them. Then again, his father wasn't fond of most people—and he didn't like to say much about his side of the family either, except to say that his parents were dirt poor.

'So poor they gave me to my uncle. Free labour, Lucky—as long as he kept me clothed and fed. These days, it would be child abuse or something, but back then, it was quite common to give your children away if you couldn't afford to raise them. And here you've grown up like a little prince—you'll never know what it's like to really struggle.' And here his father would sigh, shake his head, say something about the value of hard living.

Lucky has no idea what happened to his grandparents. His father never told him, and it never seemed like a good idea to ask. Did Pearl ever ask? Did she know? She must have. She did keep the house in Teluk Intan all these years when she could have just sold it off. Lucky doesn't even know why his father ever bought a house in Teluk Intan. Is it even close to the village where he grew up? Did Pearl ever go? Lucky imagines a twin house, exactly like theirs, in a small Malaysian town buzzing with people who can all sing along to Saloma songs and who all speak in his father's Malay-tinged accent. And the twin house—Lucky pictures it with an identical yellow stone driveway and lion gateposts and casuarinas and maybe even a cat.

Lucky smiles. Then unsmiles as he looks into his sister's closet again. What the fuck is he supposed to do about all this missing stuff?

* * *

'Why do you need to do anything?'

'I don't know. It's a bit weird, right?'

Coconut concedes that it is, but she insists it isn't his problem. 'Let her take whatever she wants, and then she'll be happy.'

'You still think it could be Pearl?' God, this cat.

'Who else could it be? She didn't have anything buried with her. For her journey. Not even sunflower seeds, Lucky.'

'She never liked sunflower seeds. Anyway, a whole *suitcase* is missing.' He pauses. 'It's very weird.' He wishes he could think of a better way to describe the whole thing.

'Pearl was always very practical. A suitcase is a good idea if you're carrying a lot of stuff.'

* * *

The cat lady believes it's Coconut who's taken the objects from Pearl's bedroom. 'Who else could it be?'

'But . . . she's a cat.'

The lady nods. 'That's right. Cats are terribly good at hiding things.'

A whole suitcase? Lucky sighs. No one seems to think anything of the damn suitcase.

Her face is a little dirty today, her hair a little messier than usual. He wonders what she did today but doesn't ask. She puts a hand on his shoulder, smiling. 'You're so funny. You know, it must be easier for a cat to hide things than to learn to talk . . .'

That special brand of sane and insane, every time.

'You should really call her.'

Lucky sighs. 'The cat psychic?'

'Yes.' The woman picks at the grubby edge of her dress. 'Maybe your cat will tell her the truth about the suitcase.'

Later, staring out of the window of the bus, Lucky wonders again if he should be more worried about the suitcase and the books and all the other stuff. If he should talk to someone besides his friend the cat lady about everything that's been happening. *Not* the cat psychic, though he's starting to think maybe he wants her job.

Lucky's phone buzzes in his pocket.

Come on. How long are you going to ignore me?

He turns off the phone screen. He isn't angry with Dinah any more, but he really doesn't want to talk to her, or see her or do anything that will invite another attempt to fix him. Because that's what she's doing, isn't it? Lucky feels a momentary flicker of anger lap at his insides, like Coconut's tongue against his chin when she's trying to wake him up some mornings. Okay, so he's still a little angry. But it's a strange sort of anger, a creature sometimes small and hesitant and deeply insecure, and other times a fiery demon.

As he walks down Swan Street, it's the small, hesitant, deeply insecure creature that joins him. He looks at the large, well-maintained houses, the expensive cars, the fussed-over gardens and the fish ponds, and the ornamental fountains, and he feels guilty that he's part of this world, this . . . one per cent? One-point-five? He doesn't know the figures because he doesn't have to. People with fish ponds don't need to know who else has fish ponds, and who hasn't.

'I have a fish pond,' he says out loud. 'But I'd give it away. I'd give it up.'

Would I really?

Lucky stands in front of the house—his house, now—and doesn't know. There are too many things he doesn't know, and this has never bothered him. Another superpower.

Inside, on the white leather sofa in the living room, Coconut is watching television. It's a food channel, and Pearl is on. Lucky smirks. Who needs a shrine when you have Food Network? And how does Coconut always seem to know when one of Pearl's shows is on?

Pearl is sitting at a tiny table at a roadside restaurant, looking like a giantess. At the next table, a couple tries not to look at the camera as they dip fresh spring rolls into small sauce bowls. Pearl waves an arm, saying the restaurant has been around for thirty years, but it's still run by the family who owns it—and it's really hard to find, even for locals. The red plastic tablecloth reflects light back into the camera and onto her face. She's a little sweaty and her hair is swept back from her face with a couple of steel hairpins, but Pearl manages to make it work. A rotund, proud-looking man brings a bowl of steaming soup noodles over to her table and is rewarded by one of her high-wattage smiles. As she half-shuts her eyes in mock ecstasy, Lucky squints at the television. Chunks of beef, chilli oil on the surface of the soup, sprigs of Chinese celery—it must be bún bò huế. He waits as Pearl digs in with a pair of wooden chopsticks and slurps down a mouthful.

'What I've got here is bún bò huế . . . because we're in Hue, and I have to have this.' She laughs. 'If you're the kind of freak that can't do anything spicy or chilli-ed, stay away from this. As you can see, I'm having this with extra chilli paste. Go big or go home, am I right?'

Lucky rolls his eyes. Her television persona—so bright-eyed, so *cringey*. But he makes a cup of coffee and sits down next to Coconut on the sofa, and they watch the rest of the episode together. They watch Pearl get on the back of a scooter and wave, and in the next shot, she's somewhere else in Vietnam. Saigon! At a little eatery he and Pearl discovered together years and years ago.

'. . . so, I ordered this by accident and it isn't a noodle dish, but I love it! Guys, this is bánh xèo.'

Accident, my ass. The night he and Pearl stumbled into that place, they shared four of those—after dinner. She loved everything about it—the crisp turmeric-laced pancake, the perfectly cooked shrimp, the ceremony of layering these together with red spinach leaves and coriander and morning glory tendrils, and then rolling it all up in a sheet of crackling rice paper.

Pearl turns to the woman who's brought it to her. 'Am I saying it correctly? Baan-say-oh? Great.' She turns back to the camera. 'Well, this is basically a rice-flour pancake topped with herbs and leaves and meat. I've asked for it with prawns, but there's also a pork option, and in some places, crab. Let's have a taste . . .' She places a slice of pancake on a thin sheet of rice paper, then grabs leaves from a large dish at the centre of the table to pile onto it.

Lucky shakes his head. It's so strange to hear her voice again. To see her face, and those feathered earrings. Stranger still to see her eat, trying to be ladylike but ending up looking somewhat like a chipmunk, fighting the urge to talk while chewing, which she often did at home, in spite of all their mother's admonishments.

'Aiyoh, Pearl,' she would say, 'how will you ever find a husband like this?'

'Nonsense lah, Mummy,' Pearl would reply. 'Who needs a husband? These days we just get men to wank into tubes and that's it. After that, they can do whatever they want. Husband! What for?'

'Oh Pearl, why do you talk like that? Surely I didn't teach you to talk like some . . . cheap fishwife.'

'Eh, Mummy, I would be proud to sell fish, okay? I'm telling you, most people don't know a good fish from a monkey . . .'

Lucky grins at the memory. Poor Mum. On screen, his sister is now making rice noodles, pouring a thin rice paste into a rectangular flat-bottomed pan.

'So, we're going to steam this in a wok, letting the pan float on top of the boiling water. Yes, just let it float. Keeps the noodle sheets nice and even! And now we cover the wok for five minutes and that should do it.'

She makes it look so easy, but, in fact, she and Lucky tried this a few times in their kitchen before she figured out how much rice paste to use for each noodle sheet. At one point, she growled, 'Fucking hell, I should just take this shit out of the script.' But Lucky insisted she keep at it. 'It's cool, keep going, you have to do it.' And there she is, making steamed rice noodles like a bloody pro. He smiles.

She grins back, shaking her hair back from her face. 'And now that I've got this free time—five minutes is five minutes—I'm going to do something life-changing, like take a selfie with my crew. Excuse me!'

She flounces off camera, and the advertisements begin.

'Lucky, she looks so much like you.' Coconut climbs onto his stomach and begins studying his face.

'Yup. Tell me something new.' He winces. 'Ow. Watch those claws.'

'Beer was first brewed in ancient Egypt and Mesopotamia.'

'What?'

'You asked me to tell you something new.'

Lucky grins and rubs her head. 'I wasn't asking you to tell me something new—I'm just making fun of you, Coconut.' Hmm. It's a little hard to explain a low-level dig like that to a cat, but he tries anyway. 'So, you said Pearl looks like me, right? So, that's not new to me. But I said, tell me something new. Because you didn't. So, I'm making fun of your telling me something *not* new.' He pauses. '*But* this beer thing—very cool.' It is, and he can be magnanimous.

Unamused, Coconut begins to lecture him about meaning what he says and saying what he means, and he lets his mind drift off.

This is surely what it means to be mad—watching your dead sister on television, with her cat, while she tells you to be a more careful speaker of the English language. Maybe it's time he accepts his madness and moves on. So many people are mad. So many artists and writers and musicians and explorers—the British surveyors who first mapped the Himalayas were surely mad—and whoever first decided that space travel should be a thing. Who is he, Lucky Lee, to say he cannot be mad? Some random, nobody-nothing coffeemaker fellow in Singapore—why, he should be honoured to count himself among the mad.

Coconut swats him on the chest. 'Are you listening, Lucky?'

It suddenly strikes Lucky that maybe, if she's really a talking cat and not some loose end of his mind, then the cat talks to him *because* he's mad. If cats are learning to speak and it's all part of a plot to take over the world and it's supposed to be a secret, maybe they need people to practise on. And no one keeps secrets better than madmen, right? Because no one believes them. Lucky imagines himself on the street, telling people that THE END OF THE WORLD IS UPON US THE CATS ARE LEARNING TO SPEAK. He snickers.

Coconut walks off him and back onto the sofa, her paws pressing into his tummy and hip bone. She lies down on her side, her tail nestled along the side of his thigh. There is nothing in the world quite like having a cat choose to press her tail against your thigh— Lucky decides it's right up there with the first cup of coffee in the morning. And as a shampoo commercial blares on the television, he hopes that when they do take over the world, the cats will confer on him some sort of Special Friend status. Or declare him One Whose Thigh Is Worthy of Tails.

TV Pearl comes back on again, and Lucky and Coconut turn their heads towards her. She demands, of course, their full attention—and she gets it. Lucky loses himself in her voice—how has he never noticed before how much like a purr it was? And in her face—so creepily like his own, except hers would never grow old now. And that laugh—it hurts him to hear it again, but not hearing it again will hurt him more. He can't put all this into words exactly; he can only watch his sister eat fish noodle soup and ache and try not to cry.

Still staring at the television, he swallows the lump in his throat. 'Coconut, I think it's time you saw a mountain.' And it's time he saw that house.

'How? Where?'

'We're going on a journey to distant lands.' He waves his arms about, hoping to convey some sense of scale and grandiosity. 'My hero trip.'

TV Pearl smiles her encouragement. Coconut purrs, pressing her tail against his thigh.

Lucky smiles back at Pearl and strokes Coconut on the forehead. The lump in his throat disintegrates. He leans back against the sofa, letting his body sink into its softness as he watches his sister take a sip of thick, caramel-coloured coffee. 'Oh my god,' she gushes, 'this is so good, guys. This is *gold*.'

Pearl laughs.

Lucky laughs.

He picks up his cup from the coffee table and drinks from it. How nice to be together again like this.

He wags a finger at his sister. 'I'm still mad at you though. You shouldn't have lied to me.'

She climbs onto the back of a scooter and blows him a kiss.

Those who play with cats must expect to be scratched.
—Cervantes

The backpack on Lucky Lee's lap

is purring softly as the bus makes its way down a long, dull stretch of road somewhere in the Malaysian state of Johor. Dull is fine by Lucky, who's had a difficult morning and is just relieved to be out of JB. Johor Bahru, a Malaysian friend once told him somewhat proudly, is the armpit of the peninsula—dirty, funky-smelling, a hotbed of petty criminals and cheapskate Singaporeans looking to get a good deal on petrol and seafood dinners. Early, so early, this morning, as he took a different, much bigger bus across the causeway, he was half-frightened to see the volume of traffic on the bridge linking Singapore to its nearest northern neighbour. Buses, cars, vans, motorcycles, all neck to neck and tail to tail, all creeping along the tarmac like some sort of never-ending millipede. So much noise—the sound of hundreds of disgruntled engines kept from going beyond the speed of a pushcart—and so many sour faces staring out of so many vehicles. He tried to be empathetic. Perhaps he, too, would be sour-faced if he had to endure this traffic jam—no, bitumen—

He sends a text, grinning at his own joke. `Was caught in traffic bitumen on the causeway. Nuts!`

—every morning, even before the work day kicked in. And then, to distract himself from his failure at empathy, Lucky tried to look for Coconut on the bridge, but he couldn't see her anywhere. What a big mistake it was to have her walk across the causeway by herself.

Later, as he waited anxiously for her on the Malaysian side, at the bus stop next to the customs checkpoint, he was seized by a further, frenzied anxiety. He was in Malaysia, in the heart of the armpit (okay, rubbish metaphor), and what if Coconut was stuck on the bridge somehow or captured and caged by some zealous customs worker? Oh, maybe he should have just done the proper thing and arranged for her to be quarantined and all of that stuff instead of allowing her to convince him 'it would be much, much, much easier, Lucky, if I just walked over myself. Cats are very good at this.'

People pushed past him, clicking their tongues. *Aiya, these Singaporeans ah, no common sense lah. Standing in the middle of the walkway.* He could sense their disdain for his Japanese organic-indigo-dyed jeans, his limited-edition sneakers, the I Love Langkawi T-shirt he and Pearl were forced to buy in Bali, which he'd finally found tucked in one of his drawers, which he'd hoped would help him blend in with the locals. He would die here, clearly. In this weird-smelling corner of the customs building near the bus stop. Pushed into it by a crowd of impatient Johorians who would spit at his broken body and take all his things.

Stop, he told himself, shaking his head.

His father would have laughed—or would he? The boy from some backwater village in Perak who found his way to Singapore—was he ever afraid of JB? He must have passed through this same customs building, or at least the same site, on his way across the Johor Straits in the opposite direction—the causeway between the two countries is nearly a hundred years old. Maybe he too was frightened of an alien crowd—not that fear or anything approaching weakness was something his father ever freely admitted to.

'Your boy is too soft,' his father announced to his mother, too many times. Like that time when he had to ask them for a bailout when his first business idea didn't quite take off. 'No business sense. And you still gave him the money for that board game company. How to make money with board games? *Cheh.*'

Cheh *yourself. I gave it a good shot—*

So Lucky was mumbling to himself, arguing with a dead man, when Coconut finally appeared, seemingly out of thin air. He scooped her up and put her into his backpack, where he'd made a nest for her out of one of Pearl's T-shirts.

'What took you so long?' he hissed into the bag.

'There was a mouse,' she informed him imperiously.

'I thought something had happened to you!'

She glared up at him. 'Don't be silly, Lucky. I'm a cat. I can take care of myself.'

He glared down at her. 'Well, stay in there and take care of yourself. Go to sleep or something.' And he zipped up the backpack before she could have the last word.

And now Coconut is awake. Meanwhile, his leg has fallen asleep. How much further? Malaysians have a different concept of distance and time, he's discovered. The driver of this tiny unmarked bus told him that the place isn't far—

'*Dekat saja*,' he'd said with a shrug

—but that was nearly an hour ago. *Should have taken a Grab*. But going into his father's old country, he wanted to be brave and intrepid, not soft, not princely, not unworthy of generations of clever, streetwise, hardworking types.

Lucky pats the purring backpack, like people will pat a baby's bottom to lull it to sleep, and looks out the window. The purring intensifies, but the bus is old and the engine sounds like it's digesting itself, so no one can hear her. They turn onto another stretch of road. This is much narrower than the road they were just on, with only one lane of traffic in each direction, and it's starting to feel like the countryside. The light has softened and the cool air blowing through the windows smells like wet leaves. Lucky stares at the trees beyond the edge of the road, tall and wiry and unpruned and heavy, at the lush clutter of plants and shrubs and ferns, scattered wherever they've decided to grow, and the city-dweller in him is disturbed. Whose tree is this, and who will trim that back, and who gets to eat those bananas?

The bus comes to a jerking halt, throwing Lucky forward and interrupting his tree-lined thoughts.

The driver shouts, 'Eh, brother, *kau mau turun tak*?'

Yes! Are they finally here? Lucky jumps up from his seat, waving wildly. 'Yes! Okay!' What a thing to ask—of course he wants to get off this heaving contraption.

He's the only one who does. And then, as the bus drives off, spitting and creaking, Lucky wonders if the driver has made a mistake. There's nothing next to the road, not even a sign for the bus stop. Across the road, there's a large grassy field that stretches on and on and on, punctuated only by a few clusters of coconut trees in the distance.

Coconut! He unzips his bag and peeps in at her. 'You okay?'

'Where are we?' She stares up at him from her T-shirt nest. 'It's warm in here.'

'I'm looking around. You stay in there and think happy thoughts.' He zips up the bag but leaves a little gap for ventilation.

He tries to check his location on Google Maps, but his phone isn't getting a signal. Lucky sighs. There's nothing to do but start walking. So he does, wishing he had dressed for this. How, though? It's warm, he's starting to sweat, and his shirt is sticking to him and the jeans feel like a portable sauna and the mosquitoes have started to bite. So the perfect outfit would have been, what, his underwear and a cloud of insect repellent? Meixi would enjoy putting up a photo of him like that on Instagram: 'My boss thinks he's too hot for clothes #OOTD #bossesbecrazy.'

And why hadn't he packed any snacks? He just assumed that there would be someplace to eat, somewhere, by the time hunger struck. *Stupid Singaporean.* Lucky rounds a bend and is rewarded by the sight of a dirt track leading off the road and through a cluster of trees. He can't see where it leads, but it's wide enough for a truck. Is this it? He trudges down the track, head and shoulders bent from the weight of his backpack. *This better be it.*

Luckily for Lucky Lee, it is it. But the universe makes him walk another two hundred metres down the dirt track to muddy up his sneakers before it offers him a sign.

Nailed to a tree and made of what looks like part of an old crate, it reads, Tiger's Eye Coffee. The thick red arrow drawn under these words points in the direction in which Lucky is walking, and for this he would have kissed the ground if he had the energy to take his backpack off, put it down, get on his knees, then stand up again and heave the beast back on. Lucky misses his trolley suitcase so, so much.

But of course it would have been stupid (and gross), dragging a trolley through all of this.

Plodding on, wishing now that he had called ahead to maybe warn someone of his visit, Lucky emerges from a cluster of trees and overgrown vegetation, through a gate and into a wide, wide plantation stretching far into the distance on both sides of the dirt track. He stops and stares. Thick and straight, rows and rows of dark, tough-looking plants.

Coffee. My god.

So this is what it looks like, in real life. He can recognize the plants from all the websites, all the photos he's seen over the years, but the actual sight of them . . . incredible. In the truest sense of the word. Lucky touches a leaf, unable to believe how big it is—it makes his hand look like a child's. He's always thought of coffee plants as small and shrub-like, perhaps coming up to his waist, but these . . . these *trees* are all taller than he is, with dense foliage and coarse, muscular-looking branches. Clusters of pink and red cherries hang from the branches like bunches of fat grapes—again, much, much larger than the coffee cherries in his mind. He'd believe it if someone told him that these trees went to the gym.

'Can I come out now?'

He jumps. He keeps forgetting about her. Letting the cat out of the bag, he tells her not to wander off. 'It's a jungle out here.' But of course she doesn't listen—she heads straight to a tree and sniffs it, then begins sharpening her claws on its trunk.

Just as he's about to lift her off the tree, there comes the rumble of an engine from behind them, and Lucky turns to find a motorcycle heading up the path. The rider waves and stops. 'Hey! Going up to the factory?'

'Yes.' He struggles to lift Coconut as she digs her claws into the tree.

The woman on the motorcycle giggles. Under the helmet, her face is plump and smiling, a little shiny with sweat. 'Get on. I'll give you a lift.'

She waits for him to get on the back of her motorcycle, cooing at Coconut as Lucky holds her firmly in his arms. And off they go—purring over the wind, squinting against the sunlight, whizzing past rows and rows and rows of coffee trees. Shaking his hair out of his face, Lucky grins, suddenly excited. It's like being in a movie. Something set in a hot, lush, tropical paradise, something like . . . *King Kong*?

'Looking for work?'

'No. Just visiting.' Lucky has to lean his bare head close to her helmeted one to speak. Now he feels like the breathy heroine of a speed thriller. *King Kong* meets *Fast & Furious*? He'd see that movie.

The road begins to snake, and he has to adjust his position behind her as she whips right, then left, making sure he leans along with her in the same direction. The air around them cools abruptly as they enter a shady stretch of overgrown, uncleared land.

As the rider dips left and Lucky follows suit without needing to think about it, he can hear Pearl announcing, 'If you can't figure out how to ride with me, I'm leaving you behind.'

Jogjakarta, maybe fifteen years ago. Their first trip to Indonesia, her first time riding a motorcycle on Indonesian roads. She'd just got her license and she'd bought a sweet little Vespa she trotted out whenever it went along with her outfit, but this was Jogja and a rented bike and not a sweet little Vespa in sweet little Singapore, and she was nervous as fuck but determined to be able to say she'd ridden to Borobudur, no sweat.

No sweat. Please. Lucky nearly laughs out loud, but another set of curves snatches the laugh away and forces him to focus on the roads.

Pearl was a sweaty nightmare from the moment they got on the back of their rented motorcycle—tense, irritable, anxious. And Lucky, watching her, forced into the role of navigator, became tense, irritable, anxious. It was a time before smartphones, wayyyyy before Google Maps was a glint in its maker's eye, and for Lucky, this meant having to deal with his sister's rubbish, arrogant riding while keeping his balance while holding onto a flapping map while trying to give directions from it. To top things off, his helmet was too big and kept flopping backwards or, worse, forwards, knocking into Pearl's.

'Fuckface! Fucking cut it out!' she yelled, turning her head slightly so that he could have the full force of her raised voice.

It was barely 4.00 a.m., and they both needed coffee. But they weren't going to get it until five hours later, after they reached Borobudur for the sunrise, sighed and gushed over it, taken their photographs, and finally sat down to breakfast in the resort-style coffee house set aside solely for foreigners in return for the exorbitant entry fee. And so, when his helmet flopped forward with a loud smack against hers somewhere on a skinny country road, just before they hit the hill-hugging stretch that would lead them to the temple, it was a coffee-deprived Pearl who stopped the bike, got off, and smacked Lucky across his helmeted head with enough force to send him reeling backwards.

Furious, clutching his head, he got off, prepared for a screaming duel by the roadside while the dull yellow moon watched and laughed. But, to his amazement, she sank down to the road, squatting by the bike with her toes pointing outwards, comical for a moment. And then she began to cry. And cry, and cry, loud and open-mouthed and ugly. In the end, it was Lucky who got them to the base of Borobudur, where they parked their dew-dipped bike under a tree and climbed up to the top of the temple, where she held his hand and didn't say thank you. But later, at the coffee house, while he sat down at a glass-and-rattan table and plotted their route back to the hotel, she fetched him three rounds of fruit and coffee, and she didn't protest when he wanted to eat mie ayam at the same stall twice in a row on the same day.

Lucky takes a deep breath and blinks, marvelling at how quickly they're progressing through the Tiger's Eye Coffee estate and yet how far they seem to be from their destination—he still can't see the factory. Damn Malaysians with their misleading, self-deprecating chit-chat. He remembers Kassim on the phone, describing his plantation as 'a small place only, not that many trees, easy to manage . . . and we have a very small factory, where we process the coffee ourselves'. Small? Bah! They've been riding for at least five minutes now.

The rider turns her head slightly towards him, raising her voice over the engine. 'Have you been here before? The coffee here is good.'

'First time!' Lucky shouts back. 'But I've tried the coffee. Delicious!' He gives her a thumbs-up as their eyes meet in a side-view mirror. '*Sedap sekali!*' He's heard Pearl say this about a thousand times in Indonesia, and thankfully it does the trick here too. The woman beams at him.

When, at last, they reach the factory, Lucky's given strange looks by the men milling about outside. *Who is this fellow*, they want to know but don't ask. *Definitely not a worker, not with those shoes.* Lucky greets them all in his rudimentary Malay, smiling, nodding, hand raised, so self-assured they assume he must be the boss's friend. One of them puts out a half-smoked cigarette. Oblivious to the attention, Lucky walks into the high-ceilinged, whitewashed factory. Weaving his way past various sorting and packing rooms, he walks across the factory floor, past some sort of showroom and a few offices, and out through a wide doorway. At least a dozen drying beds, all elevated about a metre off the ground, are laid out behind the main building. Coffee cherries are spread over each one, and as Lucky watches, two workers begin raking through the beans on one of the beds, spreading them out and turning them over to dry them out evenly.

Lucky watches them, mesmerized by the sight of so many red coffee cherries moving in waves, tumbling over each other, stirred out of stillness by the rakes, moving rhythmically through them. Over and over and over again the rakes move through the rippling sea of red, over and over again, and then they stop. The sea turns back into a plain. The workers step off the drying bed and climb onto another, then they start all over again. The sun is higher in the sky now, and the air is hot, the better for drying. Lucky raises a hand to shield his eyes, wondering if it would be weird to put on his sunglasses. The workers pause, pulling their caps lower over their faces, but they don't stop for long. They wear thick gloves of a coarse fabric, but under them, Lucky is sure their hands are rough and worn.

He takes a deep breath, admiring the workers atop their new red sea and the bright green grass he's standing on as he watches them. Beyond the drying beds, rows and rows of coffee plants stretch out into the distance, all the way to the edge of the horizon. Lucky takes another deep breath. How lush all this is, how green and how lush. How invigorating. How wonderful.

A tap on his shoulder makes him turn sharply to his right. No one—how odd. Then, he sees it. There, on his shoulder, menacing and greener than the grass under his feet, is a grasshopper. The biggest, most cruel-looking grasshopper Lucky has ever seen. The only grasshopper he has ever seen up close. There is an explosion, a rush of something—is it his heart or his mind?

He squeals. He flaps his arms. He forgets the workers, the grass, the coffee cherries, the coffee plants. At some point, as he is forced to touch the thing and sweep it off his shoulder, he forgets his name.

* * *

'Coconut! Coconut, help me!'

'Lucky, it's just a grasshopper. Not a snail or a bat.'

'Coconut! Coconut!'

* * *

'Encik Kassim.' The worker pauses. '*Ada orang.*'

Kassim looks up from his laptop. A visitor? Who can it be? The goat compost guy just called and cancelled, and he's not expecting anyone else today. Could it be the new bee fellow? But the worker doesn't know, and Kassim has to leave his office and follow him out of the factory.

'*Sana.*' He points, and Kassim's eyes follow his finger to the long patch of grass near the drying beds.

Is this a dance? A protest? An epileptic fit? The stranger in tight blue jeans is running in tight circles on the grass, arms waving about him in wild, random arcs. He stops suddenly, then starts to slap himself all over in long, sweeping strokes, first arms, then shoulders, thighs, and torso. He seems to be saying something over and over, but from this distance Kassim can't hear him. A little way off sits a small tortoiseshell cat, watching the dancing, waving man. The man turns to the cat (is he calling out to it?) then turns away and begins slapping himself again, still running in circles.

As the man begins to tire, the slaps wind down and the circles tighten until, at last, he's standing still. The cat continues to watch him. Kassim decides it's now safe to approach.

* * *

'You brought your cat?'

The voice behind him sounds amused. Lucky turns to see a man squatting next to Coconut, holding out his hand for her to sniff. Coconut obliges, then lets the man pat her on the head, very, very gently.

'She insisted on coming. Didn't trust me to take care of myself.' What rot! Fat use she was when he was attacked by that insect monster. He frowns. Did this man see him earlier, defending himself against the creature? Lucky hopes he wasn't too loud.

The man laughs, standing up. He's a little shorter than Lucky but looks taller thanks to the quiff he's whipped his hair into. 'All like that lah, cats and women.' He lifts a hand. 'I'm Kassim.'

'Hey, Kassim.' Lucky brightens up. 'I'm Lucky Lee, from Caffiend. In Singapore. We started buying beans from you guys maybe a year ago? We've spoken on the phone.'

'Oh, Lucky!' Kassim takes a step forward, grinning. 'This is so cool—finally!'

He doesn't offer to shake hands. Lucky nods, grinning back. Handshakes, yuck! Unsanitary at best, and so much pressure, sometimes literally. He likes Kassim already. And he likes him even better when the man offers to give him a proper tour, after they have a cup of coffee.

'Must *minum* kopi first lah!' Kassim laughs, the edges of his eyes creasing, as he leads Lucky away from among the drying beds and back into the building. They walk down a corridor, Lucky cuddling Coconut and looking out for grasshoppers, Kassim walking ahead, stopping to point out a few processing machines, including something that looks like a modified tumble-dryer. Kassim tells Lucky that his brother put it together himself.

'My brother's the smart one. I just make the coffee.' He grins. 'And sell it lah.'

They turn a corner and go up a flight of stairs, and suddenly they're in a pantry area of sorts, with slatted windows looking out into the plantation. It's hotter up here on the second floor, but the ceiling fans, creaking from spinning at full speed, provide some relief. Lucky sits down at a table as Kassim heads to the small stove in the corner. From an overhanging shelf, he brings down two aluminium coffee pots with long, thin spouts, each one nearly as big as the watering can that Lucky uses for the vegetable patch. Lucky watches intently as Kassim reaches out and picks up something from a container on the sink. It's the kind of coffee-making sieve Lucky's seen in local coffee shops his entire life, a metal thing like a stiff lasso, trailing a thin cheesecloth 'sock' from its circular mouth.

Oh, wow. The sock. Lucky's never seen anyone outside a kopitiam make coffee with a sock-sieve.

Kassim turns, gesturing with the sieve, wagging his eyebrows. 'You want to do it? You're the pro.'

Lucky stares at Kassim and the pot and the sieve. *Okay. How not to sound like an ass? Or worse, a city hipster.* He tries, smiling sheepishly: 'Sorry, Kassim, I've never made coffee that way.'

'Oh.' The surprise in the other man's face is obvious, but he quickly recovers. 'Ah, never mind lah, you sit down. I'll make the coffee.'

Kassim scoops coffee powder into the sieve and drops it into one of the coffee pots, then pours in hot water from a large kettle. Lucky leans back in his chair and sighs, watching Kassim stir the pot with a wooden stick. Thinking of his vintage espresso machine back home, Lucky feels like a city hipster.

But Kassim doesn't let him feel that way for long. He comes back with two mugs of strong black coffee and then, easily, almost conspiratorially, leads the conversation into friendly, familiar territory. They talk about coffee, growing it, making it; they talk about the cafe business, and Lucky allows himself to whine about decaf soy latte drinkers.

'By the way, this is really good.' Lucky holds up his mug in appreciation.

It's always incredible, no matter how many times he experiences it. The same coffee—the *exact* same coffee, from the same plantation, the same harvest, the same roasting batch—will taste completely different if it's made a different way. At Caffiend, Shawn and Lucky extract from Tiger's Eye coffee a strong, aromatic espresso, or they put it through a French press and get a milder, still-fragrant brew. He's always liked both, but Kassim's old-fashioned method, brought over to Malaya by Hainanese migrants in the nineteenth century, makes a much better cup of coffee—heady, stronger than espresso, with such an intense coffee flavour it makes Lucky's fuzzy head snap awake.

Kassim grins. 'Has to be good, or you're wasting your money, right?'

Lucky thinks about Caffiend's regular shipment from Tiger's Eye. 'True!' He takes another sip. 'You guys do your own roasting, right? This is awesome.'

'We used to, but now I send my coffee to these guys in JB, and I'm trying a new place in KL.'

For much longer than grown men should be allowed to whinge and gripe about coffee and coffee-making, Kassim and Lucky moan about subpar poseur roasteries popping up everywhere: 'the problem is that every idiot returning from Melbourne wants to open a roastery.' Delighted by the discovery of a common enemy, they hurtle on. They tut, they sigh, they commiserate with each other on a variety of subjects: ridiculous snobs who only want arabica, people who think Starbucks is coffee, idiots who think all coffee comes from Brazil. They ask the gods for deliverance: 'Ya Tuhan, how to take this bullshit?', 'An interventionist god could hand out pamphlets.' When Lucky asks for another cup of coffee, Kassim pretends to be outraged.

'Wah, Mr Lee, you come here and drink free . . . but when I go to Singapore, you have to make me as many soy lattes as I want, okay? Decaf. Extra hot. Extra foam. No excuses.'

Laughing, Lucky decides he really likes the guy. At their knees, Coconut seems similarly impressed. She circles their new friend, rubbing her face against his loose-cut jeans. As Kassim stoops to pat her, making little meowing noises, Lucky studies the jeans. They look old and appear actually distressed, stained with dirt and soil and probably coffee, with patches faded from age or sun. The hems are worn down and a little frayed, with bits of grass stuck to the edges. He looks down at his own pair, hand-dyed with organic indigo, crafted by Japanese artisans, distressed by way of being tumbled with sand and rocks in a machine. And of course the man is wearing sensible shoes, dark brown and rubber-soled, and not stupid canvas sneakers designed for walking around in malls.

Better get new shoes in Kuala Lumpur.

* * *

'Why are the stars brighter here?'

'The stars aren't brighter here. They're the same.' Lucky crosses his arms. He's forgotten how cold it can be at night in the countryside. 'But they look brighter because the city lights aren't getting in the way.'

'It's like how I look bigger when you're not around.'

'Yah. Exactly like that.'

'Okay. I want you to stand a little further away whenever there's a bird around. Or a squirrel.'

It's pitch black outside. Lucky, in all his years of travel, in all his years of gallivanting across Java and the toe of Italy and the Costa del Sol in pursuit of seaside resorts and food and wine and beer, has never seen such a darkness. But here it is, in the middle of a coffee plantation in Johor, and he's surprised by what a comfort it is. An invitation to oblivion.

Coconut and Lucky should be on their way to Kuala Lumpur by now, but instead they're standing on the verandah of the house Kassim has offered them for the night, somewhere between the factory and the edge of the estate where Lucky and Coconut first entered Tiger's Eye. Built mostly for nights when Kassim would rather not drive back to his home in Skudai, the plantation guest house is small and sparsely furnished. But Lucky's thrilled to be spending the evening here instead of on some bus to KL.

Coconut's tail brushes against his leg as she walks past him. 'I'm going for a walk. You stay here and keep safe and don't wander around.'

Lucky laughs as she bounds into the darkness. She can be so patronizing. He steps inside the house, shuts the door, and turns on the light. He checks his phone. Still no signal—and it's only 9.24 p.m. He sits down at the tiny table in the kitchen and rummages in his backpack for Pearl's notebooks. Might as well get some work done—he's still wired from all the coffee he's had today, too wired to be sluggish from the too-large dinner of fried tofu, tempeh, and sup kambing.

He opens a notebook to a page he's marked with a small Post-it. Her large, loopy script jumps out:

> Most coffee grown in Malaysia is liberica, which most people never hear of because they're thinking of obvious, more famous varietals like arabica and robusta
> → check if Indonesia and Vietnam grow liberica. So far haven't heard of any. Maybe the Philippines?
> → coffee plantations mostly in Johor, a few starting out in Sarawak

To this, in the margins, Lucky adds: 'Liberica doesn't need the elevation or the lower highland temperatures and humidity, unlike arabica.' And, rather proudly: 'Origin: Liberia. Also grown in Brazil and Colombia.' Kassim's been a great smiling fount of information.

His thoughts travel back to that morning, to the coffee plants he saw. Those leaves! He writes another note: 'Also, liberica plants are monstrous. About 6m? More than three times as large as the average arabica plant.'

He writes on, grinning: 'Much taller than Lucky, and certainly Pearl.'

The last kopi for the road

is cold. Kassim pours it out of a glass jug into a glass cup. The bottom of the jug is murky with sediment, but the liquid at the top is a clear, bright brown. Rather like tea, actually, Lucky thinks. He takes a sip, then holds up his glass against the light of the showroom window. What a pretty colour it is, almost crystalline.

Kassim looks at him expectantly, somehow managing to be gleeful and embarrassed at the same time. 'So, what do you think?'

Lucky takes another sip. 'Surprisingly strong flavour for something so light-coloured. I like it.' It tastes exactly the way it smells—earthy, intense, fruity. He smacks his lips. 'Is it weird that I'm tasting lychee?'

'Some people taste lychee. Others say it's more like a berry.' Kassim pours out a glass for himself. 'It's actually made from used coffee grinds. After I make coffee, I take out the grinds and steep them in purified water, and the next day . . . this!' He holds up his glass.

Lucky nods, reminding himself to write this down somewhere later. They've never reused grinds at Caffiend, except during that mushroom fiasco, and that wasn't even about coffee any more. But this—this is worth looking into. This secondary coffee drink is like a cold brew, but lighter, more tea-like. Lucky sniffs it. 'Smells a bit herbal.'

'No herbs at all, but the nose . . . it makes a lot of strange connections. Sometimes my wife says she can smell durian in the coffee!'

They laugh. It's nearly eleven, and they've spent the earlier part of the morning pottering around Kassim's showroom. 'No one ever comes here, but I had to have one,' he tells Lucky. Looking around

215

at the random but lovingly arranged collection of books, pamphlets, coffee specimens, photographs, vintage coffee pots and grinders, Lucky is beginning to feel like he would like a showroom too. Maybe with a little laboratory attached? Maybe his father's study . . .

'That was my grandfather's.'

'Hmm?' Lucky has absently picked up a small pear-shaped grinder, made of brass and intricately carved with spiky leaves and curling tendrils. He runs a finger over the carvings, marvelling at the detail. Where the stalk of the pear would be is a slender arm with a carved knob for turning. 'Beautiful.'

Kassim takes it from him and gently takes its two halves apart. He holds it up for Lucky to see inside. 'Handmade, can you imagine?'

Lucky cannot, so he just stares at the grinder's internal system of gears and burrs. 'Insane.'

'Totally.' Kassim nods. 'My grandfather's friend got it for him in Istanbul. You ever tried Turkish coffee? The coffee needs to be ground really, really fine to brew it like that. Most electric grinders out there today can't grind as well as this little one here.'

'Really?'

Kassim laughs. 'You go home and try!' he challenges with a smirk. 'Difficult lah. Espresso is one thing, but the grind that comes out of this is like *dust*.'

Lucky raises his eyebrows. A proper espresso grind is like fine sand, grainy to touch, only achievable with a good grinder. The grind he uses for his Vietnamese phin is much, much coarser. 'Dust? Really?' He feels a little silly for saying 'really' again, but it's popped out of his brain then out his mouth before he can think of a better question.

To show Lucky what he means, Kassim grinds a bit of coffee in the old brass grinder. It takes much longer than Lucky expects, nearly twice the time it would have taken for his own hand grinder at home to get through the same amount of coffee for the phin.

'My god.' Lucky pinches the result with his fingers. It's so, so fine, so soft. *Dust*. This would just pass through the holes in a phin filter. This would escape the metal mesh of any French press.

The next moment Kassim is insisting on making a round of Turkish coffee, mixing the freshly ground coffee powder with water and bringing it to a gentle boil on the small portable stove in one corner of the room. As they drink the coffee in an easy, comfortable silence, Lucky's heart begins to pump as if it's a creature in its own right. He stares at the tiny cup of black, sugary coffee in his hand. *Talk about strong.* It's so viscous, so syrupy, that the act of consuming it feels as much like eating as it does drinking. Lucky smacks his lips, feeling the fine coffee grinds coat his tongue and teeth. It's certainly different. While most other coffees are an infusion of flavour imparted by grind to water, the fine grind in Turkish coffee is in eternal suspension. He smiles, thinking that he might add this to the Caffiend menu. Might be fun. Much more fun because Shawn will absolutely hate it. Lucky grins.

Kassim sees the grin and returns it. 'Good stuff, right?' Then he looks at his watch and sighs. 'We should probably leave soon. You ready to go?'

Lucky nods. 'All packed. And I think Coconut's ready.'

Coconut is at the window, balancing on her hind legs, her front paws pressed against the glass. She mews, swiping at the glass. Lucky rolls his eyes. There's probably a bird out there or a hundred. If he were a bird, he'd live on a coffee plantation. Waking up this morning, surrounded by all those coffee trees, the sun just peeking through them, he thought he could stay here forever. Even now, Lucky is sorely tempted to ask Kassim if they may spend another night, but he doesn't. Better to just get on with it—who knows how long he'll stay here, given the chance? He can imagine himself in ten years, still hanging around Tiger's Eye, poking at things, drinking Turkish coffee.

'Who's that,' people would ask.

'Don't know. One day, he just showed up and never left.'

The drive through the plantation is dull. Lucky finds himself wishing for the motorcycle ride of the morning before. Inside Kassim's four-wheel-drive, the dirt road feels too smooth, too easy; the curves too tame, too polite. That heady sense of being part of a tropical-jungle film is gone, too, with air conditioning on and the windows up. In the back seat, Coconut, lulled by the gentle bounce of their cushy ride, has curled up for a nap.

Kassim takes a peek at her in the rear-view mirror. 'Such a good cat. So well behaved.'

'My sister's cat, actually.'

'And your sister's okay with you bringing it with you all the way here?' Kassim grins as he swerves to avoid a hole in the track.

'She's dead.' Lucky tries to say this matter-of-factly but ends up sounding rather cheerful. 'So now I'm taking care of her cat.'

Kassim clicks his teeth. 'Sorry, sorry.' He reaches out and claps Lucky on the shoulder. 'You were close?'

'Yah. We were.' And then, without quite knowing why, he is telling Kassim about the crash, about the three months he spent at home waiting in front of the television, about eating nothing but keropok and popcorn and dried squid and always forgetting what day it was, and about how relieved he was when he didn't have to wait any more, and yet . . . 'I felt so lost when I realized she was never coming back. Like I had missed a turn or something and ended up in some weird unknown country.' The moment he says it, he knows this is the truest summary of how he's felt since Dinah called that morning to tell him about the crash. He sighs. 'Honestly? I'm still a bit lost.'

Lucky looks out the window, at the dark green leaves and the bright sunlight winking through them, at the red-pink cherries and the brown-black soil. He's liked it so much here, and he wishes he hadn't said anything so morose and so personal and so bloody tiring now that he's leaving.

'My father died seven years ago.' Kassim checks the side mirrors, then makes a big sweeping turn into a wide road. Suddenly, theirs isn't the only car on the road any more. An old blue bus zooms past in the opposite direction, then a small lorry carrying crates of chickens. They've ended up behind an impossibly slow-moving van, but Kassim doesn't bother to overtake it. 'I'm better, of course lah, seven years is a long time. But it's not the same . . . it's not the same world any more, you know?'

No. No, it's not.

* * *

'I have to head back, but you take care, yah? Come back anytime and bring the cat too.' With a wave, his head thrown back, his quiff holding steady in the light breeze, Kassim is off.

Lucky stares after him, a little envious (of Kassim) and a little afraid (of the Malaysian railway company, KTM). But lunch has been had and the tickets have been bought, and there's nothing to do now but wait for the train and get on it like a good boy. Man. And cat.

They're at the railway station in sleepy Segamat, somewhere in the northern part of Johor. Lucky has never been here, and if Kassim hadn't decided to deposit them at this particular station, he may never have counted Segamat among the places he's seen. Not that he's seen very much of it—the town centre he's just been driven through, with its dusty, tired-looking main street and small, half-hearted shops, is only a tenth of the area of the entire district, and Kassim has told him that Segamat proper is bigger than Singapore.

'Your country very small lah,' he remarked cheekily, grinning, holding his thumb and forefinger about a centimetre apart.

While Lucky checks the train route again, still amazed at how vast the state of Johor is and at how ignorant of this he's been his entire bloody life, Coconut heads straight for the nearest platform. There are only two, one on their side of the tracks and one on the other. 'Selatan,' reads the sign on the opposite platform. South? That would be towards JB and Singapore. They're already on the right platform, then. Nice. Well, no wonder Kassim said there was no way of getting lost.

To call the platform minimalist would be an act of equivocation. Three wooden benches, very old, and an abandoned soft drink can are all that stands between the concrete structure and the word 'empty'. Coconut investigates the half-crushed can and quickly returns to Lucky's side, mewing in complaint. Lucky doesn't pick her up or speak to her. He's already told her that their best bet for getting into the train unnoticed is for her to pretend to be a stray cat for now. Not that anyone cares—the few people waiting for the train with them haven't even looked Coconut's way. She, on the other hand, appears to be studying them keenly.

If she could catch them and eat them, she would. Lucky's sure of this. He's seen that look on her face before when she was eyeing birds in the garden. It's some sort of killer instinct, according to that cat website, and it's not even about hunger. Cats just want to kill things. He's still not sure how he feels about this, sharing his home and sometimes his bed with a natural born killer.

Half an hour later, as the train pulls out of the station exactly, unexpectedly, on time, Lucky peeks into his backpack to check on the packet of nasi lemak Kassim insisted he take with him on the train. And what a nasi lemak it was.

They'd turned off into a small street just before entering the small town centre of Segamat and at a tiny makeshift shack under a huge rain tree, they had the best nasi lemak Lucky has ever had the fortune to breathe upon. The coconut rice was fresh and unbelievably fluffy; the sambal tasted of freshly pounded chilli and onions and lemongrass and other magical things. Topped with a boiled egg and a bit of fried fish. The best nasi lemak in the universe.

'In Johor, maybe lah.' Kassim looked so amused at Lucky's exuberant praise that he conveyed it in Malay to the makcik running the stall. As the old woman descended on Lucky with an extra helping of the sambal ikan bilis, he laughed. 'Next time you come back, I'll bring you here. And you can ask Mak Tijah if you can marry her daughter.'

What makes a man so cool that he can say that and make it sound like the funniest thing in the world? Or at least in Johor. And that thing he said, when Lucky asked him why the family plantation is called Tiger's Eye . . .

'What kind of question is that? "Eye of the Tiger" is a good song, what.'

Lucky snickers, looking out the window. And then, as the train rolls slowly past a village school next to a lush, green field, then a pond, dotted with small children tramping at its edges, he sighs. Isn't this the life, he thinks admiringly. Where's his interventionist god now? Why not pick him up and plonk him down here, in the Johor countryside? Lucky imagines himself wandering around, foraging for food, and sleeping in the open, quite forgetting his aversion to mud and puddles and snails and bats and other things lurking in the great, grassy outdoors. And all the grasshoppers.

They get off and switch trains at Gemas, where things are less minimalist, much dirtier, and crowded. *So* much more crowded.

All manner of people are on the platform, some with screaming children in tow, others with bundles and parcels and boxes and sacks. Most people get into the third-class carriages, where seats are half the price but exactly like the ones in the second-class carriages except for the tiny pull-down table behind every seat in second class—which is why only noobs end up in KTM's second class. Lucky, having bought his ticket just hours before, is a first-rate noob.

Two prizes for the noob, however. Lucky has managed to secure a window seat in the centre of the carriage, which comes with an actual table fixed to the wall and shared with three other seats. The only other person in the carriage is an elderly man with a pile of newspapers who takes a seat as far away from Lucky as possible, so as the train pulls out of the station and they're safely on their way at last to KL, Lucky lets Coconut out of the backpack.

She hops onto the table and presses her nose up against the window. 'Lucky, it's the sea.' Softly, so only he can hear.

He follows her gaze out the window. The train is chugging very slowly over a bridge, and their view is filled by an expanse of grey water and greyer sky. 'That's a river.' He stares at it, riveted as only people who don't grow up around rivers can be riveted.

'It looks like the sea.'

'True, lots of water. But rivers are much, much smaller.'

They move closer to the window, their noses making little patches of condensation on the cold glass.

'Fish?'

'Lots, but not the same kind.' That's true, isn't it? Except for salmon, which manage to turn into freshwater fish during breeding season—pretty fucking creepy.

Lucky and Coconut continue to stare at the river. It looks so still from this distance that even the boats on its surface look like they've been glued on. Everything is so, so grey. Lucky wishes it were sunnier.

A little later, as the train moves past the river, then through a long, long stretch of paddy fields, he gets his wish. The sky turns a pale, bright blue. The sun, coming out from behind the clouds, is almost sharp now, and the young rice plants go from a dull green to a vivid, almost virulent hue. A group of farmers walk through the water-logged fields, bending often, standing up again, almost mechanical in their movements. Clearly, this is something they've done over and over and over and over. The sun beats down on them, lighting up their faces and their clothes, but it doesn't stop them or slow them down. But in his air-conditioned carriage, Lucky wishes he hadn't wished for more sunshine.

* * *

'Ticket, ticket, ticket, ticket.'

So there *is* a conductor! It's been more than half an hour since he boarded, and he's come to assume that the Malaysian railway is a bit of a free-for-all-if-you-dare situation. Lucky sits up, reaching into his pocket for his ticket. He has two, one for the Segamat–Gemas leg and the other for Gemas-KL. Coconut is hurriedly pushed into the backpack just as the conductor walks up, her hole-puncher clicking reflexively, her ill-fitting bright blue uniform rustling in the way only flammable synthetics can.

'Ticket.' She says the word like it's 'hello', with an official-looking smile and matching nod.

Lucky presents his ticket, suddenly nervous for no good reason. He's got the correct tickets, yes? He's on the right train, yes? Suddenly, it feels like a million things could go wrong now. Eyes wide, he watches the conductor check his ticket. 'All okay?'

She returns his ticket, now punctured through its top right-hand corner. 'Okay.' She adjusts the little pouch she wears around her waist (what does she keep in there? Money from fines? Her phone? Snacks?) and turns to leave the carriage.

'Meow.'

The conductor whirls around to stare at Lucky, whose eyelids have reached their limits of elasticity. Perhaps Coconut senses this—she chooses this moment to poke her head out of his backpack.

'Meow.' And when the conductor looks at her in disbelief, she yawns.

The conductor turns to Lucky. '*Kucing kau?*'

Lucky understands enough Malay to know she's asking if the cat is his, and he decides to lie. 'Not my cat. Found it in Gemas.'

'But now your cat?' She bends forward to take a closer look. Coconut mews and climbs out of the bag, then stretches for the conductor's benefit. She yawns again, flashing her teeth and curling her little pink tongue. Then she sits up straight, looking first at Lucky, then at the conductor.

'Meowrrrrr.' *What a good cat am I.*

Lucky's mind races for a story to tell. 'Poor thing, wandering around the station. So I'm bringing her to KL to live with me and my sister. *Kesian*, right?' He hopes the word 'kesian' will force the woman to contemplate the hopeless lives of unfortunate stray cats everywhere. But why did he mention a sister? *Ah, damn you, Pearl.* Always, always, she lurks on the edge of his mind.

Coconut mews again, walking across the table towards the conductor. Lucky can't help but smile. God, that confident swagger. That unyielding self-belief. If he had a tenth of that, he'd be king of the world. Or at least want to be.

'Eh, *cutenya*.' It's taken less than a minute for the woman to fall under Coconut's spell. She reaches out and pats the little cat on the head and is rewarded by Coconut rubbing her face against her palm. 'So cute.' Done.

'Okay lah.' She pats Coconut again, smiling like a child. 'But you better take care of this cat, okay? So clever, so cute.' More pats for Coconut before she walks away, shaking her head, another anecdote tucked away for the entertainment of friends and family.

Lucky sinks back into his seat. 'You're a bad cat, Coconut.' But he's grinning like a monkey as he says it.

* * *

'See that? That's a mountain.'

'Looks small.'

'That's because it's far away.'

'Or because it's small.' She yawns.

Lucky rolls his eyes. *Behold—Coconut, the cat that made a molehill out of a mountain.*

* * *

The train canteen is small and cramped, but there's coffee to be had.

It's foul-tasting, foul-smelling, and looks like drain water, but it might keep him awake until they reach KL. Lucky yawns. When Kassim told him that it was just a short train ride, he thought it might be two hours at the very most. But it's been nearly four, including a very, very long stop at a place called Tampin. Routine train checks, another passenger told him. No one seemed surprised.

He looks out the window from the tiny table he's sharing with three other men, all busy staring at their phones. It's nearly five. The afternoon sun hasn't dimmed, but it's developed a golden tint. Squinting, Lucky takes another sip of his lukewarm coffee. *Isn't it odd?* He finds himself returning over and over again to the scene beyond the window earlier, to the rice farmers working under the sun. It's odd how in the other places he's been to, in Japan and Korea and throughout Europe, sunlight is a prized commodity, accessible mainly to the rich and rich enough to afford balcony space and south-facing rooms and coffee on terraces, and when he was there he too had chased the sun. But here in Malaysia, and in Singapore and Vietnam and Indonesia, it's the poor who stand in the sun.

And really, it could be him in the sun, couldn't it, instead of here in this train? It could be him living out there, working in the paddy fields, instead of making coffee in his cafe, sleeping in his large dramatic house guarded by lions. What if he had been born here, wherever this is, or in Segamat or Gemas? What would he be then? Who would he be?

One of the men at the table reaches out and draws a tired-looking curtain across the window. Instantly, the glare is reduced by half. Lucky blinks in the sudden shade. The other men nod in approval. Then they all return to their phones.

* * *

Coconut is gone. He's only been away for twenty minutes—fine, maybe twenty-five—and that horrible little cat has run off. He looks in the backpack again, just to make sure. Yes, she's gone. Of course he should have taken her with him to the canteen, but she was sleeping and he didn't want to wake her, and of course now everything is going to hell. Hell. Hell is other people. Someone very wise said that—Lucky can't remember who. Some French fellow. But hell is also a cat. *The devil* is a cat.

Where the hell is that little devil?

He walks through the carriage, checking all the seats, calling her name, equally anxious and angry. 'Coconut, Coconut.' *Jesus.* He's supposed to be on a superhero journey, not playing nursemaid to a cat. Good thing the only other passenger in their carriage got off at the last station.

And so when the automatic door opens a few minutes later—whoosh!—and Coconut trots in with her tail in the air, Lucky strides through the aisle like a moody 1980s rock star and meets her with a scowl. 'Bad cat.'

She looks up at him. 'Why do you say that?' She looks so small. He feels so relieved.

'Because you are.' He picks her up and walks back to his seat. 'You're a bad cat.'

'You keep calling me that, but there's no such thing as a bad cat, Lucky.' She shoots him a glare, then goes limp so that he has to struggle to hold her as she flops about like an eel. A furry stubborn cat-shaped eel.

Back at their seat, he asks her where she's been. She tells him she's been keeping Nadia company, and that Lucky should go keep her company too. 'She's nice. Soft hands.' Coconut hops onto the table and assumes a sphinx-like position. 'Smells nice too.'

'Who's Nadia?'

Coconut makes an impatient sound. 'The nice girl who was here earlier. The one who called me special.' She sounds smug.

Ah, the conductor. Lucky raises an eyebrow. Trust Coconut to go seeking attention elsewhere just because he was off getting coffee. 'Fine. So, you're special. *I'm* special.' He turns his head to look out the window. 'God, I hope we get there soon. I'm starving again.'

Coconut stands up and walks towards him, then rubs her face against his cheek, purring. Lucky feels the urge to purr back. 'Lucky, why don't you have a mate?'

Lucky moves his head away. *What?* 'What?'

'People have mates, right? Even that silly man with the bowl in front of his house.'

'Dr Chan. And that's a fountain. I've told you this.'

'He has a new mate.'

Lucky laughs. What a little gossip. And it's true—Dr Chan remarried last month, and the new Mrs Chan is the talk of the neighbourhood.

'Agnes not even cold in her grave, and he marries this China woman,' he heard Mrs Rajah tell Mrs Khoo at the market. They were all at the fish stall. Lucky wished he could come back another time, but he had to get his shopping done before his shift at the cafe.

Mrs Khoo was quick to pour petrol on the fire. 'Yah! Men are like that lah. All of them.'

Mrs Rajah prodded a large red snapper with a sly face. 'To think of all those years she cooked and cleaned for him. Ironed his clothes. Raised his children. And now he's prancing about everywhere with a woman half his age.'

'Disgraceful.'

The red snapper was flipped over. '*Disgraceful*,' Mrs Rajah echoed with emphasis, giving the fish a firm poke. She waved to the fishmonger's wife. 'This one, *kak*.'

'So disgraceful.' Standing as far away from the two women as possible, trying not to listen, trying in vain to get the fishmonger's wife's attention, Lucky was beginning to wonder if Mrs Khoo knew any other words she could use on Dr Chan. She did: 'Ridiculous. And yet so predictable, right?' She picked out three large white squid. 'The trouble with men is that they're all . . .' She suddenly spotted Lucky and gave him a hard stare. 'Useless. With one-track minds.'

'Obsessed with breasts. Have you seen how that woman dresses? Like a cheap karaoke tart.'

'Oh my god. Necklines all down to *here*.' Mrs Khoo lays a hand, knife-like, against her solar plexus.

'Disgraceful.'

'*Disgraceful.*'

Lucky's mother had been friends with the old Mrs Chan. She used to come over often when his mother was still alive, and they'd sit in the kitchen and talk for hours, over endless cups of tea. As a child, Lucky often thought they were so different. One slogging for hours over housework and children, stealing time away just to have tea with a neighbour and talk about her housework and her children; one forever wandering listlessly through her home, arranging and rearranging furniture, reading and rereading her favourite novels, planting and replanting bougainvillaea, smiling benevolently at her children from time to time. She was what Pearl used to call 'vaguely mum-like', her maternal instinct only kicking in when they were ill or in trouble or, in Pearl's case, being what she called rude and troublesome. Pearl used to fight with her all the time—maybe for the attention? Lucky never really thought about it, but it seems likely.

'If that man can get a mate, so can you, Lucky. You're tall, and girls like that, right?' Coconut looks at him encouragingly. 'Nadia smells *very* nice.'

Oh, please, no. Coconut trying to set him up? Beyond ludicrous. 'Coconut.' He picks her up and sets her down in front of him. 'I'm fine without a mate,' he tells her firmly. 'I don't need one, okay?'

The cat begins to clean her face, but she keeps her eyes on him. 'But don't you want a mate, Lucky? That bossy, grumpy one—what about her?'

Dinah? 'Bossy, grumpy one' is pretty reductive but cats must speak their truth, yes? He grins, wishing he could tell Dinah and watch her growl. 'Nonsense. Dinah and I are good friends.' *Even if I'm not speaking to her. Meddlesome cow.*

'Nadia smells very nice.'

'Coconut, go to sleep.'

'*You* go to sleep.'

Lucky sticks out his tongue at her, and Coconut ignores him.

'Maybe if you sniffed her for yourself ...' She turns towards the door.

God, how persistent. How infuriating. How . . . like Pearl. Argh. And yet . . .

Pearl had never tried to set him up. His sister could be a pain and a pushy busybody and a lot of other things, but she stayed out of his hair when it came to women. When Chinese New Year rolled along every year and the aunties asked their stupid questions and dropped their lousy hints about how maybe it was time for him to find someone to raise a brood of brats with, it was always Pearl who jumped to his aid. Pearl, whom the aunties were a little afraid of, whose love life and marital status were never up for discussion.

'Hey, let him take his time, okay?' She would dart out from behind a pillar or a cousin, brandishing a slice of cake or kueh or honeyed bak kwa. 'Too many stupid, spoilt women out there. Lucky isn't just going to drag home some random weirdo and have babies with her because you're all bored.'

And the aunties would exchange loaded looks and grudgingly change the subject, and he'd be safe for another year.

Coconut looks cross. 'Maybe you didn't need a mate *then*. Maybe you need one *now*.'

Lucky laughs. 'You're watching too much garbage TV.'

Coconut swats his nose lightly with a paw. 'We'll find you a mate and then we'll both watch less TV. But she has to smell nice.'

Before Lucky can think up a retort, she turns to the window and presses her paws against it. She mews. 'Lucky, what's all this?'

Lucky looks up and out. They've gone underground and into a long, bright tunnel. The train has slowed down to travelator speed and is still slowing down. And then it stops, suddenly but more gently than Lucky will ever expect from a train, and as he and Coconut watch from their window, people pour out of the train and onto the platform and the unnecessary but inevitable battle for the lifts and escalators begins.

'We're here, Coconut!'

It is a city named for mud, his father once told him, but all Lucky can see for now are white lights and polished, gleaming linoleum. And a bright blue arrow next to the escalator pointing up, up, up.

Well, hello, Kuala Lumpur.

The rain

comes in with the tall, thin man, sheets of it dripping off him and onto the dark carpet of the hotel lobby. The heavy glass door swings shut behind him and the receptionist looks up, her expression a well-practised mixture of politeness and disinterest. Of course, they were more accustomed to a more illustrious, certainly more chauffeured, certainly better dressed variety of guest, but there were all sorts, weren't there? But there was a vague *something* about this man that still signified to her that he was the right sort, something about the cut of his jeans and the way that ratty T-shirt hung on him, something about the backpack that suggested a great deal of money had been spent on that oddly shaped, oversized piece of canvas. And most of all she could tell from the way he walked in, dripping water and unashamed, that *he* didn't feel out of place.

'Good evening, sir.'

Pushing his hair out of his face, the man launches straight into friendish chatter. 'Wow. That rain! Nuts! I spent two hours trying to get a cab at KL Sentral.'

Before the receptionist can make a suitably polite, disinterested reply, the night porter comes running in through the door, all apologies and sad face. Unlike the receptionist's, the night porter's money-radar is an unrefined machine built by nouveau riche Chinese and pompous Arab millionaires. As a result, he ignored the tall, thin man because he didn't come in a car or taxi, because he had dared to walk. So, obviously a backpacker. But now that the backpacker has walked right into the lobby and straight to the counter, the porter realizes he must quickly compensate for his lack of attention.

He reaches out and takes hold of the man's backpack. It's surprisingly dry—waterproof? 'Sorry, sir, may I take your bag?'

The man himself is wet through. He waves the porter off. 'No, it's fine, it's fine.'

'Please, sir, I didn't realize you were coming inside . . .'

'Oh, no, no, please, I'm just happy to carry it myself.'

The receptionist checks her list. Only one guest left for today, a Mr Lucky Lee. She raises her eyebrows a couple of millimetres. What a funny name.

'Mr Lucky Lee?'

'That's right.'

The reservation is for one of the nicer rooms, with its own terrace and outdoor shower. Popular with couples. The receptionist looks up at the man as he bends over the standard paperwork, noticing now the long, dark lashes and the glowing skin. He smiles at her and she smiles back, noting the slight creases at the corners of his eyes and the sharp chin. She wonders if he's had work done. As he takes his ID out of his wallet, she eyes the black American Express and the long pretty fingers. She thinks of all the first-class lounges in the area, mostly frequented by old Japanese businessmen, and of the private clubs and their bold clientele. She thinks of the magazine article she read last month at her hair stylist's.

'This way, sir. The porter will show you to your room.'

She lifts her hand in the tiniest of waves as the man walks away. Good-looking guy. Not young, but he can pass for thirty. Maybe. Well, good-looking anyway. Definitely some datin's toy boy. Or maybe some sort of escort.

* * *

The rain shower in the rain was a stupid idea. Standing naked on his large, stone-tiled terrace under a massive shower head the size of a manhole, Lucky laughs at the ridiculousness of it. The full circle of luxe—people paying top dollar to shower in the open. Right now, for Lucky, it's a literal circle of hot water streaming down on him, and beyond that, if he stretches out an arm, he can feel cold rain striking his palm. It feels good and it feels crazy. As he shampoos his hair, the air fills with the scents of lemongrass and ginger. He picks up the bottle of shampoo. The label, in a retro cursive font, boasts of aromatherapy, essential oils, and organically grown botanicals. So much shouting for just shampoo.

Lucky sniffs. The smell of lemongrass is making him hungry. Those biscuits he ate just ten minutes ago clearly weren't enough. Maybe he'll take a walk. There must be something open. It's KL. The last time he and Pearl were here, they were out eating until way past midnight nearly every night.

The towels are so fluffy. He wraps one around his waist and stares out into the city. The rain has finally stopped.

'You'd look better with a tail.'

Lucky spins around. Coconut is at the door leading from the room to the terrace. How did she get out? He must have left the door open. *Jesus.* How long has she been watching him? 'What?'

'If you're trying to attract a mate, a nice tail might help.' Is that a cheeky look on her pointy face?

'Coconut. For the last time. I'm not trying to attract a mate.' He picks up another towel and begins to dry his hair.

'No need to growl, Lucky. I'm just trying to help.' She gives him a snooty look and walks over to an open window. 'If you need me, I'll be watching TV.' One quick jump and she's on the windowsill; another one and she's back in the room.

Lucky shakes his head. A *tail!* A walk. What he needs is a walk.

* * *

Slow night, slow night. So hard to pass time on a slow night. The rain has finally stopped but the streets are empty. Who will come out now? It's nearly ten—too late for the after-work crowd, too early for the prostitutes and the clubbers—and some of the puddles on the road are ankle deep, so no one's just wandering around, are they? Meng doesn't feel like smoking but he lights up a cigarette anyway. Kill the time. He sighs. Every time the rainy season returns, he wishes he hadn't quit his job at the shoe factory. The street-hawker life—too unpredictable. Good times are good, but bad times . . . he stares listlessly at the platter of fish on ice in front of his stall, at the three wet, empty tables beyond it. A few more hours and he'll have to throw all this fish away.

'Hello!' The too-cheerful voice belongs to a man who's suddenly appeared next to him. He steps forward into the light cast by the overhanging bulb of the street stall. There's rain on his face and he's smiling, clearly keen to appear friendly.

Meng looks up, still smoking his cigarette. 'Yah?'

The man puts his hands in the pockets of his floral-print Bermuda shorts and peers at the platter of fish. 'Still open?'

Why do people ask stupid questions? Meng sighs, dropping his cigarette onto the road and nudging it into the gutter. 'Yah.'

The man turns over an ikan pari and nods. 'One grilled stingray—this one. Extra sambal. And some sotong.' He picks out a few squid and sets them aside.

'Can.' Meng nods, beginning to smile, pleased at the unexpected business. As he fires up the grill, he watches his customer tip one of the tables slightly to allow the water to flow off, then repeat this for one of the red plastic stools. Wah, solid guy—most people wait for you to wipe everything down, and if you were busy, they made faces. He calls out in Cantonese, 'You want a cloth?'

The man waves. 'No need. I'm good.' In English. Clearly a tourist. 'Do you have beer?'

'Beer? Wait.' Meng turns, and shouts down the dim alleyway. 'Ah Kin ah, Ah Kin!'

'*Oi mei yeh?*' A voice hollers back, sharp and loud, bouncing off the high concrete walls on both sides of the alley.

'One beer!'

'Wah, *bei lei ah? Sao dong juo ah?*'

'Not for me lah. Customer!' In English—Meng knows tourists like it better when they understand you. Maybe this guy will come back, bring friends. Who knows? Life is full of surprises.

'Okay, okay! Coming, coming!'

Lucky cranes his neck, seeking the loud, disembodied voice of the future beer bearer. All he can see is a small van parked a little further down the narrow alley, next to a few tables under a bright yellow plastic umbrella. A loud hiss comes from behind the stall he's at, and the air fills with the smell of grilling fish. Lucky turns towards the grill and the skinny guy manning it. The grill is still smoking as the man adds more oil around the fish from a squeeze bottle, then presses down on the fish's wide belly with a short-handled metal spatula that looks a lot more like a paint scraper than a cooking tool. More hissing from the grill, more amazing smells. Frying onions, and something else . . .

'Hallo.' A small boy next to Lucky, holding out a bottle of beer. 'Twelve ringgit.' He puts a pink plastic cup full of ice down on the table.

'Thanks.' He pays the child, a little shocked at how young he looks. Can't be more than thirteen, and he's out here working at this time? For a moment, Lucky is awed, then horrified. But the bottle of beer beckons and he turns his attention to it. He picks up the plastic cup and tilts it at an angle, then starts to pour beer into it. He would *never* put ice in his beer in a bar, but when in Rome . . . well, actually, in Rome he would have definitely put ice in his beer. The barely-cold beer of Italy—Lucky shudders at the memory.

A woman sidles up as the child walks away. She smiles and bends her head close to Lucky's. He grips the neck of his beer bottle and moves his head slowly away from hers. Her smile widens. She's oldish but not old, her bright yellow dress and gorgeous head of long wavy grey hair rather out of place in the dingy street-side setting. '*Leng cai*,' she purrs. 'You want satay?'

Lucky stares. It's been such a long time since he's been called a handsome boy in a leery way. Five years, to be exact, and here in this city of mud.

Mit used to call him leng cai in a *very* leery way and for a while he had thought she was the one. In fact, she *told* him she was the one and he believed her. It was the voice, low and slow, that did it. And that determined, upwards tilt of her well-shaped head.

She had him at 'Hello, Pearl's brother, handsome specimen of man.'

It was the KL launch of *Tao of Bao*, Pearl's first book. The guest list was cool-ish for a book event—one celebrity chef, one street photographer, three B-list soap actresses, one up-and-coming jazz singer—but the venue was 'mad, mad cool', Lucky told Pearl when they arrived, earlier than all the guests, early enough for her to drink too much and still manage to sober up in time to give her witty little speech and work the room like a pro. Bookstore by day, bar by night, the three-storey shophouse opened out into a small, dark street in the seedier section of Bukit Bintang. The shop next door had burnt down who knows how long ago, and its skeleton clung to the side of the bookstore-bar like a mad goth girlfriend.

Lucky was holding two drinks when Mit accosted him on his way to the middle of a sunken section on the second floor, where Pearl sat on a chaise-longue, charming a couple of journalists, waiting for her brother to bring her her sixth glass of prosecco. 'Hello.'

He stopped and found himself staring straight into the eyes of a woman as tall as him. He stood a little straighter. 'I'm Lucky.'

'Gurmit.'

'Isn't that a man's name?'

She sighed and took a glass out of his hand. 'I should have known. Handsome but ignorant. Punjabi names are unisex, leng cai.'

Lucky didn't know what to say, which was strange for him. He had never been that awkward idiot boy so fondly stereotyped in romantic comedies and television shows about odd couples. He struck up conversations with women as easily as some men reformatted computers. He liked women, and they liked him.

And he definitely liked this woman. He liked how she had just called him handsome to his face, twice, and how she stood so close, like it was a natural thing to do. He liked her slightly crooked smile and her wild mass of short curly hair. He took a sip from the other glass, the one he was still holding. From her chaise longue–throne, Pearl shot him an impatient look. He ignored her.

He continued to ignore her for three days after that. The morning after the launch, while Pearl was still snoring softly in bed, Lucky crept out of their hotel room to meet Mit for breakfast at a market in Air Panas, where he had the Malaysian variant of wan tan mee, fragrant with sesame oil and dark soy sauce, and then she drove him to Bangsar for some of the fluffiest idlis he had ever had. That day and the day after and the day after that, they ate their way around KL. He and Mit talked mostly about food—the woman was obsessed and seemed to do nothing else but eat—and books—but she read far more than he did because she did PR for books—and travelling—he told her about his trip to see the Alhambra—and it was funny and awkward and silly and he loved it.

By the time Mit dropped him at his hotel in her old Nissan Sunny two days later, just in time for him to pack and rush to the airport with Pearl, he believed he loved her. One hand on the wheel, she blew him a corny, dramatic kiss with the other as she drove off ('Leng cai, keep in touch!'), and that was worth the ragging he got from Pearl for weeks afterwards about traipsing off in KL and leaving her all alone.

It lasted a little more than a year, with him travelling to KL every weekend, and when it ended, he was . . . inconsolable.

'Come on, Lucky—just another girl. You'll be fine.' Pearl couldn't keep the sneer out of her voice. She hadn't been a fan of the woman who had sewn up all of Lucky's weekends for 'too long, little brother, too long'.

She was right. He was fine, in the end. But she was wrong—Mit was never just another girl.

'Leng cai, how? Want satay? Chicken also got, pork also got, mutton also got.'

Mumbling, Lucky orders ten sticks of satay. 'Anything. Surprise me.'

She gives him an odd look, but the mutton satay she comes back with fifteen minutes later really does surprise him. The marinade is heavy with lemongrass and ginger and lengkuas and brown sugar, and the mutton is . . . tender and delicately charred and . . .

Lucky sighs happily and orders another beer via the stingray man. *Ah, KL, it's good to be back.*

* * *

'What are you watching?'

Coconut is lying in the middle of the bed. As Lucky enters the room, she rolls onto her back and twists her head to face him.

'A documentary about sharks.' She turns back to the television just as the scene changes to a close-up of a whale shark, its wide, spotted face filling the screen. Coconut lets out a startled mew and sits up, sphinx-like. 'Why are there so many documentaries about sharks? Do they taste nice?'

'Hmm. Don't know. But people love seeing dangerous shit on TV—stunts, explosions.' Lucky gestures at the television screen. 'Sharks.'

Coconut leaps off the bed and walks towards Lucky. 'What have you got there?'

'Grilled stingray, for you.'

He grins, remembering the face the stingray seller made when he asked the man to hold the salt and the sambal. 'Can I get another fish? Plain, no sambal, nothing.'

'Salt?'

'No salt. Cats can't eat salt.'

The man gave him a long look before starting up the grill. 'You know you're not a cat, right?' he mumbled in Cantonese, but sadly Lucky's movie-learnt Cantonese was just enough to understand him.

Coconut sniffs at the newspaper packet. 'Interesting. Where did you get it?'

'There's an alleyway nearby with hawker stalls. I've been there before—opens super late.'

Coconut eats her midnight snack on the terrace while Lucky looks at the KL skyline. The building next to the hotel blocks about a quarter of his view, but there's still a wide expanse of it visible from the terrace. Lucky squints, trying to identify as many of the buildings as he can. Insane. Every time he comes here, there are new structures built and being built, new lights, new roads. A few years ago, he and Pearl arrived and went straight from the airport to their favourite place for thosai somewhere in Bangsar only to discover that the entire block of shops had been torn down and the plot boarded up while the foundations of a new mixed development complex were being laid. Mixed development—the noughties term that was invented to sell the notion that it was actually desirable to live above a restaurant or a gym or a yoga studio and pay exorbitant amounts in maintenance fees and—

'Delicious!' Coconut pauses mid-meal to give him an approving look. 'I'd like to see a documentary about stingrays now.'

Lucky snickers and turns back to the city. He sends a text: Just fed Coconut her first grilled ikan pari in KL. I think she's hooked!

Later, he lifts the cat up onto his shoulder for a view of the city. 'That's KL Tower. Tomorrow we're going to the part of the city beyond that—you can't see it from here, but it's not that far off.'

Her tail hits his face. 'Where am I supposed to look?'

'Over there.' Lucky nods vigorously in the direction of KL Tower as he lifts Coconut high above his head for a better view. 'The tall thing. KL Tower.'

Coconut shifts in his hands. 'The building that looks like a pumpkin on a stick?'

'Hmmm. Yes.' KL Tower *does* look like a pumpkin skewered on a light stick from a distance. He puts her back on his shoulder, steadying her with one hand, and she puts her paws on his head for balance.

'You seem to know KL very well.' One paw presses down against his ear.

'Well, I used to come here all the time. I was dating someone and she lived here . . . lives here. I think she probably still lives in KL.' He lifts Coconut off his shoulder and puts her down on the stony terrace floor.

'Oh yes. Shit.' Coconut licks a paw and begins her post-dinner facial.

'What?' Coconut's *swearing* now?

'Shit. The woman.' She makes a noise that sounds like the cat version of a chuckle. 'You know that's what Pearl called her?'

Lucky scowls. Calling Mit 'Shit' sounds exactly like Pearl. 'No. And it's Mit, Coconut. Don't be rude. But how do you know what Pearl used to call her?'

'Oh, Pearl talked about her a lot.'

Jesus. Lucky blinks. Sometimes he forgets that Coconut has spent years in his family, years overhearing stuff like this.

'To you?'

'Yes.'

Lucky realizes that yes, Pearl did always chatter to Coconut. But seriously—Shit? Another thought strikes him. 'Did you use to talk to Pearl?'

Surely not. Surely Pearl would have told him! Lucky stares at the little cat, who looks back at him with gleaming eyes and keeps silent.

'Coconut?'

'No.'

Lucky feels happier knowing this; he doesn't know why. 'Why not?'

'She didn't need me to.'

'And I do?' Suddenly he's not so thrilled.

Coconut resumes cleaning her face. 'Don't you?'

Breakfast

puts both Lucky and Coconut in a good mood. At a small greasy shop in a lane close to the hotel, Lucky eats one fluffy roti canai after another while Coconut eats Princess Shrimp Dream from a hotel saucer he's smuggled out. Their table is one of the few laid out on the street just outside the shop and, like the shop, it is a greasy, shabby thing. Lucky tries as much as possible not to touch it. Coconut doesn't seem to care and no one seems to mind her being there. No one seems to even notice. The three women at the next table, all just as enamoured with their roti canai as Lucky is with his, don't hear the cat ask:

'So, what are we doing here?'

He looks around. The women continue to eat while discussing their new colleague, whose cologne 'smells like car freshener'. God, Malaysians will probably ignore Armageddon if they have roti canai in front of them. *Good* roti canai, of course.

'Breakfast,' Lucky whispers.

Coconut swats his knee. 'Don't be silly, Lucky. I mean here. In KL. Is this it? Are we going anywhere after this?'

He hasn't made any plans, but he doesn't want to tell her this. He has a feeling she'll disapprove. But he's never been good at planning, and though he knows Teluk Intan is where he's heading and he's going to get there at some point—some point soon—he doesn't want to rush the KL leg of the trip. Dinah would say he was procrastinating, but she would be wrong. It's not procrastinating if all he's doing is not rushing things. Only fools rush in, yes? Wise man, Elvis. Except the whole thing about fried peanut butter sandwiches, of course. Like, why? Then again, the man didn't know about Malaysian roti canai.

'I've got it all planned, Coconut. Everything. We're here for a few days, and I've got a few places to check out, like the roastery Pearl put down in her notebook.' *That* should satisfy Coconut. 'It's on her list but there aren't any notes, so we're going to take a look, okay? And after KL we'll go to Ipoh—very good coffee there too, but Pearl doesn't have any notes on it.'

'So what if there aren't any notes? Why do you need notes?'

Lucky frowns. 'I don't know, maybe I'll finish writing up her notebooks for her.'

'Did she ask you to?'

'No.'

'Then why are you doing it?'

'I don't know.' He doesn't. It's something to do.

Coconut doesn't speak for a while. She finishes up her breakfast and licks her whiskers clean. Lucky watches her and sips his coffee. It's far too sweet, but still better than the swill they're serving at the hotel cafe.

'Lucky, do you know why I'm here?'

He stares. 'You mean why you're here with me now?'

'Yes.'

He thinks about it. 'The mountain?'

Coconut makes a snort-like noise. 'That's what you promised me. That's not why I'm here.'

Eeek. Surely it's too early for a conversation like this. Lucky casts a sideways look at the women at the next table. *Theirs* is a proper breakfast conversation—dumbass colleague misusing the photocopier, where to go for lunch, whether it's going to rain later. Whatever he and Coconut are doing—not breakfast-y. It's the kind of talk that in an indie movie would happen in some sort of cool, appropriately moody setting. Like a deserted beach with waves crashing or maybe a grassy hilltop with the wind blowing. Not at a wobbly plastic table at a grubby roadside next to a ditch. Our hero, bloated from overeating, hopes the cat will quickly tell him why she's decided to come along on his trip and be Sancho Panza to his Don Quixote.

'So, here's the thing.' Why does she suddenly sound like a mafia don? 'You don't know why I'm here, but that's fine.'

'Okay.' *God, where's this going?*

'Because you see, Lucky, *I* know why I'm here.'

Lucky waits for her to say more, but she doesn't. So he pays his bill and they go back to the hotel, where Coconut proceeds to watch a British talk show and Lucky sits on the terrace and watches her through the glass doors, feeling somehow like he's disappointed her.

A little later, as he turns on the water for the outdoor shower, he realizes he's disappointed too. *Isn't Coconut here just because she wants to be, because she likes me?*

* * *

It's clearly a day for unsettling, unwelcome conversations with the womenfolk in his life.

There are five missed calls from his aunt by the time he gets out of the shower and gets dressed for the day. Five—is something wrong? Is someone ill? As his mind fiddles with these questions, the phone begins to vibrate. Aunty Dolly again. Taking a deep breath, he picks up.

No hello, as usual. 'For goodness' sake, where have you run off to? Where are you?'

'Hi Aunty Dolly. How are you?' So brightly he sounds idiotic. He slides open the glass doors and walks out onto the terrace. *Wow, it's getting hot.*

'Lucky!'

'What?'

'What are you doing? Where are you?' His aunt waits for him to answer.

He doesn't. In his head, he starts singing Queen's 'Bicycle Race'. What a daft song, but what a good one.

I want to ride my . . . BICYCLE BICYCLE BICYCLE . . . I want to ride my bicycle, I want to ride my bike, I want to ride my bicycle, I want to ride it where I like . . .

'Lucky! Are you still there?'

'Yes, Aunty Dolly. Still here.'

'Dinah says you're in Malaysia. Malaysia! What are you doing in Malaysia? Don't you have work to do?'

Dinah! 'What work? I'm just a bum in a coffee shop.'

'Lucky, be serious. Just what do you think you're doing?'

'Nothing. I'm just in KL, eating things. This morning, I had the most awesome roti canai. You wouldn't believe . . .'

'Lucky, this is ridiculous. Come back home.' Aunty Dolly takes a deep, audible breath. 'Come. Home.'

'Why?'

A pause, during which Lucky walks up to the glass door and looks in at Coconut. She's sitting upright on the bed watching television. Lucky makes a face. She's turning into the worst couch potato. Are other cats like this, or just Coconut?

'Are you by yourself?'

'No.'

She clicks her tongue impatiently. 'So, who are you with?'

'Coconut's here.'

A longer pause. Lucky watches as Coconut walks over to the remote control and starts flipping through channels, one of her front paws pressing down on the > button over and over. Ducks in a pond. Music video—Miley Cyrus? Yuck. Interior of a race car. Planes flying over a field. Old episode of *Friends*. Back to the ducks in a pond. Coconut settles back down to watch them. Lucky rolls his eyes. He would've gone for the planes.

'Lucky.' Aunty Dolly says his name slowly now, as if he won't recognize it if she says it any faster. 'Do you really think that the cat talks to you?' She says this softly, but Lucky can hear the confusion in her voice. The middle-class horror of madness.

Ah, the traitorous Dinah's been very . . . communicative. Lucky decides to go for it. 'She does talk to me, Aunty Dolly.'

Another longish pause, during which Lucky wishes he'd had time to prepare for this and Aunty Dolly wishes she hadn't heard him say quite so clearly that the cat does talk to him. Neither of them wants to continue this conversation, but it doesn't feel like the kind of talk that comes to any sort of natural end.

Doing okay?

No, I'm hearing things.

Well, good for you. Okay, bye.

'You need to come home. Now.'

'She's really quite clever. Watches too much TV, though.'

Aunty Dolly changes gears. 'Okay. Just come home, okay? You and Coconut. Let's sit down and talk. Obviously something's going on with you, and we should . . . sit down and talk. I know you've had a difficult time and . . .'

Meanwhile, inside the room, Coconut changes channels. The screen goes from some sort of temperate pastoral scene to a wide shot of what looks like a tropical Asian city. Singapore! The Esplanade with its spiky crust; Marina Bay Sands looking like a three-legged insect; the twin domes of the big, fake garden next to it. And the Merlion, casting a bored, superior look across the bay. *Another cat who thinks it's too good for us.*

Aunty Dolly is still telling him about what a difficult time she knows he's had. He interrupts her before she can start talking about Pearl. 'There's nothing going on.'

'Just come home. We're here for you.'

This makes Lucky wince. How trite and nonsensical. Does his aunt really believe she can get her way by throwing low-level platitudes at him? Here for him? How? By engaging in sneaky communications with Dinah? By being in cahoots with that meddlesome cow?

But he manages to be polite. 'I'll come home soon, okay? But not right now. We've got stuff to do.'

'For goodness' sake be sensible. I cannot . . . I cannot believe you've taken the cat with you. What do you think you're doing?'

'We're . . .' Here he pauses for dramatic effect. '. . . going on an adventure. We're going to drink Ipoh white coffee, we're going to see a mountain, we're going to see Papa's house in Teluk Intan, we're going to do so so many things . . . yes we are. We're going to have such an adventure!'

Yes, that's what this is. An adventure. He can't wait to tell Coconut.

Another change of gears as Dolly decides her nephew needs a proper earful. 'Lucky, can you be *normal* for a change? Come home! Don't be such a child!'

Why does she always end up saying this? Also, what's wrong with being a child? Is it better or worse than being an ostrich? 'No, thank you.' There, nice and polite—his mum would be proud. 'But thanks for calling, Aunty Dolly.'

He ends the call and goes back into the room.

'Is that what you're wearing?' Coconut calls out.

Lucky looks down at his denim cut-offs and Care Bears T-shirt. 'Yes.'

'Go change. We haven't met any cats yet, but if we do, I can't have any of them see me with you looking like this.'

* * *

The receptionist calls out as he's walking across the lobby on the way out. 'Be careful with your things, sir. KL isn't Singapore, you know. Don't walk too close to the road.'

Why is everyone suddenly assuming he's this hapless moron?

* * *

'So how is an adventure different from a journey?'

'A journey's more about going somewhere. But an adventure is about doing things that maybe we haven't done before. So this is kind of both.'

'You promised me we're going to see a mountain.'

'Yes, yes, we'll go see a mountain. But an adventure is more than that, okay?' He pauses, trying to remember the spiel he'd composed in his head earlier—something connecting self-discovery with trying new things and throwing caution into the sea? 'This is about me finding *me*, you know?'

'If you're having trouble finding you, how are you going to find me a mountain?'

* * *

The only KL roastery on Pearl's to-investigate list in her notebooks is a total dud. Determined to take the bus, Lucky spends a whole hour getting there, changing buses three times while Coconut alternately growls and naps in her new nest. This new nest is a large canvas tote lined with a fluffy hotel towel and slung over Lucky's shoulder as he braves Malaysian public transport for the first time in years and hopes Coconut will be good and keep her head in the bag.

The roastery is perched on a small hill at the edge of KL, with an unremarkable view of nearby condominiums. At first, the selection of house roasts appears to make up for this. The menu on the large chalkboard over the counter lists four specials: a dark-roast Sumatran, a medium Colombian, a medium Brazilian, a light Rwandan.

Lucky ends up trying the Rwandan. He doesn't normally go for light roasts, but his last encounter with a light-roasted Rwandan coffee was so good—bright, fruity, so fresh and clean-tasting—that he must take this chance at reliving it. But the coffee that arrives is thin, too sour, flat. He wonders if he should tell someone, decides that he should, and walks up to the counter.

'Hi.'

'Hi.' The barista scowls at him.

'I ordered the Rwandan coffee. It's not very good,' he tells the barista apologetically.

'It isn't?' The man, goateed and man-bunned, crosses his arms.

'No.'

The barista smirks. 'Let me guess. You usually drink 3-in-1s and you think this tastes *funny*.'

Lucky stares. *Wow. The vitriol.* 'No,' he says gently. 'The roast seems a bit off.' He pauses. 'Maybe it's just this batch, but I just thought I should let you guys know . . . maybe you can check on it?'

A shrug. 'Maybe you're just not used to good coffee.'

'No, it's really quite underdeveloped. It tastes a bit like . . . sour grass.'

'Maybe your taste buds are off.'

'Maybe you're a dick.' Lucky smiles, puts the cup of barely drunk coffee on the counter and walks out.

Where did that come from? A mew from the canvas tote makes him sigh. Pearl. That's where he gets it from. A lifetime of watching his sister cutting people down, and now he's just called a stranger a dick.

Pearl never had issues calling anyone a dick. Lucky can recall far too many instances of her being eager, in fact, to call a stranger a dick. Like the time someone trod on her toes in a crowded train and she called him a dick, then pushed him out of the train and onto the platform.

'Dick! Stupid fucking shitty dick!' Lucky can still hear her shout echoing through the underground platform, every word surprisingly and embarrassingly clear as she darted back into the train, flashing her victim the finger as the train doors shut, beeping loudly, between them.

The doors closed. As the train moved out of the station, everyone around her took a step back, staring, stupefied. She cackled and took a sweeping bow. Beside her, Lucky wanted to melt into the floor and disappear.

Lucky does not take a bow. He feels like such an ass. Somewhat liberated, but an ass. A liberated ass. Which just sounds like some form of woke porn.

At a makeshift roadside joint half an hour later, as he drinks thick frothy kopi tarik and Coconut laps water from a bowl very kindly provided by the woman running the place, Lucky still feels like an ass. He shouldn't have let that awful man get under his skin. He should've laughed. He should've smiled. He should've said something quieter, something cooler. He should've said, 'Good luck.'

Good luck with your weird sour coffee, you weird sour man.

He tells Coconut all this in a whisper, adding: 'If she were here, Pearl would have found that super funny.'

Coconut agrees. 'And she'd have been the one to call that guy a dick.'

'Oh, definitely.'

'What's a dick?'

'Not a nice thing to call someone.'

'Like "bad cat"?'

* * *

They trot together, man and cat, happy from a nice meal of grilled stingray at the same alleyway of stalls Lucky visited on their first night in KL. Coconut is still purring from being fussed over by everyone, from stingray guy to beer boy to satay lady. The beer boy had tried to give her a bit of beer ('My father says free only for the cat, mister'), but Lucky firmly refused.

Coconut is still a little grumpy about this on their way back to the hotel. 'The boy said it's okay for cats to drink beer. And he should know, right?' she whines. 'I don't understand why you have to be such a stick in the mud.'

Stick in the mud? Who even says that? It's like something out of 1980s British television—and not even the impudent *'Allo 'Allo*; much more straight-laced, like *Mind Your Language*. 'He sells beer, Coconut. It's not like he's a vet.'

'And you are. Of course.' Coconut yawns.

As they walk past rows of shops and restaurants, now closed, Lucky checks the map on his phone. 'Looks like there's a shortcut through here.'

Here is a parking lot about the size of two basketball courts (perhaps a little more, Lucky can't see all that well in the dark) in an awkward space in the middle of three buildings. It's only half-full and the only lighting comes from a street lamp in the street beyond it, which should lead to the hotel.

Coconut swishes her tail. 'I don't like it.'

Lucky rolls his eyes. 'There's nothing to like. We just walk through it and that's all.' He looks down at Coconut, who's swishing her tail in bigger loops now to convey her displeasure. 'Oh, don't be dramatic. I'll put you in the bag, okay?'

'Fine.'

Into the tote goes Coconut, tucked into the towel, and into the parking lot goes Lucky. Cat in the bag, our hero surveys his surroundings. *What a dump. Who the hell would park a car here?* So bloody dark, so damn dodgy. Even the tarmac is a mess, mostly cracked and crumbling, with potholes everywhere and blocks of concrete and an assortment of junk poking out of the ground. Lucky is forced to weave through the empty cars with his eyes locked to the ground, but still he manages to stub his toe on a broken bit of pipe. He winces. Looking up, he can see the Petronas Twin Towers in the distance, bright and gleaming, staring down at him from lofty heights. When he looks back down again, he finds himself locking eyes with the biggest rat he's ever seen. Lucky yelps. The rat dashes off and under a car.

He puts a hand to his sweaty forehead. God, KL—glitz and garbage in equal measure. He takes a breath and continues walking, swinging the plastic bag of satay he's planning to eat on the hotel room terrace. Just a little bit more of this shithole car park and they're done. He plods on, squinting in the semi-dark.

A hard push from behind nearly knocks him over. Instinct turns him around to face his attacker, but all he sees is a dull, greyish blur before he's shoved in the chest and stumbles backwards, arms flailing, onto the hood of a car. When he gets up again, he realizes his attacker has taken the bag. With Coconut in it.

A little way off, someone is running through the parking lot, darting expertly through the cars. Lucky starts to chase him, but the man runs off into the street at the other end well before Lucky can even reach the end of the lot.

Oh fuck oh fuck.

He's out of breath and his heart is racing and his mind is a big black blank. *Oh fuck oh fuck oh fuck.*

Lucky tugs at his hair. *Okay.* His wallet is in the bag with Coconut, but he still has his phone. *Okay. Okay okay okay.*

This is all going to be fine. He will sort this out. He will get her cat back.

Not okay! Not okayyyyyyyyyyy.

By the time he reaches the street, it's empty. No one anywhere except for a group of singing, drunken Japanese men in smart suits. Lucky runs up and down the street anyway, looking for any sign of the man with his bag. Five minutes later, sweaty and exhausted and mad with worry, he gives up. Not like the guy was going to hang around and wait for him to catch up. He should just go back to the hotel. Instead, Lucky sighs and sits down on the pavement.

Tugging at his hair again, he takes his phone from his pocket and sends a frantic text: `Got robbed! Wallet and Coconut gone!`

He hangs his head. Why, why did he take that stupid shortcut through that stupid parking lot? He takes deep breaths, trying to calm himself, wondering what he should do next.

And then his phone buzzes. For the first time in years, a reply: `Where the hell are you?`

The hotel lobby

is far too cold and no one has walked through the doors in the last half hour. Except Lucky himself, who has popped out three times in the last ten minutes alone to check the gravel driveway, just in case. In case of what, he doesn't know. In case she changes her mind and doesn't show up? In case Coconut manages to break free and finds her way back to him on her own? In case . . .

Lucky walks up to the double glass doors again and sticks his head out, rather unnecessarily, when they open automatically.

'Sir, everything okay?' The security guard decides, finally, that he will see if this guest who keeps poking his head out the door actually needs anything he can help with.

'Yes, yes, thank you. Just, um, waiting. Waiting for someone.' Lucky blows out his cheeks, wanting to growl and bite and claw at his eyes. Where is she? And where, where is Coconut?

He covers his eyes and tries to send a telepathic message to her. *Coconut! I'm so sorry! I'm such a . . . dick. A bad man!*

The security guard takes a few steps back from the weird guest who's now standing in front of the hotel entrance covering his eyes. Should he try to calm him down? Tell him to please go back inside and sit down on one of the nice, comfortable armchairs in the lobby? Tell the receptionist? She said he was a prostitute, didn't she? Maybe he's waiting for a customer . . . a difficult customer? The guard shakes his head. All sorts, all sorts.

A car drives up and three short sharp honks break the awkward almost-interaction between Lucky and the guard. A window is wound down, a head sticks out.

A yell. 'Oi, get in the car!'

Lucky takes his hands off his face. It's her, and it's the same beat-up 1980s Nissan Sunny he remembers. He wants to smile, but he has to sigh. What a long time it's been. 'Hey, Mit.'

She doesn't hear him. She doesn't see the security guard stare at her wondering what the world has come to. Nice-looking Punjabi girl paying for a prostitute. *This* guy.

She waves. 'Lucky! Get in the car!'

Mit drives him to the nearest police station to make a report. Sighing, wishing for the umpteenth time that he didn't take that stupid shortcut through the stupid parking lot, Lucky endures the pitying, patronizing looks from both night officers as he tells them what happened. His cat was in the bag, he says over and over again. His cat is gone. The officers ask about the wallet, but he waves them off.

'Not a big deal,' he says as Mit translates. 'I only had money in there. No ID, no cards, nothing. I put everything in the hotel safe.' Pearl's old habit—his sister saves his ass *again*. 'But my cat—I need to find my cat.'

In the end, Lucky's statement in the police report reads, in Malay: 'On February 5, sometime between 9.00 p.m. and 9.15 p.m., I took a walk after dinner with my cat in my bag. From somewhere at the end of Jalan Alor, I walked through a parking lot even though it was very dark and there were no lights. Someone came from behind and pushed me, and I fell onto a car. I did not hear the person approach. I do not know if it was a man or a woman. I did not see his or her face. I did not notice what he or she was wearing. The person took my bag. In it was a towel, my cat, and my wallet. The towel is grey. The cat is brown, black, and white. This colour combination is called "tortoiseshell". The bag is white with the words "Fold Me Fill Me Fix Me Frill Me" in black letters and a picture of a box of pancake mix. I tried to chase the person who took my bag, but I did not catch him or her and I did not see where the person went.'

Even to himself, Lucky sounds like a complete idiot completely deserving of being robbed in the city of mud.

After the ordeal at the station, Mit and Lucky drive in bigger and bigger circles around the parking lot that is the eye of this hurricane, Mit glaring down her nose at the road and everyone they pass along the way, Lucky squinting at dustbins and piles of boxes and unidentifiable lumps on the sidewalk, hoping to spot his bag. They don't talk. He's too anxious to, and she's never liked talking to Anxious Lucky, who always makes her feel like slapping him.

But she steals a long look at him the first chance she gets—who doesn't want a good long look at the ex? The Ex. The man who broke her heart so badly she cut bangs—and everyone knows curly-haired women should never cut bangs. Took a whole year to grow them out, and every time she looked in the mirror she was forced *by her own hair* to think of him. She wishes she hadn't replied to his stupid text. Should've let him hunt down the cat himself—it's Pearl's cat, and why should she care what happens to Pearl's cat?

He's thinner than she remembers, and not in a good way. He looks a little . . . limp. And the longer hair doesn't suit him. Makes him look lazier somehow, and tired. Everything else looks pretty much the same. The same sleepy, distant eyes, the same perpetual half-smile, the same weird clothes. Seriously, what's with the damn Care Bears T-shirt? And what self-respecting man wears denim shorts like these? No, they're not the same— the clothes are *weirder* now.

Once, twice, three times he yells for her to stop and throws the door open and rushes out of the car, twice into an alley and once towards a dustbin, shouting, 'Coconut! It's me!' And then he returns five minutes later looking like a wet dishrag, muttering for her to drive on, drive on.

Sometime after midnight, Lucky leans back into the passenger seat with a sigh. Hopeless. No sign of the bag or the cat anywhere.

'He'll dump the bag for sure. Let's keep looking.' They're already driving at the speed of a trishaw, but she slows down further. 'Keep looking, Lucky, keep looking. Cat's going to be around here somewhere.'

Will she? Lucky winds down his window and starts calling Coconut's name. He hopes she'll hear him—poor thing is probably frightened and hiding somewhere. 'Coconut! Coconut!' Can she hear him? 'COCONUT!'

A street vendor selling burgers stares at him, at the car moving so so slowly down the street.

'COCONUT!'

Two men in 7-Eleven uniforms on a smoke break turn to watch the car go by, one of them pausing mid-drag.

'COCONUT!'

'You know you sound nuts, right?' Next to him, Mit starts to giggle. 'I'm sorry, I shouldn't. But you do.'

Lucky puts his head on the dashboard. If he weren't so heartbroken, he'd bite her.

* * *

'Seriously. Why are you wearing your sister's clothes?'

Five years since they last sat at a bar together, and *this* is what she wants to know? Women. Cats. All mystifying. On purpose.

They're in the seediest bar Lucky's ever been to. If he had been by himself, he would never have walked in. He wouldn't even have known it was a bar. No signboard, just a door in a wall in a very narrow side street, then steps leading down into a dark, windowless room with a small concrete bar counter and maybe ten tables and a smell of stale cigarette smoke too heavy for any amount of lemon air freshener to mask, though the proprietor has certainly tried. Lucky hopes the beer will quickly cloud his senses.

He takes a gulp. 'These,' he looks down at his T-shirt and shorts, 'are comfy. And how do you know I'm wearing her clothes?'

'I didn't. But now I do.' She rolls her eyes and grins. Oh, what a grin. He's almost forgotten that grin. Almost.

Lucky takes another gulp of his beer. 'You look nice.'

She does, even if she looks like a different woman now, so unlike the cool skinny creature he remembers. She's grown her hair long, and it's softer-looking, almost tame. It makes her look older, and gentler. Less typhoon, more zephyr. And her cheeks—they're rounded now where they were fashionably gaunt before, and her skin is glowing, and even in this rubbish lighting, without a trace of make-up, she's prettier than she ever was. Like a nymph in a Botticelli painting.

Pretty-pretty Botticelli? The un-edgiest painter ever? Nymphs? Jesus. If Mit could read his thoughts, she would roll her eyes. Again.

'Thanks for coming.' He sighs. 'I'm sorry. It's been quite a stupid evening.'

She waves him off. 'Don't be silly. I'm sorry we couldn't find Coconut.'

They finish their beers and order another round. Mit tells him she'll help him tomorrow—maybe they should check pet shelters and the SPCA. Lucky nods, only half-listening, wondering for the nth time how he's managed to get himself in this ridiculous situation. Losing Coconut. Losing his mind. Why did he call Mit? Why couldn't he have done this on his own? He shouldn't have freaked out. What will she think of him now? What is he to her, right now? Some loser who managed to get robbed in KL because he just couldn't stay out of a dark car park, who can't sort his own mess out. The same loser who refused to marry her five years ago because he wasn't sure where they were going exactly, who said 'okay' when she said maybe it was better to just end things if he was so unsure. The same loser who's continued texting her for the last five years to insert something somewhere, to fill the space beyond 'okay'. *OKAY?* What kind of jellyfish says *okay*?

The kind of jellyfish who orders a third pint and drinks most of it in one long swallow. Mit watches him. He can feel her watching him.

She looks at her phone and sighs. 'It's nearly three. You want to call it a night?'

'I don't know.' He sighs. What's he going to do now? Go back to his room and let Coconut sleep out in the cold, alone and afraid? Could the robber have kept her? A robber can be a robber and still be a cat person. And Coconut is an awesome cat. But what if the man is the kind of psycho who eats cats? Or the kind who chops them up into little bits for fun?

Oh god. Pearl, Pearl, I've lost our cat.

He imagines his sister rising out of the cold Java Sea, wiping water off her face with the backs of her hands, teeth gritted, seaweed in her hair, arms raised in fury. *Lucky, you dumbass,* he hears her say. *How could you, you little shit?*

Pearl, don't be angry, Pearl.

She won't be placated with nonsense platitudes. Pearl wades out of the water and begins striding towards him across sand, looking angrier than he's seen her in years. She's getting closer, closer. Lucky is five years old again and she's scarier than the dragon at the bottom of the stairs. *You couldn't even take care of a damn cat?*

I'm so so sorry. I'll find her, I promise.

She grabs his shoulders and shakes him. *What the fuck is wrong with you!*

Why is breathing so difficult? And then he feels her hands, her large man-hands, the hands he's teased her about since they were children, they close around his neck, and what a strong grip she still has across time and sea and life and death.

Pearl, no. Please, Pearl!

Lucky raises a protective hand to his throat as his mind plummets back into the seedy alleyway bar in Bukit Bintang, deep in the half-asleep city. *Pearl!* He starts to gasp for air. His heart flutters. His head pounds. He tries to take another gulp of beer but his throat closes up. Tears run down his face and they are salty, salty like the sea, salty like her papaya salad, salty like the pancakes they made their mother once for Mother's Day with salt instead of sugar, salty like the sea the sea the sea that took her and never gave her back.

He puts his face down on the table and sobs and tries to take a deep breath and fails.

'Oh god, Lucky, what's happening? Are you okay? Oh, Lucky.' He feels an arm go around him. A hand strokes the nape of his neck.

He opens his mouth and tries to say he's okay, he's fine, there's nothing to worry about. But he can't. He can barely breathe. He cannot move. And he thinks, this must be what it feels like to drown.

The hairdryer

is the next thing Lucky hears.

Whoosh-whooosh-who-whoooooooosh. Whoosh-whooosh-who-whoooooooosh. The world's most irritating sound after vacuum-cleaner black noise.

The toilet light is on. And so is the planet's—from the bed, he can see that a long slanted ray has already sneaked across the timber floor. Lucky lifts the duvet and draws it over his head. Nope, he's not ready. Not ready for a new day. The new day can just fuck right off.

The hairdryer stops and the sudden silence cuts into Lucky's head like a cold razor.

Wait, who's in the toilet?

Mit. Yes, Mit. He has a blurry recollection of her helping him into bed the night before, of being forced to breathe into a paper bag and drink a glass of water, of having his hand held and his face wiped down with a towel. But why? The last thing Lucky can remember is the weird bar they were at—and that horrible smell of cigarettes and synthetic lemon. He turns onto his stomach and buries his face in his pillow. Oh gross. The pillow stinks of cigarette smoke. But he lies still, unwilling to move, trying to remember how the evening ended.

'Lucky, are you awake? Are you feeling better?'

He lies still and doesn't answer. He can't see her, but he can smell the ginger and lemongrass shampoo. His stomach growls in response.

Suddenly, quickly, the duvet is jerked upwards. He feels her slide into bed next to him and draw the duvet over them both.

'Okay, come on. I know you're awake.'

How? Clearly she's bluffing. He continues to lie still.

'Are you feeling better?' A pause. 'Lucky, come on. You know you breathe differently when you're asleep, right? I can always tell. So stop pretending.' She laughs softly.

Grunting, he turns on his side to face her. The little bit of sunshine sneaking in through the top of the duvet is bright enough to see her.

'Hey, Mit. Fancy seeing you here.' He yawns.

She flicks him on the nose. 'You scared me last night.'

'Sorry.'

He can remember it now. Some sort of waking dream. At the bar. And Pearl, her hands around his neck. He turns back onto his stomach. 'Sorry, Mit,' he mumbles into the pillow. 'Sorry. Not sure what happened. Must have been too tired. Old age and all.'

The bed shivers as she shifts closer. 'It looked like you were having a panic attack last night, Lucky. Have you had one before?'

Panic attack? He nuzzles the pillow. 'Don't think so.'

'Well, you had one last night.'

Well, what does he do with this piece of information? So what if he had a panic attack? 'Okay. Good to know.' Lucky shuts his eyes and tries to go back to sleep.

'Do you want to talk? About anything.'

'No.'

'Okay.'

'Okay.'

'Well, get your ass in the shower then. We need to find your cat.'

At breakfast, they're both quiet. He can feel Mit watching him as they eat their roti canai, as they drink their too-sweet milky kopi. She wants to say something—he can feel that too. But Lucky learnt long ago how to let a silence sit and not feel the need to do anything about it.

It was his only weapon against his sister. *She* could never resist the urge to fill a silence, and all his life he put up with her constant interruption of his thoughts, the quiet mornings, the sunsets, the daydreams, all the soliloquies in his teenage head in front of his mirror wondering if he should do something to his hair. And whenever they argued or she blew up over something, Pearl would stomp off and sulk and then return, wanting to talk about things, and he would shrug and say nothing. Not a single hmm or right or yes or okay to reassure the queen of the power of her majesty and the . . . subjectness . . . of her sole subject.

'Lucky, say something.' Pearl was at his door, blocking his way out. Lucky had to duck under her arm to get out of his room and as he walked away, she followed him. Down the stairs, across the courtyard, into the kitchen.

She had recorded over one of his mixtapes and was attempting round two of something between a half-apology and a justification of this deliberate, selfish act that had obliterated seven songs he had carefully, patiently recorded off the radio over the last two months. Two months! Two months in which thirteen-year-old Lucky tried to stay within two metres of the radio at all times and ran to press record if the deejay announced a song he wanted or if he managed to catch the first couple of notes before the song *properly* started. Two months down the drain because his shitty sister couldn't be bothered to look for an empty tape to record some bullshit interview with some bullshit supermodel.

Lucky looked into a fridge, wondering if he should bother with the half-eaten can of tuna from yesterday's breakfast. Pearl decided to squeeze herself into the gap between him and the fridge shelves and harass him for not responding to her crummy semi-apology.

'Come on.' Pearl shoved her face close to his and batted her eyelashes. 'You know it's lame for a boy to be listening to the Spice Girls anyway, right? So maybe I did you a favour.'

Reaching through the space between her waist and left arm, Lucky picked up the can of tuna in its cling-wrap cocoon. He turned and walked off, leaving the fridge door to swing back against her. Picking up the loaf of bread on the counter by its plastic wrapping and a plate and a knife from the dish rack, he set everything out on the kitchen island and began making his sandwich.

Pearl went over to the opposite side of the island. 'I mean, it's not like I'm being sexist or whatever. But the Spice Girls? Come on, Lucky, you can't be angry with me over the Spice Girls.'

Lucky didn't look up. He went back to the fridge, got the butter, came back to the island and began buttering a slice of bread.

'Okay, so I should have used a blank tape. Okay? I'm sorry.'

Lucky buttered another slice of bread. He took his time, making sure he covered every bit of surface, all the way up to the edges.

Pearl leaned over the cold marble, propping herself up with her elbows. 'Lucky, I'm really, really sorry. Don't be angry, okay? I'll get you . . . another tape. And why don't I make this sandwich for you, okay? You just relax, huh? Make yourself a coffee.'

She tried to take the plate and the butter knife from him, but he gripped both tightly and wouldn't let go.

'Fuck!' She let go; he almost got a knife in the eye from the recoil. 'Lucky, it's just a damn tape. What do you want? Blood?'

He looked up and smiled beatifically, then went back to spreading tuna on the first slice of bread. Spread, spread, spread. The even distribution of tuna and the perfection of tuna-to-bread-surface ratio became his only reasons for existence.

With a loud, guttural growl, Pearl reached over and snatched the slice of bread out of his hand. With a frightened yelp, Lucky dropped the butter knife and took a step back. Too late—his sister dived across the kitchen island and slapped the purloined slice onto his face, rubbing butter and tuna against his nose and cheeks and forehead. She grabbed him by the throat as he tried to resist, snarling, 'Eat up, since you don't feel like talking. Eat up!'

Blindly, he grabbed the second slice off the plate and flung it at her. Big mistake. The next moment, his neck was in the crook of her elbow, and she was jamming both slices of bread against his tight-pressed lips. 'Eat up!'

Wildly, he reached behind him and grabbed her by the hair. But the next moment, he felt her bite his arm, and he was forced to let go as she kicked him under the knees and dragged him onto the floor. One arm still wrapped around his neck, she flipped him onto his stomach and sat on his back. As he struggled to shout, she pushed the bread slices back against his face. 'What's that, Lucky? *Now* you want to talk to me?'

'Pearl! Lucky!'

Lucky felt Pearl release her grip on his neck and clamber off his back. They sat up. Their father stood over them, looking angrier than they had ever seen him. He looked at the bits of tuna smeared all over the kitchen island and the floor and their faces, at the bits of bread in their hair and clothes. And they could tell from the pinched look on his face and the funny set of his jaw that the sight of all this had flung their father back through time, to another kitchen where the cabinets were often empty and the people who looked into them were often hungry.

'Are you dogs!' he roared. 'Get up!'

They got up. Lucky reached for Pearl's hand and found it.

Their father stared at them, disgust twisting his face. He barked out in Hokkien, his language of rage, 'You dare to waste food like this! How shameful!' For a moment, it looked like he would take them both into the garden, hang them from the mango tree, and thrash them with his belt.

They hung their heads and said nothing. Suddenly, they were children again. Seven and eleven, lepers wrapped in towels. Pearl squeezed Lucky's hand.

'*Chiak liao bee!*'

Not worth the rice you eat. Teeth clenched, eyes wide, their father slammed his fist against the tuna-streaked kitchen island. Pearl started to cry and Lucky held her hand tighter.

The Hokkien tirade, when it finally ended, came down to three barked orders: 'Clean this up. Clean yourselves up. Then come see me in the study and tell me why I shouldn't throw you out on your heads.'

They cleaned the kitchen until everything shone. And for three months afterwards, they spent their weekends in the garden, sweeping and planting and pruning and weeding and trimming the hedges while their father watched them at intervals from the windows and told them to work faster, or he would sell them to his friend in Raub who ran a rubber estate and always needed extra hands. They were allowed a slice of bread and an egg three times a day. They had their allowances and social lives severely severed. And when they were finally allowed out on weekends again, Pearl went to HMV and bought Lucky a Spice Girls tape. But, by then, he had grown out of his crush on Emma Bunton.

Lucky wishes he had kept the tape. But it's now sealed in a columbarium, behind a tile with Pearl's face and name on it. He should have kept it. Not like she ever cared for the bloody Spice Girls.

I cared for Coconut, Lucky. And now you've lost her.

He nearly falls out of his chair.

'Lucky, are you okay?' Frowning, Mit reaches out a hand to steady him.

Lucky shakes his head. 'We have to find Coconut, Mit. We have to find her.'

Which is, like most things, easier said than done. Thankfully, Mit has a strategy. Like a general preparing for war, she outlines it for Lucky, using their greasy table at the roti canai joint as a mock-up map. She takes the jar of sugar from the condiments plate, tells him it's his hotel, then puts it in the middle of the table. There are, she tells him, two animal shelters within a thirty-kilometre radius of the hotel. The small bowl between them, now scraped clean of dal, she puts about ten centimetres away from the sugar jar. This is the animal shelter in Petaling Jaya, about forty minutes away in KL traffic. Her phone, the second animal shelter, goes on the other side of the sugar. About an hour away from the bowl, she tells him, but near the SPCA—Lucky's phone, which she places next to hers.

'We can cover all of it by six if we start now. And after that, we can check this area again. Onwards!'

She gets up, pays for breakfast and starts walking briskly towards the hotel, where she's left her car. Lucky hurries after her. How wonderful she is, how warrior-like. Lucky draws his shoulders back, feeling like he too must be warrior-like and cool and confident.

Coconut, we're coming! Leonidas-Lucky bellows and strides on, sword drawn.

A yell from somewhere to his left. 'Lucky! Over here!' Mit waves. Oh, he's been going in the wrong direction. 'God, you're slow today. Hurry up!'

'Coming, Mit, coming!' *Meowrrrr.*

* * *

It's Friday and the traffic is as thick as kaya. Thick and viscous and sticky. Kaya—it's been such a long time since he's had good kaya. Lucky imagines himself in his kitchen with a nice hot cup of coffee and a thick slice of soft fluffy local bread slathered with kaya and butter. And Coconut at his feet, and Mit grinning at him . . .

The car jerks forward as Mit slams the brakes to avoid hitting a motorcyclist who's suddenly veered into her lane. Lucky stares at the small motorbike puttering slowly in front of them, two adults and two children calmly balanced on its slim seat. One of the children is facing backwards, a girl about six or seven in a school uniform that looks far too big for her. Mit blows her a kiss. The child giggles and blows a kiss back. Lucky shakes his head. That's right—she likes kids. How did he forget?

Really, how did he forget? It was probably why she wanted to get married—to have kids. It was why he didn't want to. Kids? Him? Pearl had laughed at the idea the only time he had brought it up, and after an initial sputter of indignation he'd joined in. It really was funny, the thought of him being a father, having to take care of a small creature and run after it and feed it and clean up after it and carry it around. So funny, and quite quite unthinkable.

'Go go go go go! What are you waiting for? A sign? Because hey genius, that's a traffic light. IT'S A SIGN! GO! GO!'

He hasn't forgotten *this*. He shakes his head, watching her hit the steering wheel and shake her fists in the direction of the errant driver. So much for Botticelli nymph.

The sun beats down on the car as they drive through downtown KL, manoeuvring around potholes and avoiding collisions with daredevil motorcyclists and pedestrians crossing the streets at random.

In spite of the air conditioning, it's getting warm inside, but Lucky knows better than to crack open the window—all he'll get is hot dust in his face and Mit yelling at him to fucking close the window. They drive in silence, broken only intermittently by Mit's verbal abuse of other motorists and physical abuse of the steering wheel.

'Oh my god, did you see that guy?' She turns her head to glare at a car making a sudden turn into a side road. 'Got his driving licence at the supermarket.'

Lucky tries his best not to snicker. This is one of her favourites, and the variations are endless. Supermarket, pasar malam, mamak stall, burger stand, bakery. He's heard them all—in fact, bakery was his contribution.

'How's work?'

'What?' She squints at a large, blue road sign and makes a face. 'Sorry, Lucky—what?'

'Work! How's work?'

'I'm managing. You?'

'Good. I started a cafe.'

'Yes. You told me.' She sounds distant. Should he have not mentioned the cafe?

'It's going well. Shawn says . . .'

'Great.'

Oh, god. Does everyone go through this special hell with ex-girlfriends or is it just him? One moment the song that's playing is 'I Want to Hold Your Hand', the next moment she's switched the record and it's suddenly 'Happiness is a Warm Gun'.

Mit turns up the radio and they sit in silence for the rest of the drive to Petaling Jaya. As they walk into the pet shelter, she turns to him with a frown.

'Hey. Don't feel like you have to make conversation or anything, okay?'

'I wasn't.'

'Seriously. You never used to ask about my work.' She raises her eyebrows. 'So why were you asking? Small talk? Really? You couldn't think of anything better than work?'

Lucky frowns, confused. What exactly has he done wrong?

'Look, if you really want to know . . . I got laid off a few months ago. I've moved back into my mum's house.'

'Okay.' Lucky blows out his cheeks. 'I'm sorry.'

'It's fine.' She pats his arm but doesn't look at him. 'I'm fine. But let's not talk about me, okay? Let's just find the cat.'

Mit manages a smile as he holds open the door for her and they walk through a wide, poorly lit corridor towards what looks like some sort of admin office. She shouldn't have snapped at him. Poor thing— he didn't mean to rile her up or remind her that, after so many years of slogging like a pig at the agency and working every other weekend, it seems to have all come down to nothing.

But seriously, how clueless can a guy be? It's a Friday and she's here driving him around the city, hunting down this damn cat, and it hasn't even occurred to him that under regular circumstances, she'd need to be at work. Not a word, not the smallest enquiry on whether she was free to help or if it was okay to take the day off, nothing. Nothing. At first, she had just shrugged it off as part of his anxiety, but for him to glibly ask her about work like that without bothering to connect it to her being so obviously off work now—utterly inexcusable.

She sighs. Is it? Is it really inexcusable? Or is she picking on him because she doesn't like that in spite of the fact that she's ignored his texts for five years and only replied yesterday because he seemed to be genuinely in crisis, right now, she's actually really pleased they're hanging out?

And this feels so much like their old adventures, driving around KL hunting down Sarawak laksa and nasi biryani and lam mee. *Why* is she pleased? Hasn't she had enough of this feckless man and his idle rich stupidity and his stupid glowing face and his stupid bumbling randomness? She growls. Lucky turns to stare, but she ignores him. Maybe Coconut's had enough, she doesn't say.

Of course it's not his fault he's grown up rich and he really isn't any sort of rich asshole and she's never seen him look down his nose on anyone worse off, but sometimes she wishes he would have a bit of perspective. A bit of common sense. A bit of . . . gravity. That's it—gravity. There's always been something so absurdly light-headed about Lucky. Even now, even—

'Oh, they like you!' This is the surprised voice of a volunteer in the cat section of the shelter.

The room is large and white and sad, three walls of wire cages with a cat in each one. As Lucky looks into the cages in search of Coconut, the cats come to the front of their cages to look at him. They put their paws against the square holes formed by criss-crossing wires and mew and mew. Mit watches as Lucky says a solemn hello to every cat, telling them he's lost a cat and he's trying to find her.

'Guys, I've been such an idiot,' she hears him mournfully confide to two large tabbies.

'Your friend is really getting some sort of VIP treatment. The cats don't usually do this,' the volunteer tells Mit as she leaves the room. 'Back in a bit.'

'Mit, Mit, Coconut's not here.' Lucky looks haggard as he finishes his thorough examination of the cages.

She's about to say something placatory when his head snaps in a different direction, towards the door. 'Oh god, Mit, look—'

The volunteer has just brought in a box and they can hear the kittens inside before they can see them. Lucky and Mit stand still for a moment, staring into the box, mesmerized by the five tiny creatures in the foul-smelling box mewling, growling, jumping over each other. Lucky picks up a yowling kitten. It's a tortoiseshell. All the kittens are tortoiseshells, little balls of white, brown, black.

'Oh, they're like little Coconuts!' Lucky picks up another one, a stupid grin on his face.

Has he ever looked so goofy, Mit wonders, watching him balance the two kittens on his forearm and pick up a third. She never even knew he liked cats, but look at him now, meowing at kittens. But suddenly he stops and the stupid grin disappears. He nuzzles the head of the nearest kitten and whispers something to it, looking frazzled.

'Adopt a kitten? Adopt five? What about a nice cat, or two?' The volunteer decides she must take advantage of this cat-people couple while they're still kitten-struck. 'Taufik here is a real gentleman.'

Taufik only has three legs, but he manages to saunter up to the front of his cage and give Mit and Lucky a long, scrutinizing look. Lucky reaches down to pat the cat respectfully on the forehead, introducing himself and Mit. As the volunteer looks on with a bemused air, Mit notices that Lucky's managed to smooth out his anxious frown from a minute ago. Such a poseur, that man. Always remembering to put his best face forward.

'Well, Taufik. Delighted to meet you.' Lucky bows slightly. Mit rolls her eyes. There it is again, that lack of gravity.

But as he apologizes profusely first to the kittens and then to the volunteer, telling them he must go forth and find his sister's cat, the lovely Coconut, and as he fills up a donation form at the front office before they leave, she smiles ruefully. *Odd man, but at least he's not an asshole.*

* * *

As they drive towards the SPCA, Lucky is desperate but hardly daring to be hopeful. The second pet shelter had thirty-seven homeless cats but none of them were Coconut. After pledging a year's supply of cat food, which costs quite a bit more than he expected, he leaves with his shoulders sagging and his heart in his feet.

Coconut, if I find you, I'll poach and grill and steam as much salmon as you want for a year. Cod, if you prefer!

Half an hour later, he renews this vow: *Ten years!*

No Coconut at the SPCA. No Coconut! Mit watches Lucky as they turn out of the small parking lot, feeling sorry for him but knowing there's nothing she can say. He stares glumly out the window as they drive back towards the hotel, one hand tugging at his hair, the other clasped around his throat. Why does he keep doing that?

Poor guy. She's never seen him so miserable. Of course, she wasn't there when Pearl went missing and after . . . that must have been hard for him. Mit followed the news of the crash anxiously for weeks, hoping for good news, wanting to call him, knowing she should, putting it off anyway. He won't want to talk to you, she told herself. Not about Pearl.

She'd hated Pearl. She felt terrible for Lucky that he'd lost his sister, of course she did, but that woman was a horror. A crazy-ass bitch. A bully. And now she's driving around searching for the woman's cat. She can see Pearl watching her weave her way through rush-hour traffic, smiling her wide sarcastic smile.

Awww, you're such a sweetheart, Mit. All this for Lucky?

Mit thumps the steering wheel hard. *Fuck you, Pearl.*

Chai

is already brewing when they arrive. Mit's mother is at the stove, trying to pretend it's perfectly acceptable, completely unsurprising, for her elder daughter to bring home for tea the man who refused to marry her years ago and drove her to cut her hair in some horrible unbecoming style completely unsuited to beautiful Punjabi girls with beautiful Punjabi curls. Thank goodness it's all grown out now. Poor dear looked like a mop for some time. Of course she didn't tell her.

What she did tell her Gurmit then: 'Darling, he's a weak man. What were you thinking, proposing to him? Of course he ran off. He's not for you.'

She wants to tell her Gurmit now: 'Darling, he's a weak man. And he looks like a *hippie*. Please tell me you haven't proposed again. And if you have, I hope he runs off.'

Instead, she throws another cardamom pod into the milky tea in the saucepan and gives it a stir, one eye fixed on the small kitchen table where her daughter and the hippie are sitting, heads bent over a magazine.

'You did this?' the hippie is asking her daughter, eyes wide and voice rising in a tone of wonder.

Why so surprised? She's a clever girl. Distracted, indignant, Mrs Randhawa throws an extra pinch of fennel into the saucepan.

Lucky flips through the pages of an issue of the quarterly food magazine that Mit started two years ago. The style is raw and quirky and vivid, every page a bit of a visual assault (if an assault is ever

269

somewhat pleasant), bursting with a mixture of illustrations and not-quite-studio photographs. In the issue he's holding, *Ode to Sambal*, the centre spread is a rhyming ballad on being worthy of sambal sotong, with coy-looking cuttlefish in tight-fitting baju kebaya dancing along the top and bottom borders. He laughs—how bizarre, and how very Mit—and flips back to the editorial letter at the start of the issue. Mit stares back at him from the page, a figure in black and white in the middle of a colourful, chaotic market.

'This is so cool,' he tells her. *You are so cool.*

She smiles. 'Thanks. It's been my side project for a while now, but we've had to stop.' She throws up her hands. 'It's so fucking hard to get advertisers, and I don't want to ask anyone to contribute their work for free.'

'Do you need help? I could . . .'

She holds up a hand to stop him. 'Lucky. It's fine.' A little fiercely, but she softens it with a sigh. 'Don't worry. I'm not giving up, and anyway, let's drink up and keep searching.'

Her mother has brought a tray to the table with two mugs of tea and a small glass bowl of sugar. Lucky's heart sinks a little at the sight of the tray and the bowl. He's getting the guest treatment. Back in the day, when he visited on weekends, her mother would pour out the tea into mugs at the counter and tell them to come get it themselves.

'You must have a biscuit.'

From a cupboard, Mit's mother extracts a round blue tin of Danish Butter Cookies, the kind everyone in Malaysia associates with gift hampers wrapped up in red or green or yellow cellophane and presented to clients and anyone else whose favour you've curried or are currying this festive season. As Mrs Randhawa pries the tin open with a key, Lucky's heart sinks further. Festive cookies, and she's not even going to let him open the tin himself. His transition from almost-family to stranger–guest is complete.

'Thanks, Aunty.' If he had had the sense to marry Mit, he would be calling her Mum. Or Ma, or whatever she wanted him to call her. Aunty! Aunty signified nothing, nothing of the year he spent sitting in this kitchen, drinking this tea, commiserating with this woman on the potty-mouthed wilfulness of her daughter his girlfriend.

If he had had the sense to marry Mit he would be basking in the blissful domesticity of this warm kitchen fragrant with hundreds of spices, fussed over and coddled along with the 1980s Pyrex and the matching Tupperware and the Baby Belling oven that Mit's father won in an office lucky draw about twenty years ago. He would be digging through that oil-stained cupboard now, searching for that jar he knows is there because her mother never lets it go empty, the one full of peanuts fried with curry leaves. Instead, he must sit here like a good guest munching these flat pale brittle cookies that the Danes have probably never heard of.

God, did he really say 'okay' when she suggested they split? Did he really mean it when he said he didn't know where it was going with her and whether he would ever be ready to be seriously serious? Well, he was only thirty then . . . thirty-two. Life was supposed to be . . . beginning, according to all the magazines and the books and the movies, and marriage sounded too much like an end. And 'seriously serious' sounded like the beginning of the end, or worse, the end of the beginning.

God, Thirty-Two-Year-Old Lucky—what a fucking cliche.

'How's the tea?'

Lucky looks up from the magazine he's not reading. He takes another sip from his mug and smiles. 'Perfect. Thanks, Aunty.'

Across the table, Mit grins wickedly at him. She mouths, LIAR.

He sticks out his tongue and rolls back his eyes. If he had had the sense to marry her, he would have also had the honour of lying about liking her mother's masala chai for the rest of his life.

God, Thirty-Two-Year-Old Lucky—what a dumbass.

Now he's Mitless, Pearlless, Coconutless. Clueless. And on top of it all he's feeling—he smiles wanly—rather unlucky.

'What are you smiling about?'

'Nothing.' He sighs and drinks more tea. And makes a face. And sighs again. 'Do you still think we'll find her?

It's been five days. Five days of doing rounds of the same pet shelters and the SPCA every morning, then searching the area around the hotel every afternoon, checking behind every dustbin in Bukit Bintang. Twice he's been charged at by cockroaches, three times glowered at by rats. His nerves are frayed. His hopes have been dashed, over and over and over. He's beginning to wonder if he'll ever find Coconut. Cats go missing all the time and they don't always turn up. He's read online that there are many reasons why a cat may go missing (well, he lost his cat, but whatever), and one article in particular has struck him hard: 'Your Cat Might Have Found a More Favourable Environment'. The writer cautions against making a pet cat feel upset, unwelcome, or uncared for in any way. Clearly gunning for the badge of Very Special Friend of Cats when their revolution is successful, he writes: 'If your cat has everything it needs and wants in your home, it need never go looking elsewhere for a more comfortable life. Gadgets like a cat water fountain can help improve your cat's perception of your home.'

A cat water fountain, a quick Google search reveals, is a pretty nifty thing with a pump that bubbles and recycles water in a never-ending loop so that cats may drink moving water instead of the sordid still stuff of regular water bowls. Lucky can understand how it might be worthwhile incentive for a cat to remain. Entertainment and sensory stimulation and refreshment all in one burbling gadget. If he were a cat, he would demand one. He would go on thirst strike until one appeared. When they return home, if he finds her . . .

Coconut, come back! I'll get you a water fountain. A big one! We can get one that plays music if you like. Or something shaped like a fish? A bird? Anything you want!

'Of course we'll find her.' Mit raises her mug at him. 'We will.'

Lucky forces himself to take a big gulp of tea. Ugh. Tea. 'Okay. Thanks, Mit.'

Oh, Mit. Without her he would be such a mess. Mit has been delightful, a bubbling brook (a cat water fountain!) of ideas. She's put up posts and left her number on social media and on cat-lovers' forums she's found online. She's called up vets in the area, leaving a description of Coconut, asking them to keep a lookout for a small tortoiseshell with a white-tipped tail, white paws, and nice manners.

But how much longer should he keep looking? Another week? Two weeks? A month? For all he knows, Coconut's found a nice family with children to terrorize or some good-looking banker type with a cat water fountain. Or she's joined a band of street cats and is having the time of her life running after vermin, killing birds. Coconut turned brigand—Pearl would either kill him or find it hilarious.

And then there's Mit. It's been so good to see her again and talk and laugh. But it's also been . . . frightening. Lucky takes another drink of masala chai and shudders. Is there anything more frightening than someone who sees through your BS? Yes—someone who wants to trawl through your BS and pick out the bones and feathers of small animals you shouldn't have eaten.

'So, what are you doing these days?' she asked him a little over an hour ago, on the tail end of their late afternoon search through Bukit Bintang.

As they tramped through the now-familiar back lanes, some filthy, some filthier, he told her about Caffiend, about Shawn and his quest for perfect espressos and perfect water filters, about Dinah joining them for evening shifts and drunken suppers, about Meixi and the crush he suspects she has on Shawn, about customers who come in asking for decaf cappuccinos with an extra shot, about the coffee traders they've met, about Kassim.

'You like it? Being in the cafe business? I keep hearing what a tough trade it is. Cafes go bust all the time, don't they?'

'They do in Singapore. Is it the same here? Well, it's a bit of a miracle we're in our fourth year now.' They hadn't broken even yet, but they were close. Perhaps because he owns the building now, so they're not paying rent any more. Nope, he wasn't going to tell Mit this. He shrugged. 'It's tough. But I like coffee.'

She rolled her eyes. 'Lucky, it's not the same thing. I love laksa, but you don't see me trying to open a laksa stall.'

'But I do really like coffee. And some of the beans we get . . . there's this very rich Vietnamese arabica that we use in a blend—'

She cut him off. 'Very nice. But do you like running a cafe? Waking up early and all that?'

'Shawn takes the morning shift.'

'Ah.'

'I usually close up.' He tried to summon a force he didn't feel. 'I go in at least five days a week.'

A raised eyebrow. 'Wow, five days. And *now*?' She bent to look under a car that looked like it had been stolen, stripped, and dumped in the alleyway they were now walking through. 'Now that you're here?'

'Five days is a lot. And Shawn's okay with me taking time off.' Lucky looked away. He scans the alley for another dumpster to check.

'How many days a week does Shawn go in?'

No dumpster in sight. They walked on. Lucky looked at his shoes. 'Pretty much every day.' Shawn takes a full day off every couple of weeks, but that's because he's Shawn, right? Incurable workaholic, always overdoing things a little. *Enjoys* overdoing things a little. Back in architecture school, he was always the guy who submitted more drawings than required, built additional models, always inventing the extra mile and then running it. While Lucky, well, he . . .

'Sounds like you got the better deal.' Mit summed it up for him. 'And Shawn's okay with this?'

'I'm sure he is.' Or he'd have said something, surely.

'And your other partner, Dinah, she pulls shifts on top of a full-time job?' Mit's question sounded completely innocent, but Lucky knew better.

'When she can, yea. She doesn't mind.' Or she'd have said something, surely.

'Of course not.' She paused, wiping her forehead with the back of a hand. 'And you're okay with all this? Fewer shifts, fewer days. And you like what you do?' Oh so casual.

'Yes.' Through slightly gritted teeth he was trying to un-grit.

'Okay then.' She gave him a long look, then shrugged.

'Okay then.'

'Tea at my mother's?'

And here they are. And now he keeps wondering if Shawn really is fine with their arrangement, or if he somehow feels short-changed? He hadn't made any sort of fuss when Lucky asked if it was okay to take a couple of weeks off, and Lucky never thought Shawn would mind—but what if he did? Better call Shawn. Soon.

As he starts on his second mug of tea and Mit's mother opens the cookie tin again for him, Lucky wonders what Coconut will make of Mit. Mit and her big voice and her big hair. Well, they both like food. Mit has been compulsively eating the cookies on the plate in front of him and so far the cookie-scoffing ratio is 5:1 in her favour. And Mit likes cats. And he likes Mit and he hopes Coconut will like her too. It would be catastrophic if they didn't like each other. Lucky frowns and bites into a cookie. Quite, quite catastrophic. Hmm, catastrophe—a trophy for cats? He giggles.

Watching him, watching her daughter watch him, Mrs Randhawa sighs. What a hopeless daydreamer—staring into space, smiling or frowning to himself. Her Gurmit deserves better. Mother and daughter watch as he finishes the cookie and picks up another.

Mrs Randhawa allows herself the shadow of a smile. Well, at least she's got rid of those terrible cookies—who knows how old they are? And now she can wash out that lovely tin and use it for papad.

* * *

'Leng cai, you want satay?'

Mit giggles. Lucky nods, smiling sheepishly. 'Okay. And two beers.'

'Mutton again? You like lah. Twenty sticks okay?' While they think this over, the satay seller turns her perfectly coiffed grey head and yells into the alley, 'Ah Kin! Heineken *liong peng!*'

Lucky's hungry. 'Twenty sticks mutton. And ketupat. Extra sauce.'

'Leng cai, for you I bring extra, *extra* sauce.' Lady Satay winks as she walks off.

The drinks seller's son brings their beer and takes the caps off with his bare hands as Lucky watches in awe. As the boy counts out the change from the fifty-ringgit note Lucky hands him, Mit and Lucky clink bottles and take long, grateful gulps.

The boy puts the money on the table and picks up the bottle caps. 'Mister, yesterday your cat come, why you never come?'

Lucky puts down the green glass bottle before he can drop it. 'What?'

The boy shrugs. 'Your cat come here yesterday.' He grins. In Cantonese, he says, 'My father gave your cat beer. He says it's good for cats, don't worry.'

Lucky stares as the boy walks back to his father's van-turned-drinks-stall in the middle of the alley. What was that? All he understood from that sentence was 'beer', 'cat', and 'no problem'. He turns to Mit, who looks shocked and amused in equal measure. Well, her Cantonese is better. 'What did he say?'

Mit snickers. 'His father gave Coconut a beer. But at least now we know that she's around here some—'

'Cats can't drink beer!' Lucky leaps from his plastic stool and dashes towards the drinks van.

He finds the drinks seller behind the van, chipping away at an ice block with a hammer and a chisel. The man looks up as he approaches. Lucky manages a friendly wave but even he can hear the edge in his voice. 'Hey, you saw my cat last night? And you gave her BEER?'

The man stands up, hammer and chisel gripped tightly. 'A bit lah. Why so angry?'

Lucky takes a deep breath. He's not angry. He's calm. He's cool. He's going to strangle this man for plying Coconut with beer and then feed him to the cats at the SPCA. But first a word of caution, a metaphorical glove against the chest of this bad man. 'Cats can't drink beer. It's very bad for them.'

'Can! No problem.' The man waves the chisel. Lucky can't tell if this is meant to be conciliatory or threatening. He takes another deep breath and widens his stance, just in case.

It is Lady Satay who flounces up and saves him the trouble of a duel. She waves a skinny hand in the face of the drinks seller, shaking her head. 'Ah Kin, *lei bei go jek mau yam beh jao ah?*' She clicks her tongue. '*Chee seen ah lei!*'

'She says he's nuts for feeding Coconut beer.' Mit's come up next to Lucky.

'Damn right!' Lucky glares at Drinks Man, who doesn't notice.

A rapid discussion ensues between Lady Satay and Drinks Man, punctuated by finger-wags and eye-rolls on her end, sighs and grunts on his. There is no battle, only a winner. Mit translates quickly: 'Very, very little . . . just one lick . . . the cat didn't like the beer . . . total waste of beer . . . so I gave it water . . . Ah Leong gave it fish! And now she's saying, don't give cats beer . . . nobody gives your son beer, right?' Mit gives him a sideways look. 'Don't worry, looks like Coconut doesn't take after you or Pearl all that much, okay? Fancy wasting beer.'

Lucky wants to laugh but he can't. But he can feel his heart quieten. Coconut is alive and safe, not poisoned or kidnapped or trapped somewhere. But where is she now?

Coconut, I'm here!

Meanwhile Lady Satay treats him to a benevolent smile. 'Leng cai, you go sit down lah. Maybe your cat will come back. You eat and wait, okay?'

They eat and wait. And eat and wait. And eat and wait. But beer-averse Coconut doesn't appear.

* * *

'We'll find her, Lucky. We will.'

In the dark, her voice is low and crisp and calm. Lucky turns on his side to face her, but he can only make out a faint outline of hair, a smudge of nose. It's like they're back at her tiny apartment again, lying next to each other in her bed talking. He used to wait all day for this. This is the thing he's missed most—talking to her in the dark, folding his voice into a semi-demi version of itself, hearing her voice but not quite seeing her, listening for her laugh. Somehow it had all the headiness of an adventure and all the comfort of a burrow.

It still does.

And in the dark, as they edge a little closer to each other, Lucky shuts his eyes and tells Mit things he can't imagine telling her in daylight. He tells her what it was like to wait for Pearl's rescue and then for her recovery, and what it was like to stop. He tells her how it sometimes feels like time has stopped and how little he cares if it has. He tells her how much he loves cooking for Coconut, how she likes her sardines seared on the outside and rare in the centre. He wants to tell her that Coconut talks to him, but he doesn't—not yet. But he tells her about the house in Teluk Intan and how he feels he must see it but can't explain why.

He tells her, 'I'm glad you're here, Mit.'

He feels her touch his face, just like she used to, and he takes her hand and kisses it. And as her hands reach into his hair and pull him closer, he breathes a long deep sigh that feels like it's been straining against his chest for years.

'Mit . . .'

'Leng cai, shut up.'

The railway station

is predictably postmodern on the outside, all glass and concrete and steel, but on the inside, air conditioning notwithstanding, it's like a portal has opened up from the station to a busy street in the middle of the city, somewhere along Jalan Masjid India or Petaling Street. Alongside the fast food outlets, cafes, pharmacies, and convenience stores that everyone expects of any self-respecting railway station in any Asian city, Lucky finds small unpretentious shops with plastic-covered tables selling mee rebus, nasi lemak, goreng pisang, and curry puffs, stores selling clothes and scarves and underwear out of massive bargain bins, an old-fashioned barbershop, a Chinese apothecary, at least three tailor's shops. The wide central walkway under the massive steel-trussed roof would have looked wider if it weren't interrupted by a long line of stalls, each the size of a small van, peddling shrimp paste, dried fruit, coffee powder, prayer mats, plastic toys, honey, and even cookware.

Years ago, when Lucky first became a frequent visitor to Kuala Lumpur, he'd been disconcerted by the chaos, by the Malaysian predilection for turning everything into some sort of bazaar. Even KL's international airport can't do without the kuih stands and the stalls selling scarves and coconut candy. He found himself wondering, over and over again, how much kuih the average Malaysian consumed. But after a few trips, he found he rather liked this eccentricity that prevented Malaysian buildings from ever turning into the soulless, orderly things that all new buildings in Singapore aspire to be. And he loved being able to walk into a modern railway station and buy banana fritters and keropok and, if he so desired, a saucepan or a pandan cake or a paper kite. And yes, kuih.

Now, as he buys freshly made putu piring for his journey, Lucky smiles in anticipation. Steamed rice cakes filled with dark, crumbly brown sugar on a bed of soft grated coconut—god, he could eat this every day forever. When the vendor hands him a banana-leaf-lined plastic bag full of his favourite kuih, he pokes his nose in and takes a few big sniffs. *Oh, my.*

Yet later, as his train pulls out of the station, as it emerges from the dark underground into the bright afternoon sunlight, as the train begins to pick up speed and the view begins to whizz by, as he begins to eat his way through the bag of piping-hot putu piring, it is the smell of ginger and lemongrass shampoo clinging to Mit's hair that he thinks about.

The hair he'd buried his face in just an hour ago when she dropped him off at the station. Perhaps he held on a little too long, but she let him.

'I'll keep looking for Coconut, don't worry.' And then she patted him on the cheek and told him to please get out of the car before the drivers behind them came over and dragged him out.

'Mit . . .'

'Leng cai, get your ass on that train and call me tonight.' She smiled but her mouth looked tired. 'Your cat is probably having a ball without you cramping her style and denying her birds.'

'Mit . . .' God, there were so many things he felt he should say.

'Be brave. But don't walk into dark parking lots.'

Now he feels terrible for leaving Coconut behind. Oh, he shouldn't have he shouldn't have.

The day before had been another disappointment. They had scoured Bukit Bintang, tramping down the busier streets, combing the side streets the alleys the rows and rows of pubs and karaoke joints, even asking the security guards at that great big mall that Gurmit hates because her old school had been torn down to make way for it. ('It's a Singaporean mall, Lucky. It was designed by Singaporeans. Did I ever tell you that?' She had—too many times.) At night, they went back to the hawker stalls near the hotel but the stingray man, the beer boy, and Lady Satay said they hadn't seen her.

This morning, even though he'd woken up early, ready for another day of Coconut-hunting, Mit sat him down and told him no. He should go to Teluk Intan by himself, she said, and she would keep looking for Coconut, who was bound to show up when she'd had enough of street food and KL rats and back-lane exploration. He should go, because one week was a long time to be stuck in KL when he should be off doing whatever it was he was going to do. And, she wanted to know, how long did he mean to leave Shawn in charge of the cafe all by himself? Didn't he say he was going to be away for two weeks? And how long had it been now—a month? It wasn't fair for him to think he could just swan in whenever he wanted and leave whenever it suited him. She said that last bit with a pointed sort of stare, and Lucky found it hard to argue with her.

'Should we talk?' he asked instead. 'About us.'

'There's no us, Lucky. And you're . . . fixing a hole.'

'But you're still the one, right? For me.' He sounded pathetic even to himself.

'Lucky, don't make this into something it's not. It's been great having you here and everything, and I'm sorry if I . . . I didn't think you wanted anything serious. Look, I'm really sorry.' She didn't look at him. She sighed.

'You're still the one, Mit.'

She didn't say anything. He didn't know what else to do, so he packed his bag and let her drive him to the railway station.

'The woman has swept you off your feet.' This was Pearl's pronouncement years ago, a few months after he and Mit started dating. She had, and he loved it. But Pearl didn't, and it was confusing. He thought she'd be pleased. She didn't say she wasn't, but she laid cookie crumbs of caution in random conversations, finding a way to tell him she thought things were going too fast with Mit without actually saying anything outright.

'That chiffon cake I made today—what a disaster. It rose far too quickly and now it's all cracked and dry on top. That's the problem when we rush into things, you know?'

'Is that coffee a tad burnt? I should have checked if the water was too hot. But I was in such a hurry, and you know what it's like when people try to rush something delicate.'

'A *moth* in your room? Whoops, I must have forgotten to shut the door completely earlier. Well, that teaches us something, doesn't it? Take a little more time to do things properly, eh? Oh please, chase it out yourself.'

And so forth. And then, after a whole year of this, when he told her he might just, might just, might marry Mit, she said: 'I guess it's time I move out anyway.'

He was shocked; he tried to tell her no, Mit would move here and they would all be fine in this old house, but Pearl only smiled and told him she hoped he'd be happy. 'You'll be starting a family, and you'll want your space, and I don't want to be in your way.'

In his way? Lucky was hurt that she could even imagine it, let alone say it. But he put off giving Mit a proper answer. He'd wait, and Pearl would get used to the idea and then she'd realize that the house was big enough for everyone. But then she began looking at apartments nearby, and he began to worry. And then she found one, and a light went out in his head.

'Pearl, you can't go.' He looked at her across the kitchen island and couldn't imagine the kitchen without his sister in it, making him papaya salad.

Pearl looked up from the bowl of shredded papaya she was squeezing lime into. 'Lucky, don't be silly. I must.' It sounded like she was trying not to sound sad. This made him sad.

'You mustn't. I want you here. Mit does too.' This last bit was a lie. Mit would probably prefer to have a place of their own. But he'd cross that river of fire when he had to.

'Nonsense. Every woman wants a place of her own. And you'll be having kids . . .' A pause, a smile. 'You know how I feel about kids.' Pearl hated children. But the gods have a sense of humour—children adored Pearl.

'I don't know about kids.' He and Pearl had already decided that the very idea of Lucky having kids was ridiculous.

'Well, in any case, you're settling down. Building a nest. Maybe you'll redecorate, get rid of the zebra rug and the dragon. She hasn't even seen the house. She'll hate the wallpaper. Everyone hates that wallpaper.' She rolled her eyes. She was right. Everyone else hated the parakeet wallpaper. But they had grown up with it, grown fond of it; they could never dream of changing it.

Pearl gave the salad a final pinch of salt and scraped it all out onto a dish for him. 'It's okay, Lucky. It's a good thing you're settling down. At least that's one of us covered.' She sighed. 'I'll move out—better that way, you'll see. You'll want the house to yourselves once you've settled down.'

Lucky chewed his papaya salad but couldn't taste it. Settling down. Building a nest. Having . . . kids. *Changing the wallpaper.* It was frightening. He was frightened. 'I don't know. Maybe it's too soon.' He ate another mouthful, gave up, and put down his fork. 'Maybe I don't want to settle down.'

'But why? You're sure she's the one. It's time.'

Time? Was there a clock ticking somewhere? He fretted. He frowned. His sister reached out and put her hand over his. He put his other hand over hers. 'I'm not . . . sure. I don't know.'

She frowned. 'Well, if you're not sure you want to settle down . . .'

Settle down. Why, what did that even mean?

Pearl gave his hand a squeeze. 'I just want you to be happy.'

Did she? Lucky isn't so sure now. All that talk about kids and wallpaper and bloody *nests*—had she been trying to freak him out? How convenient it was that the owner of the apartment she'd found agreed so readily to forget all about the lease she'd signed once he and Mit called things off. And *he*, he was so relieved to still have Pearl that he managed to make it work—it being life without Mit, without eating roti canai in KL with her every weekend, without whispering to her in the dark, without being called leng cai in a leery way. What if he hadn't given it up? What if he had said his jellyfish okay to Pearl instead of to Mit? What if he had let his sister go instead of his heart?

Lucky's head hurts. Too many what-ifs. Stupid what-ifs. He checks the time and forces himself to look out the window, at the fields the houses the farms the trees. Another hour and he'll be in Ipoh, where he'll stay the night and figure out how to get to Teluk Intan. Can't be that far. A jolly bus ride will get him there, or perhaps a languid drive in a taxi. But not before he's had the coffee—Ipoh white coffee, in Ipoh no less. Lucky's mind throws itself out the window and into the wind, which carries it over the silver waters of Slim River, across a massive golf course and onto the coffee-scented streets of Ipoh in Lucky's imagination. But a sudden jolt in the train throws him forward in his seat, and his mind snaps back into the carriage, wanting to know:

Lucky, what if you had married Mit?

He doesn't know. And it's weird thinking of himself in the second person. But it does make it easier to say a few things:

Lucky, you fool. Lucky, you should have stayed with her.

But it would've been harder, wouldn't it? To stay, knowing she wanted to get married and have children and possibly change the wallpaper. And now? *Now* does he want to settle down and have children and possibly change the wallpaper?

Was Pearl right to prevent him from settling down? Would he have hated it? Would he have resented Mit? Would he have run after children and resented them? Would he, like his mother, be a vague sort of parent? Or like his father, a distant, imperious figure full of social baggage and eccentric quirks? Who would Lucky Lee be, if *Pearl* had let *him* go? A happily married man, consumed by wife and children and loving it? A bitter creature ripe for a mid-life crisis? Does it even matter now?

Why can't everything be simpler? Every time Lucky thinks of Mit and what to do with what he thinks of her, the thoughts fly from him in frenzied curlicues, defying his attempts to gather them, tie them together, and make some sense of them. Lucky shuts his eyes and leans against the glass window. God, who knew thinking could be such a pain? He must really stop.

By the time the train arrives in Ipoh, Lucky is exhausted from trying not to think. He misses Coconut. He realizes now what a welcome distraction she is from unwelcome thoughts. Everyone needs a cat like Coconut. Affectionate, entertaining, occasionally sympathetic, and terribly dogmatic (haha!) but well-meaning and—here his thoughts drift back to her telling him about beer in Mesopotamia—*so well-informed.* How much he misses his cat. *His* cat.

Oh, Coconut, Coconut, I'm coming back for you, Coconut.

He will have a cup of coffee—no point not having one now—and he will catch the next train back to Kuala Lumpur. He will find Coconut and he will . . . come back here and have more coffee.

Backpack strapped on tight, the plastic bag formerly containing kuih clutched in one hand, Lucky steps out of the train and onto the platform. He looks around, surprised. Nothing painfully postmodern about this station, apart from the escalators at both ends of the platform, it feels like he's stepped back into the early 1900s. Lucky walks through the cool, somewhat gloomy corridor through the belly of the building and steps out into the sunshine, turning back to have a proper look. Inside, it's a little tired and worn, but on the outside, the Ipoh railway station is a stately thing. It's everything he expects of a public building in the early twentieth-century British colonial style, with its large central dome and arched pediments and even the random Mughal elements thrown in for good measure. So typically Edwardian Baroque, but why not? Somehow this style does work in the sweltering tropics, all the gleaming cool white lines cutting through the heavy, humid air. And those thick walls are so good at keeping out the heat, not like the crappy glass-and-steel horrors everyone wants to build these days. Lucky walks up to a pillar and pats it appreciatively. A woman hurrying into the station stops for a second to stare at the strange man stroking a pillar—some pervert, no doubt—but hurries on, deciding she will not engage. Smiling, Lucky lifts the hand not patting the pillar in greeting. First rule of the effective tourist: be friendly to the locals.

A quick web search for local coffee shops takes him across the manicured garden of the railway station and into the old town of Ipoh, through streets flanked by shophouses so similar to the ones in Joo Chiat that he almost expects to turn the corner and find Caffiend there waiting for him, Shawn and all. It isn't, but there are a few cafes around, some industrial-chic, some vintage-kitsch. Rather promising, but right now he's in the mood for local coffee.

He finds what he's looking for tucked between a hardware store and a shop selling rattan furniture—a small kopitiam with a counter at the back and behind it a shirtless man wielding a sock-sieve. From a small Formica-topped table under a blissfully quick-spinning ceiling fan, Lucky watches the man spoon heaping tablespoons of coffee powder into the sock and drop it into a large coffee pot. He pours in hot water, then stirs the mixture, a long-handled spoon diving into the sieve, for a full minute. As Lucky stares, riveted, the man pours the coffee out of this pot into another, and then from the second pot back into the first one through the sieve. He does this over and over, the long trail of piping hot coffee leaping through the air from pot to pot to pot to pot like a snake. Not a drop spills or splashes as he repeats this a few more times, then puts the first pot on the counter, the sock still swimming in it, the coffee getting stronger and stronger.

'Kopi!' Lucky calls out his order. If he were the type to rub his hands in glee, he would. How wonderful! A fresh pot.

The man nods. He spoons a giant dollop of condensed milk into a small, ceramic cup, then pours black, opaque coffee over it. Coming out from behind the counter, he puts the cup on Lucky's table with an irreverent plonk, some of the coffee spilling out onto the saucer.

Not a drop spilt in the making, and now . . .

Lucky sips his coffee and sighs. He was being honest when he told Kassim that he's never made coffee with a sock, but what Lucky never tells anyone is that he doesn't dare. It frightens him, the coffee snake, the thought of so much hot liquid flying around, just waiting to scald a hand (his!) or a foot (his!) or a face (also his!). In Lucky's eyes, the shirtless (!) kopi man is a hero at par with Jason and Hercules.

So much easier to pull an espresso, pour hot water slowly into a phin or pour it even more slowly into a V60 dripper.

It's also more money, to be honest. He and Shawn could never charge anything more than three dollars for sock coffee (and even then their local kopitiam guy would laugh at their audacity), but for pouring water into a filter or over a Japanese dripper with a cult following, they can charge five, and for pressing a button at the right moment on their expensive Italian machine and frothing a bit of milk, they can charge more. His father would have been amused—he would also have tried to find a way to monopolize the Southeast Asian distribution of those drippers—but he would have seen it as a challenge; he would have wanted to elevate the old sock. Lucky sighs. They've tried to make Caffiend as Southeast Asian as possible, bringing in coffee from the region instead of the usual suspects in Africa and South America, trying to cultivate some appreciation for traditional brews, and he's always been rather proud of this. But if he can't master the Hainanese–Malayan sock, does it make him a bit of a fraud? His father would have had plenty to say about this, much of it to do with having soft hands.

Lucky drinks up the last of his kopi and wonders if he should order another. So many trains to Kuala Lumpur. He's got plenty of time. And Ipoh white coffee, so buttery and smoky and smooth, is his favourite Malaysian kopi.

The ceiling fan's rhythmic creak and hum is making him sleepy. For a moment, Lucky drowses, but suddenly he sits up straight as a plank.

Something is touching his knee. Something small and light. Something alive. Lucky inhales sharply as he prepares to flee whatever insect or rodent or hell's creature has begun its assault on him. Pushing his cup and saucer away, heart thumping, he looks under the table. Amber eyes peer up at him; a white-tipped tail is flicked against his knee.

'Hello, stranger. What took you so long?'

'Coconut! You're here!'

'Tell me something new.'

The wet tongue on his face

is what wakes Lucky up from his nap. He wasn't meaning to take one, but after he checked into the hotel, brought his backpack up to the room, and fed Coconut, he lay down on the bed and now the sunlight coming in through the curtains looks less intense and he's feeling a little groggy, but every scratchy lick of Coconut's tongue on his chin gets him a little wider awake.

'Okay, okay, you can stop now. I'm awake. Are you hungry? Are you okay?' Rolling onto his side, he checks her face and belly and paws and behind her ears. No sign of a fight or struggle, thank goodness.

'I'm fine, Lucky.' She gives his face a last lick.

'How did you get here?' He's been dying to ask her, but at the kopitiam earlier she curled up around his ankles and looked like she needed a rest. So, he put her on his lap, ordered another kopi, and just sat there and watched the kopi guy. It was a very pleasant hour.

'On a lorry. It was windy and I slept in a box that smelled like cabbage. But Miaowmiaow woke me up when we reached Ipoh so I could get off.'

'Who's Miaowmiaow?'

'The farmer's cat.'

Terrible name. There must be millions of cats named Miaowmiaow. 'What farmer? How did you meet Miaowmiaow?'

'Tompok took me to the meeting point. He was going there anyway—it's a farmers' market, and the goat's milk man likes cats. And Miaowmiaow said I could travel with him and his farmer because they were going back to somewhere called Cameron Highlands and Ipoh was on the way.'

This is getting a little nuts. 'Okay. And how did you meet Tompok?'

Coconut leaps from the bed onto the dressing table. As she paws its worn surface, looking like she would like to sharpen her claws on it, she tells Lucky about the cat network in Kuala Lumpur. 'A very fine and efficient system, Lucky. And their king is a very fine cat.'

'The cat network? They have a king?'

'It connects all cats. Every cat knows at least one other cat, and all those cats know other cats, and in the end, it's as if all cats know all cats. Quite useful.'

'And the king?'

'A very fine cat, as big as ten regular cats.'

She'd been very lucky to meet the Raja Kucing, who lives in one of the last remaining villages in the middle of the city and, as befits his status, is waited on by two families. Fresh fish is served to the Raja Kucing on a large leaf twice a day, and both families have surrendered all rights to their furniture. No cat knows how old the Raja Kucing is, but they all know he is wise and clever and once caught an owl. Any cat visiting the Raja Kucing must wait under the large rain tree next to the mosque until he appears.

Coconut wandered under the rain tree quite by accident after the bad man who took Lucky's bag dropped it somewhere in the village.

The Raja Kucing, on his first walk of the evening, spotted her and said, 'Hello, little one. You look lost. Have you come to see me?'

She looked behind her and saw the biggest cat she had ever seen. His fur was golden brown and shiny. His head was the size of a watermelon and his tail was like a feather-duster. And after she told him what had happened in the dark car park and how, after a long and scary ride on a motorcycle, she'd been tossed along with the bag next to a rubbish heap nearby, she explained she had to find her way back to her man Lucky, who was probably terrified without her.

The Raja Kucing looked very solemn. 'Oh my, your Lucky is quite incompetent. Are you sure he's worth the trouble? It might not be easy to find him, little one.'

Lucky stares at Coconut, indignant. 'What? Incompetent?'

Coconut stares back. 'Don't growl at me, Lucky. That's what the Raja said.' She sniffed. 'But I told him you're a good man most of the time.'

So the Raja decided he would help Coconut find her way back to Lucky. The cats in the village were told to keep an eye out on their city walks for the only thing that Coconut can remember about the surroundings of the hotel—an alleyway with a man cooking fish on the back of his motorcycle. (Lucky is amused to think of the street-hawker stall being described this way, but agrees it is an efficient way to put it.) On the first night, the cats didn't return with any news, but they told Coconut and their king that they had asked the cats they met in the city to help locate the alleyway with the fish man. On the second night, the cats brought no news again, but there was a lot of excitement about a woman who had started feeding cats near the Puduraya bus terminal.

The Raja was very pleased. 'It's so good for them, the nice warm feeling they get when they're able to share their food with us.'

Two days later, a city cat claimed to have met a fish man on a narrow street without cars between two buildings, and Coconut was brought to meet him by Bintang, one of the village cats. Bintang and Coconut climbed onto the back of a school bus, got off at the edge of the village, and got a ride to the city in the van of an evening-newspaper delivery man. There, they met the city cat, who brought them to the fish man she'd seen.

'It was the right man, and the right alley. And the man gave me some fish. But you weren't there.'

'I was there the next night! They told me you were there the night before, and I was waiting for you to come back. And I came back the night after that too.'

'Well, I couldn't smell you at all. So many smells in that place, Lucky! I tried to find the hotel, but I couldn't recognize any of the smells.' Coconut drops her head down. 'The other cats thought it was very strange that I had travelled in a bag so much that I didn't know what the street smelled like.'

The Raja Kucing put this down to more of Lucky's incompetence. 'Not everyone can care for a cat, little one.'

But he thought hard, and he decided it would be best for Coconut to meet Lucky at the next point in their journey. 'We will get you to Ipoh, little one. Tompok here will help you—he's travelled all over the country.'

Tompok, a large spotted cat with a crooked tail, told Coconut many stories about his travels as they walked across the city yesterday to the farmer's market where Miaowmiaow and his man the farmer set up their vegetable stall. And when they closed the stall at the end of the day, Coconut hopped into the back of the lorry and travelled with them to Ipoh, where she got off.

'I was walking around this morning and I could suddenly smell you and coffee, and that's how I found you.' Sitting upright on the dressing table, she cocks her head sideways at him, looking pleased with herself.

It is the weirdest, wildest tale Lucky has ever heard. The most ludicrous. Is he supposed to believe that Coconut has somehow found her way to Ipoh on the back of a truck, with the help of the cat king of Kuala Lumpur and his feline subjects? Lucky can't even remember telling Coconut that they were meant to head to Ipoh. And even if she somehow did manage to get to Ipoh, how did she find him at that coffee shop? It's crazy. It's impossible.

And yet here she is.

* * *

Lucky slips his phone back under his pillow and closes his eyes. The double darkness of night and eyes squeezed shut doesn't help. He can still see her text in his head.

`Hey, still no Coconut. Sorry. Will keep looking.`

Now what? Of course, he should reply, but what will he say? The truth sounds like . . . fiction. If he tells Mit that he's found Coconut in Ipoh, she'll be so confused. *Anyone would be!* And she'll want to know, won't she, how Coconut ended up here, how he found her? If he tells her that Coconut hitched a ride on the back of a vegetable truck on the advice of the cat king of Kuala Lumpur and that Coconut found *him*, Mit will think him . . . mad? Delusional? A liar?

Maybe he will just tell her he found Coconut at Kuala Lumpur station. Is even that too absurd?

Lucky sits up in bed, drawing the thin cotton sheet over his shoulders. Far-fetched. His entire life seems far-fetched. He sighs. What the hell was he thinking, charging to Ipoh like this? He doesn't even know what he's expecting to find here. A house is a house. Does it even matter now if Pearl kept it secret? That his father never mentioned it? They're both dead.

A rattle of wooden shutters, and he turns towards the window. It's Coconut, returning from her night-time prowl, leaping onto the ledge. In the reflected light from the convenience store across the road, she is green and goblin-esque, her eyes glassy and gleaming.

'Lucky, your face is all funny. Are you okay?' She bounds from ledge to floor to bed so quickly it looks like a single movement.

'I'm okay.'

'I'm so happy I managed to find you.' A little rumble begins in the depth of her chest, at the top of her belly. 'Aren't you happy I'm here?'

He reaches out and takes the purring cat in his arms. He buries his face in the warmth of her neck. 'Of course I am, Coconut.'

'If we go back to KL, we have to go see the Raja Kucing and thank him. And Tompok and Miaowmiaow.'

'Okay. We'll do that.'

Fuck it. He can live with absurd.

The driver of the pick-up truck

isn't the sweet, small-town aunty he imagined—the truck itself is a bit of a shock. But there's no time to stare. The slip of street in front of his hotel is all sewn up by the truck and two cars are waiting to pass— 9.00 a.m. is a busy time for the old town of Ipoh. As Lucky clambers into the passenger side of the pick-up, Coconut tucked under one arm, he wonders if he's anything like she's imagined.

'Hello, Aunty. Thank you for picking me up.'

His father's cousin (so technically an aunt) smiles and nods quickly, her eyes on the rear-view mirror as she changes gears, her long, bony fingers gripping the stick shift. 'No problem.'

Now that there's time to stare, he does. The woman in the driver's seat is lanky, much like his father, Pearl, and himself, and brown as a toasted sesame bun, like his father was. None of this surprises Lucky. But he'd pictured short, crimped hair; a plump, placid face; matching blouse and trousers in that same unflattering cut worn all over Southeast Asia; a small handbag full of tissue paper packets and handy bottles of Axe Oil. He'd looked out for a small car, something practical and easy to park. Instead, she rolled up in this pick-up, lean-looking in a T-shirt and jeans, her grey hair in a long, loose braid, large tortoiseshell glasses on her nose.

It's an old truck. The seats, a darkish hue, perhaps once black, are cracked like used sandpaper. There's a cassette player built into the dashboard; the radio dial is worked by an actual knob. Right now, it's tuned to a local radio station, and an ad for an electronics warehouse tries to entice them with '. . . amazing bargains on everything your family needs, from blenders to deep-freezers [sound effects here—blaring horn, cheering crowd]. Special discounts for purchases above one thousand ringgit [the horn blares, the crowd cheers again]. What are you waiting for?' After this mocking rhetorical question, the next ad starts with a jaunty, cutesy jingle.

Lucky's newfound aunt hits a button on the dashboard and kills it. 'Your timing's very good, boy. No wonder they call you Lucky, eh?' Her accent is so much like his father's that Lucky's head swings towards her without waiting for him to think about it. He hasn't heard it in over eighteen years but he will know it anywhere—that fluting quality, the Malay accent, that way of ending sentences in an upwards lilt that somehow never sounds like a question mark. 'I have a few things to pick up in Ipoh today.' She makes a swift, graceful turn out of one street and into another. 'Have you had breakfast?'

He hasn't. And so, after a quick stop at a lumber yard where she effortlessly picks up a few wooden planks and hoists them onto the back of the truck before Lucky can even offer to help, she drives them to a quiet neighbourhood. As she walks briskly towards a row of shophouses, her long grey plait swinging behind her like a tail, Lucky lags behind, looking around him. They've parked on a street of small, simple single-storey houses spaced apart, each surrounded by a surprising amount of garden. A few houses have been renovated—fancier windows here, a small extension there—but they're mostly in the original design, plain, low, and squarish with green glass louvre windows on all sides, topped by gently pitched red roofs and hemmed in by cheap wire fences, personalized only with some enthusiastic gardening, a little creativity with the paintwork, and personal brands of clutter. Discreet, dignified houses—no lions, no stonework driveways. Could his father's house—*their* house—in Teluk Intan be like these? Or would it be another monster house, like their house on Swan Street?

'Lucky, everything okay?'

'Yes! Coming!'

He walks quickly to catch up and follows her into a kopitiam at one end of the shophouse row. The smell of freshly made coffee hits him like a swift tap on the nose. Ipoh coffee—such a sweet, buttery smell.

'Kopi, chee cheong fun, okay?' The woman talks like she walks, upbeat, quick, a little soldier-like. Lucky nods without even listening and she goes off to order, gesturing to a table nearby. 'Sit down.'

Lucky sits down and puts Coconut on the wooden stool next to him. 'Behave, okay? I need to make a good impression here,' he whispers, stroking her very gently on the head.

Coconut doesn't reply, but she curls up tight and squeezes her eyes shut. Good enough.

The coffee shop is crowded, full of people enjoying a late breakfast. Five stalls line up along one side of the airy, high-ceilinged space, but only two are open. At one of them, his aunt is ordering their breakfast from two sweaty, shouty men who seem to know every one of their customers by name and food preferences. She points in Lucky's direction and they both look, nodding. As she heads back to the table, she calls out in Cantonese to the woman behind the drinks counter, ordering two cups of white coffee.

'I'm over there!' She gestures towards Lucky, who realizes he can hear her clearly even above the kopitiam din.

The chee cheong fun arrives piping hot on two pale blue plastic plates, drenched in a thin, brown gravy, a splash of chilli sauce, and covered in a fine layer of fried shallots. Lucky eyes his plate, feeling a little disappointed. The moment he heard 'chee cheong fun', his mind conjured up the stuffed rice rolls of Hong Kong and Singapore, plump with shrimp or pork. Ipoh's chee cheong fun is a much more spartan affair—just plain rolls of rice noodles, thinly sliced, with a dark sauce and fried shallots.

But what sorcery is this? One mouthful later, Lucky is ready to build a shrine to this town with marble statues of the two sweaty, shouty men, no, artists, whose fine fingers have made his pleasure possible. The noodles are impossibly soft without being mushy, firm enough not to fall to pieces as he picks them up with chopsticks.

'It's like eating silk.' And why does he feel he has to whisper?

His father's cousin smiles, nodding in approval, one hand tugging absently at the end of her plait. 'Good, right?' She adds in Hokkien: 'This place isn't famous, but it's my favourite. Every time I'm in Ipoh, I come here.'

Her English is perfect, so the switch to Hokkien feels like a test. Thankfully, all his Hokkien has been learnt at the dining table—food is the one thing he can talk about without sounding half-witted. 'Really good. The noodles are so fine, so smooth.' He's pleased he remembers the Hokkien words for 'smooth' and 'fine'.

She nods, and he can tell he's gained a few points in her esteem. 'Here, chee cheong fun is all about texture, not like in KL, where I hear they're serving it with things like broccoli and bacon.' She makes a face. 'But it's meant to be a simple dish. My mother said that during the war, chee cheong fun was a luxury only the rich could afford. It being wartime, of course there was no meat. But you see how these noodles are made to look like rolls of pig's intestines? Chinese people are like that—if we can't have meat, we'll pretend.' She laughs at his expression. 'Oh, you didn't know that's what 'chee cheong' means in Cantonese?'

The kopi arrives in small ceramic cups, and they sip it slowly. Very sweet, very strong.

'So, Lucky, why are you here?' She switches back to English, looking at him serenely over her raised coffee cup.

Lucky puts his cup gently down on its saucer and stares at it. 'My sister—she died.' He sighs. He should have prepared an answer to this obvious question. 'And my father—I was told he had a house in Teluk Intan. I just want to see it.'

'Yes. You mentioned the house on the phone yesterday.'

'Yes . . . yes. I'm thinking of maybe taking the bus to Teluk Intan? Is it far from Ipoh?'

'No.'

'Okay.' Lucky stares at the thick rim of his cup, at the coffee stains the inner edge. 'I just found out about the house. No one told me. I might have come sooner, you know, to see it. Papa's house. But I didn't know.'

His aunt doesn't say anything. They sit in silence for a while, she sipping coffee, he staring into his cup, the kopitiam clamour around them slowly ebbing as the breakfast crowd began to thin. She must be waiting for him to continue, but Lucky doesn't quite know what else to say. He knows nothing about her, except that she's his father's cousin. His father never mentioned her, but they must have been close at some point. Why else would he have included her in his will? Lucky wonders how much she already knows about him, and how much she can tell him about the house, or why his father might have made the dick move of hiding it from him.

'My father and I weren't close,' he finds himself saying before *she* can ask *him* anything about his father. 'We never got along. He liked my sister better.' *Okay, that was bad. Try again.* 'She and Papa, they just *got* each other.'

And that's it—Lucky dries up. He drinks more coffee and he tries to think of more things to say to explain how he's ended up here in Ipoh, why he called this perfect stranger yesterday and asked if she had time to meet. Of course he wants to talk to her, see this damn house. And then what? Reconnect with family? He's not sure he wants more family.

'Finish your coffee,' she tells him, her eyes kind. 'We'll take the old roads—longer drive, but nicer. More to see.'

'Where are we going?'

'The moon.' Her expressive mouth twists itself into a shape both amused and amusing. 'And then I'll take you to the house.'

* * *

'That looks like Ah Huat Ko's cat.'

'What? No!' Lucky hugs Coconut a little closer.

Aunty Bok—this is what she's told him to call her—turns her head ever so slightly and squints at Coconut. 'Really looks like Ah Huat Ko's cat.'

'No, no, this is Coconut.'

'Strange name for a cat.'

'My sister named her.'

'Such a funny girl. You look so much like her.'

'You've met my sister?'

'Pearl. Of course.'

If she hadn't said 'of course', he would have pressed her for more.

* * *

You'll never believe it, but I found Coconut! She was waiting
for me at the station.

What?

Yes!

That's insane.

Completely absurd. But it's so good to have her back!

He waits a minute and when Mit doesn't reply, he sends her a cat
emoji with hearts for eyes. She stays silent.

He turns off his screen and looks out the window. On his lap,
Coconut is sound asleep, indifferent to the world and emojis. Oh,
to be a cat!

* * *

The old roads are inconsistent: some parts full of sand and teeth-
grindingly potholed, others well-maintained and a pleasure to be
on; some parts throbbing with traffic, others quiet with defeat.
An hour into their drive to Teluk Intan, his face dusty from the
open window, Lucky has discovered how much he likes riding in
a truck—the extra metre or so of elevation does wonders for the
view. He can see over hedges, into monsoon drains, into the backs
of other vehicles, and, right now, across the entire expanse of a
large, lotus-topped lake.

'Aunty Bok, look!'

She turns, but it's Lucky and his wide cheesy grin she looks at
instead of the lake. 'We've just had a few days of sunshine after
weeks of rain—perfect for lotuses.' She returns the grin. 'You know

what? We have time—let's stop.' She nods at his phone. 'Get a good picture.'

She parks by the side of the road and together they climb onto the back of the truck for a better view. Deftly, she pulls herself up onto the top of the truck cab and helps Lucky onto it too. The lake stretches on for at least a kilometre, still and glistening, its surface almost completely covered by lotus pads and bright pink flowers in every stage of bloom. No wind, no one around, not a single man-made sound. Lucky takes a picture, quickly, then holds Coconut up for the very best view as Aunty Bok points out the nearby vegetable farms and a cluster of buildings just visible in the distance.

Taiping, she tells him. 'That's where your father and I grew up.'

'I thought he grew up in Ipoh?'

'No. He went to Ipoh to live with our uncle when he was fourteen. Maybe a bit older.'

'I never heard any stories about Taiping. He never talked about it or about his family or anything.' Lucky looks at Aunty Bok expectantly, but she continues to stare out into the lake, shading her eyes with both hands.

'Not everyone likes their family.' Steady as a cat, she climbs off the cab. 'Not everyone likes Taiping.'

'Too quiet?'

'Nonsense! Too wet. And small towns are never quiet. People do nothing but talk. Come, give me your hand.' She holds his hand as he leaps off the back of the truck, feeling like a child.

The feeling continues as she drives him through Taiping, gently talking him through the town, pointing out things he can only stare at, desperate not to spoil the experience with banal observations. The hospital where his grandmother was a nurse. The bakery, still run by the same Hainanese family since around the First World War, where his grandfather worked. His father's primary school—three identical austere blocks between a church and a massive field overgrown with small flowering creepers and lalang, that stubborn despotic grass with edges that can cut paper, wild in a way that fields are never allowed to be in Singapore. Lucky frowns. How does he know that thing about cutting paper? An old memory returns, sharp and sudden, of his father once tearing off a bit of lalang in a playground and amusing him and Pearl by sawing off the corner of a supermarket receipt.

'The school used to be bigger. There were three football fields right here, before the church sold off the land to the town for development.' In the distance, a section of land has been boarded up.

As they drive on along the edge of the town, a cemetery unfolds on both sides of the road, old and untidy, scattered with faded tombstones the size of cars and burly trees and clusters of tough-looking bushes.

'All the boys came here in the evenings to catch spiders. My brother. Your father too.'

'See that tree? That's where he broke his leg once, falling off his father's motorcycle.'

Sticking his head out the window, Lucky stares at the enormous trunk of the tree. He watches a pair of squirrels scamper up into its branches, and his eyes follow them up and up and up. Aunty Bok stops the car and Lucky climbs out, never taking his eyes off the tree. The squirrels disappear into the leaves, leaving him alone with it. At least fifty metres high, the tree towers over him, its long sinuous limbs fat as pythons. Feeling like a mouse, Lucky walks up to the trunk, wider than the span of his arms, and touches it reverently. How different time must be for a tree. It must have been old even when his father had fallen here at its feet; maybe it snickered at young Lee Joo Meng as he lost his balance. Trees are such masters of gravity. And now it sighs at Lucky Lee, at his pampered palm against its weathered trunk. *What soft hands you have, my boy.*

Lucky snatches his hand off the tree and steps back, feeling indignant.

Sensing Aunty Bok standing next to him, he turns to see her looking down at the twisting roots bulging out of the ground at their feet. 'Were you here when it happened?' he asks.

'Your father's accident? Oh no, but we all heard about it. Someone said your father must have made the *penunggu* angry. The tree spirit.' She shrugs. 'Small town.'

'Was he hurt very bad?'

'Broke his leg in two places.'

Is that why his father had that slight limp? Why doesn't he know this? Lucky pretends to yawn to stifle the sigh that's pushing against his chest. 'Pah. That's nothing. I nearly broke my face falling while rollerblading. My face! See? I have a scar.' He raises an eyebrow and points to the line across his right cheekbone. 'Children run from me in parks. Dogs dash. Cats cower. Birds bolt.'

She turns to him and laughs. It's a big, buoyant laugh. Like some sort of wild bird's. 'So like your father. He always had a joke.'

Did he? Lucky can't remember a single one, but he remembers that sly grin his father had, like he was constantly sizing up something (someone?) ridiculous.

'The apple doesn't fall far from the tree.'

'Oh no, Aunty Bok, it doesn't.' He bats his lashes and gives her a wry smile. 'But I'm a pear.'

'Rubbish. Who told you that you could be a pear?'

* * *

'Wow, what exactly is this?'

Lucky puts his mug onto the table with a loud, brutish thud. The old couple at the next table turn to look at him.

Bok grins at them. '*Wa eh soon*[5], from Singapore. First time in Taiping! *Wa chua ee lai* try *hor gar sai.*[6]' She explains that she's brought him here to taste the town's specialty kopi.

'Your nephew? So tall! And *kar eh ho kwa nia*[7]. Such nice eyes. Married?' The old woman nods at Lucky, who manages to hide his alarm at the possibility of being pounced on and set up *by a complete stranger in Taiping.*

---

[5] In Hokkien, 'My nephew.'

[6] In Hokkien, 'I've brought him here to try hor gar sai.'

[7] In Hokkien, 'So good-looking.'

Her husband leans forward. 'Wah, Singapore! Taiping *mana eh pi Singapore lau juak*[8]? Young man, you'll be so bored here. Taiping isn't very exciting, you know. *Lau lang nia.*[9]'

He hadn't noticed until the man mentioned it, but if the food court they're at is anything to go by, the town really must be full of older folk. Everyone looks at least fifty. And everyone seems to know everyone else—or at least they seem to *talk* to everyone else, in that half-English, half-Hokkien pidgin that seems to be the custom here, going by the conversations he heard earlier while she was buying biscuits at the old bakery and now at this crowded food court in the middle of town. He recalls this pidgin from their family trip to Penang years and years ago, where his father beamed perpetually and kept declaring how happy he was to be surrounded by people who spoke his language. *This* would have pleased his father. This random conversation with this chatty couple in this noisy place with its delicious smells, sticky floors, and mismatched tables. And maybe this drink?

The hor gar sai arrived in a large green Milo mug, thick, dark brown, and foaming at the top from the kopi boy's vigorous stirring. It smells of coffee; it tastes of coffee—but there's something else. Chocolate? Something like it; something viscous. Lucky takes a sniff and another sip.

'I like it.' He doesn't. 'What's in it?'

'Kopi and Milo.' Bok takes a sip from her own cup, then points at the Milo logo on it. 'Only in Taiping, okay?' She laughs. 'Maybe that's a good thing. When you said you run a cafe, I thought, he must try hor gar sai.'

'What does hor gar sai mean?'

She shakes her head at his pitiful grasp of Hokkien. 'Aiyo, Lucky. Hor. Gar. Sai. Tiger bites lion.'

Lucky takes another sip. Not that bad, really. 'Is the kopi the lion or the tiger?'

'One of life's big mysteries.' Aunty Bok winks. 'Welcome to Taiping.'

---

[8] In Hokkien, 'How can Taiping be more exciting than Singapore?'

[9] In Hokkien, 'Only old people here.'

Later, he will look back and remember that wink and know it as the instant she went from stranger-aunt to proper-aunt. But now Lucky giggles. Tiger bites lion. If Pearl were here, they would be cackling like twin hyenas at the self-styled grandiosity of this Milo–kopi hybrid. He shakes his head as his heart defies all of Newton's laws, lifting and sinking at the same time at the thought of her, suddenly wishing his father were here so he could ask him if this is a Taiping thing, this penchant for quirky names? Hor gar sai. Lucky Lee. Pearl Lee.

'Good, right?' The man from the next table has turned back around, beaming expectantly. His question is obviously rhetorical.

'In Singapore, no hor gar sai?' His wife joins, with an actual question. 'No chewing gum *and* no hor gar sai?'

Lucky shakes his head. 'Nope.'

'Don't worry, hor gar sai quite easy to make. You just keep practising.'

'Yah. Must keep practising.'

'Yah. Kopi taste too *kao*, too heavy, too thick—must add Milo.'

'Yah. Milo taste too kao, too heavy—must add kopi.'

The man nods. 'Practice makes perfect. Everything must balance.'

The woman nods. 'Yah. Everything must balance.'

Aunty Bok nods. They nod together, sagely, three grey heads watching Lucky raise his mug again to his lips.

Lucky nods back, resisting the urge to snicker. The secret of life in a green Milo mug in the belly of Taiping. Where has it been all his life? He takes a sip. Neither good nor gross, not particularly enjoyable, but therein lies more of its metaphorical powers, yes? Everything must balance. And maybe in balance, things are underwhelming. Undelicious.

The old people drink their kopi and discuss the likelihood of rain, resisting the urge to smile as Lucky solemnly finishes his hor gar sai. These young fellows from the big cities—so cute how they take everything so seriously. So cute. *Chin choo bee.*

* * *

'Thirty years!'

'Thirty-seven! I was twenty when I started teaching.'

Thirty-seven years. That's as many years as he's been *alive*. Lucky can't imagine doing anything for that long. Except living, obviously. He can't even imagine doing the same thing for . . . ten years? Five? No, not even five. Wow. He's never even stuck to anything for five years.

'Thirty-seven!'

'YES! ENOUGH!' Without taking her eyes off the road, she swats at him with one hand. 'Fine, I'm ancient! You're no spring chicken, you know.'

They laugh.

'But weren't you, I don't know, bored?' *Thirty-seven years!*

'Sometimes. But no, mostly no. There were always new things to do, new students to get to know, new things to learn. It didn't feel like I was doing the same thing all the time, more like I was building something gradually. Adding windows, doors, plants, paint. To myself, the students, the school. Does that make sense? And Rome wasn't built in a day, you know.'

'No. It was built over centuries and many times.'

'You've been to Rome?'

'A few years ago. On my way to Verona.' He doesn't add, to drink crateloads of expensive wine.

'Lucky you.' She smiles. 'I've always wanted to go.'

'You should!'

They are trading stories. As the roads weave through villages and palm oil plantations and the odd rubber estate, she tells him about teaching in Ipoh, coaching the girls' hockey team, trekking through Cameron Highlands with the young police cadets. 'Half those boys were in love with me,' she says with a laugh, but Lucky believes her. He can imagine her as a teacher, young and strident and bold, clambering over hills and rocks and teenage hearts.

Lucky tells her about travelling through Spain with Pearl, climbing cathedral bell-towers in every city, eating frozen yogurt in ancient city squares, learning to cook and eat artichokes, weeping at his first sight of the Alhambra, getting mocked by his sister. He tells her how he learnt to ride a motorcycle in Saigon, years before he actually got a licence in Singapore.

'It's a long drive, yah.'

A quick sideways look from Aunty Bok. She looks amused. 'For a seasoned traveller, your geography is terrible.'

Google Maps quickly tells him she's right. Teluk Intan, nestled against the twisting tail of the Perak River, is south-west of Ipoh; Taiping lies north-west, its nose nudging the border of Penang. *Oh right, that's why they speak the same way.* And anyone with even the slightest inkling of local geography would have realized a long time ago that even the old roads snaking towards the coast from Ipoh would never have taken them past Taiping en route to Teluk Intan.

Lucky laughs. 'Yikes.'

She sighs theatrically. 'Your fault lah. I had to make sure you had your hor gar sai.'

'Of course you did.'

'Your father hated it, you know.'

'Taiping or hor gar sai?'

Her turn to chuckle. 'Both.' She makes a left turn onto a small road. 'One and a half hours to go. Maybe a bit more. A lot more, if it rains. You still haven't told me why you're here, you know. You've been all over Europe, but you've never wanted to see any of this.' Without looking, she gestures at the scene just beyond her window.

Lucky looks out through the window on her side of the truck. Another overgrown field, full of grass and insects. At a distance, a cow. No, two cows, brown and indifferent. One of them stares through him, its eyes large and smug.

He turns back to face the road. 'I told you. The house.'

'Just the house?'

'Yah.'

'*Just* the house?'

All aunts are alike, at bottom. 'Aunty Bok, why don't you just tell me what you think I've come here for?' Lucky rolls his eyes, but he's curious.

'When you called yesterday, I assumed you finally came to say goodbye to your father. Just like she did.'

'Pearl?'

'Yah. Long ago, right after he died.'

Of course she did. She always had to be first. Even managed to *die* first. He imagines her sly smile, her raised eyebrows. *Didn't even realize I sneaked off to Perak, did you, Lucky?* No, he didn't. When had she? Probably sometime in his first semester at university, when he was staying on campus, spending all waking hours at the architecture studio.

Taking a deep breath, Lucky stares down at Coconut on his lap, then out the window. 'Well, I've come to see the house.' Quietly, more to himself than to Bok.

'We'll see it tomorrow.'

'Tomorrow? It's still early. Can't we go today?' And though he brought his backpack, he was starting to think maybe he'll return to Ipoh tonight—maybe hire a taxi, maybe take a bus—and wake up tomorrow to that lovely white coffee.

She sweeps these unuttered almost-plans aside with an impatient wave of her hand. 'By the time we reach the moon, it will be after five. I'll cook us dinner. You can help. We eat at seven.'

The moon? This is the second time she's said it. Is this a local nickname for Teluk Intan? Cute. Lucky sighs. A night on the moon. At least it has a nice ring to it.

'Okay.'

'I've waited eighteen years to meet you, Lucky Lee. You can wait until tomorrow to see your house.'

The moon

perches over the water near the end of a row of houses stretching out onto the river, a short bridge of planks leading up to its front door. Coconut trots behind Lucky trotting behind Aunty Bok towards it, feet making disproportionately loud noises on the old timber boardwalk connecting all the houses, paws making none.

It's a funny, long sort of house, clearly expanded in stages over the years—even from a distance, the wooden planks of its walls are three distinct tones of brown–grey. A dragon's head nailed above the door peers down at them as they enter, its wide, aged smile missing a few teeth. Lucky stares back. What's this? A talisman? A warning? A—*har de har har*—lucky charm? He's never seen a less frightening dragon—the stair-dragon at home would have this one for tea, washed down with a child or three.

'Lucky! What are you doing out there? Come inside.'

Leaving his sneakers and socks at the door, Lucky walks into the Moon and finds himself in a sunny room painted a dreamy, watery blue. Very little furniture, but everything looks well-used—this feels like a loved room, he thinks, very much loved. Photos on the wall. A shelf crammed with books. A desk piled high with paper, magazines, folders, and stationery. A sofa languishes next to it, the frayed ends of its upholstery moving in the breeze from the windows, tantalizing Coconut, urging the little cat to come closer, closer. As Lucky crosses the room to snatch her up, the sun-warmed floorboards creak under his feet, accompanied by hollow-ish thumps that remind him they're cantilevering over the river.

At the beginning, Aunty Bok tells him later, the Moon was just this one room opening out into a verandah that was then also the kitchen and the living room and sometimes, on hotter nights, the bed. There's a proper kitchen now, built some years ago, and two small bedrooms beyond it, built a few years later, all connected to the verandah that lengthened with each extension to the house. Coconut on his shoulder, Lucky follows Aunty Bok through the Moon's simple kitchen into the shaded verandah. Gesturing towards the end of it, she tells him that the room at the very end is his for the night.

Coconut isn't impressed with their quarters. 'A bit small,' she sniffs.

Lucky looks around. 'Not enough room to swing a cat, for sure.' The room is tiny and sparsely furnished—a bed, a chair, a chest of drawers.

'Who would want to swing a cat?' Coconut sounds offended. 'Why?'

'It's just an expression, Coconut. I don't think anyone really thinks of swinging a cat in a room.'

'Well, I should hope not.' She gives him a pointed stare. 'Least of all you.'

Lucky puts his backpack on the floor next to the bed and picks her up. 'Just an expression. Really.' He grins, scooping her up to face him at eye level. 'Though if you'd like to try it, I'm happy to help. Might be fun.' Lucky swings her gently back and forth.

'Put me down. Now. Or I'll scratch your eyes out while you sleep.'

'Nasty!'

'Lucky, you must have heard of people being eaten by their cats. Perhaps they tried to swing them?'

* * *

The moon is full and from the window of his room it looks like someone's hung a massive lantern over the river. Lucky leans out of the window, suddenly pleased to be away from the skyscrapers of Kuala Lumpur. It's crazy how quiet it is and yet not. He can hear the hum of insects rising and falling, the river washing along the bank, a lone frog in the distance, but no people sounds—no talk, no traffic, no televisions, no generators, no one.

His phone vibrates on the wooden table next to him.

Lucky, where are you?

He frowns. Is this part of some sort of stupid strategy? Does Dinah really think he will give in and talk to her if she hounds him enough?

Are you in Ipoh?

Lucky stares at his phone. For a moment, he contemplates throwing it into the river. Mmmm.

Lucky, can I call you?

He puts his phone back on the table. No, no. No. No! A few minutes later, the phone vibrates again, its screen lighting up. Lucky doesn't see this. He's gone outside to look at the moon, the wooden planks of the verandah creaking softly under his bare feet. Everything, everything, creaks in the Moon. As Lucky folds his arms on the thin railing of the verandah and leans into it, that creaks as well.

So this, this was perhaps what Papa dreamt of at night, in his big bed in his big bedroom in his big house guarded by his big lions. A fishing village on the edge of a slow, small town. This unobstructed view of the moon. This gentle river. This air smelling of rain and mud and grass and some sort of green, citrusy herb.

Over dinner, he'd been surprised to hear about his father's visits to Teluk Intan. He was even more surprised to hear that his father stayed with Aunty Bok on these trips, eating sweet potato porridge and sleeping in the same tiny room he would later sleep in himself, fishing in the river.

'He hardly ever caught anything, but he seemed happy to fish anyway,' Aunty Bok recalled with an indulgent sort of smile.

That didn't sound at all like his father. His father was never good at anything approximating leisure. Even family holidays were mostly business trips with his wife and children in tow. But clearly Aunty Bok knew a side of his father that he didn't, a side that only poked its nose out when it was in Teluk Intan. A side that bought a house and didn't tell his kids.

'Was my father planning to move here? Is that why he bought a house?'

Aunty Bok shrugged as she refilled his bowl with more fish soup.

It made him suddenly impatient, her languid, lovely face. Lucky ate his soup to hide a scowl. 'Really? You don't know? You seem to know so much about Papa.' He could hear the jealousy in his voice and he hated it.

She gave him a stare that made him feel like a cockroach. 'Lucky.' Her voice had taken on a scolding quality it didn't have on their drive from Ipoh. Lucky imagined her in class, subduing errant students, cockroaching them with that stare.

The moon is directly overhead now, pale and glowing. Like a lamp. Like a . . . pearl. No. Lucky turns his face up towards it and sighs. No. Not a pearl. Just a moon. He goes back inside.

His phone, on its last gasp of battery charge, shows him a missed call and three lines from Dinah.

`Lucky, answer the phone!`

`Please, Lucky. Come on.`

`Lucky! I really need to talk to you.`

Seriously, can't a fellow go on an adventure with his cat without being hounded? Dinah really should go get herself new friends—or a cat. A cat would soon put her in her place. And if it didn't, he would tell Coconut to persuade it to.

Suddenly, remembering Coconut, he looks around the room for her. *Ah, there she is.* On the bed, stretched out on her side. Watching him. 'Did you have a nice chat with the moon? Pearl used to talk to him too, sometimes. When she was sad. Are you sad, Lucky?'

'No.'

'That's good.'

'We're going to see my father's house tomorrow.'

'What's it like?'

'I don't know.'

'Where is it?'

'I don't know.'

'Why are we going to see it?' Coconut walks to the edge of the bed and looks up at him.

Lucky swallows the third I don't know. He can tell from the tone of her voice that Coconut already expects him not to know. He sighs as he sits down beside her. Why do all cats seem to have such judgy little faces? Or is it just Coconut?

'It's kind of my house now, Coconut. So I need to take a look, see if things are okay, if anything needs to be done or anything.'

'It's yours, but you don't know where it is and you've never seen it?'

'No. I didn't even know it existed! But Pearl did, and she's been to the house.' *Without telling me, without bothering to take me along. Without me, without me.*

Coconut purrs, rubbing her head into his belly. 'Then it's fine, Lucky. Pearl's very good at taking care of things.' Another purr. 'Like she took care of us.'

Lucky sighs. *Oh this cat and her sainted Pearl.* 'Yes, but she could've told me about the house, right? Didn't have to keep it a secret, right?'

'Maybe it wasn't a secret. Maybe she just didn't want you to worry.' Coconut narrows her eyes at him.

Lucky narrows his eyes back at her. Of course, she would take Pearl's side! After all they've been through together! After all the fish! He stands up and glares down at the little cat. 'Pearl isn't—wasn't, whatever—perfect, Coconut . . .' Suddenly, his head is pounding. It's like a dam has burst somewhere inside his skull.

'Nobody's perfect, Lucky.'

'Oh no, no, no. Pearl's perfect. Pearl!'

'Lucky, calm down.'

Calm down? What the actual fuck? Why does Coconut sound exactly like Pearl right now? Smug, so smug. Lucky wants to scream, but he will not, he will not give her the satisfaction. Not this time.

The little room in the Moon turns into the storeroom in the house on Swan Street and Lucky is seven again. 7-Eleven, the year of measles and Pearl's obsession with *Ben-Hur*, also the year Pearl wanted a Barbie doll and didn't get one, the year she was forced to continue exploring different, unconventional avenues of entertainment.

'If we're going to be spies, we have to be able to escape from a locked room.'

'Can't we just turn the knob and open the door?' Lucky was confused. His bedroom door could be locked from the outside with a key, but anyone inside could just unlock it.

Pearl smirked. 'No one locks spies into that kind of room, Lucky. We'd be locked into special rooms with special doors.'

Like the downstairs storeroom, which opened with a large, brass key inserted into the kind of keyhole you could peep through. The children had been inside the storeroom a few times before with their mother, to look for old newspapers or fabric scraps for an art project or balloons for a party. It wasn't a room they ever thought of at all, but now it wasn't the storeroom any more. It was a KGB detention cell.

'What's KGB?'

'I'm not sure, but it's the people always chasing James Bond. Maybe they're from Komodo—that's the island in Indonesia where all dragons come from.'

In theory, if you were inside the room and someone turned the key and left it there, you could push it out with a hairpin (all spies always carried a set of hairpins, Pearl told Lucky) and the key would fall onto the piece of paper you'd slipped under the door to catch it (a set of hairpins *and* a newspaper page—all good spies were well prepared). Then you'd slowly pull that piece of paper through the gap under the door and into the room, pick up the key, unlock the room. Easy peasy lemon squeezy.

Two dark heads poked into a dark storeroom. It wasn't very big, but it was deep enough that from the doorway it was hard to see into the furthest corner.

'You go first, Lucky.'

He didn't want to go first, but he didn't want her to think he was scared. The week before, she had called him a scaredy-cat for screaming when she jumped out at him from below the dining table. (He'd only screamed because he thought it was a wild animal, like a goat.) And then she told Papa, who frowned but then also laughed. So Lucky went first into the storeroom, armed with a box of their mother's hairpins and the centrefold of yesterday's newspaper, and Pearl stayed outside and turned the key.

He slipped the piece of paper under the door, then, bending a little so that he was eye level with the keyhole, began poking hairpins into it, one after another. According to Pearl, if he pushed the key hard enough on this end of the keyhole, it would fall out the other. But this didn't work. He kept trying with different hairpins, slowly starting to panic, even though he knew she could just turn the key and let him out.

'Come on, Lucky. Faster!'

'Pearl, the key won't move!'

A few more rounds of this and his sister was bored—he could tell, even though he couldn't see her, that she was crossing her arms and rolling her eyes and pursing her lips in that way she always did when she wanted to tell everyone without actually telling anyone that she wasn't pleased with how things were going. 'Lucky, just keep pushing the key. This isn't supposed to be so hard!'

But it was. And the more he jabbed at the key, the sillier he felt. Then one of the hairpins got stuck in the keyhole and he couldn't get it out—and the key still hadn't budged. Lucky gave up and yelled for Pearl to let him out.

She tried, but nothing happened. 'I think the key's stuck, Lucky.'

The storeroom suddenly seemed very dark and cold. 'Get me out, Pearl!'

'I'm going to ask Mummy what to do.'

'Okay.'

As the sound of his sister's footsteps faded away, Lucky pressed himself against the door and closed his eyes. He felt very alone. He very, very badly wanted to get out of the very, very, very dark storeroom. He would happily give up his new Lego set, the one he'd had to beg his mother for, to be out of that room. He would give up his Ultraman slippers, his Ultraman lunchbox, his Ultraman pencil-case—

Footsteps—Pearl was back! 'Mummy says you'll have to stay in there. There's no way of opening the door now.'

What? Lucky's little head spun. 'How long do I have to stay here?'

'Forever, I guess. It's okay, Lucky—I'll think of a way to feed you.'

'Pearl!'

'Are you scared, Lucky? I'm sure you're very scared.'

'I'm not scared, Pearl. I'm not.' But he started to cry.

'You must be. It's okay, Lucky, I won't let you starve. And if you see the storeroom monster, just lie very still and it'll think you're a log.'

'The storeroom monster?' Lucky looked around, frantic, wondering where it was hiding. In that box? Under the shelf?

'Are you scared now?'

Lucky didn't want to say so. He wasn't a scaredy-cat. He wasn't, he wasn't.

'If you're not scared, I'll just go tell Mummy you're okay . . .' He could hear her start to walk away and his heart quickened. He cried harder.

'Lucky? Are you okay? Are you scared?'

He wasn't a scaredy-cat, he wasn't a scaredy-cat. 'Pearl! I'm scared! Pearl!'

'Stand back from the door, Lucky.'

He took a few steps back and then a few steps more, wondering what she would do. Was Pearl going to break down the door? Wow. Could she really? There was a lot of hmm-ing and sighing on the other side, some hammering against the door. A few kicks. A few more, harder this time—and then, magically, the door swung open and light rushed in and so did Pearl.

He cried out as soon as he saw her. 'Pearl, Pearl!'

'It's okay, Lucky, I'm here. I knew you were scared. But it's okay now, I'm here.'

He didn't like that she kept saying he was scared, but he liked that she took his hand and held it tight, and he liked that she took him to the kitchen and opened a packet of Oreos for them to share. Years and years later, he found out that the storeroom door had had a broken lock for years and it wasn't possible for Pearl to have locked him in the room by turning the key. He realized then that he never even tried to open the door from the inside because he believed her when she said it was stuck, that she had staged the whole thing so that she could save him. But it didn't matter because by then they had settled into their roles—she the saviour he the saved, she the strong one he the silly the soft-handed the simpleton brother of Pearl Lee.

Still staring down at Coconut, Lucky takes a deep breath, feels better, and takes another. 'I'm not a simpleton. I'm not a dumbass, Coconut. She could've just told me. I wouldn't have minded at all! Pearl was better with money, and she was better at all that business stuff, so it made sense that Papa left it all to her. But why didn't she just say so? She was always so bossy, but she always said, "our money", "our business", "our" this, and "our" that, and it was nice, you know, that it was *ours*. And I thought it wasn't a big deal that I never had a proper sort of job, because, I don't know, our property and all was making money or whatever. But actually, it wasn't okay, was it? Because it was never ours and I was just some sort of . . . parasite! That's it, Coconut—a parasite. And if she weren't gone—dead—then I'd still be a fucking parasite. Some sort of weird mushroom. Kept in the dark about everything. Living in her house and eating her food and drinking her wine and watching her TV and, and . . . gah! If she were here, I'd bite her, Coconut. I'd bite her!'

His phone rings, startling Lucky with sharp, ascending beeps. Dinah. Again. Will she never stop? In one swift, surprisingly dexterous move, he takes the phone, leans out the window, and throws it into the river.

Coconut mewls. Lucky crawls under the blanket and refuses to answer her.

That's all, folks. Good night!

The tree

is bigger than the house. Far bigger. The truth is, from a distance, it's hard to see the house for the tree. Lucky almost turns to Aunty Bok, almost says, so where is it? But then, as he takes a few more steps and gets a little closer, he can see it peeking out from under a massive bough, watching them shyly as they walk up the dirt path towards it.

It's a small house, single-storeyed and low. It looks like it might have been white once. The roof is mostly missing; the tree has taken its place, branches bursting through the top of the house and pushing through the front and side walls, growing upwards and outwards in a thick, deep-green canopy. Some of the window panes are missing and out of these spill eager young shoots, curious to see the garden. There's nothing much to see, sadly, and Lucky commiserates with the treelings (is that a word?) as he checks out the long grass, the lalang, the prickly weeds. He picks Coconut up to prevent her from exploring. Anything could be in there. Snakes, maybe. Grasshoppers, definitely.

'It's not what I expected.'

'What were you expecting?'

Lucky stares at the house. *What on earth . . . ?* It's small, it's decrepit, it's not architecturally *anything*. No roof, no front door, missing windows—it's not even a functioning building. He walks up to it and tries to look inside, but all he can see is a massive tree trunk and dead branches and some concrete rubble. He and Coconut poke their heads through the almost-doorway—*shit, are those bats?*—and quickly withdraw, Lucky hugging Coconut a little closer for protection. Cats eat bats, don't they?

'Your father thought you'd find it interesting.'

Lucky stops. Every thought he is about to think, every muscle in his face, his hands, his feet, every square millimetre of skin, stops. All he can do is breathe because this isn't up to him at all—he can feel his lungs expand, deflate, expand, deflate, keeping calm and carrying on; he can feel his heart flutter vaguely, refusing to buy into the drama.

'Lucky?' Aunty Bok puts her hand on his shoulder and gives it a squeeze.

He nods. He doesn't know what to say, whether to ask her to elaborate on that crazy-ass thing she just said or whether to pretend she didn't say it or pretend he didn't hear it so he cannot try to figure out what she could possibly mean and why his father would think something like that and why she's telling him and whether this is important because of course this is important of course this is something of course this is something he should want to know but does it matter that he's afraid to know? Lucky blinks. He lets Aunty Bok put her arm around him.

Bok looks at the boy—*the man*, she corrects herself. But he has such a look, this Lucky Lee, like a child or a flower. An orchid.

'Not like his sister at all,' Joo Meng pronounced years ago over breakfast at the Moon.

'I don't think you should be so hard on the boy.' Bok didn't know much about either of Joo Meng's children, but she didn't like it when parents compared their children with each other—and then expected school teachers to deal with the issues and consequences!

Joo Meng helped himself to more coffee. 'Should have been harder on him. But his mother, aiya, you know Betty lah. Spoilt the boy. Now he can't do anything himself.'

Bok raised an eyebrow, then turned away. No, she was not going to get into a discussion about the late Betty. No point in speaking ill of the dead. 'Have you let him?'

'It's hard to be a father, Bok. So hard.' Joo Meng sighed into his coffee cup. 'My boy cannot lah. Just cannot. He's . . . *lembik* lah.' Soft. Joo Meng kept calling him soft. 'Too . . . lucky. Should have named him something else.'

Bok tried not to grin at her cousin. *Like what? Clever? Brave? Well, he named the girl Pearl. So . . . Bear? Bamboo?*

The boy Lucky, Joo Meng went on, had decided he was going to be an architect. He had applied for a place at the National University of Singapore and he'd got in. 'Crazy, right? Do they just let anyone into architecture school nowadays?'

That weekend, they took a wrong turn on the way to visit an old friend's fruit orchard and there it was—a very simple house, nearly finished but clearly abandoned, looking a little lost at the far end of a rectangular plot the size of maybe eight badminton courts. Bok only had a vague idea who it might belong to. Probably old Pak Samad, who ended up moving to KL to live with his son after he hurt his back a few years ago. Did it really take such a short time for nature to reclaim a patch of land? A young tree was already growing inside the house, pushing its branches out of an open window. This made Joo Meng laugh.

'Such a stubborn, determined little tree!' Leaning out of the truck window, he gave it a jolly thumbs-up. 'Good luck, *kawan*!'

A week later, he called her from Singapore, telling her it was done. He'd bought the house. Super quick deal—offered Pak Samad exactly what he'd asked for. So when the boy actually became an architect, he'd get the house. A proper graduation gift, not something useless like a trip to Bali or some other nonsense thing the boy would probably ask for.

'Hard to be a father but must try, right?' In Hokkien, Joo Meng continued, 'He'll never make anything of himself. Soft hands, Bok, soft hands. Too much like his mother's family. But never mind—let him make something with his hands, then. Let's see what he will do.'

Joo Meng didn't know what Bok learnt only much later from Pearl—that it took years to qualify as an architect. And so the lucky Lucky did get his trip to Bali in spite of his father's best intentions.

Bok keeps this bit out of the story. Who cares anymore, now? But she tells Lucky about how his sister hoped for years that he'd somehow find his way back to architecture. She can still see Pearl standing right here a few years ago, shaking her head at the house, at her father's hopeful gift-to-be. 'God, it looks even worse now. I wonder if we should just give it to him, let him do whatever he wants.' But immediately Pearl changed her mind. 'You never know with Lucky, you really never know. Maybe one day he'll get bored of all this random whatever and suddenly want to design buildings . . . and if he doesn't, we'll just hand over this weird, ratty place to him when he's forty or something.'

'Well, here we are, Lucky. I wish she were here with us.' Bok sighs. 'I'm sure you miss her.'

Lucky is thinking many thoughts but he stays quiet. He focuses on the wind against his skin, the ribbed collar of his sister's T-shirt against his neck, the purring of their cat in his arms. His telltale heart beats rapidly in his chest. He thinks of Papa, of Pearl, of all the things he'll never be able to ask them, all the things he'll never know, all the angry things he'll never be able to say. Soft hands—where the fuck did that obsession of Papa's come from? And that awful Pearl—why didn't she just come right out and say, hey there's a ruin that Papa bought for you when he thought you would be an architect, so what shall we do with it now? Lucky sighs. Lucky laughs. Is this what love is, then? The need to be understood, the need to understand. The neverknowing, the alwayswishing, the mindfuckery.

Bok watches Lucky as he gently eases himself out of her embrace and starts to walk towards the house. She brushes a tear from her cheek with the back of her hand. Ah, she's getting sentimental in her old age. Joo Meng would laugh at her if he were here.

'Lucky, are you okay?' A whisper. A warm furry face against his neck.

'Yup, Coconut, don't worry.' He puts her down. 'Just for a minute, okay? I'll be right back.'

When he gets close enough to touch the house, he does. The dewy concrete is cold and wet against his palm. He pats it a few times. *Don't cry, little house, it's going to be fine.*

Is it? He wishes Pearl were here so he could ask her. He knows that he will always, always wish this. In the shade of the tree that started his journey—let's face it, it was the tree that captured Lee Joo Meng's heart—Lucky sighs, knowing he'll have to crack this on his own. What will he do now? What would his father have wanted? Does it matter anymore? So many things to think about.

But first . . . Lucky leans forward, closes his eyes, and kisses his house on the edge of one of its corners, like a peck on the nose. 'Thank you, Papa. It's gorgeous.'

The highway

is a river of hot, glistening tarmac. Even with his sunglasses on, Lucky can feel the glare of the mid-afternoon sun. Outside, acres of oil palms whizz by. The trees are squat and steady, looking very much like stretched-out pineapples, every one the same size and height, the same distance from each other. *Attack of the Clones*, Malaysian plantation style.

'Shall I put some music on?'

Lucky stares straight ahead. *La la la la la la la la la la la.*

'Lucky, do you want me to put some music on?'

Lucky continues to stare at the road. 'Coconut, can you tell Dinah that I don't care whether or not she puts any music on? It's her car and she can do whatever she likes.'

Dinah sighs. 'Why are you being so difficult? I didn't have to come all the way here to get you, you know.'

'Coconut, please tell Dinah that she was the one who decided to come. Can you also let her know that you and I are perfectly able to make our way back home on our own?'

Coconut yawns and stretches on Lucky's lap. He rolls his eyes and scratches her neck. *Wow, Coconut, you're ever so helpful.* Dinah keeps her eyes on the road, but he can tell she's dying to turn her head and bark at him. But she won't—Dinah prides herself on being a Very Safe Driver.

'Coconut, tell Lucky that this is what happens when he's careless and loses his phone and there's an emergency.'

Lucky closes his eyes and leans back into the passenger seat. Right. The emergency. He doesn't want to think about this right now, but he supposes he must. But it's just so damn surreal. Ridiculous. Crazy.

'The house burnt down, Lucky.'

His first thought this afternoon when Dinah arrived at the Moon: 'What the fuck.' His second thought, after her abrupt announcement: 'What the fuck. How does she know about the house?' Then he realized—no, she meant the other house. The one back home. *Home*.

A lot can be done without actually thinking. Lucky Lee has known this all his life and it's served him well. As Dinah rattled off the details, all he wanted to do was go back to bed. But he sat there at Aunty Bok's tiny kitchen table and nodded from time to time without quite knowing what he was nodding at, and he dutifully finished the two cups of coffee that Bok poured for him out of her large coffee pot. He suffered Dinah's attempt to hug him. He listened to Aunty Bok tell him that the best thing for him to do right now was go with Dinah back to Singapore. He managed to pack his bag, put it into her car, climb into the passenger seat with Coconut, wave goodbye to Aunty Bok and the Moon and the river.

The house burnt down? What? WHAT!

Lucky tries to focus on the calm, structured rows of oil palms, but his mind flies over them, dipping and somersaulting, refusing to roost on any single tree or thought. It flits from wondering what's left after the fire to how the fire might have started to whether the stone lions are okay to where he's going to live now to oh no the kitchen the kitchen the wine the wine, and over and over again it circles back to: *This can't be happening this can't be happening this can't be happening this can't be happening to me.*

On top of all this, he's thinking about the house he's left behind, the house he just met this morning. What, what does he do with it?

Seriously, a house gained and a house lost on the same day? It feels like the universe is having a laugh. This morning and all its fuzzy feelings—all gone now, replaced by a weird hollow dread in his heart and head that isn't quite full-blown anxiety but isn't anything he can easily ignore. *Fuck fuck fuck.* The house, their house, the lions, the zebra the cuckoo the parakeets—is it all really gone? Is it possible? Could it be some sort of mistake? He decides it's worth a try.

'Coconut, can you ask Dinah if she's *actually* seen the house?' Lucky sighs. 'Does she know *for sure* that it's burnt down?'

'Coconut, can you tell Lucky that of course I know for sure that it's burnt down. And tell Lucky that if he weren't so damn determined to be out of touch with everything, he would have found out himself. It's been all over the news since last night.'

'Coconut, can you tell Dinah that while there's nothing I like better than to repeat myself, I've already told her that I haven't had my phone since last night.'

'Coconut, can you tell Lucky . . .'

* * *

Shawn has brought the beer. Dinah has brought their Lucky. Standing on either side of him, they each put an arm around their old friend. Catching Dinah's eye over Lucky's shoulder, Shawn raises an inquisitive eyebrow. She shakes her head. Nope, he's not good—Lucky's been quiet for hours, staring at the road, stroking the cat.

Staring up at the house on Swan Street that Lee Joo Meng bought so many years ago, Lucky Lee takes a long gulp of beer.

'Wow.'

It is well and truly dead. Everything Lucky can see from where he stands—the walls, the window frames, the metal grilles, the roof—is charred beyond any hope of repair. A sad skeleton is all that remains of the side of the house where his bedroom used to be. The walls have fallen in (how on earth does fire do this level of damage?) and all the things that once lived with him and bore his weight and framed his every day are now unfamiliar misshapes of metal, glass, concrete, and cinders. Everywhere, everywhere, there is something broken, something bent, something fused into something else.

'It's still not clear how it started. The fire, I mean.'

Lucky turns to Shawn, who hands him another beer. He nods— what is there to say? What can he possibly say now that will take all of this chaos and put it into a nice neat line and keep it there? There's a poem about this somewhere, somewhere in an old notebook in Pearl's room that is now . . . nothing. Lucky goes all the way up to the gate for a closer look, craning his neck to see if he can make out anything in the space where his sister's bedroom used to be. Nope. Nothing.

Sighing, he turns to one of the lions and then the other. They stare back at Lucky, startlingly undamaged by the fire that has wrecked the house behind them, their faces calm and composed and commiserating. Still on duty, still guarding the ruins, still keeping the great iron gate between them.

'Thank god you guys are okay.' He reaches out to touch the nose of the lion closest to him. The stone is so cool, so comforting. Lucky rests his cheek against a muscled foreleg, presses his lips against a handsome paw. 'Thank god you're okay.' He puts his arms around the lion. 'Thank god.'

Shawn and Dinah watch him for a long time, drinking their beer as Lucky continues to whisper to the lion. Coconut circles his ankles, meowing loudly.

'You think he's going to be okay?'

'Nope. Not for a while.'

They watch as Lucky peels himself off the lion, then picks up Coconut and starts whispering to her.

'Hey, Coconut. Sorry. I'm just trying to . . .' What was he trying to do? 'I'm not sure what I'm supposed to do.'

'We'll be okay, Lucky. Right?' The tiniest mew.

'That's right, Coconut.' Lucky sinks his face into her fur. 'Of course we're going to be okay.'

* * *

The door cracks open and Shawn looks into his study, at the unfolded sofa bed in the corner, at the lump lying still under the thick grey blanket. The blinds are low and closed, in exactly the same position they've been for the three days that Lucky's been here.

'Lucky, everything okay?'

'Yes.'

'Can I get you anything?'

'No, thank you.'

'Just let me know, okay? I've made you a sandwich. I'll leave it here on the table. Okay?'

'Sure, thanks.'

* * *

The lump has shifted. Now it's pressed up against the wall.

'Lucky, I got you a new phin. Come try it out.'

'Maybe tomorrow.'

'You sure? Come, let's try it now.'

'Tomorrow, Shawn.'

'Okay.'

* * *

The lump doesn't move as Shawn sits down next to it. He clears his throat. 'Lucky, are you awake?'

'Yes.'

'Dinah's here. And Anita made laksa for dinner. Come join us . . . come outside. Watch TV.'

'Maybe later. You guys go ahead.'

* * *

The lump ignores its new phone. When Shawn picks up a call and puts it on speaker, the lump doesn't reply.

'Your Aunty Maggie and I are so worried about you! Why haven't you called . . .'

'. . . if your mother were here . . .'

'Uncle Desmond says the residual soot is poisonous, you know . . .'

'What about all the jewellery . . .'

The lump makes a sad noise and throws itself against the wall.

* * *

The lump sometimes grows when Shawn lets Coconut into the room in the evenings. The little cat finds its way under the blanket and attaches itself to the lump.

'Lucky, it's so dark under here. Don't you want to come out?'

'Soon, Coconut.'

'How soon?'

'I don't know. Just soon.'

'Shall I tell you a story?'

'No, Coconut, no stories, okay? Not today.'

* * *

The lump writhes. The lump twists and turns under the blanket.

'Lucky, wake up. Wake up!'

'I'm awake, Shawn. I'm fine.'

'Lucky, it's me. Get up and put this on.'

Lucky sits up in bed. Why is his bedroom so warm? Did he forget to turn on the air con? And what's Pearl doing here? His sister hands him a suit that looks like it's made out of tinfoil.

'Pearl, what's happening?'

She rolls her eyes. 'The house is burning down, dumbass. Can't you tell?'

Lucky looks around. She's right. Flickers of flame dance all around his bed, leaping at the ceiling, the curtains. 'Fuck!'

'Come on!' Pearl grabs him by both hands and drags him out of bed. Just in time. The fire swallows up his bed with what sounds like a gleeful roar. They run out of the room and slam the door.

There's fire here too, but it hasn't reached the stairs. Sweating, cursing, Lucky struggles into his tinfoil suit. Strange—it looks exactly like the silver onesie that Pearl wore to that Halloween party when she dressed up as David Bowie and made Lucky wear a wig and go as Iman. He tries to ask Pearl if she's got a suit too, but she doesn't hear him and she doesn't seem to need one. She runs down the upstairs corridor, unbothered by the flames, turning back every few steps to make sure he's following her.

'Faster, Lucky! Faster!' She bounces down the stairs. The flames lick her feet, her dress, her hair.

'I'm coming, Pearl! Wait for me!' Suddenly he's growing smaller—or are the flames growing bigger? 'Pearl, help!' He can feel himself shrinking as he runs down the stairs, trying to get to the ground floor.

Lucky's the size of a mouse now. *What the hell?* 'Pearl!' he squeaks, frantic. 'Pearl!' A tall hissing flame starts to follow him as he leaps from step to step. He can feel the heat on his back as it gains on him. He tries to jump down two steps at once, but he loses his balance and falls over. Trying not to cry, Lucky stares down the last flight of stairs. 'Pearl!'

At the bottom of the stairs, his sister turns. 'Lucky, for fuck's sake . . .' Ah, that look, that half-smile-half-frown, why does it make his heart ache? Pearl starts climbing the stairs towards him. Lucky keeps his eyes on her face until it looms right above him, filling his entire view. She bends over to pick him up. 'It's okay, I've got you.'

But the fire—as Pearl reaches the bottom of the stairs with Lucky cradled in her hands, the flames have beat her to it. Fire fills the courtyard, the living room, blocking their way out. Lucky looks up at Pearl. What will they do now?

'Hello, you.' She turns to the stair-dragon, its regal teakwood head still untouched by the flames, its body and tail curling up and up to the top of the stairs. Mouse-Lucky feels his heart clench. It's *huge*.

'Hello, my pretty Pearl.' *Damn, dragon, what a nice baritone.* 'Has anyone told you you look just like your mother?'

Pearl grins and tosses her head. 'All the time. Come on, shall we get out of here?'

'Just waiting for you to ask—climb on.' The dragon rears its head and, with a rather violent shake of its body, frees itself from its mountings.

Lucky gasps. He never knew it could do that. And now it's floating. *Flying*.

'I could just eat him, save us the trouble.' The stair-dragon winks at Pearl, who giggles.

'Oh, don't tease him. He's had a tough time.' Careful not to drop Lucky, she climbs onto the dragon's scaly wooden back.

The dragon snorts. 'Meh. Needs to toughen up.' It turns its head back to check on Pearl. 'Hang on tight, my dear.'

With two flicks of a teakwood tail, they're off. Up and up they go, the dragon sailing through the central courtyard of the house, past the fire creeping up the walls chewing up the furniture crawling into the cupboards the drawers the pipes the lights. Pearl flings her head back and laughs. Lucky clings to her fingers and shrieks. They fly straight through the skylight and out into the night, and Lucky closes his eyes as the cool night air rushes against his face. When he opens them again, they're hovering high above the house, above Swan Street, watching as the house burns brighter and brighter.

Lucky blinks. Wow, if it weren't for Pearl and the stair-dragon, he'd be dead!

'Thanks, dragon!' he shouts from behind its massive carved head.

'You're welcome, Lucky.' The dragon glides down towards the street and stops right in front of the burning house. 'Now, off you go.'

Pearl jumps off the dragon's back. 'Take care, Lucky. Don't forget to feed the cat.' She winks at him as she puts him down on the pavement.

'Where are you going, Pearl?' Lucky watches his sister climb back onto the dragon.

Another wink, a wave. 'Who knows? Maybe Komodo.'

The dragon laughs. 'Maybe Kokomo.'

As they fly off and leave him behind, Pearl waving, girl and dragon growing ever smaller in the distance, Lucky finds himself weeping.

Pearl, he wants to shout, Pearl, come back, come back. Please come back, come back for me. But he doesn't. She and the dragon are too far off now, and he knows she won't hear him.

So instead he waves goodbye and blows her a kiss. *Have fun, Pearl.*

* * *

He wakes up whimpering, shaking, crying for Pearl. Alone. Afraid.

Before everything and everyone, before the world had faces, it was her and him in a house like a zoo. Before love and hate were words he learnt, before hurt and heartbreak were things he knew, it was her and him duking it out in a house that was their own Colosseum. Before superheroes, before rock stars, before television, travel, and too many things they wanted to do but didn't, it was her and him and a house.

It hits him, with all the force and the finality of a tidal wave: It's just him now.

* * *

By the time the sun rises, the blinds are raised and open. The blanket is on the floor. The lump is gone.

Lucky Lee is in the kitchen. He is making coffee, purple shadows under his eyes and a tortoiseshell cat purring at his feet, telling him a story.

The god of heaven

is not for us to understand. *Th'nee Kong mmm sai hor lang cai eh.* It was something his grandmother used to say when things went wrong, as she continued to heap fruit on the teakwood altar that stood in their living room and was meant to somehow connect the family to the Taoist deity. Th'nee Kong, the god of heaven, king of the sky.

Th'nee Kong mmm sai hor lang cai eh. That was Mr Thiang's first thought when he read the news that his friend Mr Lee's house had burnt down. The article said 'cause unknown', which didn't seem right—how could they not know how the fire started? So stupid. So many things seem so stupid these days—like all the young people sitting together in the cafe next door not talking to each other but playing with their phones and looking at other people on 'social media'. Talking to the friends you're sitting with is not social enough ah? Must have media ah? Direct, cannot?

The god of heaven is not for us to understand.

Walking down Joo Chiat Road this morning, Mr Thiang wonders what his old friend would say about the house burning down. He can imagine Mr Lee scolding the children, '*Chiak liao bee*, both of you! How can you let this happen to our house?' Wait—scold *the boy*. The girl, aiya, sometimes it's hard to believe she's gone. You remember but then you don't remember. That's the trouble with getting old.

He decides to turn into Swan Street, suddenly nostalgic. Ah, when Mr Lee was still alive, he'd drop by the house from time to time for a kopi, a chat, maybe ask for business advice. His friend always had good coffee and good ideas—they didn't always make sense, but they worked. Like the time he told Mr Thiang to start selling rattan furniture ('My girl went to Bali, the resorts are full of rattan things!'), even though rattan was the sort of thing that only people in villages used, so how could he sell it in a city where everyone wanted to look rich even if they weren't? But somehow Mr Lee was right. The young people who come into the store like rattan, even if it horrifies their parents, and he's sold so many rattan chairs over the years it's funny.

Swan Street looks the same as it did a year ago—or is it nearly two?—since he was last here. For Mr Lee's girl's funeral. Terrible, terrible, to die so young. Mr Thiang sighs as he walks down the pavement. The god of heaven is not for us to understand. And he didn't understand—why would a girl like that, pretty like her mother and smart like her father, end up dying before she turned forty, before she could really do anything? Why was he, Thiang Kim Poh, allowed to live for nearly eighty years now, every day growing weaker, every day opening his furniture store out of habit? Every day checking the newspaper obituaries, wondering if any old friends have died.

Ah, he's here too.

As Mr Thiang approaches the house, he sees Mr Lee's boy standing on the driveway beyond the gate, staring up at the remains of the house. Lucky Lee. He shakes his head. What a strange name for a boy. Sounds like a dog's name. Or a . . . cat's, like the one sitting on one of the stone lions, looking down at him. Nice fur, looks well fed. Definitely a lucky cat.

As for the boy . . . poor fellow looks a bit ragged. Doesn't help that he always looks like his mind is elsewhere. Poor thing—in some ways, not so lucky. After all, money isn't everything, right? Money is *good* but imagine—your sister dies and leaves you all by yourself in a big house, and then the house burns down. *Jialat.*

'Uncle Thiang!' The boy waves from the other side of the gate.

'Eh, hello, Lucky! Didn't know you were here, just wanted to have a look, you know? Ah, your Papa loved this house.'

The boy smiles, managing to look like a Hong Kong film star in spite of the tired eyes and the terrible clothes. *Wah, the children really take after their mother.* 'Come in if you like, Uncle.'

As the two men stand side by side, looking up at the house, Mr Thiang shakes his head again. It looks much, much worse than the photos he saw in papers. The roof has fallen in completely, thanks to the thunderstorms over the last few weeks, and more of the facade has crumbled. Everything looks burnt and damp, covered in soot, sodden by rain.

'It's all going to be cleared next week,' the boy explains, not taking his eyes off the house. The fire insurance investigations and everything are over, he tells Mr Thiang, and the only thing left to do is take it all down.

Mr Thiang nods. 'So can build a new one.'

The boy is silent. He shrugs.

'Lucky, something wrong?' Mr Thiang frowns. Has the boy somehow lost the family fortune, already? Must be online betting. Someone he knows knew someone who had lost more than one hundred thousand dollars gambling online, and the more you have the more you lose, right?

'No, I'm fine.' But Lucky sighs.

'Is it online betting?'

'What?' The boy looks confused. Good, good.

'Okay, very good. Just asking. Making sure.' Mr Thiang makes a magnanimous gesture. 'So, what's wrong?'

'I don't know, Uncle Thiang. I don't know if I'm ready to build another house.'

'You cannot live upstairs the cafe forever, right? Already two months!' Mr Thiang is about to say 'crazy ah?' but he clamps his mouth shut. It's never a good idea to say things like that, and he's heard people say the Lee boy is having what they call mental health issues. *Crazy say crazy lah.* Not that the boy seems at all mad—every week he pops in with a bag of fresh coffee grinds for Mr Thiang and stays for a chat. Very thoughtful! Probably not crazy.

Lucky smiles wryly. Two months? Closer to three, really. 'Yea, Uncle. It's not a great set-up.'

The army cot, for one—what a nightmare to sleep on. And honestly, it's a little creepy, sleeping in the space above the cafe. They've never bothered to do it up, so it's not even a proper room, more like an extended stair landing—no door, no partitions. The vibe, as Shawn would put it, is . . . junkyard. Cans of paint, leftover bits and pieces from the cafe renovations, old equipment from the time of his father's coffee shop, all of which he had to rearrange on one side of the space so he could set up that dreadful cot, a clothes rack, and an old coffee table that Shawn's scavenged from somewhere. He's always wondering if from somewhere among the trash there's a rat—or worse—watching him. Of course Coconut says there aren't any rats—but she's already got a new basket and she's sleeping pretty, so it's not like she's looking out for rats, is she? He glares at the little cat, who's perched on top of one of the lions, sunning herself.

'But it feels weird to build a new house so soon, you know?' Lucky looks apologetically at the old house.

'Not *so soon*! Need time to design, find contractor, build everything. Maybe one year! Better start now.' Mr Thiang pats Lucky on the back. 'Don't waste time.'

Lucky shrugs. Maybe Uncle Thiang has a point. Already, the grass is growing—literally—under their feet. The last time he was here, there was barely any green anywhere. But now, after all the crazy rain, the scorched front garden looks like it's starting to recover. Fine whispers of grass have pushed their way out of the earth; the frangipani has mustered a few new leaves.

'I just don't want to get it wrong.'

Mr Thiang looks at his friend's sad-eyed son and thinks of what the old house used to be, full of the craziest things Mr Lee could buy because Lee Joo Meng liked crazy, expensive things. He laughed. 'Aiyo, Lucky, cannot be wrong lah. You do what you like. Your house now.'

'My house.' *House-to-be. Do you, Lucky Lee, take this house . . .?* Lucky grins.

Mr Thiang claps him on the back again. 'Like that lah—smile, be happy. Do what you want. Your father always did what he wanted, you know. Always!' He clears his throat. Ah, he misses his old friend.

After he walks off, waving, Lucky kicks at a random stone and growls. 'Do what you want' solves none of his problems. All he wants is for someone to tell him what to do with this stupid feeling—what is it, reluctance? Trepidation? Plain old garden-variety cold feet?—that won't let him throw himself into this whole business of a new house. Shawn is dying to dive in, design 'something beautiful and clean and minimalist, Lucky. Think Tadao Ando, think Peter Zumthor. Completely different from the old house.'

Lucky is tempted by the thought of a sleek, modern cave with high ceilings and slivers of light, but does he want something so completely different? Shouldn't there be some spirit of parakeet–zebra–cuckoo–dragon somewhere? Meanwhile, Uncle Desmond and the aunties Dolly and Maggie want him to 'be smart and sell off the plot to a developer—the market's very good now for strata projects' and buy one of those monstrous luxury condos in the middle of the city. And not have these stone lions guarding his house? Ridiculous.

'Meddlesome cows.' Lucky chases down the stone and kicks it again.

Coconut leaps down from the stone lion and saunters over, tail swishing like she's wagging a finger at him. 'Don't talk to yourself, Lucky. People will think you're mad.'

'Aren't I?' He picks her up.

'I think you're fine.' She yawns. 'But then I'm just a cat.'

* * *

'When are we going back, Lucky?'

In their new quarters above the cafe, Lucky is half-asleep. He wakes up to see Coconut's tail dangling from the windowsill right above his cot, its tip just inches from his face. In the greenish light coming through the windows, it looks like a fiendish glowing caterpillar.

'Go back where, Coconut?' He swats gently at her tail.

'Ipoh. Isn't that where the mountain is?'

Lucky sits up and puts his chin on the windowsill next to her. 'Well, there are mountains everywhere.'

'Not here,' Staring out the window at the—moon? streetlamp? a rat?—Coconut looks a little sad. She taps her tail on his shoulder. 'No mountains here, Lucky.'

Poor Coconut. He did promise her a mountain. He reaches up and strokes her head. 'One day we'll go back and see a mountain, okay?'

She looks down at him. 'When?'

'Soon. As soon as I figure out the house, okay?'

Coconut narrows her eyes at him. 'Fine. But first, I want a new television.'

Wow, that escalated quickly. Lucky rolls his eyes, wishing he could tell people his cat demanded a television because their journey–adventure–vacation in Malaysia was cut short by the fire that consumed his family home. Of all the unsympathetic creatures of the earth, of all the cruel cut-throat beasts, cats are the worst. 'The worst.'

'What was that, Lucky?'

'I'll get you your TV.'

$$* * *$$

Clearly, Shawn has been busy. (How? When? He's at the cafe all the time!) The sketches he puts on the counter aren't the kind of slapdash thing Lucky expected when Shawn offered—oh, so casually—to show him a few ideas for the new house. Let's open a bottle of wine, he said as they were closing up, as if the wine was the thing he was staying back for. But then out came Shawn's old leather binder and from it emerged a sheaf of *annotated* sketches—plans, elevations, a cross-section, all beautifully drawn, with details on materials, colour, dimensions, even landscaping.

'So, what do you think?' Shawn pours Lucky another glass of wine.

'Wow.' He really is wowed—all this time, this effort, for *him*? He stares at the ground-floor plan again. So thoughtful, as always. The kitchen is right up front, large and central, exactly how Lucky would like to live, with an atrium beyond it for dining and sitting around and maybe a party if he ever feels like one. Stairs from the kitchen leading upstairs—perfect. No wasting time in the mornings. Perhaps Shawn should have stayed an architect; he probably misses this. Lucky looks up at his friend and wonders for the first time if the cafe has been a mistake, if with his cliched (thanks, Pearl) scheme to open a cafe in this gentrifying bit of Singapore he has somehow dragged Shawn off the proper path for Shawn.

'These are great, Shawn. Really great.'

Shawn grins. 'So you'll let me do it?' He looks so excited, so fresh-faced suddenly that Lucky wishes he could just say yes and hand everything over to Shawn. Why shouldn't he?

But he doesn't. 'Let me think about it?'

'If there's anything you'd like to change . . .'

'It's not that. I'm just not ready yet.' Lucky wonders how many times he'll have to say this and try to explain to other people something he doesn't quite understand himself. 'It's too soon.' But it's not just that it's too soon—it feels like he's missing something somewhere.

Shawn doesn't push him. Thank god for Shawn. They talk about the new bakery that's opened down the road with the long queues and the croissants that run out before ten. 'Madness—who's queueing so early?' They talk about the bottle of chianti, finish it, and open another. Shawn talks about Dinah, who's having a tough time at work and is thinking of quitting.

'What about you, Lucky? How are you doing? You know, for a while we thought you weren't coming back.'

'Really?'

'Yea. Dinah was really freaking out. You should talk to her, tell her you're okay.' Shawn tops up both their glasses. 'She thinks you had a breakdown and then ran off to Malaysia.' He pauses. 'I know things can be rough. You know you can talk to us, right?' Another pause. 'Anytime.'

Lucky nods. 'I know. Thanks.' *I'm a total jackass.* Of course they were worried. 'Sorry.'

Shawn waves this aside. 'Nah, forget it. Really.' He looks away for a moment. 'It's good to have you back.'

Lucky doesn't say it's good to be back, but he feels a warmth in his stomach that could be more than the wine.

* * *

'What do you think, Coconut?'

She sniffs at the drawings, then stares intently at the second-floor plan. 'Is that my room?'

Lucky reads the label. 'Nope. That's my study. Let's see, it says here this doubles as the guest bedroom. Pretty smart.'

Coconut circles the sheet of paper, waving her tail. 'Where's my room?'

'I think Shawn thinks we'll share.'

'I think Shawn doesn't know you sometimes snore.' Coconut bats him on the nose with a paw. 'Anyway, *you* went to architecture school too. *You* can make the house.'

Lucky laughs. Little tyrant. 'It doesn't work like that, Coconut.' He pauses, wondering for a moment if he's really going to explain the qualification process to a cat. No, he isn't. 'I can't make a house the way Shawn and Dinah can. Takes years.'

'Okay. So what can you make?'

'Um, coffee?' He laughs and rubs her head. 'Fish curry. Dumplings. Um, laksa. Nasi lemak.' All those years sous-chef-ing for Pearl! Lucky puffs out his chest. 'And noodles from scratch.'

'Not even a TV?' Coconut stares at him pityingly. 'A television is much smaller than a house, Lucky.'

* * *

'So funny.'

'Hardly! I think she's getting spoilt.'

'Nonsense—cats don't spoil.' The cat lady of Eunos hands Lucky a plastic bag of pre-packed cat dinners. Together, they squat on the wide walkway in front of the train station and begin her cats' dinner-time routine. Two by two, the newspaper packets of fish and rice are unwrapped; two by two the cats are fed.

'Thanks. I think the cats are happy you're back safe,' she says as they stand up and stretch after the last cat is served.

'It's good to see all of you.' Lucky addresses the horde of feeding cats, which seems to have grown in number since he last saw the cat lady. There must be fifty, maybe sixty cats now. He wonders where the new ones have come from.

'Maybe your cat's bored.' She looks thoughtful. 'After all her adventures.'

Lucky's told her about losing Coconut in KL ('Really, Lucky, how could you have been so careless!'), about how she met the Raja Kucing and then managed to find him in Ipoh ('I suppose she thought it was easier than waiting for you to find her').

'Other cats don't need a TV.' Lucky looks pointedly at her cats. 'Right, Gajah?' The large grey cat looks up at the sound of his name and gives Lucky a brooding stare for daring to interrupt his dinner. 'Sorry, sorry.'

'No two cats are the same.' The cat lady surveys her clowder of cats, all of them on their haunches, their heads half-hidden in newspaper packets. 'If you tried to pat Blackblack over there, she'd bite you. But her brother Brownbrown loves being stroked.' She clicks her tongue. 'Your cat didn't have to go looking for you, you know. A clever cat like that could have survived on her own in KL.'

'Well . . .' Lucky frowns. It's not like Coconut doesn't need him *at all*. Who opens all her tins of cat food? Who gives her all the little scratches she likes at the back of her neck?

'Remember what the Raja Kucing said, Lucky?' She smiles. 'Not everyone can take care of a cat.'

* * *

It's so nice to have him back. 'The moment I wake up, before I put on my make-up . . .' Meixi hums to herself as she pours hot water, cooled from boiling to exactly 92 degrees, into a phin sitting on a short glass cup.

It's so nice to have him *here*. These days it doesn't matter to her if she's scheduled for the morning or afternoon shift at the cafe—he's always around somewhere, deliciously near, mostly when he's working, but also when he's not. Sometimes he'll be at one of the tables at the back, like he is today, reading or fiddling with his new phone; sometimes he's in the little office beyond the storeroom, watching something on Netflix with the cat.

What a lucky cat.

The last drop falls through the filter into the cup and Meixi beams at it. *Yay, finally*. She stirs a tablespoon of condensed milk into the deep blackness of the Vietnamese coffee, then pours it into a glass of crushed ice, just the way she knows Lucky likes it.

Meixi starts walking down the length of the cafe towards Lucky, noting the slight frown on his face in profile as he stares at something on his laptop, wondering how she'll start the conversation. 'Hi, Lucky, made you some coffee' is so, so boring. She needs something that will perk him up, make him laugh, make sure he doesn't think of her as boring. But what? Maybe something about cats? About his cat?

At the far end of the cafe, Lucky looks up into the middle distance, running both hands through his hair. Meixi sighs and quickens her step.

To live without you would only mean heartbreak for meeeee . . .

* * *

'Where's my TV, Lucky?'

'Coconut, what the hell! Don't do that!' Lucky glares down at the ball of fur that has just launched itself onto his lap.

It winks. 'Did you think it was a grasshopper?'

'Coconut!' The nerve of her. 'How many times have I told you? It's really rude to sneak up on people. What if—'

'Hi Lucky, made you some coffee.'

Lucky jumps in his chair, holding on tightly to Coconut. He turns. 'Meixi! Ah, hello.' He stares at her, wondering for a moment if she heard Coconut speak. Unlikely—Meixi's face is the usual picture of creamy-foundation rose-blusher sweetness and calm. 'Thank you. Really good of you, but you don't have to, you know. I can make my own coffee.'

'I know.' Meixi wonders what else to say. 'I've seen you do it.'

'Ah.' Lucky wonders if he should tell her he prefers his Vietnamese coffee hot.

In the awkwardness that follows, Lucky takes a large gulp of coffee, and Meixi decides she will speak to his cat. 'Hey there, Coconut. How's your friend?'

Lucky looks at Coconut. 'Meixi, what friend?'

She giggles. 'Awww, Coconut's got a boyfriend, Lucky.' She reaches out to pat Coconut, who squirms in the crook of Lucky's arm. 'You're right, Coconut, it's time for me to get a boyfriend too.'

Meixi looks straight into Lucky's eyes. What eyes! 'I saw them hanging out at Patisserie Antoine. They look so cute together.' She whispers, as if she's afraid Coconut will hear her: 'Very handsome, a bit chubby. But you'd expect that of a baker's cat, right?'

Lucky glares, first at Meixi, then at Coconut. 'No, Meixi. Cats don't eat bread.'

* * *

'Where are you off to, Coconut? I thought we'd watch this shark show on Netflix.'

The little cat turns to look back at him from outside the window. 'I've seen it. Very fun.'

Lucky frowns. 'You've seen it?'

'Yes. Cat Steven's got a television.'

'Cat Steven? That's his name?' Lucky makes a face, torn between amusement and jealousy. 'The bakery cat?'

'Patisserie, Lucky, not bakery.' She sniffs. 'Antoine's place smells very nice. You'd like it. Lots of butter.'

Pfffft. I wouldn't. Lucky turns away so she won't see him roll his eyes. Stupid Antoine and his stupid cat and their stupid television. And who calls a cat Cat Steven? Ridiculous. And who lets strange cats into their place to watch television? Even more ridiculous. He turns back to tell her this, but Coconut's already gone, trotting along the roofline away from him towards the bake—patisserie.

* * *

'Coconut? Coconut?'

Lucky calls her name and gets no answer. He hasn't seen her all afternoon. She went off after breakfast without so much as a purr or a face-rub and now it's nearly three. He glares in the direction of Patisserie Antoine. *Bloody Cat Steven.*

His phone buzzes. `Free today? I can drop by for a coffee in about an hour if that works.`

Lucky wonders what Dinah wants to talk about. It's been a rather long time since they've hung out by themselves—so much easier not to get into a quarrel when there are other people around. He sighs. Well, he does miss her and she does mean well, even if she can be such a pushy creature. Which reminds him of another pushy creature . . .

`I need to pick up a present for Coconut. Come with me?`

Present. Bah. More like a bribe. No, an offering—like the bunga mas and weapons that the ancient Malay rulers used to send to Siam and Burma in the seventeenth century so that they wouldn't get attacked by armies of elephants. Well, as long as she didn't expect a new flat-screen every year.

The biggest electronics store
in the neighbourhood

is on the corner of two busy streets, tucked away inside a rundown shopping complex where the eighties live on. In this long, windowless space, under bright white lights, it is forever and never night or day, and the piped music is a gentle refusal to move on from simpler times. Backed by an instrumental version of Stevie Wonder's 'I Just Called to Say I Love You', big bold signs ('Big Discounts! Big Value! Welcome to Big Electronics!') usher Lucky and Dinah towards the escalators in the middle of the building, past the rows of shops offering remittance services, foot massages, feng shui readings, exorcisms, and banana cake.

'Is this it?'

'Yup.'

The nondescript entrance is the same pair of heavy aluminium-framed doors that Lucky remembers from every time he's been to the store in the last thirty-ish years. His father always said the doors were a good tactic. You see doors like these and you don't think to yourself that this is a fancy sort of store; you see doors like these and you think you're going to get a good deal.

Lucky walks in thinking he's going to get a good deal.

An hour later, he is pacing the television section while Dinah grits her teeth. He's no longer thinking he's going to get a good deal—he's wondering how televisions have come to be so complicated. Also, everything seems to be a smart TV, and he's unsure if Coconut will be

345

able to cope. She's a smart cat but is she that smart? There's also the question of the remote controls—can her paws cope with these teeny tiny buttons?

'What's the problem, Lucky? If you want, we can go to another store . . .'

Lucky thrusts a sleek white remote control at Dinah. 'Look—do you think this is too small for Coconut? Why are they making these things so damn tiny?'

Dinah stares. Okay. She can do this. Carefully, keeping her tone light, she ventures, 'Coconut needs to use the remote control?'

To her horror, the answer is yes, because the cat needs to be able to turn on the television by itself. In fact, the television is *for the cat.* Well, he did say in his text earlier that he needed to get a present for Coconut, but she hadn't connected this with his wanting to go to Big Electronics and get a new television. Amazed, she only half-listens as Lucky and the store manager, who's finally decided it's time to close the sale, talk about the best kind of screens for watching nature documentaries. Should she call Shawn? Aunty Dolly? But what would she say? What can they really do? What can anyone?

Lucky stares at the mountain on the television screen closest to him. From a distance, it's lush and green, and as the camera moves closer and over it, the ridges of a crater come into view and then a gleaming, turquoise lake. The colours are nuanced and life-like, none of the weird lurid hues of some of the other models. Lucky has to stop himself from trying to reach out and touch the water. *This is it. This is our TV.*

'That's Mount Rinjani, in Indonesia. Beautiful!'

Reluctantly, Lucky turns away from the screen to look at the store manager. 'Ah. Have you been?'

The store manager sighs. 'No. Would be nice, right, to see a proper mountain? Not like Bukit Timah Hill.'

Lucky rolls his eyes, nodding.

The excursion last week up that very hill had been a massive failure. Incensed by the cat lady's insinuation that he, Lucky Lee, couldn't take care of a cat, he'd announced to Coconut that he was taking her to see a dwarf mountain.

'Dwarf mountain?'

Lucky explained to his sceptic cat (his scepticat!) that dwarf mountains weren't the same level of cool as a regular mountain, but they were supposed to be pretty nice.

'Supposed to be? You've never been?'

'Super long ago, Coconut.' Probably a school trip, and he probably left as soon as he could and erased the memory. Lucky sighed. The things he did for Coconut! He made a mental note to go visit the cat lady soon and tell her he took his cat up Bukit Timah Hill. How many people can say that?

He prepared snacks—curry puffs for himself, cat treats for Coconut—and put everything in a basket together with Coconut herself, and off they went in a cab to the start of one of the many trails marked on Google Maps. What a walk it was to the summit! It wasn't even nine yet but it was *hot*. The tarmac path teemed with elderly women in visors on their morning walk and over them hung a great cloud of citronella from all the insect repellent. Lucky, on the other hand, having brought no repellent, was nearly eaten alive by mosquitoes and relentlessly pursued by other roving insects.

All this, for nothing. The little cat was openly scornful ('the sign over there says this is a *hill*, Lucky'), there was no view to speak of ('what are we supposed to see, Lucky?'), and he lost a curry puff to a wasp (he wasn't sure if wasps ate curry puffs but he was sure that one was eyeing his so he threw one at it). Forty-five minutes after they arrived, they were on their way back to the cafe.

Coconut sulked the entire day, upset about the dwarf mountain that wasn't a mountain at all. Lucky spent the entire day contrite, wondering why he had ever imagined that Bukit Timah Hill would pass for a mountain, even a dwarf one, even to a cat.

At the television store, Lucky considers Coconut's mountain-mania. 'Yes, I suppose it would be nice to have a proper mountain here.'

'Ah, sir, your . . . girlfriend likes to watch documentaries, issit?' It's a bit of a gamble, but the store manager's experience tells him the sullen woman staring at the ceiling is unlikely to be the girlfriend. But a fellow as good-looking as this one—there's definitely a girlfriend somewhere.

Lucky throws his head back and laughs. 'Ah, yes. Obsessed with mountains.'

And score! The manager begins to talk about the television's technical specifications and why, if sir's girlfriend wants to watch shows about mountains and wildlife and all the wonders of nature, then sir should invest in this pinnacle of Korean LED technology.

'Last time, Japanese TV better, right? Now, no—Korean all the way, sir. Let me show you . . .'

Lucky's mind drifts back to the mountain on the television screen. Poor Coconut. He did promise her a mountain.

'. . . this LED is not normal LED, sir . . .'

Of course he can't go off to Malaysia again, not now, not for the next few months. He owes it to Shawn and Dinah to do his share of the work, and it's really Shawn who should be taking a break.

'You see, sir, the colour here and here look like same, right? But not same!'

There has to be something he can do. After all, the cat lady has a good point. Coconut did go looking for him after that horrible incident in KL when it would have been easier to find someone else to live with, someone with a television and perhaps another cat to be friends with. Like that damn croissant guy.

'Sir, I get new one from storeroom for you. Need delivery?'

In a muddle of his own making, Lucky pays for the television and Dinah, lost in her own thoughts, drives him back to the cafe. Stopping at the traffic light just before the turning into Joo Chiat Road, they watch as two workmen climb a scaffold outside a shophouse.

Dinah speaks for the first time since they left the store. 'Remember our first trip to Hong Kong, Lucky? All the bamboo scaffolding everywhere!'

Lucky remembers. For the first couple of days, he'd quicken his step every time he had to walk under what looked like a very flimsy system of bamboo poles tied together. But someone later explained how hardy these were meant to be—something about the natural strength and flexibility of bamboo. Still, it was a little freaky watching workers casually scale the outside of a building, balancing on floors and floors of, well, branches.

He doesn't think about scaffolding again until the next day, when he pops over to Swan Street to visit the lions. The house is gone, the grass is longer, and there, climbing up one of the casuarinas, gripping it gracefully and fiercely by the trunk, is a morning glory vine, already beginning to flower.

A mountain to *climb*—of course.

Lucky's eyes go round with delight. Well, if Coconut cannot go to the mountain, then the mountain must come to Coconut.

The mountain of Swan Street

goes unseen at first. Its beginnings are tentative, fraught with mistakes and missteps. In these early molehill days, there are times when it disappears altogether and reappears again a few days later. But with every reappearance it is a little sturdier, a little surer of itself.

Near the mountain and yet not too near, a small tent stands, one end supported by the old frangipani that Lee Joo Meng planted when he bought the house that once stood here, the other end held up by a tall bamboo pole that his son the mountain-maker has driven into the ground.

Inside the tent, the mountain-maker and his cat are talking.

'Lucky, are you sure you can make a mountain?'

'Coconut, you have to trust me.'

The cat makes an impatient noise, a cross between a hiss and a snort. 'I trust you, Lucky. But you know that doesn't mean you can do things you can't do, right? Like catch a bird . . .'

Lucky is sure he could catch a bird if he wanted. Not a very large one, but a small one . . . like a sparrow. Or a hummingbird—wait, those are *fast*.

'. . . or make a mountain.'

'Trust me, Coconut. I've got this.'

He stares at the 3D lattice of bamboo sticks he's been working on. It's taken two weeks and quite a number of adjustments, but it looks like he's finally getting somewhere. He grins and leans back in the deck chair he's bought for ten dollars on Carousell. Somehow—he doesn't quite know how, not yet—this mountain will be made.

He picks up the cat and kisses her on the head. 'Really, Coconut, sometimes you can be such a sourpuss.'

* * *

The first thing she sees when she walks into the cafe is the cat. For a moment, they stare at each other, black eyes locking on green, and Dinah thinks, *it hates me*. Sitting upright on one of the high stools at the counter, the cat stares down its nose at Dinah. *If you were a rat*, the cat seems to want her to know, *I would not deign to run after you*. Waving its white-tipped tail—like some sort of rattlesnake!—it watches her as she walks past the counter towards the back of the cafe.

'Um. Hey, Coconut.' Dinah nods at it. *Don't let it think you're intimidated.*

It lifts its head and utters a loud, complaining meow. Dinah jumps and nearly drops her bag. *Jesus. What the fuck is wrong with this cat?*

'Dinah! Hey!'

Lucky's seen her. It's like the cat thought it had to warn him about her. *Possessive little beast.*

'Hey, Lucky! Busy day?' She forces herself to smile brightly as she joins him at one of his favourite tables at the back of the cafe.

'Nope.' He grins back. 'Not at all. Thursdays are always a little quiet. So I've done the inventory, and now I'm just bumming around until Shawn gets here . . .' He checks his phone. '. . . in forty-five minutes.'

Dinah nods. It's wonderful how Lucky's stepped up, working pretty much every day now so that Shawn's got more time for his sculpture projects. She smiles to stop herself from sighing. It's hard not to be jealous. She's been busting her ass for her boss for close to twelve years now, and she still doesn't know where she's going at the firm, whether they'll give her the very tiny raise she's asked for, whether they'll let her lead that project in Malaysia she's been gunning for. Meanwhile, Shawn's getting more commissions for his sculptures, and Lucky's . . . better these days. He's working here, he's enjoying himself. And of course he's still got all that money and very few responsibilities. And while he's not dating or anything, he's got that cat—clearly, it's devoted to him.

Just as clearly, he's a little obsessed with the cat. For days after their television-store afternoon, she wondered if Lucky was having another breakdown. Who buys a TV for a cat? But Dinah's decided she's going to try not to worry . . . too much.

Maybe he's just lonely.

So here she is, determined to spend more time with Lucky. Watch TV with him if he wants. Show him there's no need to turn to a cat for attention and affection.

'What's that you're working on?'

Lucky's been sketching. Interesting. Spread out in front of him are a few sheets of paper covered in geometric patterns, but it's hard to make them out. As she leans over for a closer look, Lucky laughs, gathers them into a stack, and places them face down on the table.

'Just some random nonsense.' He stands up. 'I'll make you a coffee, okay?'

'Sure, anything—surprise me.'

Dinah waits until she knows he's likely to have his head down staring at a filter or something, then quickly picks up the stack of sketches. As she flips over the stack and leafs through the sheets of paper, she wonders what on earth he's up to. All the sketches seem to be permutations of different geometric structures, some resembling tetrahedrals, others more like 3D snowflakes, one that looks a bit like a multi-storeyed tepee. Is this for the new house? Seems odd, but it's possible. The roof? A glasshouse? Should she ask him? No—he'll only be annoyed that she's sneaked a peek.

She'll wait. Spend more time with him. Drink coffee. Ply him with laksa or nasi lemak or both. Watch TV. At some point, he'll tell her.

* * *

'Oh, are you heading off?' Dinah looks up from her half-drunk cup of coffee.

Across the table, Lucky starts to put the stack of sketches into a large canvas tote, along with a bottle of cold brew. 'Yea. It's my afternoon off.'

'Thanks for staying back, Lucky!' Shawn waves from behind the counter. 'See you tomorrow.'

Dinah stands up and walks with Lucky towards the door. 'Where are you heading? Can I give you a lift?' She watches as Lucky picks up the cat and whispers something to it.

He turns to Dinah, smiling. 'It's okay. We're just going to hang out.'

'Well, I've got the next couple of hours free. Why don't we all hang out together?'

'Oh, sorry.' Lucky looks apologetic. 'It's a Coconut and me thing.'

'Ah.' So much for spending more time with Lucky.

She watches as they walk out the door into the bright afternoon, Coconut nestled in the crook of Lucky's arm, until they turn the corner and disappear. The air conditioning is suddenly colder. Dinah can feel her throat tighten with worry and confusion and something that feels oddly like resentment but can't be—why would she be resentful of a silly little cat?

It just doesn't make sense. What's his thing with this cat? Is it transference of some sort and he's clinging on to Pearl by clinging on to her cat? And what exactly can he be doing with it? No one walks cats or teaches them tricks or anything like that. So he's just sitting around being with the cat? And it's *their* thing and he won't even let her join them?

Dinah turns to Shawn and Meixi. 'Where do you think he's going?'

Meixi shrugs. 'Maybe they're going to go see Coconut's boyfriend?'

Coconut's boyfriend? *Jesus.* What's this, some sort of fantasy life that Lucky's invented for the cat? Dinah shakes her head. Doesn't anyone else see how unhealthy all of this is, how disturbed he must be?

* * *

The mountain is starting to peek out through the wispy leaves of the recovering casuarinas. Its square base, about the length of two cars, is nearly complete. It is nearly as tall as its maker now and much taller than his cat.

Lucky can't stop himself from grinning at his mountain-to-be. After weeks of trying out different arrangements, he's finally settled on tying bamboo poles together in a series of interlocking, irregular pyramidal shapes, all secured to the ground and anchored by concrete blocks. On the sides of some of the bigger pyramids, he's woven surfaces out of leather strips to make platforms. Coconut is in the process of testing one out.

'Very clever, Lucky. I can see myself taking a nap here.'

Lucky laughs. 'Well, you'll nap anywhere.' But he's pleased. She called him clever! He can't recall the last time Coconut—or anyone—called him clever.

A breeze sweeps through the casuarinas and into the garden, ruffling Lucky's hair, blowing a leaf into Coconut's face. It passes through the mountain, plays with the flap of the tent Lucky's erected on the spot where he thinks the old kitchen table must have stood, then dances with the random plants that have taken root in the remains of the back garden.

Coconut sits up straight on her leather platform and cocks her head at Lucky. 'You know, you don't have to make me a mountain. Don't you have other things to do?'

Lucky wonders what she's getting at. 'Like what?'

'Like look for a mate.'

He laughs. 'I think I'd rather make a mountain. Don't you like your mountain?'

'It's not a mountain yet. And maybe you don't know what you want. Maybe you haven't thought about it properly.' Coconut leaps off the platform and starts walking towards him. 'Like that man.'

Lucky frowns as he picks her up. 'What man?'

'The man who wanted a tail.'

Looking very serious, Coconut begins her tale. 'A tail, as everyone knows, is a fine and wonderful thing . . .'

and the man who wanted a tail knew this. He had spent years watching his cat and longed for a tail he could use as a counterbalance so he could leap high into the air and fall on his feet, a tail to swish around when he was annoyed. A tail, he felt, would give him an appearance of dignity and distinction. Far better than platform shoes, which he found uncomfortable. A tail would be a natural conversation piece—he imagined women at bars asking if it was real, perhaps even if they could touch it. The more he thought about it, the more he wanted a tail.

He looked everywhere for a tail that would suit him—something distinguished but not too showy, something strong but elegant. He walked many miles in zoos, nature reserves, marshlands, and swamps, staring at animals, looking for the perfect tail, and in the end he decided it was a tiger's tail he wanted. It was a thing of beauty and practicality— sleek, muscular, short-furred, and in a classic print that would work well with a suit or jeans or chinos and Hawaiian shirts on holiday.

The tigers in the zoos ignored him and so he went looking for one in the wild. He trekked through jungles in Sumatra and forests in Pahang; he roamed mangroves in the Sundarbans. When he finally found one, he offered it money for its tail.

'What would I want with money?' the tiger asked, waving its long striped tail.

'Well,' said the man, 'you can buy things with it.'

'What would I do with things?' the tiger asked.

'Well,' said the man, 'you can keep them and look at them when you're bored. And if you're tired of sleeping in trees, you could buy a comfy bed to sleep in. Or a battery-operated fan might be nice on hot days.'

'No, I think I'd rather have my tail, thank you.' The tiger came a little closer. 'Tell you what—I'll trade my tail for your head.'

The man stepped back. 'No, I'd rather have my head, thank you.'

The tiger stepped forward. 'I think I'll take it anyway.'

So the tiger ate the man, who was delicious and might have been just as delicious if he had a tail but perhaps also less delicious or more delicious.

Lucky is aghast. 'What the hell? So the guy was a dumbass. But surely he didn't deserve to be eaten!'

Coconut yawns. 'It's not in the nature of tigers to consider if things deserve to be eaten.'

Lucky rolls his eyes. 'Okay, fine—so what's this got to do with me?'

Coconut swats his cheek with a paw. 'If the man had gone looking for a mate instead of a tail, he wouldn't have been eaten by a tiger, would he?' She purrs. 'Anyway, I overheard a girl in the cafe talking about the dating app she's using . . .'

* * *

Dinah returns to Caffiend at exactly the time she expects to find Meixi gone and Shawn closing for the day. Shawn doesn't disappoint—as she walks through the door, flipping over the sign behind it so it says 'Closed', she sees him at the sink, doing the last bit of washing-up. Half the lights are off and the counter smells of the grapefruit-scented cleaner that Shawn likes so much because he thinks it goes so well with the smell of coffee.

'Hey, Shawn.'

He turns his head but doesn't stop washing up. 'Hey, left something?'

She sits down at the counter. 'No. Just wanted to talk to you.'

But she stays silent for as long as Shawn takes to finish rinsing the last four mugs in the sink, and he doesn't press her. He knows it's about Lucky—it always is—and it's starting to feel like Dinah's just looking for stuff to worry about. Lucky's been awesome in the last couple of months, putting in his share of the shifts, pitching in with the social media marketing, even volunteering to take over morning shifts for three entire weeks while Shawn's preparing for an exhibition. Finally, it's beginning to feel like Lucky's a proper part of the business and not some investor who likes to play barista when it suits him.

'So, what's up?' As he pours Dinah a glass of wine, Shawn prepares himself to defend Lucky.

'Do you think he's okay?'

'What makes you think he's not?'

Shawn listens as Dinah tells him about the trip to the electronics store. Okay, so it's a little odd for anyone to buy a television for a cat— but is it really *that* odd?

'Come on, Dinah.' He tops up her glass. 'People with pets do a lot of stuff for them. We don't have pets, so maybe it's just something we don't get.'

Dinah throws up her hands. 'You don't think buying a TV for a cat is weird? Really?'

Shawn tries his best to sound placatory. 'Of course, of course it is. But think about it. People buy jewellery for their dogs, will their fortunes to their parrots and tortoises or whatever, pay crazy amounts of money to clone their dead pets. What's a TV?' He adds: 'It's at least conceivable, isn't it, that a cat will watch TV?'

Dinah sighs. 'I suppose so.' Ridiculous, but conceivable.

'And a cat could probably learn to turn on a TV. I've seen a video of a cat flushing a toilet. Same sort of thing, right?'

'Yea. I guess.'

Shawn looks her straight in the eye to drive his point home. 'Yea. It's not like he bought the cat a *car*.'

Two cats

watch the mountain grow. They sit side by side on the grass, a small tortoiseshell cat and a big black cat, watching Lucky as he balances near the top of the bamboo structure, now nearly two metres high. He's got his self-made tool belt around his waist—the first thing he did this morning was attach a rope harness to it, which he's using to secure himself to the mountain. Yesterday, he nearly fell off it, much to Coconut's amusement. Today, Lucky is determined not to be entertainment.

'Be careful, Lucky.' Coconut calls out from below. 'You're not a cat, you know.'

'I'll be fine!'

'Take small steps. And don't look down.'

Lucky ignores her patronizing cat calls for the next hour. He has to do as much as he can by noon so he'll have time to get back to the cafe and shower before his shift. So far, it's coming along nicely—its base of bamboo pyramids is holding up well and the first level is nearly done. A few more weeks, if he works hard and fast, and his cat will have her mountain. Lucky grins to himself as he surveys his morning's work. He hasn't had this much fun in years.

The two cats are still watching him as he carefully climbs down the mountain. He stares at the black cat and then at Coconut. 'Who's this?'

Coconut stares back. 'This is Cat Steven.'

Ah. So this is the baker's cat, the television temptor of Coconut! Well, thankfully the new flat-screen has made it unnecessary for

Coconut to spend quite so much time at Patisserie Antoine, but she still sometimes disappears after lunch for a couple of hours without telling him where she's off to and of course Lucky hasn't asked—what, and let her think him clingy and needy and all the other things cats and women find so damn attractive? Clearly, this Cat Steven manages to be somewhat compelling even without the lure of a television. Lucky stares at the interloper. Is it the fur? What fur! What a sheen. And what posture—like a little black lion.

'Hello, Cat Steven.' Lucky sits down on the grass in front of the black cat.

The black cat looks him up and down with unblinking yellow eyes, then turns to Coconut.

'Cat Steven says the mountain is very nice.'

Lucky nods in approval. The cat has taste. Perhaps not a terrible sort of friend for Coconut. 'Tell him thanks. When it's ready, you two can try it out.'

The two cats exchange a long look. Coconut turns to Lucky. 'He says you may pat him if you want to, and he won't try to scratch your face even though it looks like a very scratch-worthy sort of face.'

Lucky involuntarily raises a hand to his face, torn between glaring at the black cat and patting him. He shoots Cat Steven a look that he hopes is stern and authoritative but isn't quite a glare, then pats him on the safe side. The cat responds with a throaty purr.

'Cat Steven says good butter is key to beautiful croissants. Always French butter, always artisanal.'

Lucky nods, hoping he looks thoughtful. 'I'll keep that in mind.' He pats the black cat again. 'Thanks, Cat Steven.'

Best to keep all the neighbourhood hooligans on his side, after all.

* * *

The mountain is as high as the casuarinas are tall and it keeps growing. The four bamboo poles at its core have been reinforced by a system of ropes pulling in opposing directions, much like the ones supporting the new trees on the main road. More platforms in a variety of sizes have been built within the mountain's bamboo skeleton, some for support, others for shade.

Dr Chan of 25 Swan Street, who drives past every morning at 9.12 a.m. on the way to the hospital, is frowning as he slows down at the end of the street and turns left into Joo Chiat Road. Did he see something there, on the plot where the old Lee house used to be? Must be a trick of light. They took down everything months ago.

But just behind the casuarinas—what was it?

* * *

Grinning to himself, Shawn flicks a towel at the spot right between Lucky's hunched shoulders. 'Stand up straight, comrade.'

Lucky turns around with a wry smile. God, why does Shawn find this funny?

Shawn notes the slight frown, the strained smile. 'What's the matter?'

Lucky rolls his eyes and puts his phone down on the counter between them. 'Okay, don't laugh. I'm trying to decide if I should reactivate my Tinder account.'

Ah. This is unexpected. But good—yes, Shawn's almost sure this is a positive development. All the same, he wishes Anita were here to take his place in this conversation. Shawn makes a face.

Lucky sees the face. 'You don't think I should?'

Shawn dismisses this as quickly as he can with a vigorous wave in Lucky's face. 'No no no no. Do it! If you're thinking of it, just do it.'

Lucky unlocks his phone screen and shows it to Shawn. 'Yea, but I don't know if this is still me, you know? What do you think?'

Shawn takes the phone from Lucky. He reads aloud: '"Lucky, 38. Human coffeemaker. Enjoys food, cooking, beach holidays, Italian wine, German beer." Um, how compelling.'

Lucky grins. 'Yea, yea, yea. It's Tinder, damn it. It's the photos that count.'

Shawn scrolls through the rest of Lucky's profile. First photo, chopping vegetables in the kitchen at home, probably taken by Pearl.

Nice touch, very domestic. The next two were taken on vacation. In both, Lucky's grinning madly, beer in hand. Not bad—weeds out anyone who doesn't drink. Next, Lucky trying to climb a very large statue of a frog, probably somewhere in Thailand. Super goofy—some women probably like that. The last one is of Lucky and Pearl, close up and slightly off-focus, in a posh-looking bar. In all the photos, Lucky is smiling, handsome, amused.

But the photos might as well be of a different guy. Shawn hasn't properly noticed this until now, but his friend has lost that unapologetic carelessness that turned everything he did into something of a joke. Is this a good thing? Shawn isn't sure. But he does like this Lucky, the guy who's still a bit of an airhead but who seems to care more about things, the guy who's there for him even when he's dealing with so much shit from the universe.

'. . . They're all a little different but also all pretty much the same . . .' Lucky's been talking for a while about dating apps. Shawn forces himself to pay attention.

'. . . So I might just try a new app and kill Tinder. Fresh start.' Lucky shows Shawn a review of a dating app. 'Maybe I'll try Hinge. Coconut says she's heard good things about it.'

Shawn stops reading the review. He looks up. 'Coconut said what?'

Lucky looks away. 'Oh, I don't mean literally.'

'You said Coconut says she's heard good things about Hinge. What do you mean, not literally? Your cat has *not literally* said she's heard good things about Hinge?'

'Yea. That's right.' Lucky wishes he hadn't said that. And does Shawn have to be so damn pedantic? *Okay, dumbass, think fast.* 'Not . . . literally. Just, you know, she seemed positive when I said, "What about Hinge?" So I'm thinking, maybe start with that.' Even to Lucky this sounds insane.

Hoping he sounds nonchalant, Lucky begins to babble about the Hinge interface, but Shawn isn't listening. Shawn is staring at his shoes, at the laces on his shoes, at the plastic tips of the laces on his shoes, wishing he hadn't heard those two crazy-as-fuck words. Coconut says. Coconut *says*.

If he were the hugging sort, he'd reach out and hug Lucky and tell him, we're going to get you through this. But he isn't. So he waits until Lucky's busy in the storeroom, then texts Dinah.

We need to talk. It's serious.

* * *

The early-morning brisk-walking aunties of Swan Street have taken to lingering in front of the old Lee house. It appears the Lee boy has been busy building some sort of decidedly unattractive structure in the garden. Every day, he adds a little more to it. A disturbingly large pile of bamboo sticks lies on the grass—obviously, the boy is far from done.

'Aiyo, what is this?'

'I hope this doesn't affect the property prices on our street.'

'Maybe it's some sort of outdoor gym? You know young people nowadays—can't keep fit doing simple things. My son-in-law has taken up something called bouldering. Pays good money to climb walls while pretending they're hills or cliffs. What can I say? Nothing to say.'

A few of the aunties manage to catch the Lee boy in the act one morning, as he balances across two bamboo poles, securing a third one in place. He is at least four metres off the ground, and the aunties are torn between maternal instinct and outrage.

'Oh my god, he better be careful! Goodness, what is he doing up there?'

'I told you, right? A bit cuckoo. Like his father. Just look at those lions!'

'Someone should tell him off. That is an eyesore. And if he falls down . . .'

'Needs a smack, that boy.'

Not everyone is unsympathetic. Mrs Doshi's maternal instinct prevails, and she shows up the next day with samosas, hot tea, and the safety helmet that belonged to her son when he was a process engineer. 'Don't fall and break your head, dear.'

The cats approve of her and the helmet.

Lucky isn't thrilled. Helmet hair! No. Just no. A long and trying conversation with Coconut ensues, with second-hand interjections from Cat Steven.

The cats have the last word. 'Cat Stevens says if you fall on your head and end up with jam for brains, he'll eat you and then I can go live with him and Antoine.'

Lucky puts on the helmet.

* * *

'We have to watch him closely, Shawn. He's about to snap.'

Shawn doesn't like that he agrees. But he does.

* * *

Lucky, Coconut, and Cat Steven are marvelling at the latest addition to the mountain. A large pink dragon now floats above it, anchored by a string tied tight to one of many, many bamboo poles that make up the mountain. Tugging at the string, waving its tail in the wind, the creature twirls and dips and flips, unaware of its audience.

'What do you think, Coconut?'

'It's not a bird, but I like it.'

'What does Cat Steven think?'

Cat Steven blinks and doesn't answer. Lucky pats him encouragingly. Coconut and the black cat appear to confer in a series of subtle tail flicks and earnest eye contact.

'He says it's very thoughtful of you. This will make the mountain easier for the other cats to find.'

Lucky is intrigued. 'What other cats?'

'The cats who want to find the mountain.'

'How do they know about it?'

'Every cat in the neighbourhood is talking about you, Lucky.' Coconut purrs. 'Everyone is talking about the man who's making a mountain for his cat.'

Every cat! Talking about him! Lucky has never felt so pleased to be talked about. He looks up at the mountain. Almost done. By the time he completes the final layer, the mountain will be as high as the house once was, maybe even a little higher.

And it's going to be so cool.

* * *

'Jesus. What the hell is this?'

'What's that? A kite? A plastic bag?'

Unseen, two sets of eyes peer at a helmeted Lucky and his nearly three-storey-high construction from the gate. Thank god for these dumb lions, Shawn thinks. He feels a little guilty about spying on Lucky like this—when Dinah first suggested it, he'd told her a flat no—but that guilt is fading fast, rapidly replaced by curiosity. The more he stares at this thing Lucky has built, the more he needs to know what it is.

The thing towers fortress-like over the casuarina trees, taking up most of what used to be the front garden of Lucky's old house. Made of wooden sticks (is that bamboo?) arranged within a frame, it reminds him a little of the Eiffel Tower and more of the structural models of DNA and sodium chloride molecules that his chemistry teacher brought to class. Except for the flat platform on top the size of a van, the thing is a pyramid, with a squarish core that extends all the way from the ground upwards. Shawn counts three distinct layers of interlocking sticks, each in a different geometric structure—triangular, cuboidal, tetrahedral. There are no floors or ceilings, but in every layer there are small platforms and tunnels made by weaving rope around the sticks. Some kind of playground contraption, maybe? But the spaces and platforms and tunnels look too small, even for kids.

'Pretty amazing. I mean, it looks really well made.' Shawn turns to Dinah, who's staring at the thing with a deep frown on her face.

Dinah cranes her neck, trying to see more. 'But what's he *doing*, Shawn? What's this for?' She shakes her head. 'This is so weird.'

Shawn sighs. 'Well, yes. But Lucky's always been a bit weird.' *And Dinah, you've always been an overthinking worrywart.* 'Remember the mushrooms? Remember the stupid veggie farm? He always had some sort of project going on, he was always making shit.' He pauses. 'Until Pearl . . . well.'

'Yea. I remember.'

They're silent for a while, their heads full of a different time, a different Lucky. The guy who spent weeks figuring out the ideal ratio of coffee grounds to cardboard bits for growing mushrooms. The guy who turned his back garden into an urban farming experiment in tomato and chilli cultivation.

Shawn clears his throat. 'So, Dinah, maybe this . . .' he waves at Lucky's massive structure, '. . . is a good thing.'

'Maybe.' She doesn't look convinced. 'But what is it?'

'Why don't we just ask him?'

Stepping out of the shadow of the lion he's been hiding behind, Shawn lifts the lever on the gate and pushes it open.

Lucky turns his head towards the movement at the gate, half expecting to see a cat popping by for a sneak peek. His eyebrows lift. Shawn! And Dinah! He waves them over, wondering how they knew to find him here. But he's excited to show them the mountain.

Dinah flashes him a quick smile. 'Hey. How's it going?'

Shawn wastes no time. 'Hey, Lucky. What's this?' He looks up at the structure. 'Super cool. Like an Aztec pyramid!'

Ah! He hadn't even thought of that. Lucky grins. 'Yea? It isn't even done yet.'

'What is it? Is this a sculpture?' Dinah squints at the structure. 'Art installation?'

'Nope.' Lucky waves an arm in an exaggerated flourish. 'Behold— Mount Coconut.'

Beside him, as if on cue, Coconut lifts her head and lets out a long, loud meow.

Like a warning bell. Shawn glares at the cat.

Like a siren. Dinah takes a step back.

Like a very, very happy cat. Lucky laughs. And then, seeing the looks on his friends' faces, he stops.

The arrival of the cats

takes Swan Street by surprise. Unlike Lucky, no one else has had the benefit of being told by Coconut and Cat Steven to expect the cats of Joo Chiat, Katong, and neighbouring neighbourhoods dropping in to see the mountain.

At first, no one sees them. Silent and sure-footed, they make their way to the mountain from all directions. On the streets and the pedestrian pathways, along the rooflines and the boundary walls between houses, through the back lanes and the alleyways, in the shadows of tall trees and parked cars. They pass the stone lions; they slip through the gate of the old Lee house. Then the cats climb the mountain, joining Coconut and Cat Steven as they bound through the bamboo. Some of the cats don't stay very long; others linger for hours.

Lucky is thrilled. When he's not working at the cafe, he's at the mountain, putting out fresh bowls of water and kibble and watching the cats climb, play, and squabble.

The rest of the inhabitants of Swan Street are not quite as thrilled. They stare at the cats slinking through their respectable old-money street, unsure of what to do. Where are they all coming from? Where are they going? Should someone call someone?

'I've seen at least ten this morning alone.'

'Ten? I've seen thirty!'

'They keep coming. It's like a plague.'

'Is someone feeding them?'

It is Mrs Wong at number nineteen who first notices that the cats are all heading to the Lee house. Putting down her gardening shears, she tails two large tabbies walking glibly down the middle of the street and watches as they go through the rails of the gate and climb up the crazy heap of bamboo that the silly Lee boy has built. As she stands outside the gate, wondering what can be happening, more cats arrive. First, a small black-and-white cat, then a large ginger. The ginger studies Mrs Wong with placid yellow eyes as it walks through the gate, leaving her feeling as if she's the one who's out of place here.

The next morning, Mrs Wong returns with five other neighbours. Navigator-like, she points at the cats on their bamboo playground. 'There, can you see? They're all here for this.'

'Hey, that's him!' Mr Subash points at a figure emerging from a tent holding a mug.

Six heads follow the man as he walks from the tent towards the cat-laden structure. He sees them and lifts his hand in a wave. Then he starts drinking from the mug, eyes on the cats, ignoring the group beyond the gate.

'Hey!'

'Hello!'

'Boy!'

The man, who is certainly not a boy but is resigned to being called one by every neighbour of his father's generation, turns towards them with a slight smile. When they beckon him over, he obliges.

'Good morning.'

He comes close enough to the gate to speak softly and for a moment they are tongue-tied. Mrs Wong and Mrs Tan have forgotten how handsome Betty Chong's boy is. Mrs Fernando pats down her hair. Mr Subash frowns. Mrs Doshi wonders if he might be her niece's type. When they untie their tongues enough to grill him, they find they cannot get a sensible response from the Lee boy.

'This thing you've made . . . it seems to be attracting cats.'

'Yes, isn't that wonderful?'

'What are you going to do about it?'

'I'm quite done building. I don't think there's anything left to add.'

'Aren't you going to take it down?'

'No. Of course not.'

'But all these cats . . .'

'Don't worry, they're fine.' A smile, bright and cheerful. 'But thank you for stopping by.'

* * *

'Crazy.'

'Yah. Why can't he just build a house?'

'Exactly. Surely he can afford it—I hear their father left them millions. And all that property he bought in the eighties must be worth so much now!'

'Crazy.'

'Playing with sticks at his age. He must be forty or something by now!'

'Just look at it. What an eyesore!'

The neighbours turn their heads once again towards the strange structure of sticks and ropes and who knows what else that the Lee boy has built. They stare at the Lee boy, sitting in his tent, drinking his coffee, watching the cats climb all over his monstrosity.

'Crazy.'

'But he looks happy.' Mrs Doshi cannot help but smile, watching him scoop up the cat at his feet and put it on his shoulder.

'Crazy.'

* * *

'Thank you, Lucky.' Coconut licks his nose and rubs her face against his in a rather showy display of affection (and he suspects, ownership) as they stand on top of her mountain together, looking down at the street.

'You like your mountain, Coconut?' he asks her.

He asks her every day, just to hear her say, 'I like my mountain very much, Lucky.'

Lucky closes his eyes. The world disappears except for the gentle tickle of Coconut's fur on his cheek. If he dies now, it would be a fine thing. Coconut and Cat Steven and the other cats will eat him. His bones, gnawed clean, will fall to a heap at the base of the mountain. The cats will walk over them. Over time, the mountain will collapse and cover them. The earth will take him like the sea took his sister.

'Are you okay, Lucky?'

He opens his eyes. 'Yes.' He smiles. 'I'm glad you like your mountain.'

'Your friends didn't seem to like it.'

Lucky sighs. He hasn't spoken to Shawn and Dinah since their visit nearly a week ago. Dinah hasn't tried to call, which is strange but also a relief, and Shawn and he have so far managed to busy themselves with different things at the cafe. It's getting harder and harder to avoid each other, but it will probably be much harder to have a conversation. Well, now that Dinah and Shawn both think him mad and he knows they do but he doesn't care, perhaps there's nothing left to say.

Of course that day he could have left it at 'Behold—Mount Coconut', but *they* couldn't.

Lucky put it as plainly as he could. 'I'm making a mountain for Coconut.'

They weren't happy with that. Shawn kept on frowning. Dinah kept on shaking her head.

Lucky tried to elaborate. 'She's never seen a mountain, you know. Isn't that sad? Every cat should get to see a mountain.'

They struggled with this. He could see it in their faces, and he didn't understand why it was so hard for them. Dinah's face was full of questions, but she started and stopped and started and stopped and didn't or couldn't ask them.

In the end it was Shawn who said, 'Come on, Lucky, what's going on?' He took a deep breath, and when he spoke again his voice was gentler. 'Are you feeling alright?'

'I'm fine. I'm just making a mountain for my cat, guys.'

He explained that he had promised to take her to see an actual mountain in Malaysia but they didn't manage to see one and she seemed sad about that and he had tried showing her Bukit Timah Hill but she hadn't liked it at all and it wasn't a mountain anyway only a hill and then he thought he would just make her one.

'. . . and here it is.' He almost said 'Behold—Mount Coconut' again but he managed to stop himself.

They were all silent for a few minutes. Shawn looked at the grass at his feet. Dinah folded her arms and mumbled to herself.

'What's wrong, Shawn?'

Shawn sighed. 'Well, it's a little . . . unusual, Lucky.'

Dinah exhaled sharply. 'It's a little nuts.'

'Why?'

They didn't answer. Lucky walked away and continued working on Coconut's mountain. By the time he looked up again, they were gone.

It's evening now. The sun is low and the shadows are long. Everything is golden—the tops of the cars parked along the street, the wispy leaves of the casuarinas, the manes of the stone lions, the fur at the tip of Coconut's ears. As Lucky and Coconut look down the length of the street, they see a cat turn the corner at the top of the street and walk in their direction. Lucky leans forward for a better view. Something about the cat looks familiar—something about the way it swaggers down the street, slow and lazy and lion-like.

'Oh my god, it's Gajah.'

It is. Behind him, a few more cats have turned the corner and into the street, and behind them, a few more appear. By the time Gajah reaches the mountain, Swan Street is a river of cats. Lucky and Coconut watch from their platform on the summit as the cats begin their ascent, Gajah leading the expedition.

'Wow, Coconut, I can't believe they're all here to see the mountain.'

'And you, Lucky. They're all curious to see you too.'

Gajah reaches the platform and Coconut jumps off Lucky's shoulder to greet him. By now, Lucky knows better than to interrupt or, worse, attempt to pat Gajah before the formal introductions are over. He watches as Coconut slowly, carefully, approaches the large grey cat. They study each other, both purring softly, and their eyes meet and hold the other's.

Then it's over. Coconut sits up on her haunches. Gajah goes off to explore the rest of the mountain after the briefest glance at Lucky.

'He says you're looking well.' Coconut butts her head against Lucky's right shin. 'He says you must be cleverer than you look, to be able to make a mountain.'

Lucky rolls his eyes and is about to say something sarcastic when he spots a familiar figure standing across the street, staring up at him. Their eyes lock, like Coconut's and Gajah's just minutes before. A hand lifts in greeting. Lucky waves back, then clambers down the mountain to meet her.

'Hello. I followed the cats here.'

'Come on in,' he says to the cat lady of Eunos station.

He unlatches the gate and waves her in. Surprise has got his tongue by this time, and he stands quietly by her side as she surveys his handiwork. Her eyes flit from level to level, scrutinizing the bamboo poles, the little platforms and perches, the woven-rope tunnels, the massive scratching posts he's made out of rope and used coffee sacks, the steps that wind around the mountain and spiral down its core, the sheltered platform on the summit, the pink plastic-bag dragon flying above it all. She watches the cats play, bounding up and down and through the mountain, and she smiles.

She turns to look at Lucky, still smiling. 'You built a mountain for your cat.' She pauses as Coconut comes up to inspect her. 'Is this Coconut?'

Lucky picks Coconut up. 'Yup.' Using his arm for leverage, Coconut stretches out to sniff the hand that the cat lady holds out to her.

The cat lady bends forward until she comes face to face with Coconut. 'Hello, Coconut. What a lucky cat you are.' She strokes the little cat gently on the forehead. Coconut mews in response. Lucky wonders what she thinks of the cat lady and her many, many cats.

Later, as the sky turns a deep blue and the cats begin to leave, the cat lady strokes Lucky on the forehead too. 'Good man. You can definitely take care of a cat.'

Lucky mews in response.

* * *

'That was silly.'

They're lying in the dark in the space above the cafe, Lucky on his cot and Coconut on his chest.

'What's silly?'

'You. Meowing like that.' Coconut taps him on the belly with her tail. 'It was embarrassing.'

Lucky laughs. 'Sorry. I just felt like that was what she was expecting.'

Coconut burrows her face into his neck. She purrs. 'You're not a cat, Lucky. You're a hero.'

Lucky laughs again. 'A hero? I'm not a hero, Coconut.' He sighs. 'I didn't even finish my epic journey.'

A swat on his ear. 'Of course you are.' She sniffs. 'Anyone can take the train. Only a hero could make a mountain.'

The next morning

is like many other mornings. Lucky is woken up by the first number 16 bus charging down Joo Chiat Road. Like on most other mornings, he manages to go back to sleep, but is woken up by the second bus. Also like on other mornings, he tries again and then gives up after around ten minutes of squeezing his eyes shut and tossing around.

As usual, he goes downstairs in the dark. He switches on the lights, then the espresso machine. As usual, just as he sits down at the counter and takes his first sip of coffee, he looks up to see Coconut slinking down the last steps.

As she walks towards him and leaps onto the counter, he says, as always, 'Good morning, Coconut.'

He waits for her to return the greeting and tell him about the things she saw the night before. Did she see that giant rat again, he wonders, grinning, did she chase it? But Coconut says nothing. She sniffs at his coffee, his face. She licks his cheek. But she doesn't say anything.

'Managed to catch that fatass rat?'

Coconut looks at him, blinking slowly. She yawns.

What's up with Coconut? *Maybe she's just hungry.* Frowning, Lucky opens a packet of Princess Shrimp Dream and empties it into her dish. 'Here you go.'

They sit in silence, Coconut eating her breakfast, Lucky sipping his coffee. He wonders if she's annoyed with him, but before he can ask her about it, the door swings open and Shawn walks in.

'Morning.'

'Morning.'

Shawn goes behind the counter and starts his routine checks—the milk, the beans, the water purifier. Lucky finishes his coffee, watching Shawn, saying nothing, wondering how much longer this strange unsilent silent war will go on for. Coconut finishes her breakfast, then curls up under a table to give herself a nice and thorough clean.

* * *

It's the middle of the afternoon and more than half the tables are occupied. In the narrow space behind the counter, Meixi, Shawn, and Lucky keep up a brisk pace, moving with practised ease as they take turns to ring up orders and prepare coffee, reaching for and passing each other glasses and cups and different grinds and milks. As a single organism, they look up and nod when Dinah comes through the door, then quickly drop their heads back into their tasks.

She sits at the counter and waits for a lull. Meanwhile, she watches Shawn pull two espresso shots into a mug and hand it to Lucky, who nods and takes it, then pours frothed milk over it. They don't speak. Dinah sighs. This must be hard for them.

She and Shawn haven't spoken much either. Knowing Shawn, he's dying for everything to go back to normal with as little confrontation as possible. Dinah sighs. What does going back to normal even mean? What does 'normal' mean with Lucky? How was he ever normal? With that face, that hair, that house, that sister. That life. Never needing to care about making money, getting anywhere, achieving anything. Never needing to pretend to.

Ah, but does it matter?

Last night, she went back to see the thing, the *mountain*, he'd built for his cat. The gate wasn't locked—well, there's nothing to steal now—so she walked right in and stood in front of the thing and stared it down. It stared right back, and she had to admit it was pretty impressive. How long had it taken him to design this, to figure out all these angles? And it must have been such a pain to build, measuring up and then tying all these bamboo poles together, anchoring the whole structure with ropes and concrete blocks, working while climbing up and up and up.

'What the hell are you doing, Lucky?' She didn't care that she was talking to herself in the middle of the night, in front of this ridiculous thing, in what used to be the front garden, on possibly the exact spot where she sat on a white plastic chair and watched the band play at Pearl's funeral and didn't let herself cry.

The wind whistled through the casuarinas. Two cats looked down at her from somewhere midway up the mountain. Mountain! If only Pearl were here, they would laugh at this together. If only Pearl were here.

She didn't care that she was crying now. 'Pearl, I'm sorry. I've driven him nuts.' She had, she had, she had.

Still watching Lucky–Shawn–Meixi, Dinah takes a deep breath. *Just do it. Just do it.*

'Come with me, Lucky.' She seizes her chance when the queue finally dwindles and the pace behind the counter slows down. 'You too, Shawn.'

It's hot as a grill outside as she leads the way to a small basement car park nearby. Shawn walks quickly, keeping in step with her. Lucky dawdles, shuffling his feet behind them. Dinah smiles to herself. It's the way they've walked together since they were at architecture school, prowling the gloomy corridors in search of a vending machine that hadn't run out of shitty coffee. Has it really been nearly twenty years with these two?

The car park is dark and mostly empty. Dinah walks to her car, stops, and turns to face Shawn and Lucky.

'And this is where you kill us and put our bodies in the boot.'

Dinah scowls. Shawn can be so annoying sometimes.

'No, no. There won't be space. It's a junkyard in there.' Lucky giggles. 'She'll have to tie us to the roof.'

Fucking clowns, these two. Fucking clowns. Let's just do this.

Dinah pops open her boot and steps aside. She waits as they exchange a quick, apprehensive look, suddenly allies again. First Lucky, then Shawn, steps up to the boot and looks inside.

'What's this?' Shawn pokes at a black suitcase.

Dinah says nothing, her eyes fixed on Lucky's face as he reaches into a cardboard box and pulls out a blue seal plushie, frowning. He puts it under his arm and leans forward to rifle through the box, taking things out at random. A sweater. A T-shirt with Channel printed on the front. A copy of *Ben-Hur*. She watches his face contort in disbelief as he flips open the book and reads the name written inside. He turns to look at her and she forces herself to meet his eyes.

'Oh my god. It was you.' Lucky tries to recall what else went missing from among Pearl's things. 'But why?'

Lucky grips the seal plushie with both hands as he listens to Dinah explain how she'd let herself into the house from time to time, go into Pearl's room and just look at her things, and touch them. His throat is dry from all the things he doesn't say. How dare she sneak into his home, even if he did give her a key? And how horrible, that she poked around his sister's things and then quietly took them and put them into her car, and left him thinking he was . . . what? Losing more of his mind? Under siege by a ghost? He doesn't even know any more.

'I'm sorry, Lucky. I was trying to keep them safe.' She looks away. 'You cut up her dresses and hung them in the garden.'

Oh, right. The scarecrow. Lucky nods.

Dinah wipes her eyes with the backs of her hands. 'I don't know, I don't know.' She is whispering but the car park is so quiet that he can still hear her. 'I thought you were going to destroy all her stuff. I couldn't let you do it.'

Lucky sighs. *Oh Dinah, ever the meddler.* But he's grateful for her, he realizes. The next moment, as she makes a mad dash towards him and throws her arms around him, he thinks, for the first time, how lucky he is to have her. And Shawn, whose hand is on his shoulder now, a little awkwardly. It's like a scene from a tawdry soap opera. Lucky feels an urge to laugh.

'I miss her too, you know, Lucky,' she says against his shoulder. 'But I miss you more.' She steps back and catches Shawn's eye. 'We just want you to be happy, whatever that means.'

Lucky stares at his feet. So many thoughts to think. The weight of the moment presses down on him and he wishes he could crawl under a blanket and lie very still and not talk or think or be. He wriggles his toes. He sighs. When he looks up again, his friends are waiting.

He smiles. He tells them it's all going to be okay. He watches as their faces relax, as they turn to each other and smile. Because that's what you do, isn't it, with people you love, with people who love you? Tell them it's all going to be okay. Figure shit out later.

In the evening, as they sit on the grass next to the mountain, he tells all this to Coconut. 'I never, ever suspected it was Dinah. You know, the cat lady thought it might have been you who took Pearl's things and hid them. Imagine that!'

The little cat looks at him solemnly, but she says nothing. She's said nothing all day.

'Coconut, what's wrong?'

Lucky strokes her forehead. She mews, but that's all. He checks her eyes and ears. No sign of cat flu. She doesn't appear annoyed with him—she's calm, her tail is gently tapping against his thigh.

He lowers his face to hers. 'Coconut, say something. Tell me a story.'

She rubs her head against his cheek. But she doesn't tell him a story.

* * *

It is Meixi who tells him a story, the next morning. Sleep-deprived, having stayed up most of the night watching documentaries, trying to get Coconut to say something about puffer fish sharks turtles lions hyenas swallows starlings penguins Pearl, failing, Lucky can hardly understand her.

'I don't get it. Coconut's mountain is in the papers?'

Coconut's mountain? The *papers*? Sometimes she forgets how old he is. Meixi takes a deep breath. 'It says here you've built a giant cat tree.' She shows him her phone. 'See? You're in the news, Lucky.'

So he is. The headline reads: 'Lee scion's giant cat tree enrages neighbours'. Cat tree! How is the mountain anything like a cat tree?

He takes the phone from Meixi and scrolls through the article. The photos are pretty good—he suspects one of the neighbours snuck in and took them. The angles make the mountain look enormous. And though he hates to admit it, from some angles it does look like a giant cat tree. There's a photo of him too, an old one scrounged up from someone's social media account somewhere, dressed as Iman, wig askew and eyes shiny from too much wine, at a Halloween party.

Bastards. I look like ass.

* * *

Of course the aunties call.

'Lucky, do you know you're in the papers?'

'Lucky, why did you build that thing?'

'Lucky, what were you thinking?'

'Lucky, for once in your life, can you do something *useful?*'

Lucky endures the phone calls, the same questions repeated an impressive number of different ways, the sighs, the scolding–pleading–cajoling for him to please, please take the cat tree down. He tells them patiently, in the same tone of voice he uses for Coconut when she's being difficult, that yes, he knows he's in the news, that he built the mountain, not cat tree, for Coconut and it's nice that so many other cats like it too, that he wasn't thinking anything in particular, that he's sorry they don't find the mountain useful, but no, he is not going to take it down.

'Wouldn't be fair to the cats.'

'The cats? What about the neighbours?'

'They can make their own mountains if they want.'

Meanwhile, Coconut still hasn't spoken to him and it's been weeks. She naps in the same old spots, she spends the occasional afternoon with Cat Steven and the cat-luring croissant-maker down the road, she prowls the neighbourhood at night and slips through the window in the wee hours and snuggles up next to him on his cot. They go to the mountain together in the evenings and stand on the platform and look over the tops of the trees. But she doesn't speak. No amount of wheedling, no incentive of expensive Japanese fish, no mention of

Pearl, not even the promise of a much, much larger television can get her to talk.

Another week goes by. Coconut remains silent.

Another week. Lucky stops trying to get her to speak.

Another week, and another. Lucky stops expecting her to say anything. He wonders if he will ever get used to a not-talking Coconut. *Well, cats don't actually talk.* He begins to wonder if Coconut ever really spoke to him or if he imagined it all. *Rubbish! Of course she did!* But he continues to wonder.

He thinks of all her stories, and he wishes he could hear just one more.

* * *

'Well, maybe it's time you told her stories, Lucky.'

'Me?' He has no stories to tell, but he doesn't say this to the cat lady of Eunos station.

'Who else? Don't be silly, Lucky.'

Lucky stares. For a moment, she sounded just like Coconut.

* * *

Lucky is telling Coconut a story. 'So this cool thing happened today.'

Her mountain, he tells her, has found its way into an architecture magazine. 'Imagine that, Coconut!'

She cocks her head sideways at him. Lucky takes this to mean she's trying. Encouraged, he continues. Her mountain has been called 'an elegant reprise of the Southeast Asian tropical vernacular'.

'This is a good thing, Coconut.' Well, perhaps a tad overblown— but good.

Taking out his phone, Lucky reads out to her parts of the article that Shawn sent over this morning. The little cat stares at him intently as he reads out the paragraphs gushing over the cross-ventilation, the inclusion rather than exclusion of the environment and the use of inexpensive, easily sourced natural materials, then rolls onto her back and yawns widely and repeatedly when he gets to his favourite bit: 'Lee's early architectural training clearly comes to play in the design and engineering of the structure, which cleverly combines geometric shapes and weaving techniques into a delightfully textural playground for local wildlife.'

Wait, how does the writer know he went to architecture school? He checks the byline—it's Naresh. Lucky laughs. Lovely, earnest Naresh, who adored the old house, who patted the dragon. He should have known.

Lucky skips to the end of the article. '"The Swan Street Cat Tree House could be—should be—the start of a new local movement . . ." What do you think of that, Coconut?'

She looks at him and mews loudly.

He kisses her on the nose. 'Yea. Singapore could do with a few more mountains.'

* * *

'Do you think Pearl would have liked the mountain, Coconut?' From the platform, he looks down at Swan Street, at the lions, at the roofs of the houses nearby. From right below him, he can hear the sound of a few cats running through the structure, chasing each other (well, hopefully—he hasn't seen any rats on the mountain yet).

Coconut purrs in the crook of his elbow.

He wishes she would say something to reassure him that yes, Pearl would have loved it. But she doesn't, and he realizes he doesn't need her to. It's *her* mountain, after all, not Pearl's.

Lucky smiles. He imagines his sister would look at the mountain and laugh and say a whole lot of things at once loving and unkind and funny and interesting, and she would have him laughing along with her. And his father would probably have said something about wasting time and bamboo.

'But Papa, I made it with my hands.' Lucky giggles. The wind rustles through the leaves and tousles his hair and he can almost hear Pearl giggle along with him.

Lucky looks behind him, almost expecting to see the old house rise from the ground, dragon and parakeets and zebra intact. How funny, that he doesn't miss it any more, even though he loves it still and always will.

He has his cat, she has her mountain, and they have evenings like this.

Thank you, thank you, and thank you again . . .

My mother, for first bringing cats into my life, for listening to all my stories.

Kevin Seah, for being the first to read this and everything else I write, for being the friend I phone from Penang, Florida, Melbourne, anywhere, to blather about writing. For the wisdom, the love, the unending support.

Dhruv Doshi, for all the hours, for all these years, for being Coconut's tireless cheerleader.

Ken Kwek and Jeremy Fernando, my kawans, for staying with me through this journey, for reading this novel so many times, through all the starts the stops the sighs the sweat.

Ryn Suthipradit and Abirama Thanikasalam, for opening up their homes to me and feeding me cheese and chicken and all the coffee all the coffee all the coffee as I wrote the first half of this novel.

Nishta Geeta Thevaraja, Victoria Wee, Joanna Lim, Joanna Zablocka, Gabriel Oon, Andee Tay, and Stephen Tompkins (for whom Cat Steven is named), for the friendship, for believing, for keeping me sane in all manner of storms.

Vu Quang Nguyen and Rachid Saint Jean, for making sure I didn't die that night and sending me home armed with a Korean fusion burrito.

JW, for the biscuits, for flying across two continents to walk with me in Orlando. For trying.

The Kerouac Project of Orlando, for welcoming me to the Kerouac House as Spring Resident 2022 and giving me the peace, time, and space to almost but not quite finish the second half of this novel. Thanks especially to the lovely Erik Deckers, who took me to the coolest bookstores every other weekend.

The remarkable team at Penguin Random House SEA, for all the hard work that went into putting this novel together.